SOM

GW00694070

SYNCHRONY

ANN FOWERAKER

Faith Warren, married mother of two, is a secretary in a newspaper office. It wasn't what she'd hoped for, but her dreams of university and becoming an author were lost long ago. Telling stories to entertain her lifelong friend, Di, on their journey to work and back is all that is left …. until she tells The Story.

The real trouble began with the minor characters, just unfortunate coincidences, but when do you stop calling them co-incidences and begin to wonder what the hell is going on – and how it can be stopped

This light thriller, set in the late 1990s combines romance, harsh reality and unexpected events.

SOME KIND OF SYNCHRONY

First published 2011 in e-format by AnnMade Books

Paperback Edition 2014 Pendown Publishing Cornwall, United Kingdom

Set in 11pt Garamond

Printed by Lightning Source

www.pendownpublishing.co.uk

Cover: NJM designs

To my good friends who have inspired me
– you know who you are

SOME KIND

OF

SYNCHRONY

ANN FOWERAKER

Some Kind of Synchrony

chapters

chapter one - Faith

Faith's first true memory was of Di. It was impossible to place a date on it, or even an age, though it felt like being three. Di had appeared one day at the door, a fairy princess, all light and gold, sun dancing on honey-blonde hair, dress alight with sparkling jewels. Only Faith remembered this. Remembered the first time she was really aware of Di, though she knew now that they'd known each other almost from birth. No-one else had recalled it for her, no-one else could have conjured up the peculiar feeling that seeing Di that time created in her young mind. Examining it, turning it over gently to feel the sensation again, Faith, in her thirties, could put a name to it, or rather a collection of names, 'love, awe and envy'.

Not much had changed. Faith was waiting five minutes early in the bitter cold for the car to arrive. Punctual by nature anyway, she always made sure she was on time for Di. Eventually the car turned in at the end of the road, radio blasting so loud that it could be heard above the rattle of the engine as it neared and slowed, breathing heavily into the gutter. Faith ran around to the passenger door, snatched it open and hurried herself inside. The fan blew cool air ferociously in anticipation of the engine warming up, the radio was snapped off. Di flashed a smile, her eyes already seeking the mirror as she indicated and pulled out.
'Thought it wasn't going to start this morning ! I nearly had to go back in and get Paul - well pleased he'd have been!'
'How is he?' Faith asked softly, never sure how much to press Di on Paul's drinking. Sometimes Di seemed to pour all her worries out, other times she seemed to resent the fact that Faith even knew about them, as if they might disappear if no one knew.
'Bloody hung-over - though to hear him you'd think he'd gone down with the latest virus doing the rounds - that it has nothing to do with his drinking.'
'Oh.'
'Well, what's Andy up to today then?'

'Well - he should be taking the kids off to school - then, then I think he was talking of seeing your Paul?' wondering if she had got it right.

'As long as they don't end up in the clubhouse!'

Faith was silent. The club membership had been the cause of their most recent row, the bruises blossoming yellow on her upper arm now. Membership that Andy maintained was necessary for contacts and for keeping him sane, and that she'd suggested should be the first thing to go as things became tighter, with her job being the only one to bring money in.

Di swept the car out onto the motorway.

'You all right?'

'What? Oh yeah - sure,' Faith said, remembering the grip of Andy's hand on her arm as he'd insisted that it wouldn't be long before she could quit her 'poxy little job'. 'Did you watch that new thriller series last night?' she said, dragging her mind away from the pain.

'For what it was worth - I mean were you really 'on the edge of your seat'? You could do better than that for suspense - remember that story you did back in the third year?' Di flicked a glance at Faith.

Faith remembered. She always remembered times like that; times when she gained Di's whole attention, her acclamation and her admiration. Years ago, when they were teenagers, she'd written stories for Di; tales starring Di and herself in adventures with their favoured pop heroes of the time. Usually fun romantic stuff - but exciting all the same. Then, after Di had turned away from her at a difficult time, she'd written a story edged with fear and darkness, a story that put Di into a position where she was in dire danger - and to her rescue came - Faith. Faith hadn't meant it to be read at all - but soon after their friendship was renewed, somehow she found herself showing it to Di. To her amazement Di loved it - said it was the best, most tingly-scary thing she'd ever read and told others that Faith was going to be a writer, a really great writer. And, as always, whatever Di thought and said was soon believed by the others in her school clique - Di had that effect on people. Faith had hugged that idea, that image of herself, right to the end of her schooldays.

'I mean - you could do better now - just sitting here – a really scary one,' Di laughed and tossed her head at the thought. 'A real scary one - like set in a deserted manor house - with a murderer escaped from somewhere nearby, come on.....'

'I'm not sure,' Faith hesitated, knowing that the first scary story had been driven by her own demons.

'Come on - I'm depending on you to cheer me up!' Di said, her mouth pulling a frown.

'Oh, okay. Hang on a mo.'

Di gave her an impish smile and a wink.

Faith thought herself into the creepy manor house, thought around the rooms, the air, the sounds and the reasons for them being there.

'Okay - *You have won a prize!' the card said, 'All you have to do to receive your prize, worth maybe up to ten thousand pounds, is attend this free, special, luxurious weekend for two. No purchase necessary, a complimentary weekend for all our lucky winners ..'*

'That's just like those time share cons - isn't it?'

'Don't - I'll lose it else.'

'Sorry - go on.'

'For all our lucky winners.' But who to take? Fay had not yet met the man of her dreams, and the thought of wasting the extra holiday was just too much. The answer came to her in a flash - she'd ask her good friend Di. Immediately with this thought she reached out her beautifully manicured hand and picked up the phone. She pressed in the numbers for Di's phone and in moments heard the confident buzz of the ringing tone .....'

'Bye, Di - see you later,' Faith said as she clambered out of the car.

'Yeah - ready for the next instalment - it really made the journey fly! God that creepy place is getting to me already.' A horn blared behind her. 'Keep your hair on!' she shouted back. 'Okay - see you.' she indicated and lurched back into the stream of traffic.

It was only a short walk from where Di dropped her off to the newspaper office. The streets were littered with the debris of last night's take-aways, huddling in corners where they had been cast or fluttering in the stiff breeze to wrap around hurrying ankles. Head down, avoiding eye contact, avoiding bodies, she hurried along the slippery pavement towards the refuge of the big, glass, office doors. She only lifted her head and smiled as she heard the whisper of the doors at her back.

'Morning!' she greeted the receptionist as she went on past into the lift. A couple of minutes later she arrived at her desk, where her job was to type up *other* people's words. A sudden rush of resentment flowed through her. She could have done so much better. She could at the very least have been writing her own words - hadn't that been her dream?

'Morning!' she smiled to those around her as she hung her coat up and rubbed her hands together to warm them before getting ready to work. She touched a new glossy leaf on one of her plants, feeling the tentative tug of its freshness on her fingertip, felt the dampness of the soil of another, then sat herself at her desk and composed herself to work.

The computer screen offered her a blank page and waited patiently humming to itself. She glanced at the pile of papers before her, at the tapes. Supposedly a 'personal secretary' she belonged to two different bosses. Each had their own preferences for how they liked their work presented, and for how they presented their work to her. The gentlemanly Mr Watson liked to dictate, from the sound of the constant roar in the background his dictation was mostly done while he was in the car. He liked to have the most formal style of letter, in the old-fashioned pattern. Ms Robertson however, like a short, modern but friendly style, everything blocked to the left of the page and produced hand-written scrawls which Faith had learned to decipher where others had failed.

She slotted in the tape and hooked on the headphones. Faith always did Mr Watson's tapes first as he finished at the office just after lunch time and she needed to get them signed before he left. Today she was glad to begin with the tapes, working from them would allow her mind to travel back from the luxurious but sinister country house hotel she had left it in at the end of their journey.

Five completed letters, neatly printed and awaiting only the signature before being sent away, lay to one side of her computer when she heard Mr Watson's unmistakable old-boy tones.

'Well I suppose if you need a secretary then I can give Mrs Warren to you,' he said.

At the sound of her name, Faith listened intently, looking towards the gap where the speaker should appear.

'Does she come gift-wrapped?' a voice mocked lightly. Something about the tone irked her, setting her ready to dislike the speaker before she'd even met him.

'Pardon? Um - she's an excellent personal secretary and should be able to accommodate any letters - er whatever - you may require.'

Faith could hear the usually eloquent Mr Watson stumbling in his speech, something had upset him.

Suddenly he appeared, Faith flicked her eyes to the pile of letters she had waiting for him, ready to give him a pen.

'Faith, my dear,' he coughed lightly. He seldom called her Faith, it was more usually Mrs Warren. 'This, er gentleman is Mr Wren,' he sighed. 'The photographer - with us for a while - you understand - he may need a secretary and I have assigned you to him,' he smiled apologetically.

'No wrapping necessary,' Nick Wren murmured apparently to himself, then, smiling and holding out a hand, 'Pleased to meet you – Nick Wren.' His smile brought light and amusement to a handsomely rugged face, but as his eyes seemed to hold hers longer than necessary, her impression of his arrogance was strengthened. Wary of him she touched his hand as one would a wild animal, and allowed only the briefest smile to turn her lips as she murmured a greeting.

'I won't make much extra work for you - Faith,' this time allowing his smile to reach his eyes, grey-blue eyes that danced with light and mischief. She felt herself stiffen as if challenged.

Instinctively she drew herself up, her spine straightening, her eyes narrowing.

'It's quite all right, thank you - *Mr* Wren,' she said holding formality as a shield, holding tight to her best received pronunciation. He raised one eyebrow slightly, smiled and with a slight nod of the head turned away. The physical impression was swift, the face, the eyes and the dark hair, darker than her own, burnished ebony in the concave, a deep mahogany on the convex, and cut so that it was not until he turned that the length was apparent, caught in a band at the nape of his neck. As they left she felt the blush of annoyance creep up her neck and warm her cheeks - and she'd allowed Mr Watson to escape without signing his letters.

The general murmur of people leaving their desks to head for the staff canteen drew her attention to the time. With a sigh she turned off her screen and tidied the pile of correspondence that she had been working on. Her arms ached slightly, the muscles feeling weary as if too heavy to hold at keyboard height another moment. Lightly she swivelled around and caught Susie's eye, throwing her a friendly smile - they'd go down to lunch together, catch up on the weekend happenings. At the very least Susie would fill her in on her latest love life, distract her for a little while from her own troubles. Faith was always good at listening. Other people's words and ways lodged in her memory, filling her imagination with other lives, other possibilities, but all she heard stayed there, never passed on to other ears, she was not known to gossip.

How can a salad, merely washed raw bits and a slice of cheese or ham, really cost as much as a fully cooked meal? Faith reflected, as she settled yet again for a cheese salad and a virtuous glow, before taking her tray over to the same window seat that they always sat in. Susie arrived, steaming spaghetti bolognese on her tray, and wriggled her way into the stiff padded seat.

Faith watched the steam curl wispily from the mound of mush and felt slightly nauseated.

'Well! Who's the lucky one then? I wouldn't mind working for Nick Wren, even if he's dropped out of the limelight! I'd do his copy work anytime,' Susie said pursing her lips in a mock provocative manner.

'You know him?' Faith began, yet even as she did so she realised that she had heard of 'Nick Wren'. 'Mr Wren' introduced to her in a provincial city newspaper office had meant little - Nick Wren, now she actually thought about the name, rang a bell like a long forgotten brand.

'Don't know him - just *of* him. He's won awards, and he did a big series on the stars back when I was at school. Plastered my bedroom wall with his shots. Wild man with a camera!'

Yes she remembered now, but she'd been too busy with babies back then to take much notice of such trivia. No wonder he appeared arrogant - and she'd gone and reacted like a prissy little madam. The blush began to make its way up her cheeks again.

'Hey - you're not smitten already - are you? Wouldn't chuck him out of my bed though!' Susie grinned observing the change in Faith's colour.

'You wouldn't chuck any of them out!' Faith laughed, glad to find a foil, 'You were going to tell me about the weekend? Did he come over - or what?'

'Oh - and or what. The works, oh dear, you remember I said he'd sent roses. I mean - roses!. Well on Saturday at seven he turns up, 'nother big bunch of roses in his mitt - and all togged up - like - like he was going to an opera - to sing like! You won't believe it?' Susie, bubbly blonde hair, dark eyes and full of life waited for Faith to fill in the pauses, the gaps in the script that kept the story going.

'Well - where did you go?'

'The bloody opera!' Susie squealed. 'The bloody opera - and I know b-all about opera - don't I? You should have seen me, nodding and smiling, and pretending I knew all the tunes, oh Faith! He is ever so nice - but I don't know.'

'What's wrong - I wouldn't mind being taken to the opera - not quite the worst thing in the world? Not quite anyhow!'

'It's not that - I just don't know if he fancies me? He gives me a kiss – like,' she kissed the air gently. 'his hands just resting on my shoulders. What d'you think?'

'What do you do?'

Susie shifted a little uneasily in her seat and spun her fork in the seething mass of spaghetti.

'Well - it doesn't seem right to throw myself around him - I just -' she dropped the fork and put up her hands, as if fending someone off, 'I just rest my hands on his chest and kiss him back - the same.'

'Oh Susie! You do make me laugh - what would I do without you?' Faith beamed.

'Yeah well - it sounds stupid - but when you're there it seems the only way to be - it's like being in one of those old pictures - Fred Astaire - Ginger Rogers things.' Susie was laughing too, 'I keep expecting him to burst into song!'

'Or you - "Taking *off* his top hat, taking *off* his white tie, taking *off* his tails!" oh Susie!'

'Oh - shut up!' she smiled amicably.

'If you have a moment, Mr Watson?' Faith stood by the office door with the letters in her hand. At least two of them required his personal signature, the others she could have signed on his behalf. Alun Watson's office always appeared crowded, even when he was the only person in it, and reeked of his pipe tobacco. His desk seemed to be squeezed into one side of the room, four filing cabinets stood back to back making an island on the other side and the top of these, and every section of wall space up to the ceiling, was stacked with box files - black-marbled backs all labelled, his personal news collection.

He looked up and removed his glasses, his thin face momentarily rounded by a smile. 'Come in, yes, yes, I'm sorry about that this morning. Quite, quite offhand manner. Thinks he can,' he unscrewed his fountain pen and signed the letters unread. 'There.'

'I - didn't realise who he was when you introduced him this morning, I mean.'

'Well - difficult thing isn't it?'

'I wondered - what he's doing for Central News?'

'Exactly! Nothing, him being here is just some kind of favour for the family - relative or something of Lord Boulder it seems.'

'Ahh.'

'Ahh, exactly - never mind - photographers shouldn't need a secretary at all - don't think he'll bother you too much. Any problems come and see me again.' He settled his glasses back on his face, the interview at an end. Faith smiled and collected up the letters. Whatever the reasons for Nick Wren being at Central News it was not by popular arrangement with at least one of its senior editors.

Still curious, she next sought out Ms Robertson for her to sign the letters of the day. Though an identical room in essence, the room she next stepped into could have been a world away, not just the other side of the busy newsroom. Heavily scented by Amy Robertson's favourite perfume the room appeared large and airy in comparison, with pale furniture and neat waist-high shelving adorned with a few beautifully elegant houseplants. Amy looked up from under her heavy auburn fringe as Faith tapped on the open door and stepped in. She laid the letters down at the slight smile and nod she was given.

'I understand *he's* landed you with extra work?' Amy said slowly as she ran her eyes down the sheets of printed words.

'Yes, but it shouldn't be too much - a photographer?'

Amy looked up at her again sharply, her eyes fixed on Faith for a moment.

'Not quite any photographer though, eh?'

'No. I know - I don't know what…'

'What he's doing here in this hole in the back of beyond?'

'No …'

'I do. Not been in the news much lately - buried himself it seems in the deepest countryside,' she sounded disgusted by the idea, 'A waste - playing at the simple life.'

An idea crept into Faith's mind, perhaps Ms Robertson and Nick Wren already knew each other.

'Have you - met Mr Wren before - in newspaper work?'

Amy smiled, the lips formed an almost perfect vee, the cheeks bulged momentarily, her glance was conspiratorial.

'You could say so - we worked closely on a number of 'celeb' projects back in the eighties. Some of his best work,' she let her gaze rest on the desk for a moment. 'I don't suppose he'll be here long - once he gets back into the swing of things - though it's fun to see how upset Alun's got over it.' She knew she could trust Faith with such comments, that Faith understood how things were between the senior editors of the sister papers, Central Daily and Evening Central.

Faith nodded.

'He's gone for today, I suppose. I'd imagine that Alun made sure he didn't stay until I arrived, but I'll catch him later - review old times.' Amy smiled again as she offered the signed letters back to Faith.

Faith shivered. The street lights shone sickly yellow in the thin fog that clouded the tops of the buildings and slid almost down to street level. A stream of silver reflections from the passing cars dazzled as she peered along the road. She hated waiting to be picked up here, so close to the tug of the vehicles as they swept past. She stood with her back to a post box, clinging to its solidity as the other commuters flowed along the greasy pavement. At last, one car flashed its lights and pulled in. Faith climbed in quickly, the car moving away before she had a chance to fix her belt.

'You'll never guess,' Di said, her voice laden with pleasure, her eyes fixed on the road as she drove furiously through the rush hour traffic.

'What?'

'I've got it! Personal secretary to the M.D.! God did I work for it! It's a rise – and it's a cinch of a job.'

'Great ...'

'All I've got to do is keep at arm's length from the creep!'

'Oh!'

'Oh, my arse! Faith, sometimes you sound like you come from a different world,' Di said passing her a glance as they took up their station in the lines of motorway traffic.

'Well - that's me.'

'And I love you for it!'

'I've got a new boss too.'

'Really - who's gone?'

'No, an extra. Nick Wren the photographer - have you heard of him?'

'Give me a minute - let me think.' she looked straight ahead at the windscreen, features at rest for a moment, 'Glossy mags stuff ... back in, ohh, in the eighties? Film stars – pop stars that sort of thing. Young, well back then, and *very* good looking, almost as famous as those he shot. Am I right?' she flashed a smile at Faith, knowing she was right.

'Your memory! I didn't even twig who he was - not till later.'

'If I recall he had a bit of a reputation - better not let Andy know - he'll be jealous.'

Faith shot Di a sharp glance - but she was only being her usual jokey self.

'He's a bit of an arrogant bastard, if you ask me!' Faith said trying to put herself back in the real world.

'Is that Andy or Nick Wren?'

'Oh, Di!'

'Oh Faith! Hey! What about our story then?'

Faith had known that Di would be expecting the next part of the Murder at the Manor story, and she had it ready, but it hadn't inspired her much, galloping to a plausible if dramatic conclusion. The idea was too tired - too well used. However, there was another thriller-style idea building in her mind: an idea that felt as if it were really her own, with no tired ancestry. If she let it develop, if she pushed aside all the mundane things, perhaps she could tell Di that story next. It would be something altogether bigger, a story worth telling.

chapter two – Di

The creep, or 'The Leech', as she thought of him, Mr Arnold Lechwood would be getting the best personal secretary he had ever had, Di thought, though a secretary was all he was getting if she could help it. The rise was important, it would mean that they would have enough to pay their mortgage and still be able to eat. If, and this was the big IF, if Paul would lay off the drink. He was costing her more in whisky that in groceries, and it was making her sick. Paul, her Paul.

She'd fallen for him the first time they met, tall dark and handsome: everything that she'd been looking for. He was ready to work hard and, more to the point, had the right contacts to make the building boom work for him. Together they'd made a brilliant team. Her accountancy and office skills turned a one-man-and-his-dog operation into a tidy little building firm. They weren't into building high-rises or anything grand - just plenty of neat houses for the new first-time buyers, the new to ownership class of people, her class of people - but the punters were never to know that. Though never quite as well spoken as Faith nevertheless she put on a good show, besides, she could get away with things that little Faith couldn't. Dear Faith, dear little Faith, always such a dark sweet natured girl. Di knew there were times when she had turned against Faith, provoked her, just to find out what would happen, what went on behind those large dark eyes. Yet she could never leave her for long.

And of course where Di and Paul went, Faith and Andy followed. Andy, as Paul's right-hand man, had fallen as hard as the house prices. The men consoled each other - Di didn't think that was the best way for her Paul - he needed to be fighting, on his own, getting it all back together. She was holding the world together waiting for him to be ready - her world, all she'd, they'd, worked for. And she wasn't going to let it go.

'Paul? Paul?' The house, cold and feeling damp told her to expect no answer. 'Damn!' she'd have sooner found him glued to the television than out, for out usually meant at the club

house, putting the drinks on the slate. For the sake of show -
for never letting others know how bad things really were, she'd
made sure the slate was paid at the end of each month - up until
now. Now she was going to have to do some really hard
thinking, and some hard talking. It was time. It had to be time.

There was one thing about being brought up where there was
little enough to go round - you knew how to make do when
the hard times came round again. She sliced a small onion into
a glass casserole dish, dabbed some marg on it and set it to
soften in the microwave. Quickly, she peeled carrots, potatoes
and swede, and chopped them roughly. Stirring a spoonful of
flour into the softened onions she made a coarse roux, then
blended in a can of tinned tomatoes and added the other
chopped veg. She browned the small quantity of diced chicken
that she'd bought and added that to the casserole and put it
back in the microwave to cook while she went upstairs to
shower. When she came down it was all cooked through. Some
fat dumplings, livened up with a few herbs, and their meal
would be complete and there would be enough to go in the
freezer for another day too. Not quite what they'd been used
to, at the peak of the business they'd eaten out more nights than
they'd stayed in. It was as if it was going to go on forever. She
sometimes had the nagging doubts, sometimes she urged Paul
to salt away some of the largesse, savings for a rainy day. But
the rain was never going to come, he said, and any money that
was not ploughed back into the business, buying other plots of
land that he 'just happened to know might be released as
building land' was theirs to live well on. By selling up everything
and taking out a mortgage on the house they'd once owned
outright they'd been able to keep the creditors at bay. There
was nothing else left: not a single plot of land; not a cement
mixer; not a wheelbarrow - just her and Paul and their home
on mortgage - and she wasn't going to let that go.

The door banged shut. She heard him hang his coat on the
end of the banister, kick off his shoes, wander into the sitting
room, then return. The door to the kitchen opened.
'This place is bloody cold.'

'There didn't seem much point in turning on the heating just for a couple of hours - the Calor's on in here, close the door.' He looked at his hand still holding the door handle, released it and stepping inside he leant against the door until it closed.

'Dinner's ready.'

'What is it?'

'Chicken casserole.'

'Stew again?'

'Don't! It's a meal .. it's good food .. it's ..'

'Don't give me a lecture.'

Di bit her tongue, let her heart beat five times, took a slow breath. 'I've got some good news -'

He sat down at the kitchen bar, looked at her, flicked the long hair back from his forehead in his usual manner. He was still a very handsome man, eyes the colour of dark honey, thick chestnut hair, a good body. Just looking at him made her fall for him all over again, stirred her body from its weariness.

'I've got that promotion I was after.'

His eyes flickered, slid away from hers. 'Good, well done,' the tone all wrong.

Di's heart squeezed, disappointment flooded through her. She got up abruptly, ladled the casserole out into large bowls, almost banged them down before them.

'Well, we've got to eat.' she said. He hung his head slightly, not looking at her anymore. He picked up a fork and poked it about in the mass of vegetables. He ate a piece. Di sat and began to eat her own, the hot lumps searing her throat, tight as it was with anxiety.

He pushed his bowl away - still half full.

'What?'

'Not too hungry.'

'But you must be!'

'Had a bite at the club ..' he ducked his head as if he expected her to throw something.

'At the bloody club - oh Paul - why? It costs the earth for nothing there!'

'We all did, okay? I can't stand there and say "Oh no, I can't eat with you, I've got to watch the fucking pennies."'

'You didn't have to stay! You didn't have to be there at all - you could - you could have made something up. An appointment. - anything! Anything would be bloody better than hanging around the clubhouse all day. How often did you do that when you were in work? Hardly ever! Just being there singles you out as a loser - they all know! There's no real point in belonging! We never really did belong there!'

'You fucking never belonged there you mean. Never even been in a restaurant that didn't dish up fish and chips before you went with me. You forget. You drag me down to your level every time. It was *my* fucking capital that got my business off the ground and where did I get that from, not from some council house in a poxy little village - from my inheritance - from Grandpa's house that he left *me*!'

'Yes, yes but look -' she began, but stopped. She had been going to remind him of how things were before she came along - and she knew that would only lead to a deeper more dangerous row. Time to play the peacemaker - he was tired, probably a little worse the wear from drink. 'Look, love, we'll be all right. We'll keep the house, something will turn up - some opportunity to get business back on the road.' she added gently.

'Yeah, yeah. I'm - I don't know why I said that - I'm tired - tired of it all,' sounding too weary to believe her, 'I'm off to bed, okay?'

'Okay,' she said softly. He'd be asleep again when she'd finished clearing up and putting the house to rights. Did she really care? Thank God they'd not had children. What must it be like for Faith? Faith and Andy's saving grace had to be the minuscule mortgage they had on their tiny place, Faith's salary couldn't keep them all otherwise, and Andy was about as useful around the place as Paul even if his whisky consumption was much lower. Would she tell Faith about this latest row? Could she? Would Faith feel Paul's disdain in the telling? After all they'd grown up as next door neighbours, in identical houses in a row of eight. She looked at the washing up, turned and ran a bowl of hot water, she wouldn't use the dishwasher - there was hot water in the tank and the electricity bills were high enough already. She stood watching the bubbles wink and break, not seeing but remembering.

She'd loved to go and play at Faith's house, to escape the torment and row of her three brothers. Faith's mum was so quiet and there was plenty of room. Faith was an only child, there was some reason why they couldn't have any more; some reason that dropped behind a whisper whenever it was spoken of. A 'woman's problem' of some kind. As she grew into her teens she understood more, but never heard the precise details of the problem, but she did take in the other shadow in Faith's family. They said it was the disappointment - her father had desperately wanted a boy - and had got a girl, and no second chances. He'd fathered a boy elsewhere, and left Faith's mum to go and live with the mother of his son when Faith was just thirteen. Suddenly it was as if Faith's mum had caught the plague. People only talked about her in hushed tones, they avoided her, no one knew what to say. There was a lot of 'who knows what goes on between man and wife' and 'it takes two to break a marriage' and 'poor little Faith' yet they kept their distance in case it was catching. Even Di had abandoned Faith for a time - shunning her as seemed to be expected by her parents and peers. But it didn't last long - none of it. Faith's mother never seemed to get over it - drifting through life, keeping house, working at the village shop, looking after Faith - though everyone else soon forgot the scandal.

Scandal? An everyday event now - even in the area that they'd grown up in some now didn't bother getting married in the first place. And here, in the leafy new suburbs, it was a time when all the other wives, and the recent divorcées, rallied round to keep everything shipshape for the latest casualty, handing out tips on how to get the most, the best deal, from the split. She was right. They didn't belong. And it didn't matter how much Paul talked of 'his inheritance', his home conditions were poorer than hers, a touch of 'fur coat and no knickers' as her mother had put it. His family 'owned' their home, one in a terrace near the centre of town, but owed more than they'd paid off. His mother liked to 'eat out'; Di suspected that she merely couldn't cook. His father worked for the County Council, an official of some pomposity, and made much of his position and his membership of the local Conservative Association. There was something in that. The 'connections' that Paul had came through that clique - those in the know with their fists on the rubber stamp.

The water was almost cold, the dishes looked up at her through the scummy mess that had floated free. Di shook herself and whisked the scourer around, dried the dishes and cleaned the table quickly. 'Hang the ironing' she thought, if she headed off to bed now Paul might still be awake, the thought brought a smile to her lips. Making up after a row was often the best - they both tried a little harder.

Di hummed happily to herself as she made coffee and poured herself a bowl of Special K. No frowning at the skinny woman on the box today. Last night she'd been right to forget the ironing. She'd massaged Paul's ego back into shape, and a little more! The booze had been little enough and taken early enough before so as to shake loose some of his little inhibitions and yet not interfere with performance. He'd even smiled this morning, and suggested she might not want to get up just yet. Sadly she had to - but then, she told him, there was always tonight.

She checked her hair in the mirror, called out that she was leaving and plunged out into a frost-bitten morning. Even the garage door seemed frozen closed. Groaning, it gave and she dived into the gloom, glad to get out of the wind.

'Start, damn you,' she muttered as the engine whined and whined. Suddenly it caught, giving a jolt and shudder as it did so. She pumped her foot a few times on the accelerator, the exhaust fumes billowing off the back wall and coiling round the sides of the car. Slowly she pulled forward, stopped, went back out into the icy wind to close the door, daring the engine to stop.

She rounded the corner. Faith was not in sight. She rubbed harder at the screen to enlarge the clear patch. No Faith? Then again there had to be a wind-chill factor of about minus ten degrees - she wouldn't have hung about herself - though she hadn't expected Faith not to be there. Level with Faith's house she pressed the horn a couple of times, short bursts. She rubbed the side window. The light was on in the front room, showing as a wedge near the top where the curtains were not quite pulled tight. A light appeared in the hall - went out - the front door opening. Faith appeared, bundled up in her old sheepskin coat, a tasselled triangular scarf wrapped around her neck, across her face. She ran to the car, dragged open the door, slid in, slammed it shut and fumbled with her seat belt. 'Okay?'

'Yes - fine - sorry,' Faith's automatic answer came muffled by the scarf as she cupped one hand to her neck. Di paused a moment then put the car into gear and pulled away. Di, catching the movement out of the corner of her eye, noticed Faith turn towards her, as if about to say something. She waited - then Faith's face turned away again.

'Do you ever go to the club nowadays?' Di asked suddenly, as much to start the chatter going as anything.

Faith laughed, it came out hard and cynical. Di looked at her old friend again - this was not usual - Faith had the only laugh she had ever thought of as being musical, a laugh that rose and fell like the sound of wind chimes.

'Scarcely, it's hard to both be out.'

'Ah - I forgot. It's just - well we had this row about the club. Paul keeps running up bills there - it's all I can do to clear them. I'm getting sick of it, and oh God, Faith - he gets so, so defensive when I suggest we drop membership - how do you manage?'

'You don't know? You really don't know? Andy - well he *insists* he stays a member - but I think you'll find most of his drinks go on Paul's tab, I'm sorry, I've tried,' she rubbed her neck again, like a nervous tic.

'What?' Di took her eyes of the road to look at Faith for a moment. 'What - you mean I'm slogging my guts out and waving my arse around The Leech so Andy can drink with Paul? Oh come on!'

'Di! It's not me. Paul - Andy says - Paul feels 'responsible', feels he owes Andy something. I've tried - I have - there's only so much I ...'

'Wait till I see that wretch. Bloody hell - it's bad enough footing his bills, let alone,' her voice trailed off. Both women stared out of the front windscreen, concentrating on the traffic ahead and around them. The silence filled the car like a fog coming down, blinding their thoughts to further conversation. Within the fog a message tapped itself out on Di's subconscious, a worry that nagged at her but would not become clear. She felt it was something to do with Faith, yet even to think of Faith clouded everything again with Andy and Paul and her own anger.

chapter three – Faith

Her neck was stiff this morning; the after effect of a letter from the school.

'What's this?' she'd asked Andy, opening the letter that Jilly had given her just before going to bed.

'Can't guess - an envelope?' he raised a slack-faced smile from his position on the sofa, half dozing, half watching a quiz show.

'No - it's a letter from school,' she scanned the contents, ran her eyes back over the lines again. 'Oh - Andy!'

'What?'

'What? You may well say 'what'. The children were late to school every day last week! Every day! What the hell are you doing? They're all ready to go when I leave for work - all ready.'

'Yeah - well. It doesn't matter- it's only primary.'

'It matters! It gives them a - a bad reputation with the school.'

'So send them a letter- an excuse.'

'And what do I say next week then?'

'Faith, have faith,' he'd said, standing. 'Have faith,' he gave a short laugh at his own joke, resting his hands on her shoulders, looking down on her. A gentle squeeze, reminiscent of their first days. Days when he'd squeeze her shoulders then, slipping his hands under her arms, he'd pick her up, bringing her up to his height to kiss her. But not this time. 'Faith - don't fuss! I can't stand it.' a little shake, 'I - can't stand it.' a harder shake. She tried to twist from his grip - he held tighter, his breath, rank with drink, came faster, his eyes fixed somewhere just beyond her. She felt sick - her heart thumping, but he kept shaking her like a dog with a rat. It was all she could do to stand, her mind a whirl, a blank of nausea. He stopped, clasped her to his chest, held her head there, his heart thumping in her ear, the sound of his breath rasping through her frame. And then he was sobbing, great gulps, his fingers stroking her hair. She stood, dizzy, scared. Stood still, waiting. Suddenly he dropped his hands and stepped away, turned and walked away, leaving her to sink to the floor.

This morning, for the first time ever she'd wanted to talk to Di. She'd wanted to say - 'it's getting too much, I can't take much more, help me' - but it was hard, and then Di was not 'at home' to anyone else's troubles, and so she'd kept the words inside. She'd been late because she wanted to make sure Andy was at least awake and prepared to take the children to school, and that had been difficult. She'd stood by the bedroom door daring herself to open it for at least five minutes. And when she did, it was as if he remembered nothing - as if he'd never noticed that he'd slept alone.

'All right?' he'd mumbled.

'Yes,' she'd stared across at him, his large frame creating a vast mountain range from the duvet, 'Just - the children are all ready for school, just don't forget. Bye.' and she'd turned and fled. In the kitchen she'd spoken to Jilly, quickly, quietly. 'Don't make a row, but make sure Daddy knows when it's half past eight, okay? Okay?' and she'd hugged and kissed the dark-eyed child, and kissed the blond top of Jon's head, and run for the door - late.

The silence would not be broken. It was the longest journey into work that Faith had ever endured, and the more she held her head still, the more her neck seemed to ache. The more she tried to find something to say, the more her mind was filled with all those things that it was better not to say at the moment.

'Bye, see you -' she said, holding the door a moment as she climbed out, but was cut off by the tug of the door in her hand as Di edged the car forward. 'Bye.' she shoved the door hard, making it bang shut, and stepped sharply out of the way of the wheels. For a moment she watched the rear lights weave their way into the pattern of the traffic, wondered how she'd broken the fabric of their friendship yet again, without meaning to. The cold wind that sliced into her ankles brought her round and she turned quickly to head for the office, stepping right into the path of a man.

'Sorry! Sorry!' she said quickly and hurried off. It was dangerous to stop, to say more, to look. A few steps and she felt a hand on her arm. A melt of fear ran through her.

'Mrs Warren? Faith?'

She paused, half turned, dared to look. Nick Wren.

'Are you okay? Sorry I barged into you - I wasn't paying attention,' he said, his voice rich with concern.

She sighed. 'Fine,' her hand touched her neck. 'Fine - I - rushing for work.'

'Come on then - we'll brave it together,' he said, opening his eyes wide a moment, allowing a sparkle of amusement to light them up. Faith found a smile touch her mind, despite herself.

It was as if his body shielded her from the wind, she felt warmer, safer. They walked side by side slower than she usually walked alone. At the door he allowed her to go through first, she turned to him as the doors closed, loosening her scarf from her neck as she did so.

'Thank you.' she smiled.

'Pleasure's all mine,' he said, and turned his hand to indicate the lifts, 'going up?'

She nodded. They stepped over to the lifts together.

'Have you worked here long?'

'Just the last four years - since my youngest started school.'

'Children? What have you got?'

'Just the two, Jilly, she's nine now and Jon - he's nearly eight,'

'Then you must have had them young.'

Faith blushed, annoyed with herself that she'd liked what she'd heard. 'We've been married twelve years!' she said sharply.

He just smiled - a warm, understanding smile; a smile that transformed his face. And the lift stopped, the doors gasped open and let the noise and bustle of the busy room come in.

'Thank you.' Faith said automatically.

'See you later,' he said softly.

Faith found it hard to concentrate on her work. The ache in her neck kept reminding her of Andy, and the memory hurt. What had happened between them? They had always been the odd couple in the foursome, but still a pair. Di and Paul - well matched, tall and beautiful, the perfect couple - and Andy and Faith. Andy, Paul's best friend from the blood-brother-bonding days of their childhood, had grown to be his right-hand man. Evenings, when they'd all get together and the boys would drink a few over the top and get to reminiscing, their 'do you remember' stories were full of the type of pranks and adventures that only boys seem to delight in, semi-cruel in a childishly savage way, the prototype boys for 'the Lord of the Flies'. And Faith knew just who would be the leader, and who would follow, as they tormented the life out of a victim. There was something frightening about the hidden power of a natural leader, about the charisma that meant that their ideas always sounded exciting, daring and possible. What frightened her most was how much she wanted to be part of it, as if she knew deep within her that if she were not part of it all, then she would be in danger, the danger of becoming the victim.

She'd revelled in their foursome, part of the power-block, part of the beautiful couple. Where Paul and Di were so well matched, and so in love, Andy was scraping the ceiling at six foot three and at least fourteen stone, and there was she, a foot shorter and, in those days, just under eight stone. He always called her 'little' Faith, and for a long time they were just together because Di and Paul were together. He'd put his arm around her shoulder as they all walked together, cuddle her up to him when Di cuddled up to Paul. Kiss her, his hands squeezing and rubbing her breasts too firmly, in the back of the car while Paul and Di said good-night in the front. Somewhere along the line they became a twosome, recognised in their own right. And was it love or relief she felt when he pressed her in to 'letting' him? She knew it would happen. They had Paul's parents' house all to themselves for the weekend, a small party was arranged for the Saturday night, a carefully selected group of Paul's choosing - he had no need to throw wide the doors to cultivate acquaintances - and Faith and Di were to stay the night. Faith hadn't wanted to at first, hadn't wanted to leave her mother all alone, hadn't wanted to lie to her, but Di said she needed Faith. Di called on her friendship - and she stayed the night.

She was terrified. Not so much at the idea of having sex - she knew the facts, and with Di's help was prepared - no, she was irrationally scared that Andy might crush her, stop her breathing with his sheer bulk. Sometimes, when he held her with her face pressed against his chest, she felt as if she would suffocate, it was part of that, she supposed. When it happened, he was remarkably light on her, remarkably careful - as if she might just break if he wasn't. She believed then that he must love her; that she was in love with him. What had happened between them that he no longer treated her with such care?

Once she'd finished the work for Alun Watson she took the sheets over to his cramped office. The door ajar she tapped and stepped in. Alun looked up and removed his glasses, Faith presented him with his letters.

'And there are a number of queries that need you attention, here and here,' she added, her tone confident and crisp, laying down two pieces of incoming mail that she was unable to deal with alone.

'Fine, fine.'

'I have something for you, Faith.'

Faith jumped, she had not noticed Nick lounging against the wall behind her, box file in hand.

'Um - yes. If you could - um.' she swallowed. 'If you bring it across to my desk, I'll do the work as soon as possible.'

'Fine, fine.' he said, his words a mimicry of Alun's.

Faith looked from him to Alun. The thin man forced the cap back on his fountain pen firmly and laid it down slowly.

'Thank you, Mrs Warren,' he said carefully. She collected the papers and left, seconds later the door to the office banged shut, the two men still within.

Faith felt a sudden weight on the back of her swivelchair, causing it to turn slightly under her.

'I'm sorry,' Nick said, close to her ear, then turned and perched on the corner of her desk, looking down at her. 'I'm afraid your Mr Watson's pomposity brings out the worst in me. I hope I didn't embarrass you? Let me make amends - buy you lunch?'

Faith let out an involuntary huff and looked down at her hands poised over the keyboard. Something about his obvious self-assurance made her want to hit him - it was as if he thought he could have whatever he liked just because he was 'someone' once. 'Once' - she grasped the idea and turned her face back to his.

'I always lunch with a *friend*, Mr Wren, thank you.' she said politely, coldly. What she was not prepared for was the look that flitted across his face. She might as well have hit him. It was the look of an often-beaten child, a wincing at pain that is covered swiftly by bravado, in case another beating is given for being afraid. His eyes, usually alight with amusement, became momentarily dull, as if seeing nothing before him. All in a fleeting second - gone so swiftly that by the time the pain had registered and she tried to soften her words he had stood and walked away.

She looked at the words on the screen. They jumbled themselves, making nonsense. She knew she'd hurt him - yet couldn't understand where the power of the weapon came from. Was he just so used to being accepted that he was annoyed by being turned down? And that was as silly as him asking her to lunch in the first place.

'Lunch, Faith?'

Susie stood almost where Nick Wren had been, looking at Faith with concern.

'What? Oh! Yes - I'll just save,' she flicked the cursor to the save icon and blanked the screen. She smiled up at Susie and pushed her chair back. As she stood the ache in her shoulders reasserted itself - she moved them forward and back tentatively. Susie watched her. 'It's tension. Makes you tighten up all the back and neck muscles,' she said cheerfully as they walked towards the canteen. 'Not that I'd mind that sort of tension,' she smiled quickly at Faith. 'Did I really hear you turn down lunch with that gorgeous hunk of man - to lunch with *me*?'

'Yes - I suppose you did. And I suppose you're right - there is something ..' Faith paused, lost for a moment, standing before the salad selection, seeing only Nick Wren's face. 'Yes,' she said brightly, turning to Susie. 'He *is* quite attractive - isn't he?'

'Oh yeah – like you've only just noticed!' Susie laughed as they paid up and headed for their table. But what Faith had only just noticed was that she could see his face in her mind; that somehow she'd held it there, and the realisation strangely moved her.

'At last!' Amy Robertson sighed extravagantly when Faith brought her letters in to sign. Faith glanced at her watch. Not late, earlier than usual if anything.
'There's only one letter that I think you need to reply to, I've put that on the top. The others are pretty standard.' she said tentatively.
'Yes, I'm sure.' Amy scanned the letter and put it to one side. She scanned each of her own drafted letters and signed them, not once looking up. 'There, thank you.' she said briskly, leaving them lying on the desktop. Faith began to gather together the letters. 'I've missed Mr Wren again I see - unlike some?'
'Sorry?'
'I wasn't a gossip columnist for nothing, you know. Always have contacts, dear. I understand you arrived together - most friendly.'
Faith blushed. She hated her traitorous face - the way it offered everyone an insight into her feelings of anger or embarrassment.
'And invited to lunch - indeed?'
'And turned down,' Faith said, straightening her shoulders until they hurt. 'Anything else, Ms Robertson?'
'No - but perhaps when you see him again you'll let him know I'll be glad to see him. No - forget that - say I enquired after his health.'
'Health?'
'Yes, dear. That'll be enough,' she said, looking back at the work on her desk, dismissing Faith from her presence.
The whole atmosphere was wrong. How could one man upset the working atmosphere of the place in two days? She returned to her desk with the horribly creepy feeling of others watching her. Everyone knew how fast and maliciously the office gossip could travel. It really didn't take much - and there had been at least one nasty incident when a jealous husband had been the eventual recipient of the tittle-tattle. A rumour with a bedrock of truth as it happened; it split families and ruined chances of promotion where the whole thing might have blown over in a

couple of months without the rumour machine. And here she was - a subject - spoken of - so quickly, on so little, with no basis at all. How dangerous, how stupidly, seriously dangerous, it was.

chapter four - Faith

Faith felt cold and exposed. She'd been standing in the fine drizzle hard against the post box for over half and hour, her hair now dripped small ice-cold tears down the back of her neck, her sheepskin coat felt slimy to the touch as she pushed back her cuff to peer at the time. Di was never this late. She surely wouldn't have just left her? The atmosphere in the car had been grim - but they'd not exactly fallen out with each other. The supermarket carrier bag was cutting into her hand, yet she daren't put it down, she moved her fingers, one at a time, to let the blood flow through them again. She shivered. And what was she going back to? She didn't want to think of home at the moment, it did nothing to warm her, she felt cold right through to her heart, as if the rain had found its way into her veins chilling her whole being. Yet somewhere inside a spark of warmth flared. The Story. It flickered before her mind's eye for a moment - and warmed her. The Story. She'd let it run - see where it went.

The girl, the 'heroine' is small and dark, with eyes of deepest brown. She has a wonderful smile and a beautiful voice, speaking or singing. She is intelligent - she's been to university, got a degree in - English. And her name is - Faith? Hope? Charity? Her name is Hope - Hope Jones. She is a journalist - not a beginner - someone who has worked her way through the local rags, through the small-town weeklies and has now landed a position on a large regional newspaper, the last stepping stone to a National.

Faith could see her, see herself, a few years younger, a little slimmer, with that certain go-getting gleam in her eye she'd never quite had in reality. The beginning of *The Story*.

A horn sounded sharp and raucous just below her rib cage: she jumped. Di's car had pulled in tight to the kerb, trying not to get crunched by the press of traffic she was blocking, her face pushed forward to the screen, mouthing words, waving one-handed at Faith to hurry. Faith hurried. She slid, wet, into the passenger seat - the indicator already flashing Di's intention of returning to the flow, the tyres squealing a little as they pushed away from the pavement.

Faith adjusted her coat collar slightly, trying to get a section of dry to nestle against her skin, wishing she'd remembered her scarf, imagining it huddled at the foot of the office coat rack.

'What's up? Didn't you see me coming?' Di snapped as soon as she was comfortably in the main flow heading for the motorway.

'No – day-dreaming I suppose.'

'Lucky you!'

'You were so late.'

'Not my fault - *I* can assure you. One day, one day as that man's secretary, and I'm wondering if I did the right thing. The paper work is zilch - as I knew - but the demands!'

'Harassing you?'

'Too sneaky for that - no, *advice*.' Di put on a voice, plummy and cajoling. 'My dear, my dear Di, a little of your feminine intuition, how do you feel about the move towards weight training - bulging biceps - toned torsos?'

'What's that got to do with their line of business?'

'Some idea - so he says - of creating body workshops alongside the clubs. And if you can believe that you'll believe..' she waved her hand to finish the sentence. 'It was like that all day - in and out of his office to give him *advice*!'

'Could be worse.'

'Could be a hell of a lot of things,' she sighed extravagantly. 'How are you? Sorry I was so - you know - this morning. The men - huh?'

'Yep.'

'Come on then, Faith, cheer me up,' Di flashed a tight smile at Faith, her eyes betraying a trace of tiredness.

'A story?'

'Great.'

Do I tell her The Story? Faith thought. Dare I start it when I'm not even quite sure where it's going to go? One step up from a daydream; one step away from a fantasy, like a crystal pebble rubbed for luck until it reflects the face of its owner, it may reveal too much. And it's all mine, what if she doesn't like it? Dare I share it? Shall I? Shall I?

'You could do another thriller - how about a maniac hitch-hiker.' Di said nodding towards a dark figure with a drooping card reading 'London' held listlessly up for those joining the motorway to read and take pity.

'No - no. I have an idea for a story. It's just.' Faith stopped, unsure of how to explain it.

'What?' Di took her eyes off the traffic to look at Faith again.

'It may be long - a very long story.'

'Great.'

'I mean - days, weeks long.' Faith, her eyes dark and shining as if filled to the brim with her dreaming, turned and looked at Di.

'I'm ready - nothing else to do!' Di said brightly, snapping a smile, glancing at the traffic, checking out the look on Faith's face once more before settling back to driving and listening.

'Okay. It's called 'The Story'. As in a newspaper story?' she waited. Di nodded. Faith smiled to herself, a small tight smile that belied the feeling within. She felt as if she stood on the edge of a precipice, just as she'd done one adventure weekend they'd all been on, back before the children came along; rock-climbing and abseiling. The instructors told them all what to do, how safe it would be to hang out into space, feet pressed to a vertical face of rock. Her heart had thumped so hard she'd had difficulty hearing and understanding what they said. Then it was her turn. Shaking, unbelieving, she'd stood on the edge of the precipice. "Lean back, lean back." the instructor said. And she had leant back, over the abyss. Back and back, until it was too late to change her mind and she had to step - to walk down the rock face. It was brilliant! Lean back, lean back.

Hope Jones stepped up to the entrance of the newspaper office and the doors paid their homage and slid sibilantly aside, making way for the newest journalist to join City Press. She felt proud, pleased, to be entering this impressive hallway not as an eager applicant but as a new member of staff. Steadying her usually quick walking speed she approached the receptionist and introduced herself pleasantly. She had learned very early on in the

*business that it paid to be nice to everyone because you never knew who
would be the first to hear about a story or to know someone who did. The
receptionist smiled a plastic smile and assured Hope that she was pleased
to meet her. Shrugging her shoulders mentally, Hope headed for the large
set of lifts, her own image, distorted and erratic, flashed back at her from
the shiny stainless steel doors.*

*Inside, facing mirrors made the lift crowded even as she rode up alone to
the third floor and gave her a chance to check that her glossy brown hair
was neat and business-like, that her cheeks were not too bright with
excitement. Feeling good about herself - feeling confident, she stepped out
of the lift into the busy newsroom, her eyes quickly scanning the range of
offices down one side for that of the Senior Editor. Bestowing smiles to all
who were idle enough to catch her eye as she headed down the newsroom
she called up the image she'd retained of.'*

Of? The senior editor - this was going to be Di - a name?
The most famous Di - Princess Di. Windsor? Spencer! And a
first name? Di Harvey - Harvey? Bristol Cream Sherry. Come
on- don't be silly. She leant her head back, eyes closed, thinking.
'You all right?' Di sounded concerned.
'Mmm - shh.'
'Image of?' Di prompted.
Harvey Jones - Joan? Joan Spencer? No no. Harvey, Harvey,
Harvey. Bristol Cream Sherry. Oh! Sherry? Sherry Spencer?
Okay.
'Okay - just getting the name right - okay?

*She called up the image of Ms Spencer. She knew the reputation of the
woman as an editor who accepted nothing but the best; of an editor who
could be as sharp as a guillotine with staff who did not measure up. What
she'd not been prepared for was her physical beauty. The tall, strikingly
attractive woman who had leant forward to touch her hand in greeting at
the interview could have appeared on the front cover of a fashion magazine.
Her honey-blonde hair, cut to halo a strong but fine-featured face, and her
eyes of palest blue served to create the suspicion that the facade was all there
was. It wasn't.'*

Faith flicked a glance at Di. Her lips were turned up in a
smile, though her eyes remained fixed on the road ahead. She'd
recognised herself, even in the hyperbole of the fiction. Faith

felt a tingle of delight run round inside her head - pleased to have made her friend smile again.

'*She stopped just before she reached the open office door. She could hear Ms Spencer's clearly modulated tones, and judged by the pauses that she was on the phone. Not wishing to appear and be waved away, or told to wait, Hope bided her time, waiting for the call to end. She didn't have to wait long. Standing as tall as her five foot three would allow, she stepped into the doorway and tapped at the open door. Instantly the face behind the desk looked up and gave her a smile so radiant that Faith - Oh - sorry! that Hope was almost taken aback, thinking that someone else must be in the room, or standing behind her.*

'*Welcome, welcome to City News. I have high hopes of you, Hope - no pun intended.*'

'*Thank you Ms Spencer.*'

'*Well - we'll keep the formalities for meetings, shall we? You may call me Sherry otherwise. Would you like a coffee?*'

'*Thank you.*' *Hope said quietly, the warmth of the welcome making her feel off balance. She'd been prepared for a short sharp beginning - not the introduction to a coffee morning.*

'*Two coffees,*' *Sherry spoke into the intercom on her desk, looked up and raised a beautifully curved and eloquent eyebrow.* '*Milk?*'

'*Thank you, yes.*'

'*One with milk,*' *Sherry added to the box before releasing her finger from the button.* '*There,*' *she smiled at Hope again, and Hope couldn't help feeling as if Ms Sherry Spencer was playing some kind of game with her, some initiation rite, some strange test - only Hope didn't know what it was.*

Later that day, seated at her assigned desk and getting to grips with the computer system that served the whole of the newsroom and beyond, Hope felt a little deflated. Sure, she had to get to know how to work her way round the system, how to call up information from the fantastic background log that the paper kept, how to retrieve one of the millions of photographic images from store - but she felt she'd rather find out as she worked on a piece. She'd really wished to be assigned to a story straight away so that she could show them what she could do, how she could really dig for that extra little nugget that would make her piece just that bit special, different to any other article on the same subject. She was determined to make her name as an investigative journalist though she knew the road to be difficult, that it took a lot to be accepted by editors as having the right sort of 'nose' for the job. Often it would be a lucky break that would place the journalist in the investigative league - but once you were there the leeway to work more independently was granted, and greater credence would be given to suspicions raised or ideas suggested. She sighed and leant back, closing her eyes for a moment.

'No use sleeping on the job,' a warm baritone voice sounded behind her.

Instantly her eyes snapped open, though she just controlled the urge to sit straight to attention, maintaining her leisurely pose for a second before moving slowly to upright and turning her chair to meet the eyes that belonged to the voice. Eyes of sea-grey flecked with deep blue contrasted well with his dark glossy hair and enlivened a handsome but somewhat rugged face. He leant forward, adding a pleasant smile to his charms, holding out a hand in formal greeting.

Oh - he's got in here. Nick Wren - at least his name-change should be easy - I'll call him Christopher - Chris. And a different bird - something with black plumage - Crow? Rook? Raven!

'Chris Raven - welcome aboard,' he said.

'Hope Jones,' she said shaking the outstretched hand and smiling back at him, 'What 'er?'

'Photos.'

'Oh - perhaps we'll have to work together sometimes - I'm a journalist.'

'You don't say,' his rich voice mocked her.

She blushed, annoyed with herself - annoyed with him.

'Pretty obvious, I suppose,' she said quickly to diffuse her own anger, and looked down to avoid his eyes.

So pretty, so fresh and real, he thought, as he took in the shine of her chestnut coloured hair, the curve of her dark lashes as they met the bloom of her cheek. Fresh, delicate and a delight to savour. He was almost caught staring as she suddenly lifted her head to flash her challenging dark eyes at him.

'Oh yes?' Di said suddenly 'Who's the fella?'

'What?' Faith, like a sleepwalker disturbed, felt disorientated, dragged back into reality from the dream.

'The fella! The one who's making eyes at you in the story - certainly doesn't sound like Andy and it'd better not be Paul.'

'No! It's someone I made up - just - made up.'

'Just as well - else Andy had better watch it,' she laughed.

Faith's heart still thumped unevenly against her ribs. The story had for a few moments filled her with so much life and joy that she had been living it. Feeling those eyes appreciate her, feeling admired, making her feel beautiful - for a change. Real life, the rain on the windscreen, the never ending swish of the wipers, the proximity of home came crowding in on her, driving the words far away, back into the recesses of her mind.

'Go on.'

'I can't.'

'Go on - you can - you usually carry on when I interrupt,' Di said, a slight note of a whine hiding behind the coaxing.

'Not tonight - bit late. I'll carry on tomorrow - if you want?' Half hoping that Di would say she didn't want - that the story was too slow, not gripping enough. Anything so that Faith could return it to her pocket to caress and shine up for the dark times, for her own moments of escape. And yet - now she had begun - wanting it to go on.

'All right - I'll let you off! But I'll think about it all through 'til tomorrow,' Di laughed easily. 'Here, you haven't got any more heroes like that about the place for my Ms Sherry Spencer, have you?'

'Ah - you'll have to wait and see on that one,' Faith replied, truthfully - as she suddenly recognised that even she didn't know who or what was in store for Sherry just yet. And that was proving to be the best bit - the unknown being discovered little by little as she let the story unwind. The outline she had in mind being filled and made alive by the words and the characters they made, and by the characters and the way they behaved within her imagination, as if they held a life of their own, autonomous and wilful.

They were home. She reached for the door handle finding her mind grinding to a halt, being brought down to the ground. It was as if she felt no need for any other life just at the moment

- no desire for any other company - she had embarked on The Story and it filled her with impatience.

chapter five – Di

Lights were on all over the house Di noted with a little irritation, but at least it meant Paul was at home. She recalled Paul's petulance at her obsessive turning off of lights behind him in their early days - days when like now they had little enough money to waste. 'Just like my mother!' he'd said in final and winning thrust. Leaving the lights on was one defiance of his upbringing - and even though she hated to see the waste of money she would not be compared to his mother. She opened the front door to a house of light and warmth filled with the sound of an old Sting LP. As she dragged a bag of shopping through to the kitchen, she heard Paul upstairs joining in the refrain at the end of the number. She smiled - singing was not one of his good qualities.

He came thumping down the stairs bringing the scent of newly showered man into the kitchen, his face grinning.

'What?' Di said, smiling back at him. He came over to her and wrapped his arms around her tight and kissed her. And was kissed back. 'What?' she said again. 'Work?'

He kissed her again, lightly, and released her. 'Yes! With Billy - remember Billy?' he said, sweeping the damp hair from his forehead with his fingers.

Di remembered Billy. Great friend Billy - bought the majority of the plots that they'd owned from them - market price mind, rock bottom, no favours. Yet somehow he'd made it seem like a favour - and Paul seemed to take it in the same way. She nodded.

'He's got the go-ahead on the ten-house site up at Ridgley,' Paul rubbed his hands together 'He needs a site manager - and a foreman. He says we'll do. Andy and I are going to see him about it at the club tomorrow.'

The ten-house site at Ridgley had been one of theirs, their largest and most recent investment, before their delicate balance of finances had come crashing to the floor.

'When's it going to start?' Di said softly. Plenty of sites had been given the go-ahead by planning, only to remain idle as the market for new houses was just about non-existent.

'Soon - he's changed it all round see? He's gone for the top of the market - well you know the smaller places are no good - too many cheap repossessions up for grabs, so he's knocked it down to five houses, five-bedroom jobs, with a decent bit of land. He's got interest already!' Paul sounded almost as excited as if it were one of his own projects. Di's heart felt squeezed. It should have been theirs - their new scheme, it didn't seem right for Paul to be enthusiastic about working for someone else.

'That's really great - Andy too?' she said, aware that her face felt tight with her unvoiced thoughts.

'Andy too! Come on - pack that stuff up - let's go out, have a bite - bottle of wine?' He pulled her to him again, nuzzling her neck, his warm breath melting her reluctance.

They drove out of their smart cul-de-sac, away through the five, four and three bedroomed detached residences, each in its own island of neatly kept and barely bordered levels of green, and headed towards the centre of town. Here they passed the rows of terraced houses, the wide flash shopping centre and then on into the original narrow backstreets that were once all there was of Leventry. They managed to park on a single yellow line outside the dark facade of the seventeenth century church and ran briskly through the cold glistening streets to 'The Cloister', a small, not-too-extravagant restaurant, a favourite haunt in their better-off days.

They skipped starters and chose carefully from the attractive handwritten menu, salmon en croute for Di and steak au poivre for Paul, with a bottle of a crisp dry Soave to keep it company. Paul leant forward earnestly, engaging Di's eyes with his.

'I've got an idea.'

Di leant forward a little more, her eyes widening, inviting him to tell her.

'If we do well, Billy'll take us on again. It's all a matter of keeping to schedule - it's always going over schedule that mucks up the costing - isn't it? I mean, *we know* what a screw-up in cash flow can do, don't we? Anyway, it could be a start to getting back into business.'

'How could it?' she said, not seeing how it possibly could be - capital was the only real asset that could get them back into business on their own. 'Billy won't pay a fortune - you can be sure of that.'

'I wasn't thinking of just that - working for Billy - I was thinking of getting the business back on its feet - raising some capital. If we've both got work then we can afford it.'

It was the real reason why they'd given up so much just to make sure they weren't declared bankrupt: the possibility of raising new venture capital in the future.

'How? I don't see banks lending to building firms just now.'

'On the house.'

'No! No, not a second mortgage.' Di felt a sense of panic fill her as she recalled how close they'd come to being homeless, destitute. 'I'm not risking the house - it's all we've got.' she could feel her face flush and knew that her eyes had instantly filled.

'Yes, precisely.'

'Not a second mortgage, please Paul. There must be another way - could we try a - a partnership, or something?' The trouble being finding the partner who'd trust them. It would need someone with a wide interest and plenty of money looking for something to do. Di's mind flickered to her new boss. Lechwood had a finger in many pies but none in the building trade as far as she was aware - he might even need building services if he went ahead with his multigyms-attached-to-clubs idea. She wondered, would he be tempted? What would it take?

The food arrived. Paul smiled and winked at her through the aromatic column of steam that lifted from the vegetable dishes as the lids were removed.

'We'll be all right. You'll see,' he said as his knife sliced off a generous portion of steak, his keen appetite restored.

She looked at the jewel bright carrot slivers, the satin-skinned French-beans and the gold of the flaking pastry on her plate. So easily destroyed - she drew her knife through the salmon, the flakes lifting and turning to reveal their soft pale undersides, the pink spilling out to clash with the orange and green. There had to be another way, a way without threatening their one security. In the meantime, at least, he would be in work.

'I bet Andy's pleased,' Di mused later as she used her fork to tease apart the brandy-snap basket that held her favourite dessert. 'Faith'll be. I've the feeling...' she stopped, the wine must be going to her head, she couldn't share this particular thought with Paul - Andy's best friend. She had a feeling Faith was unhappy - that perhaps lack of money was only part of the problem.

'What? What about Faith?' Paul sounded altogether too curious.

'Faith - Faith's been telling me a story.'

Paul's eyes narrowed. 'Something about Andy?'

'No! Not that sort of story, a made up story. You know, I said she used to when we were at school - and some other times. It makes the miles go, you'd be amazed. This time she said it's going to be a really long story - not just an hour or so.'

'What's it about then, this story?' Paul leant comfortably back, glass of wine in his hand. And Di began to relate the story so far, and the story as Faith had told it on their journey home seemed to flow from her like a recording, the pictures that she'd created in her mind leading her through the narrative.

'Then I broke the spell,' she said, 'but we were nearly home so I have to wait for the next instalment tomorrow.'

'She makes it up as she goes along? Sounds more like she's reading it to you from a book.'

'It does, doesn't it. Faith's always been like that - not just, um, 'the two girls arrive at a creepy house' more like "the two girls cautiously approached the dark shadowy building, the ivy clinging darkly to the worn stone walls, the windows blank in the moonlight." real story stuff.'

'You can do it too - 'the ivy clinging darkly' - sounds right to me.'

'Ah , but I was quoting Faith again, from another story.'
'Oh, oh well, you can never tell what goes on in some people's minds, do you want to guess what's in mine?' he leant forward and smiled softly at Di.
'Hmmm!' she smiled back at him, not needing to guess.

The house greeted them with a lingering warmth, just about held over from earlier, even though Di had flicked off the central heating switch before they'd left. Once again the household chores remained untouched as they made love, long and sweet until they rested back against the pillows, bodies touching from shoulder to hip, comfortable and sated. Paul's steady breathing soon told Di that he had drifted into sleep, while her mind worked on the new information of the day, on the possibilities that Paul being back in work could open up for them. Even as she thought about them the same panic ran round her frame, causing a slight shiver. She couldn't allow Paul to risk the house. It meant more to her than he could ever understand. He'd even talked of the 'better option' of renting back in their early days, highlighting the flexibility of being able to move round the country to where the work was, where the building opportunities were. She'd put a stop to that idea then, thank God, he had no conception of life in the rented sector, of the uncertainties that it held. No, she'd made sure that they'd invested in their own home and that it was not part of the business, not liable to be sold off to pay business debts. The mortgage had been taken out to pay off those debts, and she managed to pay the mortgage - just. But she'd have to find an alternative to his idea, and soon, for the light was back in his eyes, though she was glad of it.

Possibilities? They seemed so few and so small at the moment and each one led her in impossible circles of wishing and knowing that her wishing was just beyond what could be expected of real life. Real life didn't pan out like a story. In real life the escaped murderer does not get himself trapped and captured by two girls enjoying a freebie weekend at a creepy hotel - in real life they'd have ended up mutilated, raped or dead. Faith's new story felt more like real life, so far, nothing beyond belief. Faith's story. It had sounded almost word perfect when it had left her lips as she passed it on to Paul, and he was right, it really did sound as if Faith were reading from a book. And the story was already intriguing - the characters attractive and the hint of sexuality subtly given.

She lay in the cooling darkness and re-ran the story again while sleep evaded her. Paul stirred, rolling onto his side. Di pulled the duvet higher to cover his shoulder and slipped from the bed. She pulled on her long velvet dressing gown, wrapped it firmly across her breasts and tied the belt tightly. Quietly she drew out a drawer and pulled out a pair of thick walking socks from near the back, barely used since their 'outdoor activity' fad, and snuggled her feet into them. Paul's rhythmic breathing did not falter as she opened the door and carefully closed it behind her.

She padded down to the kitchen and boiled the kettle, making a pot of tea and taking it, a mug and a bottle of milk, she returned upstairs to the spare room that had been turned into an office for their business. The computer was the only remaining part of the business that had not been sold off. The fact that she'd been able to get a little work from home using it had saved it, along with the pitiful price that second-hand computers commanded. She turned it on, sipping the hot tea while she waited for it to boot up. The blue-white light of the screen eventually showed her a blank page. Di took another gulp of hot tea, set the cup down on the floor and rested her hands over the keyboard. 'THE STORY' she typed at the top of the page. She looked at it for a moment, then sat up straight and began to type: *'Hope Jones stepped into the entrance of the newspaper office as the doors slid aside making way for the newest journalist to join City Press.....'*

It was three fifteen when she finished. She created a file called 'Faithstory' and saved her night's work. Her hands were freezing, her fingers felt stiff with the cold. She warmed them momentarily between her thighs, then reached out and switched off the computer. She left everything as it was and crept back into the bedroom, stripping off her socks and robe at the last moment before sliding into bed and curling as close to the glowing heat of Paul's sleeping form as she dared without waking him with the coldness of her touch. She felt strangely satisfied, as if the typing up of the start of The Story had been a good job well done. She'd do the rest, for Faith, a present, the whole story written down. She'd have to get it right though - a tape? Faith wouldn't notice a tape recorder under the noise of the engine, would she? A tape recorder, then the typing would be even quicker, and more accurate. She had been aware, as the words hit the screen, that there was some lack of music in them, a beat missed here and there that she didn't quite get right. The whole sense was there, that was the most important thing, she hadn't missed out anything important, just the odd word, or particular turn of phrase. A recording would make it perfect, she thought, as she drifted off into sleep.

Paul woke early for a change and had the kettle boiling before Di had left the bathroom.
'Di? Di?' he yelled up the stairs, 'Where the hell's the teapot?'
Di, her mouth full of foaming toothpaste suddenly remembered her foray into the 'office' with the teapot. She spat the paste out.
'I've got it - just coming,' she yelled back as she dashed across the landing and grabbed up the tray. She trotted down stairs and slid the tray onto the kitchen bar. 'Pot needs emptying,' she added, turning tail and haring back up to get dressed. As she rooted through the drawer for a pair of tights without a ladder she thought about the pages she'd typed up. In the middle of the night it had seemed a good idea, now she mulled the idea over again and gave it full consideration. It still had merit, not least as a gift to her friend.
Paul poured two mugs of tea and sat drinking his at the bar. Di grabbed the box of Special K and shook some into a bowl, drowned it in milk and began to munch ruminatively.
'What's that?' Paul said, pointing towards her face then touching his own lower lip. 'Just there - white?'
Di ran her finger along just beneath her lip, feeling the chalky mark. Toothpaste? She tasted it to be sure. 'Toothpaste!'

He smiled and shook his head a little as if she was going dotty.
'Paul, where's the small tape recorder?'
'What for?'
'Ohh - nothing. Just an idea.'
'Dunno - I think I saw it in a wall-unit drawer - or in the desk?'
'Never mind,' she munched on, trying to remember where it was, keeping one eye on the time.

She found the tape recorder, but its batteries were flat. A quick search of the drawer where she kept such things told her that she'd have to buy some; a quick look at her watch told her that she'd have to buy them en-route, no time to zoom off to the newsagents before picking Faith up. That would make it harder to organise she thought, as she stacked the dirty dishes in the dishwasher and closed the door, she wiped down the bar, turned and ran upstairs again. She flung wide the wardrobe door and dragged a large leather shoulder-bag from the shelf. She opened it wide, the faint scent of neglect wafting from its interior. Within seconds she had transferred everything from her usual bag into this capacious one, and added the recorder, with not even a bulge. It would do. She dashed back down to the kitchen and gave Paul a fleeting kiss as she grabbed her keys from the hook.

The air outside was damp and clammy, warmer than it had been for the last few days, a faint mist hovering on the edge of visibility. The car started sweetly and she rounded the bend just on time, and there, reassuringly, was Faith. Di saw her look up as her headlights straightened towards her, saw the small pale face hiding within the hood of her jacket, before the face was tipped away from the glare, the head drooping a little as she drew near.
'Hi.' Faith said, her voice as soft as the incipient mist.
'Morning! A small detour this morning - won't take long,' Di said brightly, her idea burning in its secrecy, like palming a penny sweet while making a five-penny selection.
Faith did not reply, instead, when Di flicked a glance in her direction, she seemed to be searching for something in her bag.
'Lost something?'

'No, just...' her voice trailed off. She snapped something shut, closed the bag and pushed it into a heap in her lap, knuckles white on her clenched fists.

'You okay? Won't be a tick,' Di said as she pulled into the kerb beside the brightly lit front of a small newsagents.

The light was very white inside, colour-draining, the assistant looking more dead than alive. She picked up a tube of Polos and put them down on the counter, 'And a pack of four double A batteries, please,' she said nodding to the display next to the cigarettes behind the counter. The batteries looked as if they'd been around a long time, with dust on the top surface of the packet. Beggars can't be choosers, she thought,   handing over a fiver. A quick mumbled recitation of price came back followed by her change and receipt.

She dropped the change into her purse, ripped open the battery packet and fiddled the slim cylinders into the back of the recorder, checking in the brightness the black on black markings for which way to put them in. With no time to do a test to be sure, she just checked that the spool turned as she switched the machine on, and left the shop. Her heart beat a little faster as she opened the door. Faith didn't even look up. 'Okay!' she said, to drown the gentle hum while she turned the engine on. Engine on, bag tucked between the seats on the floor behind her. 'Let's go - want a Polo?'

'No thanks.'

'How about some story then?'

'Di, did Paul say anything about some work?'

'Yeah, with that Billy. Well anything's better than nothing, isn't it? Andy pleased?'

'Yes. Yes, I just…'

'What is it Faith?'

'I don't think I believed him.'

'Well, there you are, it's true!' she flashed a smile at Faith.

'True.' A small silence, 'Do you really want more of The Story?'

'Oh, yes please, I was thinking about it half of last night,' Di said, smiling within herself at the amazing truth behind her words. 'You've got to go on.' Fingers crossed that the tape works, she thought.

chapter six – Faith

Faith left the car reluctantly as they reached her home that first day of telling The Story and waited as she watched Di drive off, feeling as if somehow she was taking the magic with her. The car's rear lights turned the corner and Faith turned and walked slowly to her front door. It stuck when she tried to open it one-handed. It always did in damp weather. She put down the bags she was carrying, knowing that she would have to throw all her weight against the door to make it budge. She turned the key again, then let it flick back. For a cold moment she knew she didn't want to open the door and go in - then in a sudden flush of guilt she thought of Jilly and Jon, turned the key and shouldered the door open.

The unexpected aroma of pizza, unmistakable in its amalgam of cooked cheese and oregano, stopped her for a moment, standing in her own hall, a rabbit poised for flight. Then Andy appeared, filling the kitchen doorway.

'Thought I heard the door,' he said and turned back into the kitchen. Faith grabbed up the shopping bag and her handbag, pushed the door shut with the vigour it required, and followed him. Two large size Pizzas stood on the table, one with the lid flopped back and a ragged wedge missing. Andy held the remains of this piece in his fingers as he lounged against the worktop.

'Thought we'd have a pizza tonight - got the kids a video out too,' he smiled then popped the thick crust into his mouth and chewed contentedly, wiping his fingers on his jeans then folding his arms. Faith could read the signs, he was waiting for her to ask 'why?' She was so good at it, providing all the right cues, she thought bitterly, learnt from an early age, reading all the unsaid signs, attuned to the nuances, responding as was best. Too good for her own good.

'Any special reason?' her line.

'Good news,' his line.

'Well? Come on, tell me,' as if a character in one of her own stories, the intonation correct, the face tilted ever so slightly in inquiry, as if enjoying the game.

'Paul's got us lined up with some work - good money, soon. What did I tell you?'

'That's great, doing what?'

'Managing a site, together like. Paul over-all, me his right-hand man, like the old days. Come here,' he tugged her to him and hugged her, his large arms heavy around her shoulders, pressing where her shoulders still ached from the evening before. 'We'll be all right now, eh?'

She nodded into his chest. No way could she have spoken, her throat felt full of bile, her heart beating too fast for comfort. How long until she felt safe in his arms again?

She looked in on the children as she passed the lounge, she could just see the back of their heads, one golden, one dark, as they sat on the carpet, backs to the sofa, eyes fixed on the gaudy moving images that screeched across the screen. Children's television - she wondered what video Andy had got for them. Jilly suddenly looked round as if sensing a presence. Her wide eyes creased with her smile and she turned back to the television. Faith climbed the stairs slowly. She still felt cold, she longed for a deep hot bath and an evening of silence, instead she peeled off the heavy sheepskin coat, kicked off the court shoes, the smart navy-blue skirt, jacket and cream blouse, hastily replacing them with loafers, jeans, tee-shirt and thick cable-knit jumper. She brushed her hair vigorously trying to reshape it before it dried completely. She put the hair brush down and looked at herself in the mirror, really looked at herself, not just at her hair, not just at the fit of her clothes. Who was she? From the outside it was impossible to tell what went on inside the mind. Where was she real - as an image - as real as one of her own characters - as a mind, and imagination - unseen but full of life and creativity? What was the difference?

'Faith?' Andy bellowed up the stairs.

'Coming!' and to the mirror, softly, 'See you later.' Faith walked from the room with the eerie feeling that her refection actually watched her leave. The over-large geometric pattern on the wallpaper in the hall offended her sense of proportion, as it had from the day Andy had chosen it, so she kept her eyes on the plain carpet as she walked slowly down the stairs. She had been waiting for the day that the accumulation of scuff marks and handprints would mean it needed replacing, hoping to get her choice in first, but since the business had folded she'd given up on that idea and just tried to avoid looking at it.

'I'll put the video on, love - if you zap the pizza we can eat it while we watch - "The Nightmare before Christmas".'

'Okay. What was it called?'

'Nightmare before Christmas.'

'Is it ...okay for the kids?'

'It's a Disney,' he shrugged.

Faith heated the pizzas up again, cut them into suitable wedges and stacked them onto two large plates. She carried through a tray with small plates, paper napkins and drinks on. The film was already rolling. She returned with the pizza. No one spoke, they each reached out for a slice and began to eat, their eyes barely leaving the screen. Faith sat herself on the sofa, carefully manoeuvring her legs to avoid clipping Jon in the ear with her feet as she curled them up beside her. She ate one slice of pizza, slowly. The film was Disney but weird, the style was musical but the characters were out of a horror film, the children were enraptured but Faith couldn't concentrate. She sat with her face reflecting the moving light of the screen, her eyes open but turned inward, seeing herself in the role of Hope Jones.

Hope was one incarnation of what she'd wished for herself, for when Faith Evans was at school there had been the possibility of greater things. From the first year at the Comprehensive she had been noticed by the English department. Her grades had been excellent in this subject, and due to her clear and creative grasp of the language she managed good grades in most other subjects too.

Jilly and Jon gasped simultaneously as something ghastly suddenly happened, Faith's eyes focused for the moment it took to assure herself that all was well, then returned to the classroom of her childhood.

'Whose parents are coming to the GCE choices evening?' Mrs Brockford asked at the end of double English. Hands went up all round the room. She smiled as she looked through the top of her bifocals scanning the forest of hands. 'You may go

- um - Faith, just a quick word before you go, please.' Her words all but drowned in a scraping of chairs.

'Miss?' Faith, small for her age, stood beside the teacher's desk.

'Aren't your parents coming to the meeting?'

'I don't know Miss - they haven't made up their minds - I think.'

'Well, ask them. I particularly want to talk to them.'

'Yes, Miss,' Faith said quietly. She drifted out into the throng of the corridor wondering what Mrs Brockford wanted to say to her Mum and Dad in particular, oblivious to being pushed and shoved by the other pupils heading for the canteen; she thought how little they even spoke to each other at the moment.

   Her mother had come, had sat wide-eyed beside her daughter as Mrs Brockford had her say.

'You know that Faith is one of our more able pupils,' she said, her head nodding slightly to encourage the passive face before her to engage in the conversation. Mum's eyes brightened. 'Faith should do extremely well at any GCE subjects she chooses, and I wanted to talk to you about looking forward to A-levels and a University place after that. You see, some subjects have to be dropped at this early stage and a careful consideration of the options open to Faith needs to be made depending on what career she wants to follow,' she paused. Faith sensed that this was somehow as difficult an interview for Mrs Brockford as it was for her mother. 'You understand?'

Yes! Yes! Yes! Faith said in her head, as if she'd always known. Yes, that's what I want, University! The word filled her mind with towering libraries, black flowing gowns, green lawned spaces between grand old buildings and the idea of being part of it all.

'Yes, but I don't know - I, I'll speak to my husband,' Mum's eyes flicking downward.

'Well, consider it. There's time - I'm sure Faith will do well, whichever subjects she chooses,' Mrs Brockford finished lamely, her eyes seeking out those bright, shining eyes of her pupil in an effort to understand the limp reaction of the mother before her.

   That was the real start of the dreaming. The dream of leaving everything for University, for a life of words. The possibility hung in the firmament of her imagination, bright and shining, a light to guide, a gleam of hope. She began to flick through the careers guides in the school library, looking for those that wanted a Degree in English as a basis, her heart settled on that of Librarian, surrounded forever by her beloved books. Her daydreams now saw her as a County Librarian, a position she could safely imagine herself to be comfortable in, smartly dressed and independent, or on daring days, as a journalist, a professional writer, writing stories for magazines in her spare time, aspiring to a novel. She continued to work hard, and made her own selection of subjects with no input from her parents apart from her Mum's scrawled signature on the bottom of the page, her Dad having left by then.

'More Pizza, love?' Andy broke into her reverie. She eyed the greasy shining wedge on the plate before her and shook her head, her throat constricting at the thought of the cold congealed mass entering her mouth. Andy scooped it up, folding it between thick fingers and chewed a lump from the end mechanically as his eyes locked back onto the screen.

Faith felt a shudder of disgust run through her. Disgust at what she'd allowed herself to become when her dreams had been so golden, so full of a different kind of life. The film credits ran, Jilly and Jon remaining motionless as if still absorbed to catch the last minutes before being sent up to bed. 'Come on you two, bed,' Faith said, her voice a cross between admonishment and laughter at their delaying technique. Both children turned mock sad faces towards her, before melting into heart-breaking grins. How could she have wished for any other life that did not include these two?

She chased them upstairs, saw them each showered, story read and tucked into bed, delighting in their banter about the film they'd just watched. She returned to find Andy breaking open a second can of lager and settling himself down on one end of the sofa. They had been married long enough for Faith to recognise the pattern. Andy had *his* chair, the armchair directly opposite the television, Faith often occupying the sofa along with the children. When he invaded the sofa he expected her to come and curl into his side as she had always done in their early days, and as it had always been, this was his foreplay - a signal understood that tonight he wanted her. Faith hesitated in the doorway a moment, her mind a whirl of indecision. She'd always just joined him whenever he sat on the sofa like this - what would happen if she didn't? Her indecision held her transfixed for too long, Andy looked round.

'Come on - what you standing there for?' he said, his hand giving the space beside him a pat.

'Just - I was thinking of getting a drink,' she turned, moving quickly back into the kitchen, her heart beating fast. She stood in the kitchen and looked at her reflection in the large dark windows. What could she do? She snatched one of the remaining two cans of lager from the four-pack Andy had bought, and poured out a glass, watching with impatience the foam rise quickly up the side. She drank, the froth tickling her nose, the cold fizzy liquid gulped down as if she were trying to drown herself in it. She was. She poured the remains of the can into the glass, bringing it foaming to the brim once more, and sure she could feel the alcohol already dulling her senses, walked with her glass back into the lounge, back to sit beside Andy.

He was careful not to rest his full weight upon her, not to squeeze the breath from her, but was cursory in his love-making. They both knew what they were there for. The sooner they came together, the sooner it was over, the better. Each differing objective attained in the same hasty coupling. Andy sighed, rolled his bulk away, turning himself to sleep, his back to her. Faith lay in the darkness her heart leaden. She didn't love him. Gentle or not - there was nothing she could label as 'love for him' left inside her. Why had she ever believed she did?

The dream of University was one she kept to herself, sensitive to the reaction it would have gained from many of her friends. There was no one else from her village, except Di, that was even likely to get good grades at GCE, and the friends that she'd made from other villages couldn't protect you on the way home, she was too much of a target already. It wasn't until later, after her hopes had been shattered, that she even told Di. After that terrible time, that lost time, when suddenly their household had lost its function, a wheel without the hub, spinning aimlessly, going nowhere. There was nothing she could do. It was, of course, her fault. Her fault that she was born a girl, that 'something' had gone wrong, that there would be no son to follow. Her fault - but there was nothing she could do to make amends. Her mother withdrew into herself, turned her back on the gossiping world, mechanically carried out the tasks she always had done, cooking meals for three, laying the table for the absent man, shopping for his favourite foods rather than her own. The house rang to the constant play of the radio, too loud, loud enough to drown the sound of gossiping neighbours in her head.

He'd taken everything of his, carefully and coldly packed up his clothes, his few odds and ends, memorabilia, toothbrush and comb. It was a decision of rationality rather than anger or haste. There was no hate, just disappointment, a cancerous disappointment that had eaten into their relationship until there was nothing left, and in the scales against this vacuum there was the incalculable weight of his son.

Nearly three weeks after he'd gone, Faith came home to find her mother crying, for the first time. She was sitting on the kitchen floor, one dark sock of his clutched in her hands, rocking and sobbing in a cracked cry like the sound of breaking branches. Faith paused for a moment at the door, uncertain what to do, then went to her mother and hugged her. Hugged her so tight she was afraid that she would hurt her. Mother and daughter sat together on the cold lino and cried, coming to terms with reality.

Mum changed after that. No more pretending that he would be home as usual, no more catering for a taste that had left the house. She began to look for work, and was lucky that just at that time the long-serving assistant in the village shop was retiring as her arthritic fingers were no longer able to open the paper bags or pick up coins from the counter, Doreen got the job. She was unfailingly prompt, neat and polite. She served all those who had shunned her with the same smilingly blank face that she offered any customer, took her meagre wages and looked after the house for herself and Faith. She created a life she could accept. To Faith it had meant the end of the life she'd hoped for.

A great writer. Di's prediction. It had been then that Faith had confided her hope of University to Di, then when the hope had been crushed, couched in terms of, 'now I'll never have the chance to go' it didn't sound so bold. Di hadn't heard the ache, the wistfulness behind the words. Di had cheerfully offered the option of joining her on a secretarial course that she was aiming for after GCEs.

Lying in the darkness, Andy's low snoring punctuating the hours, the path that had seemed hard enough and the only one possible at the time, showed itself to be nothing more than Pilgrim's 'easy wide road - down'.

chapter seven - Faith

The mistiness of the day seemed to suit her mood this morning. The car came, she climbed in - a thought nagging at her. Her handbag had been moved. When she'd gone to grab it before heading out of the door it was not on the floor beside the bed, but on the chair.

Inside the car she opened it, purse prominent. She knew before she even snapped it open that money would have gone. Money to cover the price of some pizzas, a few cans of lager and a video - a quarter of the week's shopping money. She snapped the purse shut. A few quid, a few less bruises? And Di, brittle bright this morning, sparking with energy, waiting for the next part of the story. And Faith delivers: Hope's first assignment, something paltry, a civic reception being held to announce the new joint venture - City Hall and Private Investment - the dream team to build a new leisure centre complex.

Hope felt let down, assigned to running around on a job the merest rookie could do - all offered on a plate of duplicated sheets of information - names, dates, places, prices - and hype, hype, hype. The only column that could come from this lot would read just the same as that in any local rag. Hope thought bitterly and turned her gaze away from the celebrations laid on, the glasses of bubbly and thumb-nail sized nibbles offered by gliding waiters. She wandered to the window, allowing the buzz of self-congratulation to slide into the background. They certainly had a terrific view from the new City Hall. What was that? Through the latticework of the bare twiggery of trees at the perimeter - a rushing of bodies - a movement of people in a hurry. Every nerve in her body became alert. The mere movement suggested protest, and suppression. She looked round the room again, stuffed black and white suits, bow ties bobbing at throats, fat jowls shaking, elegant women in clothes that cost more than the whole of her wardrobe. She sauntered to a table, deposited her glass and made her way out of the door, down the brightly lit marble-mosaic entrance hall and, with a nod and a smile to the doorman, made her way out.

The noise caught her attention first - an angry noise, repetitive, chanting. The words didn't matter - the anger did. She came to the security barrier, was saluted as she walked out, listening, guessing the direction in which to go. The great encircling fence seemed so much more threatening from the outside, close up. The sounds grew louder. A knot of people, a few placards, home-made, and a string of dark blue looped around them. They weren't going anywhere. And now she could hear them. 'Parks not Shops! Parks not Shops!' A pathetic slogan, lacking everything that was required of it - yet it had something. Controversy. Her senses tingled. She noticed a policeman turn and look at her, she smiled, then turned and walked away, just far enough not to be noticed but to still be able to keep an eye on the knot of protesters. She saw her target about ten minutes later. A respectable looking woman, with sensible shoes and well-cut hair, was leaving the area and walking alone across the street and along the pavement towards her, she stepped back behind an advertising board, to emerge just after the woman had passed, then to quicken her steps to catch her up.

'Do you think they heard? In there?' she said, her voice breathless as if she'd been hurrying or as if tremulous at the audacity of the protest. The woman looked round sharply, her mouth open, her eyes wide for a moment.

'Who knows - they kept us about as far away as possible, didn't they?'

'Yeah -' then guessing, 'too late really, just when it's all finalised?'

'Well - we've tried.'

'What about the press - I mean, I came very late - what's been done?'

'Didn't want to know. There's just not many green spaces left right in the middle - certainly none for businesses to get their hands on. Stands to reason - the City own the only prime sites - the developers have the money, and not just for the building.'

'Have we any proof?'

'Who are you?'

Crunch time. 'Hope Jones, new press correspondent for the City News. And that's New correspondent - as in freshly interested in anything your group has got to say.'

The woman eyed her carefully. 'Do you know who I am?'

'Nope - I just picked you out from the group of protesters.'

The woman pressed her lips together to make a tight line.

'I daren't be named. I shouldn't have even allowed myself to go on the protest - but I did. Joan Hemingway,' she held out her hand. Hope offered

hers in return. 'County Librarian,' Joan finished, her voice dropping to a small self mocking laugh.

'I know I said I was new - but I am an experienced journalist. I'm also ready to hear your side of the story - even if it's been turned away before - can we find a quiet place, get a coffee or something - tell me what the protest is all about?'

Joan Hemingway looked at her for a moment as if scrutinising her title page, getting the gist of her from the inside-cover blurb. 'All right - this way,' she said.

The cake shop had a coffee lounge upstairs, with few customers at this time of day, they sat on the blue shiny seats opposite each other, comforting the steaming cups of coffee.

'We don't have any real proof - not of the kind we could take to the police - but,' she stopped, squeezing her fingers tight around the cup, the knuckles whitening, the skin flushing bright against the hot china. She looked up, engaging Hope's eyes as if trying to read her character there. 'We have a sort-of mole, someone who saw a document that indicated that there were considerations being paid, that were not public - nor in the public interest.'

'Bribes?'

'That's a dangerous word to use without the evidence - but that is how it looked and that was only the start - we found out more.'

'And the papers wouldn't chase it up?'

Joan shook her head, her lips compressed into a tight line again.

'Can I talk to this person - the one who saw the information first?'

'I can ask - but is it worth it - as you say, it's all been finalised?'

'But no one's started digging up the park yet - there's still a chance, and I won't let you down, this is my field - digging up the truth.'

Joan drank her coffee, tipping the cup up high, draining the lot. The cup landed with a note of finality in the saucer.

'All right. Meet me here, this evening at six. I'll be able to tell you then if she'll meet you, or not.'

'Great, fine. Six o'clock - thank you.' Hope said as they stood to leave. She waited a while, selecting a celebratory sticky bun to take back to the office with her and allowing Joan to leave alone. As Hope returned she was already planning her formal covering of the afternoon's shindig and dreaming up scandalous headlines for what she hoped might follow.

She was just putting the finishing touches to her report when Ms Spencer herself stepped up to her shoulder. Hope was drowned in a wave of 'Poison' as Ms Spencer leant near enough to read her copy neatly created in two columns below a blocked-in yet un-chosen title, 'Headline, Headline'.

'That's fine,' Sherry murmured lightly in her ear. 'Why don't you bring a draft copy through when you've finished?' she added as she turned away.

Hope looked at the bland words on the screen - if that was 'fine', wait until Ms Spencer saw what she could really do, she blanked out the words 'Headline' and began to write in the title that she had settled on to top her article - 'Leisure Centre Partners Celebrate' then just to see how it would look she wiped that and topped the piece with 'Leisure Centre Sleaze' - it made her smile - it certainly had a better ring to it. Her finger was just over the delete button to wipe the fantasy words when Chris Raven appeared at her elbow.

'Wishful thinking! Couldn't you have booked a hungry photographer in for the party?'

'Don't! You made me jump,' she let the cursor eat up the letters and retyped the proper title. 'And you wouldn't have appreciated the company - I didn't.'

'I can tell,' he said, turning and sitting himself on the corner of her desk, pushing aside the bag with the bun in it. 'What's this?'

'A reward for playing super-sleuth,' she said as he picked up the bag and peered in. 'Get off!' she laughed as he pinched a piece from the end of the bun and ate it.

'Mmm - but I prefer coffee icing - next time.'

She made a snatch for the bag, he lifted it away just before her hand reached it - then presented it to her almost ceremoniously, raised an eyebrow, smiled, pushed himself off from her desk and sauntered away. She found herself squeezing the bun with a silly smile on her face. Putting the squashed bag down, she frowned to settle her mind again then checked her work and ran off a draft copy, sitting back while it purred its way out of the printer.

'Two coffees - one white,' Sherry said to her intercom as soon as Hope appeared in her doorway. 'Take a seat,' she indicated the pair of two-seater sofas that faced each other in the window niche of her office.

Hope looked at the desk, then across to the coffee-table ensemble, mentally she shrugged, the lady was the boss, and smiled her acknowledgement as she moved across to the sofas. The view from the window was impressive, and the obvious reason for the positioning of this cosy corner.

The assistant brought in the coffees on a tray, sweeping straight over to the coffee table and placing it carefully down.

'Anything else, Ms Spencer,'

'That's fine,' she smiled at her assistant, 'Close the door - thank you.'

She turned her attention to Hope, still looking out at the view, not wanting to seat herself until Sherry had done so. 'Hope, sit down - biscuit?'

'No thanks,' Hope said, sitting fairly central on the sofa as Sherry had just done opposite her. 'Here's the draft,' she said offering the sheet of paper.

'Thanks,' Sherry took it and laid it beside her. 'Are you settling in?'

'I think so, I ...' to push or not to push, give it a go. 'I am used to slightly more demanding tasks, but I understand I've got to start somewhere.'

'You need a little time to get to know the city, I think I will be able to use your talents better if you've had time to find out how the place works first. And I do think you have talent,' she picked up her coffee cup and looked hard at Hope as she sipped. Hope felt as if she were being appraised right at that moment. 'Do have a biscuit - it'll make me feel less guilty.' Sherry added taking a chocolate dipped Viennese finger and biting the end off. Hope took a biscuit; Sherry smiled.

'Tell me what brought you into journalism in the first place,' Sherry asked.

'You'll have to tell me later!' Di laughed as they turned into the street where she let Faith out of the car.

'What? Oh yes -' Faith felt the jerk back to reality as if it were something tangible, the twang of an elastic band, stinging. She gathered her bag back onto her lap, ready to clamber from the car quickly. 'See you later,' she called as the car pulled in tight and she opened the door.

The cold air woke her up, pulling her coat closer she walked swiftly towards the Newspaper offices, wondering a little about why Hope had gone in to journalism and what it was about Sherry that made Hope feel uncomfortable when she was being so friendly.

The first thing Faith saw when she arrived at her desk was cardboard document wallet propped up against her screen. She didn't hang her coat up straight away, as was usual, but instead picked the wallet up, scanned it quickly in the process of opening it, no name, and lifted the flap. Two sheets of paper, an unrecognised scrawl, then she saw the name - Wren. She placed the file down carefully and went over to hang up her coat. Her scarf hung dusty and listless from the peg, she tucked it in the pocket of her coat as she hung it up and returned to her desk.

For one fleeting second, just before she recognised who the work was from, she had felt a frisson of excitement pass through her. She had thought it was from Chris Raven! Ridiculously, her mind was playing tricks on her, confusing the story with reality. She sat down and removed the sheets from the file: Two letters to type - with a note for two copies of each to be provided. Nothing more. What did she expect? She put them back in the file and turned her attention to the work left by Mr Watson first.

Susie was away. Faith collected her meal and almost without thinking picked up a sticky iced bun. She sat alone in their window seat, not really feeling like making the effort to integrate with another group just for the day. It made a good observation point. There was Joan Ernest from Accounts, the woman she had based her picture of Joan Hemingway on, and beside her Annie Morecombe, Personnel, both laughing at, or with, the young man seated opposite them. By the way Annie Morecombe was colouring up the laughter had been general, but had touched the easy-blushing Annie in some way. Faith empathised. Tommy Salmon could be both attractively funny and an acid wit, enough to cause confusion and consternation in any sensitive woman. She watched as the two women leant forward a fraction, their bodies showing their interest in what was being said, one head greying, smartly, if formally cut, the other a coppery mass of curls pinned back just enough to keep them under control. They laughed again, leaning away suddenly, glancing at each other, eyebrows raised. Obviously some tittle-tattle, a little scandal-mongering, a laugh over lunch. Faith hoped it had nothing to do with the gossip Ms Robertson had accused her with yesterday.

'May I sit here?' his deep voice rumbled.

Faith's heart jolted her back into the present, the pungent aroma of curry suddenly strong.

'Yes, um - if you like,' feeling the instant heat of a blush hit her cheek.

Nick Wren slid himself into the seat opposite her blocking her view of the other table, but not before she had time to see Annie nudge Joan and feel their eyes lock onto her table.

'I hope you didn't mind finding work waiting as soon as you got in this morning, I left it very late last night.'

'No, not at all - I, I, haven't done it yet - was it urgent? You should have said.'

'No. Not urgent, don't worry,' he smiled, his eyes catching the light. He began to eat his curry, wielding his fork deftly in his left hand. 'Not bad really,' he indicated the dish before him, 'What's the salad like?'

'The same every day,' she found herself smiling, her stomach tight and her heart beating a little too fast. 'I pretend it's slimming.'

'Not that you need worry - what does the bun do?'

Faith looked where he was looking, at the plate with the sticky bun sitting accusingly on it. For a fleeting moment Faith couldn't think how it got there - it was Hope's. Too ridiculous to explain she laughed. 'Ah! It looked lonely.' And he laughed, his eyes catching hers, holding them for a long second, suddenly to pull away to guide his fork in arranging the pearly rice and golden curry into a neat mouthful.

They ate in a strange silence for a while, the clatter of the staff canteen going on around them. The silence in their bubble was so complete that Faith felt as if she could hear her own heart beat, that every mouthful seemed amplified, a chorus of crisp sounds. And this silence enhanced other senses, the flavours heightened, the colours brightened. The garish arrangement on her plate seemed far too much to eat.

He slid his cleared plate aside. She could feel him looking at her, yet hardly dare look up, hardly dare let herself meet his eyes. She carefully folded up a single lettuce leaf into a small parcel, and delivered it into her mouth. Her knife and fork consigned the remains of her meal to one half of the plate before lying themselves neatly side by side on the other half.

'Not so hungry today,' she murmured, half apologising to herself, half to the starving of the world. She picked up her tea cup, raising her eyes.

'Then you won't be wanting the bun?'

'What? Oh, no - no, you have it - if you like,' feeling foolish.

'Mmm - I might,' he looked amused, 'though I'd prefer coffee icing - next time,' he added softly.

chapter eight – Faith

Like a tower of brightly coloured children's bricks the words tumbled haphazardly through her mind. They were so familiar, yet recognising them made no sense - a dizziness, a wave of déjà vu, and she remembered them. They, along with the sticky bun, belonged to Hope. She smiled brightly through her confusion as he ate the bun before her.

She was in two minds whether to tell Di about the strange coincidence that had occurred. She thought it through while waiting for her lift and decided against it - Di would probably read more into it than there was. She'd been half expecting a caustic remark from Ms Robertson when she had delivered her work to her, but the senior editor was too busy to waste time on talk, quickly signing the copies, flashing a smile at Faith, and returning to her conversation with two earnest young journalists who obviously had hold of something they, at least, believed to be hot.

When the car arrived she was all ready to take up her story where it had left off, leading Hope through a very friendly meeting with *her* senior editor.

That evening at a few minutes to six Hope wandered casually into the coffee lounge over the cake shop and ordered a coffee. She was soon joined by Joan Hemingway and another woman. The newcomer had masses of wavy red hair and the pale and freckled complexion that usually accompanies it. They sat side by side, opposite Hope.

'Hope Jones,' Hope introduced herself offering her hand across the table.

*'Annie Wise - though I'm not so sure I **am** being wise - being here,' she laughed nervously.*

'I always protect my sources - no one will ever know except me,' Hope reassured her with words that she'd imagined saying a hundred times. 'Tell me what first alerted you to something - suspicious.'

'To get things straight, I work as a clerk cum receptionist at Prospectus Properties - do you know it?'

Hope shook her head, 'Go on.'

'Well we're, **they** are part of the consortium that makes up IDRA - you **have** heard of them?' Annie looked sceptically at Hope.

Hope nodded. She had heard of them, just, even met a few of them in their stuffed shirts at the celebrations. She wasn't about to explain the paucity of her knowledge for the moment.

'I had this big stack of filing to do - usually I just run through it quickly to make sure it really goes in the right file - you know? Well, I scanned this letter - odd, I thought, it was really rough, not typed up by one of our girls, bad spacing, old-fashioned style of layout. That made me read it. Properly. It was - like - reading between the lines? Do you follow?'

Hope nodded quickly, her blood singing its way through her veins.

'The gist of it was that the 'agreed contribution' would be paid to the 'appropriate beneficiaries' at each stage of planning, increasing in proportion to the 'final agreed result'. Well - it was weird, and it was addressed to Mr T. Trout, at City Hall. That's the name of the clerk to the planning officer.' Annie blushed a little. 'I play badminton with him, as it happens, so I know him. Well, I filed the letter then, when I saw him next, I sort-of apologised for the poor quality of the typing on the letter - by way of conversation - said I thought it was probably a new typist - though we didn't have any really. He seemed quite - curious. Things for his office are usually addressed to the planning officer - not him. And he didn't recall any letters at all from Prospectus Properties. I wouldn't have thought any more about it - except Tommy came back to me on it.' She looked hard at Hope as if trying to ascertain whether she was totally trustworthy. 'What made him come back to you?'

'He'd made a few enquires - asked if there had been a letter addressed to him. The secretaries had looked sharply at each other, one coloured up. So he pressed them on the point. It appeared that the planning officer had asked them to forward any letters sent to Mr T Trout straight to him, the planning officer - saying that he, Mr Trout, was under suspicion of subverting planning rules. The secretaries had reluctantly complied, though they both said they didn't believe it, but were surprised when a letter addressed to Mr Trout did arrive. So Tommy did a bit of his own digging, and with his access found out more - stuff that suggested that an ancient covenant that had been placed on the parkland as a condition of its bequest to the city in the sixteenth century was being misrepresented in such a way that the leisure centre could be covered within its terms of reference. Do you see?'

'Why would anyone make a copy of such a letter for the files - it seems suspicious to me?'

'They may not have realised - we've got an automatic file-copy set up on all our machines - they print out whenever the printers are not on line for immediate work - so who ever typed it up may never have known about the file-copy.'

'Right! And you took this to the protesters group?'

'No - I did,' Joan put in. 'Annie just happened to tell me - I passed it on.'

'What did they do with it?'

'Tried to get to see the original copy of the covenant - however it appears that the original was substantially water-damaged in a flood in 1988, all that is available to the public is an attested photocopy supposedly taken before the '88 flood - then they tried to get the press interested. One reporter seemed a little keen - at first, but he soon told us that he couldn't do anything without proof - and at that time the only real proof we had was an unsigned letter addressed to Tommy.'

'And Tommy?'

'He was livid! He didn't take kindly to being put under suspicion - he joined our cause. Very quietly though - he daren't make his views known - besides there was always the chance that he could find out more later.'

There was a pause in the conversation, Hope could feel the air vibrating with the words left unsaid - waiting to fill the gap.

'And did he?' she all but whispered.

They nodded.

'What happened?'

'No one would listen - it was as if the whole council, all the press, everyone, had turned a deaf ear.'

'Odd, I mean, usually we'd kill for a story like this. Give me an idea of what you had and if it's within the law I'll get it printed!'

'It's a photocopy of the original deed of covenant, when you compare them it shows how it's been changed.'

'How the hell did you get that?'

'A student, well a university professor now, he'd been doing his thesis on the Marchmonts and had asked the county records office for a copy, he still had it in his files.'

'Surely the protesters could take that to court?'

Joan gave a pitying look. 'An untestified photocopy would have no standing in law - *we* could have altered it.'

'Oh - well, still I'll try - it's worth it,' Hope smiled bravely at the two women. They smiled back - but she could see that they did not have high hopes.

As soon as she got into the office the next morning she asked Ms Spencer's assistant to find her a slot in the editor's day to discuss a story. An appointment booked for half three she returned to her own desk and typed up a series of notes about the case - delving back into the paper's own archives for any item concerning the leisure centre from the first time the idea appeared in print. There were letters too - letters from residents living close to the park who objected on aesthetic grounds and from people who had lived in the city for all their eighty-odd years and could remember things being said - things that meant that the park had to be a park - a green open space for ever and ever. There was a hell of a lot of 'hype' - some articles read more like advertisements: the benefits to the city of a new leisure centre; the advantages of well-lit well patrolled shopping malls; and the prestige associated with such a wonderful new arts, leisure and shopping centre for the city. Others took the form of attack, denigrating the present facilities: the cost of park upkeep; the menace of the park at dusk; vandalism; druggies; queer-bashing; and even dog-mess were brought out against the park. She ran herself off a copy of each item as she discovered it - finding that the only pieces in the 'Pro the Park' pile were the letters.

She didn't like it, the press coverage stunk! It was already twelve o'clock and she had one very important visit to make before she put her proposition to Ms Spencer. Pushing herself away from her terminal she grabbed her jacket and was heading out of the office when she all but bumped into Chris Raven.

'What's the hurry?'

'Do you know where the park is?'

'Yeah?'

'Where then?'

'What for?'

'Forget it!' she snapped and began to walk swiftly away - she'd find out where the park was soon enough. He caught her arm, her body swung round to face him with the momentum.

'What?' she said, her eyes flashing with annoyance.

'From here it's tricky - I'll take you,' he smiled, his eyes sparkling, 'Okay?' he added opening both eyes wide for a second.

'Fine - yes, thanks.'

They walked out of the offices together rapidly, him keeping up with the pace she set. His transport was a motorbike. Hope gulped when she saw it. She'd never ridden on a motorbike and was slightly scared by the thought.

'We can take my car,' she said quickly.

'What? We'll never get through the lunch hour traffic!'

'But, er - I, I'd need a helmet,' she stammered.

'Here,' he took a helmet from the box on the back and began to adjust something inside, glancing at her head, returning to the fixtures. 'Try that.'

Hope put the helmet on - it felt heavy, her head feeling over-large, her neck feeling very vulnerable, suddenly too weak.

'Fine,' she murmured as he placed both hands on the helmet on her head and felt the movement for fit. He looked down, their eyes meeting, his hands still resting on the helmet. She could hear her heart pounding in her ears. He patted her shoulder and turned away to put his own helmet on, while she stood breathless for a moment.

'I've never ridden one of these before,' she said suddenly.

'What a bike - or a Harley?'

'A motorbike.'

He grinned. Just hold on tight and don't fight the machine - if I lean - lean with me.'

Hope nodded, her throat tight with both fear and excitement.

He sat astride the machine, and nodded to her to join him. She stretched her leg and reached it over, having to steady herself against his back. She used his body as a lever to pull herself up on the seat centrally, both feet well off the ground.

'Feet on there,' he said turning his head and pointing back at a small bar. She put her feet up and felt herself being pressed closer to his back. 'Hold on tight,' he took hold of one of her hands and pulled it round his waist. She wrapped the other around as soon as she felt the machine roar to life. She glued herself to his back, moulded her body to fit tight to his, her breathing shallow, her grip so tight that her fingers almost slipped with the tension. They seemed to travel so fast - the wind blasting against the cheek not pressed against his jacket and tugging at her jeans. Cars appeared close and fast, a lorry terrified her into closing her eyes until she sensed that

69

its ominous presence had passed. When they pulled up and Chris cut the engine she was trembling so much that she wasn't sure if she was going to be able to stand, she unlocked her joints and slithered off the seat, to find that she could at least do that.

'You did great - with me all the way,' he grinned at her as he removed his helmet. Aware that her face was still a numb mask she contrived to smile back at him while she fumbled at the chin-strap. Chris stepped over and unbuckled it with a flick of his finger then lifted the helmet from her head. Suddenly she felt free, she gave her head a shake to loosen her hair, and caught his eye. He held her look, dangling the spare helmet by the strap, he leant forward, his eyes never leaving hers, unsure enough to be searching their dark depths for her responses. And she, drowning in the sea-grey brightness lifted her face to his, enough, just enough to take the kiss, and to give in return.

'Oh, Hope - as soon as I saw you,' he murmured, shaking his head as if unbelieving. She smiled, there was something about him that she couldn't quite pinpoint, something that registered with her in a way she wasn't used to, but her blood sang and tingled as it usually did when she thought she'd found a really good story, one to hit the jackpot. 'Chris,' his name suddenly felt different in her mouth, more significant. They kissed again, longer, deeper, until suddenly aware of scrutiny from a pair of elderly ladies heading into the park.

'You didn't tell me what you wanted with the park.'

'Well - before I stir up a hornet's nest over the place I thought I ought to get to see it first,' Hope said as they followed the elderly ladies.

'I thought that it was all cut and dried?'

'Yeah - just that there is something awfully fishy about it all - did you know that there was a…' she stopped herself, Chris had been around a long time on this paper - he must know all about the previous attempts of the protesters to put their ideas forward, and what had he done about it, something, nothing?

'Did I know what?'

'Do you know anything about the attempts of a previous journalist to get some of the protester's views put forward?'

'John, John Tarrent. Your predecessor, went from here with brilliant references, working on the Edinburgh Times, I believe.'

'Friend of yours?'

'Drinking acquaintance - you might say - nothing more. What is this?'

'I get the feeling,' Hope began finding she wanted to believe in Chris more than she wanted to doubt him, 'That there has been a conspiracy to keep the whole leisure complex scheme sweet and uncontroversial. With the media helping to make sure that nothing gets under the skins of the public, that the truth doesn't get ferreted out.'

'The truth being?'

'That the City Council is breaking an ancient covenant on the land to allow the speculators to build, and certainly not for altruistic reasons.'

'That's strong Hope - that's tantamount to accusing them of taking bribes.'

'Yep,' she nodded.

'What are you going to do?'

'I have enough - just - to make a speculative story that might bring a few worms crawling out of the woodwork, I'm seeing Ms Spencer this afternoon to get the go-ahead.'

Chris was quiet, his gaze fixedly forward.

'What?' Hope asked after a moment or two.

'Good luck - it's worth saving isn't it?'

Hope looked. She suddenly realised that they'd walked a good way without her even taking much notice of her surroundings, being so engrossed with her thoughts.

The park undulated before her, well trimmed grassland, attractive plantings of trees, with mixed sizes, from large deeply glossy evergreen oaks to flittery dancing aspens. Bushes warmed the feet of these trees with leaves of fiery red, creamy or acidic yellow and every shade of green from white to black. Here and there, sun-warmed niches held a traditional-style park seat, usually complete with an elderly person sitting enjoying the sun. A mother with a double buggy and a toddler running behind her came over the hill and sauntered down towards them, she smiled and said a cheery 'good-morning' as they passed.

The light seemed different here, as if it held the glow of the sunlight longer and, now that they were well into the park, even the sound of traffic was largely gone. An island of peace in the centre of the city. What had the letter from the elderly resident said? 'The park was the green lung of the city and should be forever!' Now she understood. It was a prize, a gem, something that the city should be fighting to keep - not selling to the highest bidder. That was the crunch - it wasn't the city's interest that was being taken into consideration - but considerations were being taken into account

- or should that be accounts - Swiss or offshore probably! She'd give it all she'd got - not just for the story, but for the people.

Sherry greeted her with smiles and solicitously offered her a chair before seating herself.

'What is it, Hope?'

'I believe I have evidence of a fraud - of a broken contract - involving both businessmen and city councillors.'

Sherry leant forward, her eyes a little wider. 'Go on.'

'It appears that the city park was given to the city under a covenant - which states that the land must be held as a open space in perpetuity. A park! The city fathers have had a word or two changed, enough for them to be able to sell off the only large green site left within our city. The document now reads 'open to the people'; just enough of a difference to make a hell of a lot of difference to some people's pockets.'

Sherry was standing now, pacing slowly about the room - she came to rest behind Hope as she finished speaking, Hope twisted in her seat to look up at her. Sherry rested one beautifully manicured hand on Hope's shoulder.

'Hope,' she gave a short light laugh. 'There's nothing in this story,' a smile of commiseration, 'It's been gone through before - there's really nothing there,' her smile tight and fixed on Hope's large dark eyes.

'What if there was some evidence of a cover-up, and evidence of bribes?'

The pressure from Sherry's hand increased, she squeezed Hope's shoulder tightly, leaning down so that her face was close. 'What evidence have you got?'

Hope felt a surge of triumph - she had caught Sherry's interest - perhaps now she'd be able to dig out the real goods.

'A letter and a photocopy of the original covenant, there will be more, the - my informants - they need to know that they can trust me, they've been badly let down by the media before.' Hope rushed her words, trying to make it all seem more concrete.

Sherry released her shoulder and returned to her seat, when she looked up at Hope her eyes seemed large and bright.

'I can't let you do this - it would be a total waste of time. Hope, you have so much talent, don't waste it on this story. I had one of my best investigative

reporters pursue it to the limit - there was nothing the lawyers would let us use. Forget it. Please,' her voice soft and caring.

'But did he find out ...'

'Forget it!' her voice suddenly sharp, then with a smile, 'That's an order, Hope.'

chapter nine – Di

'Forget it!' her voice suddenly sharp, then with a smile, 'That's an order, Hope.' Di stopped typing and rubbed her hands together, her fingers were cold. The story was looking really good as it came out on screen - and so much better now that she had the tape. There was the odd word or two that was drowned by the roar of a large lorry or when Faith dropped her voice and looked out the side window simultaneously, but it wasn't often that Di had to struggle to recall the story and fill in the gaps. The hardest part now was deciding where to stop. A story this long seemed to cry out for chapters, yet Faith just told the story, no gaps for a new chapter heading, in fact, until she went on it was impossible to know if any particular place was suitable. Like this spot, when they'd got home yesterday evening this seemed like a good place to finish a chapter, but having heard two more instalments Di was not so sure now.

She changed the tape and warmed up her fingers ready to continue, one of the great things about bashing all this into a computer was that you could change things later - like adding the page breaks and chapter headings, right now she was catching up with the tape and enjoying hearing the story again.

'Why so glum?' Chris Raven said as soon as he saw her emerge from the editor's room. Hope turned her large dark eyes up to him, she felt unable to speak, just shook her head and looked back at her feet.
'I think you need a drink - come on,' he smiled and took her hand. Pausing just long enough to pick up her bag and files from her desk they left the newspaper offices together, watched jealously by Ms Sherry Spencer, from her window.
The journalists' pub stayed open most hours and always had a few hacks dreaming up their stories in odd corners. Hope usually disliked the rank atmosphere of such places, stale beer and smoke, but today she couldn't care less. Her mind was whirling now. The refusal of her story had two effects upon her, the first was disappointment, but the second was determination. She was right - the press coverage did stink and now she was surer than ever that there was a conspiracy to keep it all quiet. When

Chris brought her over a half of lager she was ready to boil, he barely had time to get settled before she assailed him with her theories and plans.

'Okay,' Chris said eventually, placing his empty pint glass down carefully on the stained beer mat, 'so, you'll get nowhere with our wonderful editor unless you have a lawyer-proof case.'

'True but...'

'No buts, what we have to do is find that evidence.'

Hope looked up at him. 'You said 'we'.'

He nodded and opened his eyes wide for a second, a smile tugging at his lips. Hope leant forward quickly and kissed him, her hands grasping his, being caressed in return. 'Wonderful,' she said softly, 'let's make plans.'

'Not here - too many ears.'

Hope glanced quickly round, the place had begun to fill up. 'Okay, meet me my place, twelve Lockyer Gardens, about seven?'

'Do you want a lift home?'

'No thanks! Besides, I'll need my car to get here in the morning,' she smiled, but was aware of the colour stealing across her cheek as she left the pub. Chris leant back and watched her leave, astounded by the effect she had on him when he had felt immune to all emotion for so long.

'What are you doing?' Paul asked as he came into the spare room.

'Typing.'

'I can see that - funny. What is it?' he stood behind her reading the screen.

'It's Faith's story.'

'What the hell are you doing messing around with that, I thought you had to put together a business proposal to show your boss.'

'I've done that. Besides, I don't think this is a waste of time, I started doing it just to give to Faith, to cheer her up a bit, thought I'd give it to her for her birthday, if she's finished telling the story by then.'

'Still, must take a helluva lot of your time.'

'Yeah, but look, have a read at what I've typed up so far. I think it's really good, might be worth sending to a publisher.'

'Go on - Faith?'

'She's a good story-teller. You never know.'

He looked over her shoulder again. 'Any printed off?'

'No, I'll do that later, when it's finished, no point in wasting paper and ink,' she said turning back to the keyboard.

'I'll check the business plan then.'

'Oh sorry, I took it in yesterday. I left it with Lechwood just when he was feeling good about himself. It was perfect timing – honest.' To be really honest she didn't want Paul checking the business plan that she'd put forward because she knew that he would have felt honour-bound to add some of his own surety, and that would have meant the house. No, she'd put this plan forward on a different basis, a bigger slice to the investor than was normal and her own signature, not Paul's. She hoped she'd never have to pay the surety that Lechwood would deem his right if the business failed.

'Okay, love. When do you think he'll have considered?'

'Give it a week, I'll ask after that, don't want to be seen to be too pushy.'

'A week?'

'I know the man, he'll take advantage if he thinks we're desperate.'

'You're the boss,' Paul smiled and leant over the back of her chair wrapping his arms across her breasts caressing them. 'Finished here?' he nodded towards the screen. She turned her head a little and took the kiss that she knew was waiting. 'Okay, I'll just close it up now.'

'Don't be too long,' Paul said lightly as he left the room and headed for their bedroom.

Di woke early and lay quietly in the darkness going over the story that Faith had been telling. It was amazingly well fitted together for a story being told straight out of her head - she guessed that Faith must take time in between tellings to make up the next section. The tenderness and passion that Faith had managed to get into her telling of the sequence Di was just about to type up had been exquisite - just the right balance to make every red-blooded woman want to reach out and make love to the Chris Raven character, and yet Faith had held back, had not allowed Hope and Chris to end up in bed together.

They had kept their main aim in focus and had sought out the protesters' group again and through them had two more contacts to make. The first of these was Tommy Trout. Di had burst out laughing the first time Faith had used the name. 'No one can be called Tommy Trout!' she'd said. But there was a reason, as Faith quickly explained, she was using the faces of people she knew for some of the characters, not just herself and Di, and to help her keep track she had changed these names only a little bit, so one Tommy Salmon from work had become Tommy Trout, and besides what did it matter. Di had wondered why she bothered changing the names at all, but Faith had said she just felt that it wasn't right to take someone's name as well as their personality, that would feel a bit like stealing something, like the tribal people who thought that a photograph would steal their soul. Di had laughed but had regretted her interruption as Faith was not ready to go straight back into the story and sat for quite a while saying nothing, and Di constantly conscious of the tape turning had coughed and hummed a little to herself while waiting.

Tommy Trout had made his appearance as a witty and quite dashing man in his mid-thirties. He and Chris had taken an instant dislike to each other, with Hope noticing the way that Tommy sneered as he noticed Chris's long hair. Hope had waved Chris away, suggesting that he should get along to their other appointment. Chris had gone, aware of the other man's instinctive hostility but reluctant to leave his precious Hope with another man. Hope had then been able to talk to Tommy and find out all he knew - and to elicit from him further names to contact and a copy of all that Tommy had been able to pass on to the protesters.

As she watched the digits on her clock reach those that meant the alarm would tell her to get up Di thought that she would have added a little more sexual tension between Hope and this new man, if it was her telling the story. The alarm peeped and was turned off; Paul stirred and turned round, his hand sliding down her flank. She patted his hand and slid out of the bed, heading for the bathroom and getting dressed.

Di made a note to check the batteries and put a fresh tape in the recorder before she went out to work. Faith had left off the story just as Hope was saying goodbye to the dashing Mr Trout with him suggesting that they could meet another time, that he could find out more, especially for her.

Paul joined Di just before she was ready to go off to work, made himself a really strong coffee and smiled blearily at her through the steam rising from its rim.

'Leave it - I'll do it,' he said as she started to run the tap to wash the few breakfast dishes.

'Thanks love,' she said quickly drying her hands and going over to kiss him.

'Don't let the bastard work you too hard.'

'He's only in for the morning, thank God, he's at the Blue Angel interviewing in the afternoon,' Di added as she gathered up her bits - handbag, tape recorder, coat, keys. 'See you later.'

He listened for the sound of their car roaring off down the road before he picked up his cup of coffee and padded upstairs. In the spare room he put down his cup, switched on the computer then left it to boot up while he fetched a jumper from the bedroom. By the time he came back it was all ready to run. He surveyed the menu and selected a file that looked like it could be the new business proposal. It wasn't. He tried again. And again. And yet again until he found himself looking at a page he was sure he had already opened once and rejected. He cursed the shorthand that the title space forced on the user, then decided to take a more methodical approach and begin at the top of the menu and open each file in turn. The eleventh file he opened was titled 'Faithstory'. Even as it began to fill the screen he realised that this was the story that Di was typing out for Faith yet instead of exiting he began to read.

Paul sat back. He'd got to the end of the last piece that had been typed in and he was annoyed. He wanted to read on - yet that was all there was. Perhaps Di was right, perhaps Faith was such a good story teller that this could be turned into a book that could be published. Making a mental note to read on as

Di typed up the pages he exited and opened the next file: 'futurep'. He took a couple of moments to check the date before he realised he'd hit on the right file at last. He read the opening paragraphs swiftly and nodded at them in agreement - then he came to a paragraph setting out the very advantageous investor returns. It pulled him up short. He re-read the terms, then sighing heavily he acknowledged the fact that times were hard and that Di had always had her finger on the pulse when it came to borrowing requirements. Finally he came to the last paragraph. It was couched in slightly less business-like terms, calling upon 'their friendship' and assuring him that she would be responsible for all financial transactions, and offering no other form of surety than his sure knowledge of her business administration and her promise to remain as his secretary even if their business took off.. Paul didn't like it. This was not how business was conducted - what would this bloodsucker want if the venture failed? There was nothing explicit in the document but an uneasy sensation of anger and mistrust grew within him, though he didn't know who to aim it at. Di had always done everything possible to make their business a success. Everything - anything? He recalled the times when Di had told him laughingly about her boss - The Leech. Times when she had hinted that the only thing that kept him at bay were the harassment rules and the fact that she was such a good secretary he'd be hard put to find another to match her standards.

He quickly turned off the machine and went downstairs. His mind was whirling - he knew that he had to do something about that business proposal - something to put it back on a proper business footing. Di could be such an innocent sometimes, Paul felt the anger flare again within him, not at Di but at a boss who would read the wrong sort of promises into Di's naive offer. He grabbed up the Yellow Pages, flicking through it roughly. Here: Nightclubs: B's, Barn, The; Blondz; Blue Angel. That was the one. He noted it was in Westgate Street and flicked the Yellow Pages closed again. It was almost lunch time, he opened the fridge and took out a chunk of cheese, taking a bite out of it while he pulled a couple of slices of bread out and buttered them. He sliced the cheese straight onto the work top, finished off the sandwich with pickle and sliced it in two. He sat down to a table still cluttered with breakfast debris and thought hard, not even tasting the cloying mass that he ate. He scooped the crockery into the sink, popped the bread back in the bin, the butter and cereals in the cupboard. He had to get moving - the washing up could wait until he got back. He rang for a taxi then dashed back upstairs to shower, shave and get smartened up, putting on a business suit, a sober deep blue, a quality silk tie against a crisp white shirt. He checked his appearance just before he heard the toot of the taxi from outside. He shrugged himself into over three hundred pounds worth of dark wool coat and left the house.

Westgate Street was just round the corner from one of the most notorious streets in the city and it wasn't hard to find the club as the Blue Angel's neon sign was glowing dimly even in the middle of the afternoon. It was only as he approached the blue and white striped entrance porch that he wondered how he expected to get in. If Lechwood was conducting interviews then the place may not be open - and even if it was and he was permitted to become an instant member of the club then it was unlikely that he'd be able to get to see Lechwood himself. Still, he was here now, he might as well have a go. The door was open, just inside a large man of approximately the same age as Paul leant against a table and inspected his fingernails. He straightened as soon as Paul stepped within the door frame.
'Member, sir?'
'No - I understand Mr Lechwood will be here this afternoon, interviewing.'
'That's right - follow me, sir.'
Paul followed, amazed. There were about twelve broad steps down and then the man opened a blue baize door and allowed Paul to go in front of him.
'Interviews!' the man shouted into the dim room, 'Go on in, someone'll show you the way,' he added to Paul and closed the door behind him. Immediately a pretty petite woman appeared at his elbow and asked him to come with her, leading him straight up a second set of stairs to an office.

'Your name?' she asked.

'Paul Harvey.'

She opened a second door, 'Mr Paul Harvey,' she said through the gap and stepped back to let him through.

chapter ten – Faith

The weekend faced her, a desert, drained of imagination and words, filled with the prickly day to day living, the catching up of housework and general distractions of having the house full. Then, centrally, there was the arid mountain range of Saturday night. She had successfully blanked out her thoughts on this subject since the celebratory night of the pizza, lager and video, yet it was there. It was as if she could turn her head a little too quickly and catch sight of her feelings, chained up, huddling in the dark corner, thoughts and emotions that would make her feel nauseous if she looked them in the eye.

To avoid 'turning her head too quickly' she kept her face turned towards the simple domestic chores, mechanically channelling her energy through her hands. She worked hard and fast all through the day exhausting her body, allowing her mind to carry the story on a stage or two, ready for the telling on Monday. A bright new Monday, Andy going off to work, the children sure to be on time by going into school with a neighbour, and Di waiting to hear what happened next.

She'd successfully sent her heroes on the trail of finding out the truth behind the city hall and IDRA set up, Hope, having gained another lead from Tommy Trout, was just about to set off to contact her, and Faith knew just who it would be this time, her good friend Susie, and the name change was simple, Dudley became Moore.

'So you see, if I can get to talk to this Susie Moore then I may have found a way into the records kept by IDRA,' Hope finished breathlessly. Chris sighed and wrapped his arms around her, kissing her lightly on the top of her head.
'It's like holding a firework,' he said softly, 'trying to hold onto you, isn't it?'
She tipped her head to look up into his eyes, her own, slightly puzzled.
'And it's wonderful,' he added, 'you fill me with your light.'
She smiled, eyes sparkling, and hugged him tightly. Though holding a live firework is dangerous, he thought, I'll still hold on.

Susie Moore had a pleasant smile ready for her when she walked up to her desk at IDRA Holdings, she rose a few inches and offered her hand across the table.

'How can I help you?'

At the front desk she'd asked for an appointment with the consortium manager, as Tommy had told her this would get them straight through to her private secretary, Susie. Now she was here Hope felt that they had to move quickly on to their true business.

'Tommy suggested that I came to see you,' Hope said, *fixing her eyes on the attractive yet homely face before her. The eyes widened slightly and she betrayed herself by clasping her hands together as if to prevent them flying away.*

'Yes?'

'You let him have some evidence about the park project,' Hope began, *but saw the alarm in Susie's eyes almost as soon as she let slip the word 'evidence'.* 'It's all right - I'm a friend - won't say a thing - it's just I need to know a little more, I need to find the connection between the two groups. Sure they dine together at civic functions and that but there appears to be no other links apart from the one rogue letter from Prospective Properties to the planning department, the one Tommy told you about. I need to find some kind of deal between them, something passed from one group to the other, it's too big to be simply a buy-off between odd guys here and there.'

Susie nodded, she'd come to that conclusion a while back and had also decided that someone at Prospective Properties was pulling an extra fast one on the rest of the IDRA group in order to gain some preferential treatment when the go-ahead was given. She had looked then, but found nothing. And as for 'dining with city hall' her boss didn't even do that unless it was a major state occasion! She'd looked for just the sort of evidence that was being asked for, but had found none.

'There's nothing - however,' *she paused, was she right?* 'However, I do wonder how much Miss Johnson knows. This project is very much her baby as manager of the IDRA consortium, she might not like it if she thought Prospective Properties were trying to pull a fast one - she might be interested in that enough to allow you a little access.'

'What's she like? Would she be mixed up in all this? I, mean if she's running it for IDRA she must know everything that goes on, surely.'

'She's managing it now, but it began with a different manager, Mr Perkins, but,' her voice dropped, 'he's dead, car went off the road between Glossop and Manchester, brakes failed.'

'Oh dear, I am sorry,' Hope said to fill the sudden silence.

'So you see - well it could all have been in place before Miss Johnson took over.'

At half past five her family gathered to eat the meal she'd made and Faith abandoned Hope and Susie to her subconscious, leaving them to sort out the details of arranging an appointment with Amy Johnson, a woman created in the image of her own boss, Amy Robertson, and the first name swap that came to mind. This she knew was going to be Hope's big mistake, though it would not become apparent until much later. At least she hoped that Di would not spot the turning point too easily, nor resent the aspect of Sherry Spencer that would soon show itself in the character that Di knew to be fashioned upon her. It would be all right, Di must understand how this story-making went, how sometimes the characters had to do certain things to carry the plot forward - after all, if their lives were all as dull and uneventful as their own, then the story would not be worth telling. She looked across the table at her children tucking into the home-made chicken burgers she'd done for tea and gave a glance sideways at Andy, one hand filled with half-eaten burger, the other gripping a folded back TV magazine.

'Bloody rubbish on a Saturday night,' he grunted laying the magazine down on the table.

'Have we something on tape?' Faith asked, hoping they had, as an early night was the last thing she had in mind.

'S'pose so,' he stretched, lumped the last bit of his burger bap into his mouth, chewed once and stood up. He seemed to fill the room, towering over the table as he stood beside her, his shadow huge and dense as he blocked the light from the central bulb. 'Could do with getting out a bit,' he said.

His day had been spent in the garden ostensibly getting a recalcitrant muddy area ready to receive paving slabs and the new title of 'patio'. She knew what 'getting out' meant - a trip to the club, and if going solo, without Paul, he would need a little cash in hand. Faith's mind flashed between peace for the evening with the chance of her being too fast asleep when he returned and the possibility of his being too drunk to notice that she was already asleep but not so drunk that he'd leave her that way.

'Well, with you starting work on Monday there should be a few quid spare,' she said, trying to smile. It seemed to work.

'Yeah, well - that's what I thought,' he said leaving the room, taking his shadow with him, heading upstairs towards the money.

The children watched a little television, argued and were sent to bed. Faith made herself a hot drink and took it up to bed with her, sipping it while she absent-mindedly read a library book. After a while she put the book down as nothing of any sense was going in, finished her drink and went to clean her teeth ready to sleep. Sleep didn't come easily though and she allowed her mind to return to the story, taking it that one fatal step forward, letting Hope make an appointment to see Amy Johnson. Meanwhile Chris was following up another lead and had been talking to a very interesting man, a man who kept records, rack upon rack, filing cabinets full, all carefully labelled in his meticulous way. The records that Alun Holmes kept, Faith's sobriquet for her other real-life boss Alun Watson, covered anything to do with the history of the city council from its Royal Charter granting it permission to hold a market in the eleventh century to the list of members of the council serving on each of the sub-committees during the current term of office.

Chris had expected a professor of history to be a dried up old husk, dust ingrained in the lines on his skin, so Alun Holmes came as a little bit of a shock, younger than Chris himself by the look of him, he wore his erudition with a laconic smile and his hair almost as long as Chris's own.

It amused Hope to redesign her boss in this way.

'Come in,' he said leading the way into a brash office, all white furniture and black filing cabinets. He caught Chris's raised-eyebrow look as he surveyed the room. 'I like order - in some things,' he added with the briefest

flick of his fingers to indicate the rows of filing cabinets, 'now how exactly can I help you?'

'I'm not sure how much Mr Trout told you of our researches - but it boils down to the fact that you appear to be the only person we know of who had sight of the original document before the water damage, to acknowledge that there may be some difference between the original and the attested copy that is being used for the current planning applications.'

'I would agree to that.'

'Is it possible that you remember who was with you when you took the copy?'

'No, I didn't take it, that's not how it works. I had requested that particular document from the archives. Not one that is generally released - but a letter from my professor persuaded them that I was a serious student and deserved special treatment. Have you seen the copy that I sent to Mr Trout?'

A shake of the head from Chris - they'd been very reluctant to reveal its whereabouts to the press.

'Ah, well, then you would not appreciate the difficulties in copying such a document. It was part of an extensive will, five closely written pages, each being over A3 wide and long. Each sheet needed four sheets of A4, that being the only size of copier available to the records department at the time. Just taking the copies was a tricky task as the pages were joined at one corner and the join sealed. The archivist, after my second request to work on the document, asked how many more times I may need to see it and when I told him that I had only completed the first page he opted to take the copy for my study rather than risk such a valuable piece in the hands of a student.'

'Who was the archivist? He should be able to corroborate the accuracy of your copy.'

'Mr Grantham passed away sometime in 1989. They said he was distraught by the damage caused to his precious archives by the flood in 1988, and never truly recovered. But why is it so important that the copy is verified?'

'Didn't Mr Trout explain what's going on? That there appears to be some kind of deception being played upon the people of the city, to allow the city council to sell off the park to developers.'

'But they can't do that - not under the deed of gift.'

'Exactly, it appears that the copy that all the legal precedent is being taken from is not worded in precisely the same way as your copy, a few words changed mean that as long as the public can have access to the space it can be anything, leisure centre, shopping mall - anything!' Chris found himself feeling quite emotional about the idea.'

'No - Mr Trout merely wrote to me as a member of the planning office saying that he had learned that I "may have information relating to the Marchmonts and in particular to their philanthropic acts towards the city and would I be so good as to furnish him with any relevant details". I recall his letter particularly as it was one of the most old-fashioned letters that I have received in a long time, but I photocopied a section of my thesis and sent a few copies of some original documents to illustrate the points brought up in the thesis. Pure vanity, even though I can see the flaws in my early work; it was a work of love - and you are always fond of such things. If only he'd explained fully before.'

'Why?' Chris felt a suspicion that perhaps this man might know more after all.

'Well - I'm surprised that no one has come up with it before - certainly any self respecting archivist should have pursued the matter. The Marchmont deed of gift was entailed in the will, as I have said, and all wills had to be proved in the Bishops' Court. The copy that was held at the City archives was from the Marchmont estate archives, and as such was the personal property of that family. A contemporary copy would have been lodged at the bishops' court and the records kept there.'

'Would have been?'

'Well, yes, always - however sometimes these have been lost, damaged, even destroyed. Many were destroyed during the blitz, burnt rather than blown up, sad.'

'But the Marchmont will?' Chris prompted.

'Safe, at least it was the last time I had sight of it, few years back now, but then the records at St Catherine's House in London are usually well looked after.'

'God! Do you mean there's another original - one that can be read, that the City haven't, haven't…'

'Not easy to get to see, city luminaries would have little difficulty however. Perhaps they just are not aware of it, but then, the archivist should at least be aware of the possibility.'

'Unless he doesn't want to be,' Chris muttered, *'Thank you, thank you so much, this may just be the break we have been waiting for. How do we get to see - no. Perhaps you would help us further at a later date?'*
'Delighted, that park is something special you know, not just an open space it's a memorial to Leonard Marchmonts' two elder boys who died of the plague and a thanksgiving for his third, who survived.'

Faith was suddenly aware of the sound of the front door shutting. She listened in the dark to Andy's heavy footsteps as he moved from hall to kitchen. A tap ran. The fridge door closed. A short silence. Then he was on the move again. Heavy slow tread up the stairs, the click of the bathroom light, a cascading of water finishing with two short bursts and a fart. No sound of the lid being replaced, nor the tap being turned on. Faith moved further towards the edge of the bed, shrugged the covers higher around her shoulders and tangled the sheet in her fingers, feigning deep, deep sleep. Andy came in the room, his shoes shuffling on the carpet suggested that he believed her to be asleep. The bed dipped, leaving her clinging to a hill-slope, a waft of lager, vinegar and chips swam round her senses as he flopped the covers over himself and turned on his side, away from her. Faith breathed out, gently, slowly and subsided into sleep.

chapter eleven - Di

'You did *what?*' Di screeched.

Paul, over Monday breakfast had just decided he'd better let Di in on the new deal that he'd struck with Mr Lechwood. He had been considering her reaction all over the weekend, had once or twice thought of telling her the whole story making a big joke of it - saying how he'd almost got the job of nightclub manager for the Blue Angel by walking into the interviews. Something had always stopped him, he knew that Di wasn't going to be pleased, but now he had to say - she'd go ballistic if Lechwood let it slip before he'd owned up, and as she had to be out of the house in a few minutes this was as good a time as any.

'You should have let me see that proposal before you sent it off - you're, oh Di - you're too trusting.'

'I'd arranged that - I knew exactly what I was doing - after all I did arrange most of our deals in the old business, didn't I? Didn't I - or did you go sneaking round behind me picking up pieces and fixing things - no - I thought not!' Di slammed the recorder into her bag - glanced at it - felt a moment's irrational impulse to take it out and smash it on the kitchen counter, but viciously zipped up the bag instead. 'You know - you know what annoys me most? You knew I didn't want the house put in jeopardy - you knew that, that was my reason for turning to the man in the first place - my only reason! And you go there and offer just that to him - do you think he'll consider any part of my original proposal as having changed? God - the thought of Lechwood listening to your drivel - what damage it's done to my reputation with him?'

Paul was standing now, not knowing what to do - Di had a temper on her at times but he thought this was the worst he'd been the target of. Oh he'd seen her in action all right - with suppliers who did not supply on time, or enough, or the right quality - with late payers - what good that ever did, but never aimed at him before. He moved towards her, hands reaching out to hold her - holding her always had the right reaction at other times, but all of a sudden he felt that he may have just misjudged the situation.

'Di? Di - love? Come on - I thought it was for the best - honest, Lechwood and his type will always want their pound of flesh - and your words were - well - he'd misunderstand them, that you can be sure of!' He'd reached her, hands rubbing gently on her upper arms. She closed her eyes, shook her head.

'Oh, Paul - too late now - never mind. You better get a move on - you've got to be out too.'

'I'll wash the dishes,' he offered with a lopsided rueful smile.

'What - like you did on Friday?' Di threw as a parting shot, glancing at her watch, gathering up her things and heading for the door.

'Oh, well,' Paul sighed as he heard the door close, 'better do these dishes.'

Between her house and picking up Faith, Di had almost decided to forget taping the story, Faith didn't know what Di had planned, she would have no cause to feel let down, then, just as Faith ran round the car to get in she changed her mind again and pressed the record button. It was just as well as Di scarcely heard any of the story that Faith told her, the details pouring out without hesitation. No pauses while names were conjectured, no ruminative silences while Faith closed her eyes and pictured something that just made the whole thing come alive. Di didn't listen hard to the story, aware that she could listen later, but she noticed the flow and once again concluded that Faith made chunks up ahead of the journey.

Did she see an avaricious gleam in Mr Lechwood's eyes when he greeted her that morning? She was waiting all day for him to refer to the arrangement in some way. It was as if by waiting for him to speak she was preventing it for as soon as she cleared her desk ready for the following morning he called her into his office.

'Sit down, my dear. About your proposal, your joint proposal,' his thick eyebrows crawled as high up his deeply ridged, oily forehead as the flesh would allow.

'Yes, I, understand my husband came to see you - I really would rather that you considered the original proposal - alone.'

'You don't agree with my interests being protected, with a small guarantee being on the books?'

'I don't mean it like that - I had hoped that you would consider the proposal on its merits.'

'On your merits, you mean. However, I am a business man, the revelation of a hitherto unknown security leads me to question the approach made in the first place and to decide that it is probably best that I take the security later offered as there must have been some doubt in your own mind to have withheld the information from me in the first place.'

'I understand - though there was no hiding our 'security' from you - it was my personal choice, reflecting nothing on my expectations of making our new business pay.'

'No - I'm sure you could - you are an excellent and hardworking person - and the statement of the affairs of your business show that it was the throw of the dice that sank you, not bad management. No - I'll back you - if you'll back yourself, as your husband offered, and more than that, if you can get the business organised and running in a fortnight I'll put the building of my first gymnasium extension in your hands.'

'Thank you.' Di felt like a cut bloom, all glorious show and suddenly rootless. 'Thank you - I'll tell my husband, and I'm sure I shall be able to give our reply first thing tomorrow, thank you,' she added holding out her hand for a business-like shake. His thick soft fingers laid themselves lightly around her hand, his forefinger stroked her inner wrist once. It sent a shiver running around her frame, which she disguised quickly by picking up her bag.

'Till the morning,' he said and smiled.

'Yes, good evening, sir,' she said, trying to put formality firmly between them.

Paul wasn't home when Di got in, she took the recorder out of her bag, put the tape in the drawer in the wall unit, picked out a new one and put it in the recorder ready for the morning. The house was cold, though the day had been tolerably mild for November, so, feeling the recklessness of someone with two incomes coming in she turned on the heating and decided to take a deep hot bath while the warmth permeated the house. She armed herself with a pencil and notepad and set off upstairs, she always thought well in the bath, and there were a myriad of things to contemplate now.

Deep in fragrant water she let herself almost float for a few moments before thinking of yet another point that must be dealt with if they were to get the business off the ground at the same time as bringing in money. The most obvious course was for Paul to tell dear Billy that he had another opportunity and that he could stuff his site manager's job - obvious but not the wisest choice when you took into account Billy's influence in the building trade. No, she had to work out a way of making sure that they could set up a firm and make sure it ran sweetly without letting down Billy or Lechwood. There had to be a way. Would Billy accept Andy as his site foreman instead of Paul? She doubted it - what about Andy running their show until Billy's contract was finished? Well, what about it? To start with Di wasn't sure that he had enough wit to keep everything on track and secondly she had always felt that Andy resented Paul's successes, which wouldn't make for the most efficient manager. Yet an outsider could strip a contract, rob it blind and be none the worse off himself at the end - it had to be someone with some kind of stake, even if it was some crazy friendship that went back to childhood.

She was suddenly brought out of her contemplations by a rattle on the bathroom door.

'Hey - what's this locking the door on me? You won't get your back scrubbed like that!' Paul's rich warm voice came through the door.

'It wasn't locked against you - besides the water's cold now.'

'Oh - who have you had chasing you round while I've been working my rocks off down t'mill?'

'Go away with you - I'll be down in a minute - put the kettle on if you want something to do!' she said, the laughter clear in her voice. She never could stay angry with Paul for long, and there was far too much for her to sort out without a nagging resentment taking up needed brain space.

By Friday Di felt that she'd never worked so hard in her life. Since telling Lechwood that they would take up his offer she had spent all the time she had after work and sometimes during her own lunch break, making arrangements for the hire of the equipment and delivery of materials that they would need to fulfil the gymnasium project. Paul dealt with the finding and hiring of men required, as he had always done, selecting those he knew by reputation or by past experience. There were enough to choose from and fortunately rates could be trimmed accordingly. It was something that Paul did well, his natural leadership and camaraderie somehow engendering the feeling that it would be a pleasure working with such a man.

The problem of who to set as their site manager was resolved by Paul's straightforward refusal to let anyone else take the job on except himself. He'd persuade Billy that Andy could do the job for him just as well as he could, he said, but that he'd stick with it right up to the day he had to start on the new project. It had seemed reasonable to him, offering to keep on right up to the last minute.

When he told Billy on Friday afternoon it wasn't that Billy didn't like the idea much: Billy didn't like the idea at all, swearing that if he saw Paul sulking round his site after he left his office he'd have the friggin' law onto him and not even saying whether Andy would be taking over or not. Paul, thinking that he could always take on Andy himself if things didn't work out, deliberately left off telling Andy that he wasn't going back until Monday, not wanting to cause upset if it wasn't necessary.

Monday came after a hard weekend working at the new business and Di felt that going back to work would be something of a break. Her mind had been fully occupied making sure that every aspect of the paperwork had been covered, running up a new letterhead, re-working their accounting programme, getting letters off to people and firms that she'd gained verbal assurances from during the week. Harvey Construction was back in business and though exhausted she was elated.

Di was aware that she had barely spoken to Faith as they drove to and from work but Faith's happy telling of the story went on and filled in the journeys though she'd not had time to type any of it up. This was temporary, Di reasoned to herself, if she still had no time to type the tapes up after the business actually took off, then she'd forget the whole idea - if she did have time then at least she'd have every word down on tape and nothing missed. She had been so preoccupied since coming home on Friday that it was only as she was about to go out that she remembered she'd not put a fresh tape in the recorder. She scrabbled to find the pull-strip to release the fresh six-pack of tapes that she'd bought for the next week, giving up she stabbed through the cellophane with her fingernail between two cassettes and ripped off the clingy covering. She flipped out the full cassette from Friday and inserted the fresh one, and headed out for work.

'Andy!' Paul spoke cheerfully into the phone mouthpiece his eyes scanning the neighbours opposite as they bundled themselves out of the house, one standing listening at the door for a moment or two before joining the other in the car that stood billowing out fumes into the cold morning air. 'Andy - I'm not in work this morning. I've given notice, this job for Di's boss that I mentioned - I've got to get it sorted.'
'Well - I thought you were just dreaming - if you could get an outfit up and running …'
'Yeah well - I didn't want to count chickens and all that.' He paused, judging that he'd better give Andy some kind of warning. 'I offered to work out the week for Billy - see his new man in - but he had other ideas - I put in a good word for you, so, er, be seeing you.'
'If he's given you the push what about me?'
'Oh, well, he didn't say anything definite, I reckon you're still in there, nothing to do with me leaving.'
'Oh, right, thanks - but what ..'

'Bye, see you,' Paul cut in and let the phone clunk down as he heard the word 'thanks' and the hesitant 'but' that followed it. He didn't want to say any more until he heard what Billy had decided on.

Paul made himself a fresh cup of coffee. The ridiculous thing was that he had very little to do to get the project running. He had his men, Di had the hiring of the machinery in hand and the materials ordered. He could look over the plans that Lechwood had supplied again, checking out any problems, sorting them before they arose, yeah, he'd do that after his coffee. He picked up a tape and stuck it in the kitchen player, expecting some easy listening stuff, instead he heard Di's voice, 'Morning!' the background rumble of engine, a car door bang and 'God it's cold again!' from Faith, engine revving, driving off with a gentle roar. Like eavesdropping, he was mesmerised, sipped at his coffee as the general greetings and grumbles turned into the monologue of The Story. He'd missed quite a bit, he could tell, the story he'd read left off where the photographer had got himself invited back to the dishy young journalist's flat, he recalled being piqued at the finishing point, sure that there was a bit of spice coming up in the next section; here they were talking about going off to separate appointments.

' Heads or tails?' Chris said flipping a coin.
'Don't be silly, heads,' Hope smiled at him. It really didn't matter which of them interviewed the new archivist and which the IDRA manager, but to choose by a flip of the coin seemed silly.
'Tails! You choose,' he said.
'But - oh - I'll take the archivist - I've always been keen on history.'
'It's a deal - see you in the 'Printer's Devil' about seven?'
'Okay - any change leave it on my answerphone at home,' Hope said as she gathered up her bag ready to go.
'Take care,' Chris said coming over to her, drawing her to him gently and holding her close to him for a moment, 'see you later.' as he bent to kiss her lightly and to be kissed back firmly.

'Hope Jones, City News, good of you to see me.' Hope held out her hand to shake that of the City Archivist. The smartly dressed attractive woman of about forty-five, her hair smoothed back into an immaculate chignon, shook her hand briefly and smiled.

'How can I help?' she asked with clear home-counties syllables.

'I'm interested in the Marchmont Will, I understand that it was damaged in a flood?'

'Yes - a disaster - so many irreplaceable records damaged.'

'Are there any duplicates of the Marchmont Will? I mean I was told that there usually were, especially of the more important ones.'

'Yes, there usually are - however in the case of this will it was one of those that was destroyed during the blitz - leaving only the estate copy available.'

'Destroyed in the blitz?'

'Yes, unfortunately it happened to many documents and when the original was damaged I was asked to seek out any copies that there may have been and …'

'Sorry, you? I thought the flood happened when a, Mr, um, Grantham was archivist,'

'Yes, I was one of the assistant archivists at the time.'

'I see – sorry, please go on.'

'I investigated the possibility of there being a second copy, however the set held by the Bishop's Court were lodged in the Cathedral archives during the war and they suffered a direct hit, the whole area was ravaged by fire - everything was lost.'

'I see - and no one else has looked for another copy?'

'No - we are talking about the sixteenth century, they didn't just run off copies for the sake of it - each one had to be laboriously written by hand and this one is long and detailed. The only recorded copy was at the Cathedral, so there can be no originals left.'

Hope suddenly felt chill and decided not to even hint that she knew that another copy did exist.

'Thank you - I had just hoped.'

'Don't we all - such a loss to the city archives, a will that has shaped the face of the city for the past four hundred years.'

But not for much longer, Hope thought to herself, 'Well, thank you for your time,' she added aloud.

'Not at all, was that all you wanted to know?'

'Yes, really. It was just background work on a piece about the new leisure complex, the bit about the blitz will work in nicely, thanks,' Hope ducked and bobbed her thanks in her haste to leave. She had no reason to mistrust this woman but something deep within her told her that something was wrong, like the dull ring from a cracked china bowl.

Chris was just wondering why he seemed to meet the most attractive women at all the wrong times. At IDRA's headquarters Susie Moore had just shown him into Amy Johnson's office where Amy had indicated that he should take a seat while she just finished the phone call she was taking. She replaced the receiver and turned a smile upon him. He felt himself smile back.

'Would you like a cup of coffee or tea?'

'No - er, yes - coffee if you're..'

She didn't wait for him to complete his stumbling sentence, depressing a button she asked for two coffees to be brought in, then smiled at him again.

'And how can I help the gentlemen of the press?'

'I'm aware, Miss Johnson, that you took over this operation after it had been set in motion.' And that you're just too good looking to be true, he thought.

She inclined her head to show her assent and did not correct the 'miss'.

'We have had some information that might suggest some kind of fraud being carried on using your office as a front,' he saw the hurt in her eyes at once, and hurried to reassure her, 'not that we believe you to have anything to do with it - on the contrary we believe it may have been put in place by your predecessor and well hidden.'

Her voice when it came was low and tremulous, 'What is it?' her green eyes large below her thick auburn fringe, suddenly vulnerable. Chris felt the need to make her smile again.

'Someone at Prospective Properties sent a letter to the planning department - it looked like part of a deal - one that IDRA should have been dealing with.'

'But PP are part of the consortium.'

'Exactly - that's why the letter seemed odd, it appears to involve bribery for preferential treatment.'

'Have you got this letter?' she looked decidedly more cheerful already.

'Yes, I've a copy with me - I was hoping we could work together on this one - that we could do a scan through your files to see if any correspondence matched it in style?'

'If that's all,' she glanced down and away coyly, a small blush hitting her cheek.

'Well, yes, you could explain how it all works, then later perhaps you'd ..'

The door opened and Susie came in carrying a tray of coffee and biscuits, one glance at her innocent face brought Chris back down to the ground.

An hour later and now on first name terms they had worked through all the files. Nothing, nothing in any of the correspondence from Prospective Properties bore any resemblance to the letter sent to City Hall. Amy Johnson had been so open with the files, so eager to help that Chris felt that she was on their side and found himself opening up to this hurt-child of a woman.

'You see Amy, this isn't the only thing we've found - it's possible that the original will giving the land for the park to the people of the city, or rather the copy of it, has been tampered with.'

'What? How could it?'

'People in high places - money can work miracles.'

'How - how was it changed?'

'Well - there was a copy made before the original was damaged - it wouldn't be too difficult to amend the copy and have it re-copied - the difference of a few year's photocopying technology.'

'But the original would show the difference up.'

'Not if the relevant parts were those obliterated in the flood - and not if there wasn't a second contemporary copy of the original.'

'And is there?' Suddenly she seemed too interested, something in her voice made Chris remember who he was talking to.

'Not that I've seen - or know of,' he added, 'and I have taken far too much of your time - thank you for being so helpful.'

'Not at all - willing to help anytime. Mr Raven?'

Chris looked down into her shining green eyes. 'Yes?'

'Chris, let me know how you get on? It sort of - well it would affect me - wouldn't it?'

'Yes, and thank you again,' he said as they shook hands. He turned, decided not to say any more and left.

As soon as he was out of the door Amy Johnson was dialling a number, her eyes glittering as hard as emeralds, at the other end of the line a phone began to ring.'

chapter twelve – Faith

'But that's wonderful,' Faith smiled up at Andy after he told her how he'd been made manager of the site after Paul had left Billy in the lurch.

Billy had been downright rude about Paul, had wanted to know if Paul had offered Andy a job in his new set up. Andy, with an open face and the first touch of bitterness he hadn't even thought of before, said that he hadn't, that Paul had just said he'd left Billy to start up on his own and left it at that. 'What a shit,' Billy had said 'Thought you were supposed to be mates?'
'Only when it suits him,' Andy had answered vehemently with a bright streak of vision that had always seemed to elude him in the past. Swearing some kind of allegiance to Billy, Andy had been offered the job and had accepted gladly. It wasn't quite how he told it to Faith, worried that she might say something to Di, for though he now nursed a thin thread of antipathy towards Paul he had no wish to alienate a long-term mate.

Faith had realised that Di and Paul were starting up Harvey Construction again. Di had mentioned that she was working on the paperwork and on ordering materials. What Faith hadn't thought of was how Paul was going to manage working for Billy and getting his own business off the ground. Now it was obvious, he'd left Billy's concern and nominated Andy to take his place. She couldn't wait to see Di the next day to let her know how pleased Andy was. It would be good to have something to talk about, it seemed as if Di had been in a world of her own for the past week - happy to let Faith ramble on with The Story. Faith wasn't even sure if she'd been listening, she'd seemed so preoccupied, perhaps she'd better check whether Di wanted to hear anymore at all. Come to that, did Faith want to go on? The past week The Story had moved on to the turning point and it was from there that it became difficult - where Di would begin to learn the real character of her alter-ego, Sherry Spencer and Hope would get the hero. Perhaps she'd ask her tomorrow.

'Di?' Faith started after she'd clambered in the car and they were on their way again.

'Yep?'

'Do you want me to go on with this story? I mean you don't have to - you seem a little, sort of far away - like you're not listening.'

'Of course I do.' Di looked towards her, her face earnest as the tone of her words.

'You don't have to say that just to please me - honest.'

'Honest - I've been a bit distracted, but just letting your story sink in is a bit of a rest. God! I don't know what I'd do without it - it makes this bloody interminable journey go so fast.'

'Well - if you mean it,'

'Go on - I'm waiting - really, I am!'

'Okay, if you're sure, right, Amy Johnson's spoken to the new archivist and arranged some kind of meeting - now,'

We have a problem ladies, some greedy slime-ball has drawn the attention of the press back to the covenant covering the use of the land. We need to sift through all the contacts and sort them out - the whole project is at risk.'

'But, surely there's nothing to find - let them loose their hounds.'

'Marie?' Amy said coldly

The smart archivist stood up to face the six women in the room, all of an age, all immaculately dressed and close to positions of power within the city, her face was crimson.

'I - I may have made an error back in '89 when I first sought a second copy of the Marchmont Will. It, it was destroyed in the blitz - and there usually are only two copies. It may be that there were three of this one.'

A sharp intake of breath was the only sound in the room.

'And if there is another copy there's only one place it will be - St Catherine's House.'

'Then it needs to be dealt with.' Hedda's deep voice cut in.

'Not so simple - I, I don't think we could get to it.'

'Nonsense! You're the bloody archivist aren't you - request it for a display or something - surely they do that.'

'Yes, but it would only draw attention to the fact of its existence.'

'You mean we may as yet be the only ones who suspect there is another original?' Felicity asked quietly.

'I don't know - I haven't even checked it out yet - I wanted to know what the Dorm thought first.'

'So, we are not even sure that there is a third copy - but suspect it. They cannot be sure otherwise they would have exposed our photocopy as a fraud. Discretion. I say we get hold of this document as soon as possible, those who hold it probably have no idea of its detailed content, in our hands it is out of the reach of anyone else.'

'But we couldn't destroy — '

'We need only keep it safe for the time it takes for the work to be irreversible, and in the mean time, as Amy says, we must sort out the vermin problem,' Hedda interrupted.

'I'll see our friend in the press - she'll be delighted with a visit from me,' Antonia smiled.

Susie Moore arrived home at the usual time and ran her Nova right up into the narrow drive. She'd just got out of the car and was reaching back in for her handbag when she felt the door press against her and started up suddenly cracking her head on the edge of the door frame, the pressure from the door eased and she came upright rubbing her head and cursing.

'Damn, ow!! Damn -' but even these sounds dried in her throat as she saw the two balaclava-clad forms that stood before and beside her.

'Just a few questions, Susie,' a deep soft voice said with a nod. Susie nodded. 'That's right. Now, somebody's asking questions about Prospective Properties and the Leisure Centre deal?' Susie nodded. 'Good, that's right, now, who are they, and why did they come to you?'

'What for?'

'Wrong answer,' the voice didn't change but the eyes narrowed and the head lifted slightly, a quick glance at the other person. Susie felt herself shoved forward, reached out to save herself from toppling, felt her hand snatched up and slammed down on top of the door, the door pressed back towards its frame. So quickly she barely had time to think and by the time she tried to resist it was too late, her attempt to snatch her fingers from the icy jaws of the door frame were met by a punishing crush as the second person leant on the door.

'Who and why?'

'They ..' the slight lessening of pressure allowed the blood to rush through her fingers bringing a new pain with them 'Ahh ... they're from the press - City News.'

'Better, and why did they come to you?'

'They didn't, I'm just Miss Johnson's secretary, it's her they wanted to see.' The eyes narrowed again, Susie tried to pull away but the door crushed suddenly tighter.

'Ahhh My fingers, my fingers - they'll break, ahhh!'

'Why you?'

'I - I know someone - owww! They're in the protest group. NOOO!!'

A leather-gloved hand slapped across her face yanking her head back as it cupped her mouth.

'Quietly!' a voice hissed in her ear.

'Names, my dear?'

'Mmmim,' the hand was removed, but held hovering nearby. 'It was about a letter - bribery - something.'

'Not what - who?' the eyes flicked a glance upwards again and the door bit into Susie's fingers. She screamed into thick leather.

'Again?' the gloved-hand eased away.

'Trout,' Susie's voice came as a whimper.

'Trout?'

'Tommy - at - at the City planning office - forgive me, owww!'

'Good girl,' the voice came as if speaking to a cowering dog. 'You won't be telling anyone about our little chat - you're far too sensible for that, I know.' Suddenly the car door opened, her arm snatched free, her body buffeted hard, expelling all her breath and they were gone before her body had even slid to the ground. She sat there on the icy cold slabs shivering and holding the fingers of her right hand, cradling them, red raw, throbbing and unable to straighten, tears falling unchecked.

Tommy was just settling down with a glass of wine and the TV when the doorbell rang. He glanced at his watch before answering the door, a quarter past seven. He had the impression of a tall attractive woman through the spy-glass in his door, though the vision was distorted by its fish-eye lens and the way the woman kept turning away as he looked. He unlatched the door and she threw herself into his arms, crying 'Oh Tommy!' and knocking the breath out of him, making him stumble back just as two masked figures leapt up to and through the door. They slammed the *door behind them just as he became aware of a tiny pricking pain just beneath his ribs and looked down. The blonde looked straight at him, the mask was good, and close fitting but obvious now.*

'Don't try anything, this knife needs only to slip in a few inches to touch your heart,' a deep rich voice tainted by the scent of rubber spoke in his ear. He froze - his mind whirling, wondering what he could possibly have, or know, that needed such threats.

'God! You're getting a bit blood-thirsty aren't you, just as well we've arrived, else I don't know if your friend Tommy would be alive!' Di laughed as she negotiated a place to pull in where Faith could get out of the car.

'Oh! He'll still be alive when they finish with him - just,' Faith laughed at Di's mock-shocked face, 'See you later!'

Telling the tale had put her in a good mood, as if all the violence in the story had got something out of her system, some deep-seated anger. She turned with a lighter step and saw ahead of her Nick Wren enter the Central News building. A spiral of burning and freezing spun through her, alternately melting and chilling her core, leaving her momentarily short of breath and shocked. She slowed her steps. She felt betrayed by her body, or was it her mind? Whatever controlled the uncontrollable. Bewildered, she resumed her progress into work. It was true that Nick Wren hadn't been about for the last few weeks, off on some kind of project someone had said, but she wouldn't have said that she'd missed him being around. That was it, it had been like the feeling associated with seeing a ghost. That's all, seeing him had just triggered off some old memory, creepy she decided, as the lift doors opened onto her work level.

Faith could tell that Susie was excited and dying to tell her something by the way she winked and said 'See you at lunch today!' when she passed her desk. What it could be - and what it probably was fluttered in and out of Faith's imagination during the morning while she transcribed the letters left for her by the editors and prepared some drafts of other work ready for them to peruse at a later date, by lunch time she was ready to hear.

'Oh, Faith, I can't wait to tell you.' Susie gushed as soon as she took her plate of Lasagne off her tray.

'Go on then,' Faith looked at her friend's glowing face as she removed her own salad lunch from the tray and then left it there, leaning forward, a mirror to Susie.

'Faith, last night we, well you know how funny he is - all that proper gentleman stuff, opening door for me and all that, even if it all goes wrong sometimes like the one at a club on a spring that slipped out of his hand and nearly catapulted me back into the street,' she laughed, 'well I began to think he didn't want me, you know. So last night, I pushed it a bit and - well, wow. It was like I opened some locked door - oh you wouldn't believe it - so - so considerate, and well, caring, making sure I was, there, ready, - oh, you know, kisses, everywhere, and compliments, soft murmured words of love,' her words grew soft and low, her face glowed and her eyes sparkled in remembrance.

Faith was genuinely pleased for Susie, really happy for her and kept the smile on her face even when inside she began to hurt, began to ache for the soft words and the caressing care. Until, somewhere at the very back of her mind, deep in her sub-conscious, the longing took on a shape and a face and with a sudden stab of recognition she lost her smile.

chapter thirteen - Di

Di found herself more intrigued by Faith's story now that it had assumed a little bit of bite, the element of danger set her mind thinking back along the other characters that Hope and the decidedly tasty Chris had met in their investigation and found that she was unsure of those who'd appeared in the later tellings, though she could remember the character of Tommy Trout and found she actually wanted to know what became of him in the hands of these nasty women. She'd just finished a stack of filing when Mr Lechwood appeared beside her desk.

'Di, my dear, would you come into my office for a moment,' his oily voice oozed into her ear driven by a wave of expensive aftershave.

'Take a seat,' he waved at the comfy chairs off to one side.

Tentatively and folding her long legs as demurely as possible she sat down opposite her boss and waited.

'I have to go away for a few days. I trust you,' he coughed lightly into his closed fist, 'I want you to run this office for me while I'm away. There should be no problems that you can't handle and no decisions that I alone can make that cannot wait until my return - though you'll have an emergency number if need be.' he looked at her steadily for the count of ten. 'Well.'

'Well - yes sir, if you are confident, of course.'

'Good,' he reached across and patted her knee, caught her narrow-eyed look and immediately removed his hand. 'Good - I'll let you have that number before I go this evening.'

'Excuse me, sir, but for how long will you be away?'

'Not sure - should be less than a week - but I'll keep you informed, anything else?'

'No, no sir.'

'Thank you, that's all.'

Di stood carefully and left his office. It shouldn't be difficult to continue running the office without Lechwood about as it was him who took up so much of her time anyway with his habit of using her as a sounding board for his ideas, and come to that, his foible of entering into unnecessarily lengthy correspondence was time consuming too. In fact, the idea occurred to her that, with no-one looking over her shoulder, she would have sufficient spare time to type up Faith's entire story to date. Having made up her mind to commit the story so far to disc and to bring the tapes into work Di was really looking forward to hearing the next episode by the time she collected Faith from outside the newspaper office.

She was even a little early collecting Faith, she realised as she spotted her still walking towards the post-box that marked their collection point. Di beeped the horn a couple of times as she slid the car into the kerb and switched on the tape recorder. Faith looked round hurriedly and dashed to the door as soon as she saw who it was.

'Oh, sorry, was I late?' she gasped as she fumbled for the seat belt and the car pulled back out into the stream of traffic.

'No, relax, it was me early for a change - Lechwood's taking a short break of sorts, a working vacation- if there's such a thing,' Di was smiling, feeling that she was beginning a sort of holiday of her own. 'Good day?'

'All right. Susie was in good form today, full of the joys of love,' Faith said and found those foreign sensations swimming through her again.

'Aren't you going to go on with the story?' Di asked into the silence that Faith left.

'Oh, yes sure. Where was I? Oh Tommy - in trouble,' she laughed lightly, then began.

'What do you want?' Tommy asked, his voice small in terror.

'Just a few answers to a few questions, I'm sure you'll help us, won't you?' the knife point pressed cold against his skin. He nodded.

Tommy thought hard, he determined to remember as much about his attackers as possible. He decided that all three were women by the size of their leather-clad hands and this shocked him. Not that he'd been overpowered by three women but that they were doing this to him at all. It was as if his mind had split to operate on two levels. One level was filled with fear while the other became overly analytical, noting his own feelings as well as taking notes on his observations. The way that they tied him to a hard chair, arms taut behind his back seemed melodramatic, like something seen on a sixties cop programme, the way that the rubber-faced woman spoke to him was altogether more terrifying by the fact that her accent was polished middle-class and the glint in her green eyes was steely hard.

'We understand that you are involved in a bribery attempt by someone at Prospective Properties to get themselves a better deal on the Leisure Centre Complex,'

'No! No! That was nothing to do with me!' Tommy blurted. 'Someone set me up - sent that letter to Planning and let the Head know it was on its way. I never even saw it until - I had nothing to do with it!'

'Until what?'

'Nothing - just I didn't see it straight away - the office intercepted it.'

'So how did you come by it?'

Tommy was silent, he didn't want to mention how he'd found out about the letter, did not want to bring the lovely Annie's name into it.

'I'm waiting, Mr Trout.'

Tommy tried to think of some way of deflecting the question. The rubber-faced woman suddenly turned and marched out of the room. He heard her walk through to the kitchen. There was a crash and the sound of breaking glass. Her footsteps returned, in her gloved hand she held a vicious-looking shard of glass.

'You really ought to have safety glass fitted in your kitchen door, Mr Trout. You could do yourself a lot of damage if you tripped and fell through the glass.' By now the shard was within a centimetre of Tommy's right eye, caressing the skin. Tommy swallowed, his skin prickled all over, he tried to breathe gently, tried to remain as still as stone. 'Now, I'll ask you again - how did you find out about the letter?' The glass moved away from his face. He breathed.

'Someone at Prospective told me that it had been sent, then I asked in the office and the secretaries told me what had happened to the letter.'

'Who - at Prospective?'

Tommy shook his head, the glass flashed, a searing pain burnt his cheek and there before him again was the glass, tinged with a smear of pink. The gash felt two inches wide, but he couldn't see or reach to touch, to find out. A warm trickle flowed down his chin and dripped onto his shirt, he stared open mouthed as the bright spot soaked in a widening red blotch as it was joined by another drip, and another. He looked up. The eyes behind the glass hadn't changed. He felt himself shudder as he recognised determination and total disregard for his plight.

'Who?' the voice grazed his mind.

'Annie Wise - but she just told me that she'd filed this – poorly-typed letter - apologised for the state of it - she didn't know what it was about.'

'Good - well done. You see there is an easy way. Now, we know you're in the protest group,' Tommy stiffened, began to shake his head but a glance from his persecutor soon made him stop. 'as I was saying, we know that, what we want to know is what is it that the protesters have that they think could change the plans - even now?'

Tommy looked blankly at her, the rubber had an unhealthy sheen, its makeup done in a slightly old-fashioned way, it reminded him of Margaret Thatcher. What did she mean - what had they got? The woman moved the glass closer to his face, all the time staring into his eyes.

'A photocopy of the original - the original before the flood.'

'Attested?'

'No.'

'There must be something else.' The woman looked down, suddenly she snapped her gaze back up to Tommy. 'Where did it come from?'

'What - oh - I wrote to..' he hesitated, another name, God forgive me.

'Who?'

'Does it matter?'

'Who?' The word and the flash of the glass came together. Tommy sucked in his breath, expelling it in a short scream of pain.

'Fuck it - Professor Holmes. History at Louton University.'

'You are a silly man,' she said softly, her voice full of contempt. 'What else do we need to know? I'm sure you'll tell us now.'

The sound of a woman's voice, a refined accent full of apologies for disturbing her, combined with the use of Tommy's name meant that Annie unwisely buzzed the door release that let the rubber-faced woman and her accomplices in and up to her flat. Annie felt the familiar vibration that told her the lift had arrived on her floor and opened her door. At first she saw nothing wrong, a female walking towards her, then she saw the others come out behind the woman. In the next few seconds she almost shouted a warning to the woman, then realised they must all be together and fled back into her flat, the door almost shut before it jammed against the woman's foot. Annie leant all her weight against the door and began shouting, hoping a neighbour might hear.' Go away! Go away! Oh God!' she felt herself pushed bodily across the floor her soft shoes finding no purchase on the carpet. Suddenly she was shoved hard, sandwiched between door and wall, then the door was snatched back and closed, the latch dropped and a leather gloved hand clamped over her mouth, and others hands pinning her to the wall.

A hand tangled itself in her long curly red hair and tugged sharply. Annie let out an involuntary squeal of pain. There was a tearing sound and she was twisted round for a wide strip of sticking plaster to be slapped across her mouth, the antiseptic smell cloying her breath, the edges tugging at the fine down on her cheek, pulling the soft skin taut. Dragging her by her hair, her hands now tied behind her back, the woman led her through to the bedroom.

They sat her down facing the long mirror.

'Let me explain,' the woman said, looking over her shoulder into Annie's face in the mirror. 'We want the answers to some simple questions, I'm sure you will help us, one way or another. First, are you part of the anti-leisure-centre-complex protest group?'

A nod.

'Good, well done. Tommy has told us about the letter you showed him, do you know who sent it?'

A shake of the head.

'Are you sure about that?'

Nod.

'Fine, now I'm going to remove the tape and you are going to keep quiet, understand?'

Nod. The woman fumbled to grip the edge of the tape with her gloves on, then with huff of annoyance she stripped off the glove to reveal a beautifully manicured hand with nails varnished in a delicate shade of lilac. The nails found the edge of the tape and ripped it from Annie's face leaving it burning with thousands of pinpricks. The glove was replaced and in her hand the rubber-masked woman now held one of Annie's own ornamental candles, the fragrance of sandalwood wafted to her as the flame burned.

'Now, what did Tommy bring to the protest group?'

'What do you mean?' Annie whispered.

'He wrote to Professor Holmes and got something important back, what was it?'

'I don't know what you mean.'

'Lovely hair you have,' the woman said lifting up a hank, letting it trail over her fingers. 'don't you find it gets in the way?'   Annie stared at herself in the mirror, watching her hair slip through the gloved hand. 'What did Mr Trout get from Professor Holmes?'

Annie was silent trying to decide what to say, whether these people knew already or not.

'I'm not sure.'

'Wrong answer,' the rubber-faced woman said her voice scythe-sharp as she grabbed up a hank of Annie's hair, gave it a twist and dangled it over the flame. The stench of burning hair replaced the sandalwood as her beautiful red hair flared and coiled singed to carbon, dropping away as ashes. Annie screamed and tugged, a hand slapped her hard across the mouth, and the flame moved away, the smouldering ends of hair crushed in the woman's gloved hand. Terrified, Annie began to speak, her voice shaking with the effort to speak rather than scream.

'I'll tell you. I mean - a photocopy of the Marchmont Will - I'm not sure it was important - our lawyers said it was no good - unattested, or something. That's what I meant - when I said I'm not sure!' She was crying now but noticed the way the three people looked at each other. The woman nodded.

'Who else saw the photocopy?'

'Everyone in the protest group, too many to name, I don't even know them all.'

'What is the group working on now - to try to stop the scheme?'

Annie hesitated. The woman picked up a second hank of hair, gave it a single twist and stared at Annie through the mirror.

'There's some journalists, they're, they're following up leads - trying to find out,' her voice broke off.

'What?' The flame flickered beneath the twist of hair, the ends curling and singeing in the heat.

'Who's behind it,' Annie whispered. The hair was suddenly dropped. The woman turned away and walked to the far side of the room, beckoning the others to follow. Annie watched them in the mirror, heard the woman say the name 'Hope Jones', caught a steely glance from one of the hooded partners, and willed herself not to hear anymore.

'You won't be talking to anyone about this evening's little visit. After all, we know you, we know where you live and where you work. Short hair will suit you. Goodbye, Miss Wise, and thank you for being so —

111

helpful,' she said as she loosened the bindings around Annie's wrists and walked out of the room.

Annie heard the door to the flat slam and wrenched her wrists from the bindings as she made her way to her phone, perhaps they could be caught at the main door if the caretaker was in his flat, but the phone was dead, ripped from its socket.

'Oh, hello, Antonia,' Sherry's usually confident smile was absent.

'Aren't you going to ask me in?' Antonia said in her husky voice as she stepped past Sherry into her spacious apartment.

'Oh, of course - I just didn't think - after - after what you said,' Sherry trailed behind her guest as she walked confidently through the lounge towards the bedroom.

'I know darling - but then you've not kept your hounds in check - have you?'

'I have - you know I have.'

'Then what's the delightful Hope Jones sniffing round at?'

'Hope? Nothing - I told her - there's nothing in the story - to leave it alone. It'll be all right - please.'

'Please what?'

'Please leave her alone, she - she'll do as I say, she's just enthusiastic.'

'Really? And so sweet with it,' Antonia spat as she grabbed and wheeled Sherry by the arm and pinned her against the bedroom door. Her nicotine scented lips clamped down hard on Sherry's, she resisted, but Antonia was always stronger, her body toned by workouts and weights at the gym.

Despite her fear Sherry felt herself soften and respond as the tongue began to explore her mouth. Antonia pulled away, just a little.

'Oh I've missed you, little bitch,' she whispered and kissed her again. 'Come on, we've things to discuss - after.'

chapter fourteen – Faith

Faith stole a glance at Di as she revealed the secret of Sherry Spencer's character. She wasn't sure if she imagined the heightening of colour on Di's cheek or whether it was real. She ploughed on with the story, leaving the 'reader' in no doubt that Sherry both loved and feared the woman Antonia and that Antonia had picked up on Sherry's proprietary interest in Hope. 'We're nearly back - shall I go on to the next bit?' worried that she'd gone too far with a character that Di was identified with. 'What?' Di glanced round at Faith.

'Well, next the story goes to the University - the women,'

'No - no, I think you'd better stop.'

'Stop the story - forever?'

'What are you talking about? I mean till tomorrow.'

They took the slip road and were heading down towards their end of town.

'Where do you get it all from? All this stuff - you know, the women - vicious and lesbian and all?'

'I make it up - it's the same with the men, sexy and smouldering and such - not much of real life in that either is there?' Certainly not with Andy, Faith added to herself.

Di smiled, gave a short laugh, 'No, I guess not!' tension relieved. 'See you tomorrow,' Faith called as she left the car. She went straight indoors, dumped her bag, put the kettle on and went back out again to walk down the road to collect Jilly and Jon from the neighbour who was looking after them.

Back home she chased the children upstairs to change out of their school uniform and settle down to learn their spellings while she prepared the evening meal. For a while she was so busy she had no time to think of anything else, but by the time the meat and vegetables were simmering nicely for the cottage pie and she was peeling the potatoes to make the topping the pace had eased, the children had checked through their homework and gone into the living room to watch Star Trek and only then did she allow herself to wonder where Andy was. He was usually back by six. When the meal was ready, the cheesy topping to the fork-ruffled mashed potatoes turned a crispy golden, she decided that she would give the children their meal and wait until Andy came home to eat with him.

Jilly chattered on about her friends at school, and the endless petty bickering that went on between them, all through the meal. Jon ate with his usual one-track gusto, clearing his plate quickly and asking for a slice of cake before Jilly was half finished. Faith partially cleared the table, wiping away spills and crumbs, before taking the children upstairs for their bath and bedtime story. It was only as a delaying tactic, as a last chance to stay up later, that either of them asked where Daddy was. Jilly saying that they couldn't go to sleep because Daddy hadn't come to say good night, and Jon quickly joining in with the idea that they could watch television quietly until he did come home. Faith struggled to keep a straight face as she told them they would do nothing of the sort, that they would go straight to bed and she'd send Daddy up to say goodnight when he came home. She allowed the smile to light up her face at last as she kissed each of them and snuggled them down.

Andy came home late; too late to go up to say goodnight to the children and in no fit state to do so.
'Where have you been?' Faith began until she registered the smell of lager and the soft look that his face took on when he'd had too much to drink. 'You never drove home like that?'
'Shut up, don't be a bloody nag woman. Fetch us some coffee.'

Faith watched him as he lurched into the living room, then turned on her heel and went to put on the kettle, a hard knot forming somewhere in her chest. She heard him stomp upstairs and listened as the kettle boiled unheeded, wondering if he would disturb the children, relieved to hear the flush go in the bathroom then his heavy tread go on through to their own room, and the creak on their bed. She made the coffee; black and strong, heavily laced with sugar. It made her shudder just to smell it. She carried the scalding mug upstairs carefully. He lay sprawled on his back across the bed, one booted foot up on the duvet, one still trailing on the floor. He must have sensed her standing there, or smelt the coffee, for he lifted his head just enough to catch sight of her before letting it fall back. 'Stick it on the side,' he said and belched resoundingly.

'I've got cottage pie waiting for you - if you're hungry,' she added as she discerned the vinegar and grease scent of fish and chips.

'Nah - ate with the boys, God they can put the stuff away, though,' laddish admiration in his voice.

Faith shuddered. This Andy she couldn't take. She felt sick with hunger, and sick at the thought of food - or bed. 'Your coffee's there,' she said and quickly returned downstairs.

Faith slid out of bed as quietly and carefully as she'd slid into it the night before, making sure she did not disturb the snoring bulk of her husband. He was still partially dressed, had taken off trousers and boots only, drunk half of the coffee and fallen into a deep sleep. She wakened the children warning them that Daddy was not feeling well and not to make a noise, showered herself, dressed for work and went to prepare breakfast. Suddenly a screaming match of 'DO!' 'DON'T' filled the house as Jilly and Jon reached crescendo on some argument. 'Shut up - shut your flaming row!' Andy roared as Faith ran upstairs to sort things out and quieten them. 'You!' *slap*. 'And you!' *slap*. He struck out at both children as Faith reached the bedroom door, 'Shut up - and don't start squawking or I'll really give you something to cry about!' he added as he turned to leave the room and saw Faith.

'What?'

Faith could feel the blood rushing through her face. The slaps had been wild, uncontrolled, flinging the children back onto their beds with their force. 'How dare you - they're children - our children!'

'Well it's 'bout time they learnt!'

'Just because you went and got yourself stinking drunk and feel like shit it doesn't give you the right to beat up our children.'

'Beat up? Beat up? Where do you get off woman? You smack them when they're naughty - go on - say you don't - see!'

'What - it's not the same – not...'

'Not often enough if they can't behave themselves. What's the time, shit, I gotta get moving, out the way,' he finished pushing past her. She went into the children's room to hold them close, soothe Jilly's silent body-shaking tears and Jon's stiff, frozen frame.

Faith was seething inside as she waited for Di to collect her. She would have liked to keep the children off school and take them somewhere special, give them a treat, anything to help them forget, but it wasn't an option and besides Jilly had wanted to go to school, had kept asking when it was time to go to Debbie's, the daughter of the neighbour who looked after them and took them to school each day.

The car rolled up and Faith climbed in, finding it difficult to even open her mouth to say 'Morning', her lips seemed compressed shut, sealed with anger and sadness.

'What's up?' Di asked and busied herself with getting the car on its way.

Faith gave a short deep sigh, yet her lips remained closed. She felt as if she were a pillar of ice within a mask, as if she could look out through the eyes of this strange living creature but experience no emotion, no feeling, no understanding of the form she inhabited.

'Hello! Faith?' Di turned and looked at her on a straight stretch of road. 'What is it?'

Deep at the core of the ice pillar there was a change. A pocket of heat, the glow of anger. And it grew, the thrumming of the wheels on the tarmac seemed to feed the fire, the anger melting the ice, filling the void, her teeth ached, her breathing quickened. She would tell, she would.

'You look awful, bad night with the kids? Have they got this sickness bug that's going round?'

Was it the word? Suddenly her stomach lurched, the melt water threatening to overspill.

'Pull in!' Faith, one hand cupping her mouth the other reaching to unclip the seat belt.

'I can't just ...' a look, pulling over to the hard-shoulder, 'Okay, okay!'

Faith struggled to open the door, just about made it to the grass before vomiting up her breakfast. Di came round behind her, a bundle of tissues from the car in her hand. Faith was shaking now, the sweat instantly on her skin cooling rapidly.

'Looks like you've got the bug too,' Di concluded her earlier thought of troublesome sick children.

Nearly half way to work, Faith thought as they passed the M6 turn off for Rugby. The wave of sickness had passed and with it the conviction to tell Di about Andy. Andy - Paul's best mate after all. She shook herself.

'D'you want some story?'

Di glanced round surprised. 'No, not if you're feeling rough.'

'I wouldn't have offered if I was feeling like that,' Faith snapped, then sensing Di stiffen, 'I mean - take my mind off it.' And she meant it.

'Yeah - sure,' Di threw her an encouraging smile, 'Ready when you are.'

'Where was I? Um - had I sent the Dorm down to the professor?'

'Not yet - you were about to.'

'Right, here goes.'

'Professor Holmes?'

'Speaking.'

'Professor, I am doing research into the Marchmont Will and my dear friend Tommy Trout told me that you could help me.' The voice on the phone was deliciously sexy.

'Well, yes, probably.'

'It just so happens that I have to stop overnight, here, in Louton, perhaps I could talk to you this evening?'

'Well - how about first thing tomorrow?'

'Oh! I have a lunch-time appointment in Birmingham I cannot miss. It was rather cheeky of me to even ask, but I did so want to meet you - perhaps I can make it back down this way soon.'

'No - this evening - I can manage this evening,' he said thinking quickly that he could miss the sherry and nibbles at the Head of Faculties if he really wanted.

'Just give me a time - I'll be there.'

'Yes, um. We'll say seven, I have a late tutorial at six-thirty, I um, seven then Miss?'

'Humbold, I look forward to it, until later,' the rich voice promised.

Alun Holmes tidied away some loose papers, stacked some student essays into a neat pile and glanced at the clock again. Ten minutes past seven. If she wasn't here in ten minutes he was going, there was still time to change and announce that he was feeling better, better enough to take sherry with those who controlled his purse-strings.

He didn't hear them enter, there was no knock, he just felt the draught of the swiftly opened and closed door at the moment that she spoke.

'Good evening, Professor,' just as sensual as on the telephone, he turned a smile ready on his lips and was still grinning as his eyes registered the rubber mask, the two dark clad figures even as they buffeted him back into his seat and set about binding him with tape. It was so fast, for three seconds he wasn't sure it was happening and then it was too late to stop it.

'What the hell?' he began to shout, the thought of screaming for help came to him at the moment that a leather gloved hand slapped across his mouth, and he told himself that it did not matter, that the rest of the faculty would be out of earshot anyway, swilling sherry elsewhere.

'Now, a civilised man doesn't want to cause problems, does he? We only have a few questions and I'm sure you'll be happy to answer them.'

He stared at the face, a grotesque distortion of Princess Di, but recognisable for all that, he tried not to even blink.

'My dear friend Tommy Trout did come to see you, but I suspect that others have been here too on account of the Marchmont Will - you see I really am interested in them. What did they want to know? What could you tell them that Tommy Trout couldn't?' She nodded at the woman who's hand stifled Alun's words, the hand moved away, the blood rushing to his lips as the pressure released.

'I'm not sure what you mean - they were interested in the will, they had seen a copy of the photocopy I took when I was a student, they wanted to know more about it - something to do with the covenants being broken.'

'Go on?'

'Well - that's all - I told them how it was that I had the copy, that it was a true copy, that it was possible to check as there was a third copy lodged in London,' he stopped, he saw her whole body tense, the eyes within the rubber mask flashed and communicated to the other two. He saw that they hadn't known about the third copy and that he'd just told them something he should have tried to keep from them, whoever they were, people with tactics like this were not to be trusted. He comforted himself a little that the documents were well looked after, only open to proven scholars, yet a sinking feeling told him that this would be no barrier to the woman before him.

The news the next morning carried word of a terrible fire at the University of Louton, the whole of the history faculty building had been damaged or destroyed by fire. It was reported that the seat of the fire appeared to be in Professor Holmes' study and that the Professor was the only casualty from the conflagration, having narrowly escaped with his life. He was now confined to hospital in a dangerous condition, with fifty percent burns and that it would be a while before the investigators could even talk to him to help solve the mystery.

Inside his blistered and flayed skin, beneath the singed scalp, in the mind burning with vengeance and the need to speak, Alun Holmes saw them take his precious notes, his neatly filed information from carefully labelled files and tip them into a bonfire pile of loose papers before they dropped the match and left, leaving him still taped to the chair.

'What did they do that for? Burn the place?' Di suddenly cut in.

'Oh - to destroy evidence - to kill the Professor - it needed to happen for the story.' Faith answered shortly. She'd wanted to drown herself in the telling, not answer silly questions.

Chris picked it up on the national news printout. The name leapt and fired his memory, he could see the man, the study, the neatly labelled filing cabinets. Fifty percent burns! Christ – it'd be a miracle if he lived. A sudden shudder ran down his spine. He had a horrible suspicion and he had to see Hope, and quickly.

Hope was working on a set piece for the next day, bashing away on the keys as he came up behind her and gently laid his hand on her shoulder, his thumb caressing her neck. She looked up smiling into his frowning face.

'Meet you in the 'Printer's ASAP,' he said and nodded to show he meant now, and left her.

The lager tasted sour and Chris didn't know if it was a dodgy batch or the taste of ashes in his mouth. Hope arrived, a bright elfin creature dancing quickly to his table, her eyes glancing at his barely touched pint.

'What is it? Not that I was ungrateful for the interruption, that stuff they've got me doing is just so much dross.'

'You remember the history professor I interviewed about the Marchmont papers?'

'Of course - he changed everything!'

'He's been - well there's been a terrible fire at Louton Uni - in the History Department, with the seat of the fire being his office - and him in it?'

'God that's awful,' then a moment staring at the condensation on the outside of Chris' glass as a scene of horror played itself quickly across her imagination and the questions began to tumble in, pillars of suspicion grew and fell. She looked up at Chris, saw in his clear grey eyes that he too had suspicions. He raised his eyebrows a fraction, an invitation to comment.

'And you think - wonder if it might be connected?

He nodded, 'Connected, that's the word. I tried to get hold of Mr Trout at his office - it appears he has taken a few days off to get over a minor accident. It was, well I thought we had to talk.'

'Could be coincidence - let's get in touch with all those we interviewed before we jump to conclusions - and, and let's get it ready to publish, there's got to be enough to push past the lawyers now.'

'Okay, we'll go for it. Just one more check to be made, on the original copy of the Marchmont Will, then we'll roll. I'll do that, you contact those that you interviewed and I'll do mine,' he said and took an ill advised draw at the lager, 'Those that are left,' he murmured, standing, leaving the rest of the drink where it was.

'And that's where we'll have to leave it. It's getting really nasty,' Di said as she turned into the end of the street where she dropped Faith. 'I mean - not that I don't like it, it's making an exciting story but it's not like your other ones, is it? I thought there was going to be more, you know, romance in it.'

Faith sighed, 'Well there's Hope and Chris, they're falling for each other,' she gathered her bag and checked the traffic as they pulled up, 'I can't help it - it's the way the story goes,' Faith added as she left the car.

The way the story goes, she thought bitterly, as the reminders of her own life crashed back in from the sidelines and she felt swamped beneath them. I can't help it - it's going on, it's nasty, getting nasty and something is happening to me. Am I falling too? No? I don't know. Murmuring to herself she headed for the doors and caught sight of him as she had once before, not far behind her, raven hair flying in the breeze, leather bomber jacket, jeans, something of the buccaneer about his reflection in the glass as he almost caught her up just before she opened the door. Then he was there beside her, his arm reaching past her, pushing the door open wider, and smiling down at her.

chapter fifteen – Faith

'Good Morning, *Mrs* Warren,' his eyes appeared to catch the light, his smile hit her just below the ribs and she felt her heart race, and thought how apt that hackneyed phrase was. She tried to smile back at him, casually, and form the words 'good morning' but they would not come. A fathomless sigh surged up from deep within, releasing the pent-up anger and bitterness, pushing a tide of tears before them. She turned away and almost ran to the open doors of the lift, swinging herself round and pushing the button before he had moved from where she left him. She watched the glow on the button, listened, the doors began to close. He was running, actually running, just dived in through the doors as they grasped at him with their rubber jaws.

'What was that about?' he said, his voice light but betraying some hurt, confusion, as he punched the button for the top floor.

The lump in her throat choked her; Faith just shook her head, eyes filling with tears. She leant back against the lift wall feeling its vibration through her spine. Tears ran down her face in silence, she could feel him looking and turned her face towards the corner, caught sight of her reflection moving, heard the lift slow to her floor.

'Something's wrong - obviously - not just the shock of seeing me so early in the morning,' his voice lifting to self mockery. The doors opened, he punched the top floor again and they slid together and the familiar drone started up as the lift surged upwards. Faith couldn't believe what was happening. She was usually so strong emotionally, could usually control her feelings, but the tears still leaked out from beneath her lashes and actually dripped to the floor. Ridiculous. Unfair. She gathered her facial muscles and forced them to smile, she raised her head to face him, brushing away the ridiculous tears with her fingers.

'Sorry - just caught me at a bad moment,' she grimaced again, 'I'll be late for work,' she glanced at the ascending lights, four floors to go to 'his' level. He was looking at her in a strange way, as a dog listens to a new and puzzling noise.

'If there's anything? Anything. Perhaps I can help? I want to - if I can...' his voice so hesitant, his bright eyes searching hers. 'I'm okay really,' she pulled together the bright smile again. 'Really,' and met his eyes for a fraction of a second, all she could stand.

The lift purred to a halt. He pressed the button for her level and stepped out, turned, 'I mean it.' he said, 'Anything,' and watched her as the doors closed.

Faith worried that the gossip would be all round the office by the afternoon; that Nick Wren had chased after her into the lift. She smiled across at Susie, her eyes still reddened by the tears. Susie made matters worse by winking back.

Faith felt strangely guilty when she took the finished letters to Alun Watson, as she stood before his beloved collection in the box-files all round his room. Despite her short tempered assurances to Di she didn't know why the 'Dorm' had treated Alun's alter ego so badly, why she had told the story in that way. Looking down on his balding head she thought briefly of the long hair and youth she'd given him in the story and smiled, so that as he glanced up, signing finished, he only saw the smile.

It was all right, Susie's wink had been more on her own account, not anything to do with rumours running around the office. She was full of the joys of love and life and barely stopped speaking to eat her lunch. Her man, the shy, gentlemanly top hat and tails man, had proposed - and she had accepted. Susie's lovely hands with their surprisingly slender fingers fluttered as she spoke or were momentarily captured for her to stroke her ring finger, as if preparing it for that evening when they were going to look at rings.

Faith listened and remembered. It hadn't been like that for her, she was sure of that now. There had been the sense of something being settled, of a problem being sorted out, of a place in the world. And now she was sure that it was not the right place.

Susie's words filled the lunch hour. When Faith returned to her desk there was a portfolio file propped against her screen. Her heart recognised it as Nick Wren's and lurched before she could analyse the reason and find that despite herself she wished she'd not spent quite so long at lunch. The note pinned to the front told her that it was not urgent and that he'd collect it in three days time when he returned. And that last caused a small sinking sensation beneath her breastbone. It was fortunate that it wasn't urgent as most of her afternoon was taken up with a sheaf of letters for Ms Roberton, and getting them typed, signed, sent and filed, filled the rest of the day.

Di was early again and being spoken to by a young policeman as Faith ran across the pavement to the waiting car. The policeman stood back a little and watched her as she threw him a small smile and climbed in the passenger seat.

'I'll have to judge this better,' Di said as she wriggled the car back into the flow of traffic, 'I've been causing an obstruction! Though he was very nice about it - what do they say about when policemen start looking younger?'

'You're getting old!'

'That's it - he'd only be fit for a toy-boy, I'm surprised they let him out alone - nice looking young lad like that. Now come on, I've been worrying all day about the professor and the rest.'

'Really? I mean, that's really good, okay, okay er they were just checking things out, right?' Faith said relieved to plunge straight back into the story, no chance for contemplation, no chance for confessions.

Di nodded.

'Chris is checking up on the remaining original Marchmont Will, okay,' Faith began.

It didn't take long for him to find out that such a document existed, and to also pick up from the delightfully homely sounding woman in the records office that he was not the only one who had enquired that day. 'You'll be able to see them on display there soon, the City Archivist wants to do a special display for a civic anniversary and has asked for them,' she sang merrily at him. He was suddenly certain that he was right, that the fire had been no accident.

Hope rang the office of IDRA. Susie's voice came on the line, cheerful and snappy. 'I. D. R. A. , how can I help you?'

'Susie - it's Hope Jones from City News?'

There was a small silence, then, in a similar cheerful tone, but cracking at the edge, 'I'm sorry, madam, you seem to have the wrong number.' and the buzzsaw of the tone as the line disconnected. Hope looked at the hand-set, the suspicion grew, took on a more solid form. She dialled again this time calling Tommy Trout's home address. The phone rang just twice before it was picked up, Tommy's voice said the number and requested that if there was any message that it should be left after the tone. Hope took a deep breath then ' Tommy - it's Hope Jones, City News - could you call me, home or office, the numbers are ,'

'No! No - I won't be calling you,' Tommy's voice cut in, 'and if you've any sense you'll get out - there's something really bad going on - you'd be better off out of it!'

'Tommy - what is it?'

'Let's say I had some visitors who've persuaded me I don't want to be in the protest group any more,'

'Who? What happened?'

'Just don't ring me, call on me, be anywhere near me - and for Christ's sake leave it alone - for the sake of your pretty little face,' his words choked off in something that sounded like a sob, and the phone went dead. For the second time Hope put down the phone with a dreadful shiver running through her body. She wondered how Chris was getting on with his contacts and began to put together their information into some sort of order, to write the story around the facts, to be ready to hit back with that most powerful weapon, the Press.

Chris heard Susie's voice when he rang the IDRA number but merely announced that he would like to speak to Miss Johnson. Amy came on line and despite himself her face and figure came into Chris' mind. He identified himself to Amy and mentioned he was chasing up some loose ends and did she have anything to add, especially about the Prospective Properties' interest in the Leisure Centre.

'Nothing that isn't completely confidential - even from you,' Amy Johnson said, a smile behind the firmness of the voice.

There was a smugness in her voice that set Chris' hackles rising. There was no fear, no concern. Something that Professor Holmes said came back to him 'the archivist should be aware of it' and yet the City Archivist had only just asked for the document and had denied all knowledge of it before. Was it possible that there was a connection? There was someone he had to see, someone who had access, albeit illegal, to all sorts of personal information about people, and that was just what he was looking for.

The phone beside Hope rang, surprising her out of her concentration; she picked it up while still reading the last sentence she'd written.

'Hope Jones.'

'It's Joan Hemingway,' her voice imperious and sharp. 'Have you seen Annie lately?'

'No - not lately - why?' Hope asked with a chill feeling touching her skin.

'She's - she's been upset by something, or someone - she cut all her hair short. That may not seem much but she's been growing it out long for a couple of years. She won't tell me - all she said was to keep away from you and your long-haired friend. Has he done something to her?'

'Chris? No - no how can you think that. But something might have happened. And you're ringing me?'

'I never was one to let sleeping dogs lie, I feel there's something serious going on. It worries me.'

'I think you're right — but..' What could she say? There have been threats, accidents, something nasty in the woodshed? 'Tommy has been threatened - don't say anything - I don't think he wants anyone to know, and there's Professor Holmes - of Louton University ...'

'I read about that! Oh God! I didn't make the connection!'

'So - take Annie's advice - watch out - keep away from us. We're going ahead to print - just tying up loose ends.'

'Oh, God. Take care, there's a lot at stake.'

'I know. Take care yourself, bye.' Hope replaced the handset slowly. Take care. The sooner this went to press the sooner everyone would be safe. There was no point in terrifying people when it was all out in the open.

The phone rang again. She smiled as she heard Chris' voice.

'I may have found a connection but we'll not be able to use it as proof. Amy Johnson, from IDRA, and the City Archivist both attended Saint Theresa's Boarding School, Kent, same year, same class, and went on to London University together. Interesting?'

'Interesting - but you're right we can't use it. It makes me wonder ..'

'Me too, and wouldn't you know, the Mayor's beautiful wife was a classmate as well!'

'No?'

'Yes! I've a friend who's still looking - there could be more, oh and I had my friend check our editor out, she seems okay, at least she didn't go to either the same school or the same university as these three.'

'But - can't we use it - somehow?'

'Not without getting the whole story blocked. Are you done?'

'Nearly.'

'I'm coming over - this can all come out later - if we can find legitimate proof.'

Chris stood at her shoulder and read to the end of the page. 'It's good. Lawyer proof?'

'I think so this time, just a little worried about the intimation that whoever is behind the conspiracy may also be capable of arson.'

'It wouldn't be the end of the world if they cut that bit, okay, back it up, print it off, then I'll take a few shots of it.'

'What?'

'I'll photograph it, I've got all the rest already - I'm a photo-journalist remember?'

Hope smiled at him quizzically as he removed each page as it was printed and aimed his camera at it.

'There you go,' he smiled at her, 'into the lion's den, good luck, I'll meet you at your place about four o'clock.'

'Where are you going? Don't you want to present this with me?'

'It's your story, love,' he winked at her, 'see you later - we'll celebrate!'

'Bye - see you,' suddenly Hope felt nervous, so much seemed to ride on her getting the okay on this story. By the time she wondered where Chris was going she was alone.

She sat opposite Sherry Spencer as she read through the article. The visuals: photographs, copies of documents, were spread over the desk. Sherry read intensely, never looking up until the end. Hope read her own words upside down. Ran a mental check list, found everything in place.

'I'm impressed. Though I thought I'd told you to leave this alone?'

'Yes, but you see...'

'I do see. You have the makings of a fine investigative journalist.'

'So it will run!'

'I doubt if it ever will – sadly,' Sherry shook her head and lifted her beautiful face to look at Hope, 'You see our lawyers would never allow it to run.'

'But surely - I thought I'd covered every libel aspect - there's nothing, almost nothing, that can be refuted - the evidence,'

'Not for suggesting that one of these women is responsible for attempted murder?'

'Well - not in so many words - not yet - Professor Holmes has yet to speak.'

'If he ever does,' Sherry added softly.

'Yes -' Hope left a small silence, as if in memory.

'So there it is - a brilliant piece with no possible way that I can run it.'

'Miss Spencer - just take it to the lawyers - see what they say - I'm certain the majority will run.'

'No - I can't. It would be wonderful, I know. I'd love to do it for you - but I can't - it would harm your chances in the future.'

'You're dismissing it out of hand?'

'Not like that.'

'I've worked so hard to make this a full story - to prove actions - you just can't spike it!'

'I have to this time - look your chance will come - I'll make sure some good work comes your way -just leave this alone.'

'No!' Hope began to collect together the papers. 'No - I'll be damned if I will. What have they got on you? I'll take it to the Nationals - somewhere with guts!'

'No - stop.' Sherry put her hands over Hope's, 'Leave them - leave them with me - I'll go to the lawyers, see what they say, okay? If they give the green light, I'll run it - okay?'

Hope looked into Sherry's eyes.

'Promise.' Sherry said lifting her burning hands. Hope lifted her own hands - leaving the papers where they were.

'When?'

'As soon as the lawyers say so.'

'And you'll send them down today?'

Sherry nodded

'Okay - I mean - sorry, I get over possessive with a story.'

'I understand - you've so much potential, Hope.'

'Thank you,' Hope said finding the colour rising in her cheeks. 'Thank you - when will you hear?'

'Soon - now you go home and have a rest - take a couple of days off - see you back on Thursday.' Sherry said, ushering Hope towards the door.

'We'll know by then?'

'Oh yes - definitely.'

'Thank you.' Hope repeated as the door closed. 'Yes!' she hissed to herself her eyes sparkling.

'Antonia?'

'Speaking - Sherry?'

'I - I've had Hope Jones in here - she's got such a story — it would pass the lawyers, just - and she knows it. I had to say I'd run it just to get her to leave the copy with me.'

'So?'

'So I can't let it run - it all but names certain friends of yours ...'

'So don't run it.'

'But she says she'll take it to the Nationals. Listen Antonia, it's a story they'd run!'

'So we'll make sure she doesn't take it to them - won't we? I'm so sorry you've failed us in this - I was just getting to like the idea of having you on board in this little venture.'

'I've not failed - I just can't do any more. Antonia? Antonia?'

'What is it?'

'You didn't have anything to do with the fire at Louton University, did you?'

'What a pathetic and silly question. How the devil you made editor I'll never know.'

'Antonia - don't hurt her.'

'Don't be silly,' Antonia sneered as she cut the connection.

Sherry sat holding the phone - cradling it - listening to the purr. She thought of the news reports of the fire, her mind's eye seeing the flames leaping around the bound man, of Antonia, of that cruel streak in her nature. A sudden knock on her door brought her back to reality, the sub-editor ready for their meeting.

'So that's it? Di asked, 'She'll get it published?'

No - didn't you realise - Sherry has spoken to Antonia - and Antonia is one of them, the Dorm - and the worst!'

'Oh - yes, I see. Of course.'

'And they'll not let it get published - will they?'

'No, I suppose not - what will they do?'

'You'll just have to wait to find out - there's no time now!' It was true, they were nearly home. 'Besides,' Faith went on 'the Story's nearly finished anyway.'

'Well - it's still been a helluva long story - weeks worth - long enough for a book I'd say.'

'Well I don't know - it's just been the story.'

'Well I do - have you got another ready for when this is finished?'

'You don't want another one already - like chain story consumption!'

'I do!'

'Well, I might have an idea or two tickling around,' Faith smiled at the thought of pleasing her friend, perhaps with a more pleasant role model next time.

chapter sixteen - Di

Work was amazingly simple with Lechwood out of the way. There were no time-wasting calls for coffee - or chats or lengthy and rambling dictation sessions. Most phone calls could be dismissed as the boss was unavailable, some just required a potential appointment to be made with confirmation when Lechwood returned.

With so much less to do, Di spent the majority of her time typing up the tapes. Hearing the parts one after another the story really sounded crisp and thrilling - Di could hardly wait for the finale. It also set her thinking. She'd only intended to print out a copy to give to Faith, but now she began to wonder whether The Story really might have the makings of a real book.

Di ran the word count as she at last came up to date, well over sixty thousand - she wondered aloud to herself whether that was book length and resolved to find out.

'How many words d'you think there are in a book?' she asked Paul over dinner.

'How the hell would I know? What do you want to know that for?'

'Just a thought.'

'You could count a page and times it up.'

'Of course,' Di said a little annoyed with herself for wondering aloud in the first place 'What have you been doing today? I've been expecting you to produce some paperwork for me to deal with by now.'

'Don't you worry about the Leech's extension - you'd better not!' he laughed. 'We're on track fine - fine, don't you worry.'

'But there's been nothing at Lechwood's end - he'll wonder what's going on.'

'Pages don't stick bricks together love,'

'That's as may be - but the paper's important - you know that.'

'It'll be there - eventually - along with our first tidy profit, then we'll be on our way!'

'Paul! What are you up to?'

'Don't worry we'll be okay.'

'Now I am worried - we'll be okay - who won't?'

'No one, no one that won't miss a brick or two,' his expansive nature got the better of him, he reached out for Di. 'Come here, let's have a cuddle. What do you think,' he whispered in her ear, 'just a little get-back at our friend Billy - the oh-so-kind buyer of our ten-house plot at bargain basement prices?'

'Oh, Paul, I actually thought you were grateful to that slime-ball - buying our plots then offering you a job.'

'Well - the job was handy - shook me out of the dumps, didn't it?'

'Sure.'

'But that's not all, I've got a little scam - no need to look like that - he'll never notice, but it'll help me a little and make me feel a whole lot better.'

'What about Andy?'

'He's okay - foreman, it's a living wage.

'You know what I mean - when Billy finds out your scam.

'No mud will stick to Andy - honest. He's my oldest mate, isn't he?'

'Yeah - but you'll be careful, won't you? I never did like Billy, he's not one to cross,' she said distancing herself slightly from Paul, enough to look him in the eye.

'I'll be careful, sweet,' Paul said pulling her to him again, giving her a reassuring kiss that somehow transformed itself into something altogether more sensual.

Di was quite excited as she took the car out the next morning. Faith, she thought, should be finishing the story today. There couldn't be much more as she'd warned Di that the ending was coming up. Faith was standing outside waiting for her as usual despite the chill nip in the air typical of a day two weeks before Christmas.

Faith looked small huddled in her sheepskin coat but glanced up brightly and hurried to get in the car.

'Morning,' she mumbled as she closed the door and shivered.

'You could always wait indoors you know - I'd toot you.'

'No thanks - I'm fine.' Faith said firmly.

'Okay, just so's you know.'

There was a silence between them, the car grumbled its way towards the motorway.

'So - come on then - here I am on tenterhooks, what's that nasty piece of work Antonia going to do?!' Di caught Faith's small smile as she was prompted into her own story.

'What Antonia does is to call up the Dorm,' Faith began, 'and alert them to the problem of Hope and her Story.'

Things moved very swiftly once Antonia explained the problem. She was harsh in her determination that the solution should be a permanent one - partly through some kind of jealousy, partly through the fact that she had not been able to control the situation, and Sherry Spencer, as much as she had believed she could and had promised she would.

Hope arrived home still in high spirits. She'd bluffed it out and her story - correction their story was going to press! She was certain that the majority was bombproof - and a few small cuts wouldn't matter - it would all come out once the facade began to crumble. She stripped off exuberantly and sank into a deep scented bath. She'd rung Chris to let him know, left a message on his answer phone, and arranged to celebrate later.

The warmth was going from the water when the doorbell rang. She lay a moment thinking that the caller would go. Just as she relaxed the bell rang again, more insistently, then paused, then rang again. In the next pause she clambered from the bath and towelled herself vigorously just dry enough to slip a towelling robe on and tie it tight. It had to be Chris - there must be some urgency for him to stand there and ring and ring. Even as she raced to the door the bell clamoured again.

All right! hang on!' she called 'Chris?' she asked as her fingers turned the Yale lock. A deep grunt of affirmation came back as the lock drew. The door flew open, knocking her back.

Antonia closed the door and dropped the latch.

'What the hell!' Hope began, though answering herself in her head. This woman must be one of them. One of the clique they'd identified as having a finger in the very meaty pie of the leisure development. Her words were snatched away with her breath as the woman grabbed a fistful of Hope's damp hair and marched down the hall with her dragging and screaming in pain.

Antonia turned the key in the lock and opened the back door. For a moment, despite the pain, Hope thought she could run for it. The masked faces were simple and horrific and the eyes in them held her as the wild woman held her hair

They crowded in with not a word spoken. Too late Hope tried to scream for help while the door was still open, her cry was cut off by a shove in the ribs that winded her and a hand across her face.

'Be gentle!' growled Antonia 'There mustn't be any marks.'

'Is there a way through to the garage?' a masked face asked.

Hope stared blankly her mind still whirling over the statement that there should be no marks on her, Antonia twisted her hair in her grip until Hope shrieked

'The garage?' Antonia hissed.

Hope tried to nod, then felt the grip on her hair relax, and did nod. Her tongue didn't seem to be reliable enough to speak

'Where?'

Hope looked back over her shoulder.

'Show me - there's a good girl.' Antonia's deep tones husked into her ear. Hope moved, they all moved, along the passage to a simple side door. This door, once opened, led via four steps down, into the garage, and there was Hope's red Metro snugly parked, ready to drive out.

'Good - now come along and get dressed.'

Thank God, Hope thought, her state of half undress made her feel so vulnerable.

In her room she spun-out the time selecting clothes, ending up with a pair of light blue trousers and a pure white cotton shirt. The whole time she could feel the eyes of the woman on her, watching her every move with an intensity that was obsessive.

'What do you want?' Hope tried, thinking that if the rubber-masked woman talked she would not feel her eyes on her so much as she dressed

'One thing at a time - get dressed.'

Finding the gaze unsettling Hope turned her body away and tried to dress demurely.

'Good - come, now - some work on your computer next, I think,' Antonia said as Hope buttoned up the cuffs on her shirt.

Outside her room an escort waited, they led her to her own desk, making her sit almost by will-power alone.

'First, you'll open your files - you know which ones.'

'Well - it depends - who are you?' Hope still tried to stall for time, but time for what she wasn't sure.

'You know, Hope — you know only too well. The files on your latest story.'

The screen flashed its usual messages until it called for her password. The feel of a cold blade against her cheek ensured that she entered the code and that the last draft of the Leisure Centre Scandal story presented itself: LCS6, and was deleted. Hope wished she was not so careful with her file designations. LCS 1 to 5 were soon found and deleted also. Her rack of backup discs was run through until the LCS disc was found - and pocketed by the one of the rubber-masked women.

'Now,' Antonia said, leaning over Hope's shoulder, close enough for the unpleasant smell of warm rubber to fill Hope's nostrils, 'We'll just add a few memos.' Her gloved finger hit the Caps lock and proceeded to write -
FAILURE IN LOVE AND WORK IS TOO MUCH.
TOO MUCH!! then on another page - I AM ALL ALONE IN A CITY THAT HATES ME and on
another - I WON'T GO HOME A FAILURE - THERE IS A WAY OUT!! H.

'There my dear,' the deep voice whispered in Hope's ear 'You've been depressed for a while - thinking about failure - not being able to cope with it. There's no need to sign it is there, after all only you knew the password - it'll be just as good. Not long now, come.'

Hope couldn't move - delaying tactics weren't in it - their intention was now crystal clear and she could see no immediate way to escape them. When she didn't move the other two grabbed her, and with arms locked behind her back, toes just touching the ground, they frogmarched her away.

Sherry paced up and down her office. Her mind's eye was a riot of horrific possibilities. There was the simple 'push under a passing lorry, or train', the 'nasty fall from the top of the multi-storey car park', the 'run-away-car-crash'. Always she saw Hope's frail petite body smashed; Sherry had few illusions about Antonia's beautiful brutality. She looked out of the window once more then strode to her desk.

'Get me Raven's home number.' she snapped into her intercom. The reply came quickly. Sherry paused and took a deep breath before punching the number out.

It rang six times before she heard Raven's gentle drawl saying 'Hello?'
'Raven, it's Sherry Spencer - look, I know this may seem a strange call - but - look, I think Hope may be in danger, extreme danger'
'What do you mean by danger? What exactly?'
'I don't KNOW, just - your investigations have stirred up a hornets' nest of some of the most,' she paused, it was beginning to sound a little too detailed, too close to home, 'some very dangerous people - they may have been responsible for setting the fire at Loudon University'
'Shit! Where's Hope now?'
'I had half wished she was with you - but as she is not - at home?'
'Yes - yes,' he remembered her message, cut the call.
Sherry sat back; her hands trembling and her top lip salty with sweat. Antonia would kill her if she ever found out - and she would enjoy it.

'This do?' One of the women held up a bomber-style jacket of Hope's.
'Fine - put it on her.' Antonia held the blade of the kitchen knife close to Hope's face as the other masked women forced Hope into her own jacket, back to front, and pulled the zip up her back, forcing the neckline high up her throat. Hope struggled to break free but their hands grabbed at her and held her down. The blade flashed close to her eyes. Antonia laughed through the rubber mask.

'Didn't you talk to your friend Mr Trout? Didn't you see his face, little girl' her eyes glittering as the knife danced this way and that even as they tied the ropes to the wrist-ends of her jacket Hope seemed to hear Tommy's warning to 'stay away —for the sake of your pretty little face'. She winced at the thought of what that had really meant.

Suddenly they snatched the ropes around, crossing her body, pulling her arms down with them, then tied the ends together behind her back, creating an effective straightjacket. They brought her college scarf from her chest of drawers and bound her legs together near the ankles.

'You've destroyed all my files, this isn't necessary — what are you going to do? Whatever —there's no need - you know — not now. Oh - please - there's no need for this.' Hope's pleas were met by silence as they continued their preparations. If only they'd stop and talk.

'My editor has a copy of all my material - she'll publish it no matter what you do - you won't stop the truth getting out just by - even if - you stop me.' She stopped, something she'd said had drawn the rubber-masked one's attention, she felt a zing of hot blood course through her veins. Then Hope realised, from the eyes, that the woman inside the mask was smiling, and the zing turned to ice. She stared into that terrible face and knew that this woman had every angle taken care of or thought she did. There was no way she was going to tell them about Raven's set of information. No way at all. And, as if to back up her resolve, they finished their work with a gag that made her feel sick with every breath.

The light was going, the computer screen glowed as the only light in the room, but the women did not turn on a light, just looked towards the window, and nodded as the street lights flickered into life and glowed sulphurously into the room.

'All right - now.' Antonia said softly. The other women moved forward to Hope. Something about them seemed so mechanical, something that sent a desperate wave of panic through her. As soon as the first gloved hand touched her she threw herself away from it, struggling wildly, hitting herself against the table. Remembering their earlier instructions to leave no marks, she didn't care what marks were left - as long as someone got suspicious. 'Stay still.' Antonia hissed, 'Otherwise it'll be worse.'

Hope grunted a 'Huh!' through the gag and twisted her body away, out of their grip again.

Suddenly she was snatched up short, Antonia's fist tangled in Hope's hair, yanking it up, pulling her bodily. Then the blade was at her eye level, the glittering eyes of the rubber-masked woman staring past it. The malicious look in those eyes stopped her struggling for a moment. It was just long enough for the others to take a firm grip. They grabbed legs and arms; lifted her bodily out of the room and into the garage, as she twisted and writhed in their grip. She could hear their laboured breathing through their masks; hear them grunt as they kept her under control. At the steps down she folded her body, then threw it out straight, even if they dropped her as they fell down the stairs it seemed her best chance. She felt them stagger, her body loosen fractionally in their grip, but the steps were so short they found the bottom and their balance too easily.

Antonia opened the car door and the others manhandled her into the driver's seat, stretching the seat belt round and clipping her in. They closed the door and turned the key in the lock. She squirmed and wrestled within her makeshift straightjacket, feeling her hand pull part way up one sleeve, tantalisingly close to the armhole, if only she could get one arm forward, perhaps she could force down the jacket. The movement in the rear-view mirror caught her eye, and she froze.

One of the masked women straightened up from the rear of the car and moved forward, in her hand she held a garden hose. Hope's mouth went dry. Her insides contracted in a wave of nausea. She froze, eyes wide as the end of the hose was calmly inserted through the passenger door window, the window wound up carefully, just enough to secure, but not enough to cut-of the flow through the pipe, and the door closed and firmly locked.
'Such a pity you couldn't follow orders.' Antonia husked as she opened the door and turned on the car's engine. 'Goodbye - Miss Jones.'

Chris dialed Hope's number before leaving. The phone rang unheeded. It made him pause for a moment. Did it mean she wasn't there at all, or that she was unable to answer it?' He shoved his helmet on forcefully and went to his machine. The deep roar of the Harley sprang to life as he pushed away. He'd go to Hope's place first, see if there was any sign of her around. The traffic was slow as he hit the homeward bound jam but he wove between the lines of cars in a way he never normally did, usually too conscious both of safety and the gleaming paintwork on his bike. Today it didn't matter.

He throttled back and let the engine die to roll silently into Hope's driveway. There was the drone of an engine somewhere. No lights on in the house, but a blue glow like a TV from her lounge. He dismounted, rested his helmet on the seat and walked slowly towards the house. The sound of the engine suddenly became focused, the noise coming from her garage. He ran forward, bending to grab the garage door handle, twisting it savagely, half expecting it to be locked. It turned and with a heave whistled up to crash against the bars, half slid forward again until his hand steadied it back as he stepped forward into the dark interior.

In the light from the streetlamp he could see Hope, her face pushed forward to the windscreen, eyes wide. She turned her head towards the passenger window and it was then he saw the hose pipe, he ran round and snatched it out of the window. Then he raced back round to the driver's side to yank unsuccessfully at Hope's door, then back to the passenger door to wedge his fingers in the crack, desperate to make it move; it held firm. Changing tack he scanned the garage, found a hammer in Hope's DIY kit and smashed the window. Glass flew in amber-lit crystals showering Hope as she turned her face away. Chris opened the passenger door, knelt across the crunchy seat and turned the ignition off, unsnapped the seat belt and flicked open the door lock. He was backing out of the car as the house door behind him smashed open. Light poured from the opening in a searchlight beam across the garage for a second before the gap was filled with people.

Chris dashed away, backing round the car to Hope's side, wrenching open the door, watching them make their way down. They moved warily keeping their backs to the wall. Chris had begun to pull Hope out when they suddenly rushed round at him from both sides. They stopped. Now he could see that they wore masks and one, the mask more elaborate, a grotesque female face, stepped closer; a carving knife in her hand
'Mr Raven - how opportune.' Antonia spoke, her voice clear and polished even through the rubber mask. She stood near the rear of the car; knife flashing in the light from the house door. The other two, he was aware, were standing at the front of the car, between him and the open garage door.
The knife-woman advanced slowly then stopped as she realised that Chris was not going to leave his position beside Hope's open door.
'What's this?' she said, her voice disdainful, 'A newspaperman who has no questions? Who are you? Why are you doing this? - come now Mr Raven, surely you are curious?'
'I don't need to ask,' Raven said and turned his head at the sudden movement behind him. It all happened at once, one of the women snatched down the garage door, the other ran towards the light switch and in that moment the knife-woman slashed forward at him.

It was an inexpert thrust and as Hope screamed 'Chris!' through her gag, he turned and fielded it with his leather clad arm, then charged his weight forward into the woman to knock her off her feet. He heard the knife clatter and at the same moment the garage lights blinked themselves alive, filling the garage with their fluorescent glare.

'Get him!' the knife-woman screeched as he swivelled to snatch the gleaming blade from beneath the car.

Antonia launched herself at Chris just as he turned to straighten, and in an automatic action he brought up his fist to ward her off. The knife sank deep into her stomach. The mask askew she sank back. In horror Raven released the knife as it pulled itself gently from his grip

Suddenly his head was yanked back and he was pulled off balance as one of the other women swung her weight on his hair, as he turned and stumbled the other one jumped on his back, bringing him to his knees. Ignoring the tearing pain from his scalp, he swung his body to the side and rolled with all his might, smashing this woman against the wall. She hit the wall with a sickening thump, he felt the impact through his own body, felt her grip loosen as she slid from him, then he lurched forward, the sudden release in tension tipping the woman swinging on his hair back on her heels. Lunging further forward, his feet scrabbling for purchase on the greasy garage floor, he head-butted her in the chest, sprawling over her as she fell back. Her fingernails sliced across his face, scratching to find his eyes. He rolled aside, coming to a crouch, ready to defend himself again, but the woman scrambled up and ran, back up the steps and into the house.

Chris looked over to where Hope sat, half in and half out of the car. He stood and, dabbing at the score marks across his face, walked towards her. His scalp burned as if half his hair had been torn out by the roots, but worse, his left arm ached to the core. He tugged at the jumper that made Hope's gag, his arm screaming at him as his fingers worked at the knot to loosen it.

'Thank God - Chris - we can't stay here - are you okay?' Hopes words tumbled from her as he bent to untie her ankles.

'Sure - you?' he asked as she turned her back to him so he could untie the ends of her jacket.

'Now - now I am,' she shuddered. Her arms eased forward as the zip juddered down, the blood rushing back into her fingers setting them prickling. 'Why the straightjacket?'

'It wasn't meant to look suspicious – meant to be a suicide. I guess they'd take this lot off after I'd gone - Chris, look! She's coming round!' she nodded towards the woman slumped against the garage wall. The stunned woman shook her head from side to side, her eyes still closed, Chris moved over towards her, Hope's scarf his hands.

'Go call the police - there's a lot explaining to be done.'

Hope went into the house cautiously, ready any moment to find the third woman. The back door stood wide open showing a rectangle of dark backyard, and the door beyond that hanging open.

Chris bound the arms of the stunned woman with the scarf then went to look at the knife-woman. She lay perfectly still; the knife at the centre of a dark pooling stain, a well made-up face was revealed where the grotesque mask had slipped. He felt for a pulse, though he already believed she was dead. He was right, and his own pulse raced as he thought of the likelihood of being had up for manslaughter. He stood quickly as he heard a noise, and nearly collapsed, leaning against the wall for support. Blood oozed from the wrist of his jacket.

'God! You're bleeding!' Hope cried as she came around the car to him and saw the blood streaking his hand. *'Wait there - I'll get something.'*

She returned with bandages and antiseptic. Chris eased himself down and together they took off his jacket. The slash through the leather was quite evident once they looked for it, the slice in his arm bleeding steadily, his shirt dyed red with the blood. The police rang the front door bell just as Hope finished dressing the gash.

'There', Faith said, 'The End.'

'What? You can't say "the end" and leave them like that?' Di objected, glancing round to see if Faith was joking.

'I can - that's "the end".'

'But there's so many loose ends to tie up.'

'Well - yes - but they're pretty obvious aren't they? The real end has come, the showdown with the baddies - I could go on to say that Hope's story gets taken up by a national paper - page one stuff - then there'd be a manslaughter trial - perhaps, Hope's own story "I was there" stuff hits page one again, makes a packet, and then she and Chris ride off into a rosy sunset on his Harley Davidson - how's that?'

'And Sherry Spencer?'

'Oh well - either she retires out of conscience or she carries on as if nothing has changed - perhaps she goes to print before the nationals - besides, it doesn't matter to the main story.'

'Oh.'

Suddenly Faith remembered that Sherry was Di's character.

'Well, whatever - she was only being bad under duress - really she's a dynamic young editor, probably gets taken on by a national on the strength of her work on the story.'

Di smiled, she realised exactly what Faith was doing, and appreciated it.

'Well it was an absolutely brilliant story. How do you do it? All that fight scene, so vivid - you don't really have a secret life do you?'

Faith smiled to herself. 'Things like that, it's as if I'm watching a film, describing the action, yet at the same time feeling the pain. That's all.'

'All, she says, all! That's bloody brilliant lass - that's what it is. I always said you'd make a brilliant author. Mind you,' she cast a sneaky smile at Faith, 'I'd have had a bit more raunchy stuff going on. You've got that sexy hunky guy and they barely get a smooch - let alone a leg-over. If I'd been writing it I'd definitely have had a bit more romance at least - no, a good dollop of sex, thrown in - more Jilly Cooper.

'Well - I didn't!' Faith blushed as her mind filled in the details, running a movie she could never describe to anyone.

'Sorry! Don't mean to criticise - God only knows - I couldn't have put the rest of the story together with or without a sex scene. It was fantastic. The best.'

They drove for a moment or two in silence.

'Nearly there,' Faith sighed to break the silence.

'Yep - well, what is it - do we start a new story tomorrow?'

'I - I don't know.' Now it came to it Faith felt shocked that the grand work had been finished and dismissed so quickly. She wanted to run it round a little more in her head before she began to let other images take its place. 'Let's just see, eh?'

'Fine, fine,' Di said, wondering how she'd upset Faith, knowing there was something wrong and hoping that her plans for The Story would make it all right again.

chapter seventeen – Di

There were no more big stories in the weeks before Christmas. No more short ones either. But that didn't worry Di too much, they had plenty to chat about, moaning about Christmas and the extra work it caused, wondering what to get for which child in Faith's case, wondering whether to visit in-laws in Di's.

Di spent some of her new 'free' time finishing the typing up of Faith's story. When it was finished she printed off a full copy and took it home in a large used envelope she'd found in the office. She threw it on the bed along with her coat and bag and returned downstairs to start the dinner. She'd just about got the goujons of beef simmering in their red wine sauce when Paul arrived home.

'Hi, love, you're home early!'

'Had to stop work, hitch in materials. It's sorted now, we'll be going in early tomorrow, to get on with it.'

'Paul, what's up?'

'Nothing - just, nothing.' he headed up the stairs. Di set the oven, wiped her hands and followed him. He was sitting on the edge of the bed taking off his shoes.

'Do you want the shower?'

'No, you go first.' he lifted his head and flashed her a smile. That was all right then, she thought, as she whipped her dressing gown from her chair and disappeared into the bathroom.

She was surprised to see Paul still sitting on the edge of the bed when she returned. The manuscript was out of the envelope and split into two uneven piles. Paul dropped one page on the smaller pile and picked up another from the larger as Di walked in the room.

'What're you doing?'

'Reading this - this is Faith's story isn't it?' he said pretending he'd not seen any of it before.

'Yes, and take care of those pages, I'm getting it ready to give her for a Christmas present.'

'Mmm, okay.'

'Shower's free if you want,'

'Yeah, sure - in a minute.'

Di shrugged, got dressed as Paul continued reading and then went downstairs.

Half an hour later she called up the stairs to him to come down to eat. He arrived just as dishevelled as he was when he came home.

'Did you find out how long a book is?' Paul asked as he finished eating.

'Well, sort of - why?'

'How long is this story of Faith's then?'

'Sixty-nine and a half thousand or so words.'

'And how long are books normally?'

'Eighty to a hundred thousand, depending - mind you those Mills and Boon books are half that. Hang on - why?'

'Because - well, let me finish it first.'

'Paul! What are you thinking?'

'Nothing I suspect you haven't already thought, talk about it later,' he said as he left the table and headed back upstairs.

Di looked into their room two or three times during the evening. Each time Paul flashed her a smile but turned back to the pages immediately. Each time she went away again and found some other work to get on with.

It was almost time for bed when Paul came down the stairs with a bounce in his step and a slight smile on his face. Di knew that look, it usually preceded an idea that Paul thought to be clever or audacious, she waited wondering what he would come out with.

'What's missing from this story of Faith's?' he asked quickly.

'Well - I told her I'd have spiced it up a bit - you know.'

'I know - just what I was thinking too. Enough to make up the missing few thousand words do you think?'

'Faith said she couldn't put that sort of thing in her story. But then you know her - she's kinda shy like that. Look, what exactly have you got in mind - Faith wouldn't want anything extra put in for her.'

'No, not for Faith. Look, I was just being nosey - slid the pack of papers out of the envelope, five minutes later I was hooked, I had to know where this story was going. Now, I know I don't read a hell of a lot - but if I do it's really got to grab me. You saw, this story did that. If it did that for me it's got to be worth a try with a publisher.' He looked at her, eyes alight, then smiled suddenly, 'But you think that already - don't you - that's why you asked about how long books were?'

Di nodded, 'And you think so too - and we can't both be wrong?'

'Except, it needs those extra words - and it needs some spice - look how about talking to Faith about it. Surely she'd want to have a go if there as a chance of finding a publisher - making some money?'

'Well - okay - but what if she doesn't like the idea,' Di said, knowing in her bones that Faith would not want to write-in the sex scenes that were needed, 'what then? Do we drop the idea?' she'd run this scenario through in her own mind once already.

'Well - then we could have a go at writing them ourselves - it can't be that hard?'

'I don't know - Faith sort of just comes out with it and it sounds right, but I had a go myself and it didn't ring true. However, together, who knows, but I think we try it first, not ask Faith.'

'Why? If you say she can do it so well?'

'Look Paul, Faith's my oldest friend, I know she'll say "no". I get the feeling she might even say "no" to contacting a publisher. What I've been thinking is to try adding that spice in, then try a publisher as a collaboration - joint authors.'

Paul sat back and stared at her. 'You mean - if it's a seller - take half the profits!'

Di had the grace to look a little shamefaced, but she soon met Paul's eye again. 'It wouldn't even be a seller if I'd not taped it and typed it up, it still might not be a seller unless we can spice it up a bit, it would be a collaboration.'

'Come here you! Your mind!' he drew her to him and hugged her, his lips brushed her neck, his tongue flickered on her ear lobe. 'I think we need to go and do a little research for this book,' he whispered into her ear.

Later Paul scanned through the sheets of the story and picked out the places he felt the lead couple should be getting it together. When he showed Di she agreed with all but one of them. They sat down and began writing their first piece to fit in where Hope's first suggestion of the Leisure Centre Sleaze story had been rejected and Chris Raven had offered to help and they'd agreed to meet at her house later.

Raven rode his Harley right up Hope's drive and stopped it outside her door. He felt good when she came to the door and opened it before he'd had time to stow his helmet. Smiling, he walked up to her, bending to kiss her as he reached the door. She responded with a light kiss then turned to lead the way in, saying 'There's a lot to think about,'

'You could say that,' Raven said as he took off his leather jacket and let it fall beside the sofa. She came to sit beside him with a lot of papers in her hands

'These are copies of all the press cuttings about the Park scheme, this lot', she held the thickest pile, 'are all for it, and these,' she waved a few thin sheets; 'are the only printed defence - letters from residents mainly.'

'Let me see,' he said leaning closer to her. She smelt good to him. So close to her again he was having trouble concentrating on the business in hand, he had a desperate hard-on and wanted to think of nothing but the feel of her skin and the softness of her lips. He cleared his throat, 'Hope.' She turned to look at him and he knew that she was not entirely focussed on the papers in her hand. He reached out and took hold of the papers and her hand, pulling her towards him, her eyes widening, her lips parting. She let the papers drop from her other hand as she turned to him, her fingers stroking his strong shoulders and the nape of his neck. He drew her towards him, his hand resting gently on her shoulder they kissed and he felt as if he would burst. Her tongue flickered on his lips and he responded, dipping his tongue deep into her sweet mouth as she allowed small sighs to escape, his hand sought her breast and cradled it feeling the nipple harden and rise. They broke away from each other for a moment, eyes locked Hope stood, held her hand out to him. He took it and allowed himself to be led gently upstairs.

In her room she twitched the blinds to half closed and turned to face him.

'Hope?'

'I'm sure,' she said answering his unasked question as she came close enough to be wrapped in his arms again. 'Raven,' she whispered, her hand lightly enveloping his erection through his jeans 'I want you.' He kissed her again his hands sliding down her body, caressing her curves slipping into creases. Her hands pulled at his t-shirt, tugging it from his waistband, running up over his chest. He slid his hand inside her top, slowly sliding it across her silky back, feeling the taut strap of her bra under his palm. He was filled with a desire to stroke her whole body, to kiss and caress every inch of her, unrestricted.

'What do you think? Leave it there or go the whole way?' Di asked as she typed in the last sentence.

'Faith would leave it there,' he said, 'but I'm not sure – this sort of stuff works on people you know, God I'm feeling that randy myself just thinking it up.'

'Mmm,'

'Well if it went further they'd be geared up ready for the next bit,'

'Or if we left it they'd be tantalised wondering how far they'll go in the next bit.'

'What for, they've got to know she's going all the way, why not add to the word count with a bit more – detail.'

'Okay – but, we'll have to be a bit careful of the way we say it. I think we've been a bit close to the mark already.'

'As you say, now where were we?' Paul said sliding his arm round his wife and squeezing her breast.

Di gave herself a hour off the next day and took herself to the Library. She soon found the Writers Guide and spent a while reading an article about submitting manuscripts. She noted that it had to be double spaced, that there had to be what appeared to be a ridiculously large margin all round, until she came to the reasons, and sent loose in a card wallet. The next chapter suggested that sending direct to a publisher wasn't necessarily the best way to go about it. It appeared that an agent was a good idea if she didn't want to spend time researching publisher's lists and having to wait for weeks while some poor office-hand ploughed through the slush-pile, as unsolicited manuscripts were called. To find an agent you just needed to send the first three chapters, a full synopsis and an author biography. Flicking through she found the list of agents and jotted down the names and addresses of three who said they specialised in the sort of novel that Di felt theirs was.

Back in the office she set up the computer to print out the unaltered chapters again with double line spacing and wide margins while she worked through some invoices and filed some letters. She had just taken the last chapter out of the printed tray and slipped it into a card wallet, already straining with the bulk of paper even at this unfinished stage, when the door opened and Mr Lechwood walked in. She gave an involuntary 'Oh!' and felt her face begin to redden as he surveyed the office. The card wallet was on her chair, out of sight, and she recovered herself quickly by laughing a little and hand to chest, 'Mr Lechwood, you startled me!' she exclaimed in a girlish manner. He seemed different, his eyes beadier than usual, his manner stiff. 'Would you like coffee, sir?' she tried. He nodded and went through to his own office.

A while later she tapped on his door and entered carrying his coffee tray, his French breakfast cup, percolated coffee and flake brown sugar.
'Take a seat my dear,' he ordered, 'how has business been while I've been away?'
'Well in the office it's been fine – nothing I haven't been able to cope with. I have made some provisional appointments that await your confirmation – would you like to go through them now, sir?'
'Not just yet, not just yet. Tell me how has your husband been getting on with my extension?'
'Very well, as far as I'm aware, sir.'
'And how are you aware?'
'Pardon?'

'How, exactly, are you aware of the progress being made?' his voice was hard and querulous. 'Have you been along to inspect the site?'

'No, Mr Harvey has informed me that all was progressing well,' Di began before recalling that Paul had talked of a hitch in material supply only the evening before. 'Though there has been a minor delay in some of the material supply.'

'A minor delay?' he said slowly. 'The extension just happened to be one of the projects that I looked at on my way home yesterday. Five o'clock and not a soul on site – I'd remind you, Mrs Harvey, that you gave me your personal guarantee that this work would be completed on time,' his eyebrows raised, eyes resting on her blouse before fixing her with a stare too long for comfort.

'I'm sure,' Di said, recovering, 'I'm sure that, to a trained eye, the work would be seen to be progressing well, and as to the absence at the site, my husband sent everyone home early yesterday because of the materials and because he expected them in all very early this morning – he himself left for the site at five this morning.'

'We shall see – you can tell your husband that if he goes over contract time he'll be very sorry.'

'We've never gone over contract time –'

'No?' he cut in, 'But then I only have your word for that – whereas I do know that you nearly went bankrupt once before – and that was with your own very careful eye on the work.'

'I trust my husband – he'll do a brilliant job for you, and on time – I guarantee it.'

'So you said before,' he replied giving her a meaningful look which, instinctively, made her cross her arms.

Di smuggled the thick card wallet out of the office that evening, glad that she'd got the bulk of it printed off before Lechwood's return . In his present mood it wouldn't be advisable for him to find her using his office time, equipment and materials for 'homers'. She was still preoccupied with wondering about the problem of the contract time and the extension when she picked Faith up. It was true she hadn't kept a close eye on things, even though she'd asked Paul from time to time, badgered him for documents, invoices, and such, he hadn't been forthcoming, too full of himself and the scam he was working. She'd left it too long; she had to sort things out now even if it risked undermining Paul's new-found confidence. She wondered how much importance she could put into her request without letting him know that Lechwood had already been along while he was off-site and was sceptical as to their completing on time. In this self-imposed meditation she didn't notice how quiet Faith was during the journey.

'Don't you sometimes wish that life was as simple as a story – and all with happy endings?' Faith said suddenly as they pulled up outside her home.

'What? Simple stories like your last one? I hope not!' Di laughed. 'Suppose not,' Faith muttered as she gathered her things together and left the car. It was only as she watched Faith's small figure lean itself against the house door that she suddenly felt the poignancy in the way Faith had spoken and noted that their whole journey home had been wreathed in silence.

'Paul,' Di began after their meal was cleared away, 'you'll have to give me an idea of the progress you are making on Lechwood's extension – he came back today, he'll be wanting some kind of report.

'God! He's not said anything has he?'

'Why, what's wrong?'

'Nothing an extra week wouldn't solve.'

'No, no. He's not going to allow that Paul. You signed a contract with really heavy over-run penalties and Lechwood would delight in taking them.'

'I know – don't you think I know? It's just a problem with my source of supply – a little more limited than I'd hoped.'

'This is not the time to arse around with ripping off Billy – you've got to put this work on track. How long to end of contract?'

'A month – give or take.' he snapped, standing up and walking over to the window, whipping the curtains closed as if they could shut out any problems he might have.

'What the hell's that? Thirty days or what?'

Paul looked at the ceiling a moment his hands stuffed in his pockets. 'Twenty-seven – we finish on the sixteenth.'

'That's not a month – and that's counting Christmas Day and New Year – Paul!'

'We'll do it somehow – promise.' he gave her his best smile.

'I'm coming to take a look'

'There's no need.' his voice sounded flat and final.

'There is; Lechwood. I have to see for myself.'

'What the hell for – don't you believe me?' his voice rising.

'Of course – but I've got to look that creep in the eye when he asks me – that's all!' Paul shook his head and turned away from her, spun on his heel and left the room. Di felt a tightening in her chest, a feeling of hurt. She just knew that Paul was having problems and that he didn't want her, of all people, to know about them, and that if they were that bad then she had to get down there fast and see what could be done. It had happened before, sometimes an outsider's eye could spot the way out of a tricky situation when those working on the job were just too close to be objective.

She clattered the dishes as she vented her frustration at Paul's delicate ego. When she casually looked for him later he'd gone into her 'office' and so she left him there and went to call Faith.

'Hello?' Faith's eldest answered the phone.

'Hello Jilly, Mum there? It's aunty Di.'

'Mumm! Mum!' echoed down the line, followed by footsteps.

'Hi?'

'It's Di, look how are you fixed for an extra early start or a late evening?'

'When?'

'Tomorrow – I need to take a look at the project Paul's doing for Lechwood.'

'Okay, whichever. I can get into work at any time – leave any time. After would be easier to arrange for the children.'

'Right we'll make it after – I'll be two hours late – perhaps you could nip out for some last-minute Christmas shopping –

everything's open late now.' Di tried to make it sound a positive idea.

'Perhaps – see you,' Faith murmured distantly.

'Right, okay – bye,' Di finally finished feeling somehow rejected both by Faith and Paul. All she had to look forward to was the invidious prospect of inspecting her own husband's building project. Drawing breath, she crossed the fingers of both hands and held them together in some kind of silent wishful prayer.

chapter eighteen - Di

It was an enormous effort to keep up any conversation in the car as they drove to work. Di's mind was split between her intention to send off some of Faith's story to an agent and the dread she had of going to inspect the building site. By Paul's reaction and behaviour she was already fearing the worst, yet wasn't sure what the worst would be. The extension should be basically finished, all walls in place and services connected. There should be, at this stage, merely the cosmetic work, the plastering and the fixtures and fittings, basins, benches, cubicles, shower fixings, sanitary ware, mirrors and such to be added. What state was the work in for Paul to need an extra week at this stage?

'Penny for them?' Faith asked after one prolonged silence.

'Uh – just worried about the extension. Lechwood's a tight fisted B and he'll want his pound of flesh if we're not spot on time.' Di said, whilst in her mind's eye seeing the pound of flesh in the terms that she was sure that Lechwood would be wanting to take his dues. His eyes strayed far too frequently to her breasts as it was, his lecherous traits not quite sublimated by his smart suit and his suave manner.

'What's wrong?'

'Trouble with supply of materials, it seems.' Di tripped out Paul's reply, though certain there was a whole lot more to it than that.

'Oh dear! And with the holiday that's going to get a whole lot worse!'

'Don't tell me!' Di knew exactly what the building suppliers were like – closed when you needed them most, quoting a delivery date in weeks when you needed the stuff in days – the thought sent a small shiver through her.

'Have you decided what to do with your two hours of freedom?' she asked to change the subject.

'Oh,' Faith said desultorily, 'I'll probably do a tour of the shops – I've got all the presents I'm going to buy and so with any luck I'm sorted for Christmas.'

'Oh – I'm sorry!'

'No, it's no bother. As you said, two hours of freedom.' Faith added in a voice that betrayed a certain wistfulness.

There was no sign of Lechwood at the office when Di got there. She unlocked, set the coffee to percolate and switched on her computer. She'd sorted the mail and prepared it for Lechwood. As there was nothing in it for her to deal with and she had no work outstanding she called up the first three chapters of The Story ready to print three sets to send out to the agents she'd listed. The phone rang just as she was debating whether to start printing off some more of Faith's story on the off-chance that Lechwood would not be until later. Speak of the devil, Di thought as she recognised her boss's voice.

'I'm on a tour of operations, my dear, hold the fort for this morning.'

'Yes, sir. Shall I leave the mail until you return?'

'Yes, yes, unless there is something you can deal with that would only bore me,' he laughed.

As soon as Lechwwod rang off Di pressed the print icon and the first three chapters repeatedly printed themselves out. Even while they were being churned out, Di was working over the printed copy of the synopsis she had prepared the previous evening. Today she tried to read it as if she did not know the story and was trying not only to inform the reader of the progress of the story but also to lure them on to read the first three chapters and to want to read the rest. As she read, she marked places to change and wrote large question marks in the margin. As soon as the last chapter was sent to the printer she pulled up this synopsis and began working on it. She knew in her bones that this was important but was struggling with the words. She had the gist of the story in place, but making it sound as exciting and page-turning as she knew the story to be, was proving more difficult. As she glanced at the clock and it warned her she had barely an hour left to work in – she wished that Faith was in on this – Di knew it would be so easy for Faith to turn this pedestrian list of events into a new story of its own.

Sighing, she started again opening a new file on the synopsis, she began. When little Hope Jones was sent to cover a hack reporter story about the new City leisure scheme she did not know it would become the story of a lifetime and need her to risk her life getting it…. This Di felt was much better. She typed on, weaving in the main characters and their 'accidents', culminating in the Dorm's attempt to assassinate Hope and their ultimate defeat.

By twelve she was finished. She printed off three copies and three title pages and stuffed everything into an old envelope. There was a local building supplier's spreadsheet of prices on display when Lechwood returned to the office.

After work, Di left the office with a heavy heart. She had no doubts that she'd find her husband and his gang up working, they needed to put in all hours possible until the job was completed and Paul had promised the men a bonus if they got finished on time. It was a calculated promise, no more than he'd have to pay for a week or twos work and that without the £1,000 a day fine Lechwood would require if they went over.

Even in the poor light from the street lamps Di could see that her worst fears were realised. The windows gave back no gleam, being still holes in the wall. That, at this stage was little short of disaster. Her heart was thumping by the time she stepped through the metal grille and confronted Paul in the 'reception area'.

'Oh Paul!'

'Don't start,' he muttered, 'the men are still here.'

'So they darned well need to be – where the hell are the windows?'

'It's one of the hitches in supply.'

'Legit supply or …?' Di said with a raised eyebrow and from Paul's expression knew what the answer was immediately. 'Just give me the details, now, before we go. What else is stuck in the pipeline?'

'Not a lot … A consignment of sanitary ware.'

'Same again. Now show me round.'

'You'll not say anything.'

'Of course not,' Di cracked a smile, but inside she was seething. This was going to be very expensive if they didn't do something about it very quickly.

After the tour Di turned to Paul. 'Paul, the men seem to be working okay – unless this was just for show – so why the hell is this project – what? Two weeks behind?'

'Only one week behind Di!'

'No! Two flaming weeks because as sure as hell you haven't planned to have no Christmas or New Year break! Have you?'

'No! I didn't plan in enough time for supply hold ups – that's all!'

'But you found plenty of time to work up some kind of scam to rip Billy off, eh?'

'That didn't take time, some of that supply was quicker than usual,' he couldn't resist a smile.

'But some of it fouled up, didn't it?' Di snapped back.

'That's not the point.'

'That's the whole bloody point – a thousand a day – think about that Paul – your signature to such a deal when I'd already given my guarantee!'

'Yeah and I know what that lecher would want of your guarantee.'

'Yeah, and I bet you'd have made sure he didn't get it, instead of farting around with scams.'

'Shut up about scams!' Paul hissed.

'So, just give me those figures – I'll see you at home – what'll it be – nine – ten?'

'Hmm – when you see me,' Paul turned his back as he sifted through some papers. 'Fat chance you'll have of getting it in time anyway.'

'You leave that to me, as you should have done before!'

'It's too late tonight.'

'Oh thank you! I wouldn't have known,' Di spat back as she turned to leave.

'Di?' Paul said quietly, 'Di.' as she left.

Di doubled back through town to pass the newspaper offices on her way home. She was still angry but her mind was already planning exactly what she was going to do. She was so preoccupied that she almost forgot to stop and pick up Faith. She'd agreed to come and find Faith in the newspaper offices as the timing of her arrival was uncertain. Just in time she remembered and swung into the side street beside the office and found a parking space with surprising ease. Locking up, Di walked quickly round to the glass doors and pushed her way through into the brightly-lit foyer. Her gaze travelled swiftly round and she quickly realised that Faith wasn't there so she marched up to the receptionist and asked her to put a call through to Faith. The receptionist smiled and dialled a number. 'Mrs Warren shouldn't be long.' she said sweetly.

However it was nearly ten minutes later when the lift doors opened to reveal Faith, and in the company of none other than Nick Wren. Di recognised him immediately, with his 'trademark' long dark hair loose and glossy, and had to acknowledge that he was even more gorgeous in life than she thought he'd be. Faith coloured up when she saw Di and that made Di raise her eyebrow a little, but the 'goodnight' he gave Faith was the same as the 'goodnight' he gave the receptionist, and by that time Faith was by her side.
'Sorry, have you had to wait long,' Faith began.
'Ten minutes or so.' Di did not feel like prevaricating.
'Oh – sorry , but they had to call round – I wasn't on my floor.'
'So where were you,' Di asked as they pushed back out into the cold air.
'Top floor – delivering some typing to Mr Wren – it was lucky for him I had time to kill – he had some typing he wanted doing as soon as I could – so of course – I could do it straight away.'
'Yes, lucky him,' Di said as she unlocked the car.
'Di – What's wrong?'
'Nothing, and everything. Paul's fouled up on ordering some stuff – we're going to be behind on the contract if we're not careful.'
'Oh, I see,' Faith said in relieved tone.
'He's a bit of alright, though isn't he?'
'Who?'

'Nick Wren, much as I remember him from the photos, long hair and all, bit more sort of worn in — rugged looking now, but then we all are. I certainly wouldn't tip him out of bed — that's for sure!' Di said, flicking Faith a cheeky grin and noticing that, even in the poor light, Faith's face was glowing again.

Once at home Di threw a ready-meal in to defrost and slid the contents of the old brown envelope out. Once more she checked the synopsis, the title page and the chapters. She turned on the computer and re-read the letter she'd prepared to go with the packages; then printed it off three times. She was sending them out in the name of Diane Faith and so she practised a few signatures before signing at the bottom of the letters. She packed each lot with their SAEs into a loose-leaf wallet and slid each into a stout jiffy-bag, ready to be posted the next day. She swapped the ready-meal from defrost to heat and returned to her computer. Opening the internet she found builders' suppliers and soon had costings and estimated delivery dates. Selecting one that appeared to be able to deliver before Christmas she put in an order, with a no delivery before Christmas — no deal, clause, leaving Lechwood's e-mail address for confirmation in the morning.

Di retrieved her meal and between mouthfuls found the window suppliers and selected two that might be able to meet their needs. To each she put in a request stating that she was trying the other and the first one to get back to her with a firm delivery date before Christmas would get the order, again she left Lechwood's contact, not only would she get to read it earlier but his name seemed to carry clout in the most unexpected places.

Shoving the ready-meal tray in the bin, Di poured herself a glass of red wine and sank onto the sofa in front of the television. By the time Paul came in she had dozed off.
'It's all right for some,' Paul said as he came into the living room and woke Di.
'And what do you mean by that?'

'Snoozing in front of the telly all evening'

'Snoozing be damned! I haven't stopped working since I came home until late!'

'Okay, Okay, I was only joking.'

Di glanced at the time – half eleven – even with the journey Paul had been working till very late, she felt a wave of contrition. 'I'll get you some dinner,' she said getting up, 'won't be long,' she went to give him a peck on the cheek as she passed. 'Booze?' she said sharply. 'You've not been working till late – you've been down the pub?'

'Well you know the men – working late like that – I had to buy them a pint.'

'Had to be damned – you're offering them bonuses don't forget – so what time did you quit?'

'About nine,' Paul said surprised.

'Nine! Huh – well you can zap your own meal then – I'm off for a well earned kip!'

'Di! Di – don't be like that!'

'Don't Di, Di me! I've had it.'

Paul followed her up the stairs – tried to hug her to him.

'Get off Paul! I'm tired. Really tired! Just forget it.'

'Tired, okay, tired,' Paul muttered, 'I'll be up soon love.'

'And I'll be asleep!' Di snapped back as she closed the bedroom door on his retreating back.

Her heart was thumping and she actually felt her jaw working as she ground her teeth. This was the limit. Not only a full day at Lechwood's but then the rest of the day on the extension and the unholy mess that Paul had got himself into. She had not felt so tired and angry since their business went bottom up. 'And he needn't think he'll talk me round tonight either,' she muttered to herself as she turned off the light.

chapter nineteen - Faith

Two hours to waste and nothing to do in them, it wasn't as if it was often that Faith had time just to herself. The newspaper offices never closed down, putting out a morning and an evening paper as well as freebies and specials meant round-the-clock working, the presses rolling almost non-stop. For the majority of the secretarial staff, however, the day was more normal and swiftly the area where Faith worked, emptied. Susie chatted for a few minutes but when Faith explained that she was going to be about for a whole lot longer Susie apologised and said she had to go.

Faith tidied her desk and checked she had no outstanding work she could do. She was just thinking that it would have been a good time to do any of the extra work that Mr Wren came up with, when, as if conjured by her thoughts, he arrived.

He stopped when he saw her, looked slightly surprised then, checking the wallet in his hand, he came towards her. She smiled at him. She couldn't help herself, just seeing him had sent a warm rush through her body. Seeing him hesitate, his boyish uncertainty filled her with a feeling she could not define but it resembled the love she felt for her children.

'*Mrs Warren*, working late?'

'Not exactly, Mr Wren,' she replied with a small smile. 'Idling away two hours while I wait for my lift, but if that is work for me I'll gladly while away the time doing that.'

'Oh, no. No need.'

'Not work for me then?'

'Yes – work, I'm afraid, but not for you to do at this time. In fact,' he grinned, 'I insist that you do not do it now, that you come and have a coffee, at least, with me.'

Faith suddenly lost all confidence and composure. 'I don't think I could.'

'Nonsense!'

'The – you don't understand how it is here.'

'The gossip machine – you mean? They've all gone home. Besides, I'm talking coffee in a respectable coffee house, not the canteen, and coffee is not adultery.'

Faith felt the heat in her face in an instant, she turned away saying 'Really?' in case he saw and divined her secret thoughts.

'Really – come on – I really need a good cup of coffee. That's all – coffee and not to be alone.'

Suddenly she saw him sitting alone – perhaps too often, a single man, a cup of coffee.

'Oh. All right.' she said softly, picking up her coat, 'All right.'

'That's better,' he smiled at her, his sea-grey eyes catching the light and sending messages of their own. 'And, *Mrs Warren*, please call me Nick, and may I call you Faith?'

She grinned and nodded, but in her head tried his name.

They left the building together, but Faith held back, a step or two behind, as if they just happened to be leaving at the same time. She waved goodbye to the receptionist as usual and paused again outside the doors to pull up her collar before following in the direction that Wren had taken. It was as if he knew what tactics she was using and did not wait for her. As they rounded the building he slowed and she caught up easily.

'Okay?' he smiled.

'Yes – yes thanks.'

'There's a good place about two streets over, 'Le Croissant', do you know it?'

'No.'

'No – and neither do most of that lot at the offices' he smiled at her again. 'All ready for Christmas?',

'Just about.'

'You've got Jilly and Jon's presents then?'

'Yes – they're easy,' Faith began, realising that amazingly he'd remembered her children's names. 'The difficulty is deciding which ones from the list not to buy,'

'And your husband?'

Faith was silent long enough for him to turn his head and look at her. For some stupid reason, him asking about Andy, had filled her with a sick sinking feeling.

'Faith?'

She just shook her head as she heard his voice, tinged with concern, repeat her name.

'Here it is, and not crowded at all, which make's a change.' Wren chatted easily, 'Coffee – how do you like it?'

'Milky – no sugar,' she managed, and scanned the room for somewhere unobtrusive to sit. A table against the far wall, beside a huge pot-plant seemed to offer the best camouflage so she tucked herself in there behind the Swiss-cheese plant.

She watched as Wren turned, tray in hand and saw her. His slow smile was one of acknowledgement of her choice.

'About the only place to hide,' he said as he sat down. The tray bore her coffee, his coffee and two sticky buns; one plain, one coffee. Faith looked up at him and it was as if a blade of ice sliced through her, followed by a sheet of fire. Nothing had ever made her feel this way and it was with great difficulty that she made sense of his words.

'Let's tell tales – I'll tell you my life-story – you tell me yours.' Faith found herself looking into his coruscating eyes, mesmerised, her impulse was to reach out and touch his face to see if it was real and the yearning to pull his hair loose from its band was almost unbearable, she did not dare move.

'Faith, are you okay?'

She nodded.

'Okay, I'll start. I was born in October in fifty-seven, in a small village, the third of what was to be six children.'

'Six?' Faith was drawing herself back together slowly.

Wren nodded, 'Your turn.'

'Well, some the same. Born in a small village – in April sixty-three but I was an only child,' she smiled shyly, 'that right?'

'Fine, okay. I was never settled at school. Only really any good at art, sport, and English and left as soon as I could to take up a junior reporter post – gained I may add through my illustrious uncle pulling a few strings.'

'Who was that?'

'Questions are not allowed at this stage of the game. You see it means you can still control just how much you want to tell me.'

'Oh!' Faith felt that she would have far more questions than he would. 'Oh, yes, school. I loved school. I was,' she stopped, what the hell! 'I was considered to be especially good at English and my teachers had hopes of me heading off to university.'

'And didn't you? Ah – no questions!' he grinned. 'Me again. Right, I did some photography for the paper – that got me noticed. There was, they said, something special about each one. I was encouraged to spread my wings and then, lucky break, one of the rising stars I'd taken shots of made it big and wanted my pictures for his publicity. That was the start of *Nick Wren – photographer to the stars*.' he sounded sardonic and bitter.

Faith's mind raced with questions but she stuck to the rules and formed her own section instead.

'My father,' how to put this, 'My father prevented me from going to university, then Di and I left school and went to secretarial college. We met and married two friends and here I am,' she finished up as quickly as she could to hasten over the parts she did not want to divulge.

'And here you are Faith, and I feel,' his hand touched his own chest briefly, 'that you are unhappy.'

She stared, then nodded mutely and turned her stare to the table top.

He was silent for a moment, then, 'I also feel,' he said quietly, 'I also feel that I am falling for you.'

That made Faith snap her head up and at that their eyes met. Faith's heart was beating so hard now that she was sure he ought to be able to hear it.

He nodded slightly, 'It's true – sounds odd perhaps, you'll say I hardly know you – but it's true.'

Faith shook her head slightly but his fingers touched hers and her hand responded, taking hold of his hand.

'Oh, God!' she sighed, the electricity of their touching scorched through her body

'And I think you feel the same way about me, don't you?'

'Oh, Nick, but…'

'I know, don't say it, you're married.'

'Yes... No...' she stopped and breathed deeply. This had to be a ridiculous dream. All the women that this man had known – stars, models, what-have-you, and he says he's *falling for me*. He must make a habit of saying it, a good line.

'I am married – and, you see my father left my mother and me,' as if that would explain everything, feeling the shame sweep over her again.

'And?'

'And, I don't know – I just can't think of doing that to my children. I love my children. Do you understand?'

'Faith, I wouldn't dream of asking you do anything to upset your children. Don't fret,' he withdrew his hand from hers and as he did she felt as if her core were being siphoned away. She turned her dark eyes on him and he held her gaze with his own. 'Drink your coffee before it gets cold,' he said softly. She did so automatically, leaving the bun untouched.

'Come on, we can walk and talk for a bit,' he smiled at her in a way that made her want to cry. Nodding, she told herself that this wasn't really happening.

They stepped out into the dark evening, the street light sulphurous, the shop windows a merry show of fairy lights. Nick took her hand as if he had always held her hand and led her gently along the street towards the darker office blocks.

'Nick,' she tugged her hand slightly, loving the sound of his name in her mouth.

He tightened his hold gently. 'Two anonymous people in this awful anonymous city – relax Faith,' he held her hand closer to him, pulling her closer, his body sheltering her from the breeze. She felt cosseted, cared for.

Suddenly he sidestepped into a darkened doorway and spun her round towards him. The kiss came before she realised what he was going to do and yet her face was tipped up towards his as if by instinct. His kiss became their kiss, her body responding in a way she had never known before. She could sense the hunger in his kiss, finding an echo in her own body and it thrilled her.

'Forgive me?' he whispered into her hair when they parted and he still held her close, 'I could not bear not to have at least kissed you. Now, Faith, tell me that you are happily married and that you love your husband, then I'll keep clear, make sure I never find myself alone with you again.'

Her pulse was beating in her ears. His words came and went as the waves on the shore, but she could not answer.

'Faith?' he kissed her again, his thumb massaging the nape of her neck. Her hand reached up in the darkness and her fingers found the band that held his hair back, she pulled it loose as she had longed to, slipping the band over her own wrist as she did with Jilly's, and ran her hand through the length of his hair. All the while his eyes searched hers by the gleam of the city lights.

Suddenly she tightened her hand into a fist, tangling it into his hair and pulled him down to her, kissing him with a fervour that made her whole body tremble and, this time, it was his turn to respond.

'Faith – beautiful Faith,' he murmured and kissed her again his arms holding her close.

'Nick,' she began as he nibbled her lower lip, kissed her chin, nibbled her earlobe, kissed below her ear, and down her neck. The sensations were almost too much to bear.

'Mmmm?'

She pulled herself reluctantly away. 'You're right. I'm married. I love my children.'

'Not good enough, Tell me you love your husband. Tell me you are happy.'

Faith leant her head against his chest and the sigh that escaped her turned into a sob and as his hands gently massaged her back she wept.

'Faith, my love – tell me?'

She shook her head, her whole body trembling.

He unzipped his leather jacket. 'Tuck inside, it's warmer.'

She could feel his heart beating now, and the muscles of his chest.

'Tell me – since I met you I've watched your face. A face I wanted to photograph from the first moment, a face that has shown a growing unhappiness,' he stopped. She listened to his heart beating, to his breathing, she wanted to stay there forever. 'A face I love, hurt?' he whispered into her ear, 'Deliberately?' She nodded against his body. Gently he pushed her back so he could see her face.

'Hurt? Deliberately? Physically?'

She nodded dumbly. She doubted if she could have ever found the words to say that Andy hurt her, shook her, pushed her, frightened her until it was beyond her understanding.

'Your *husband?*' his words came out thin and sharp. Again she nodded, closing her eyes against his gaze.

'Bastard! Bastard! Faith – that can't go on! No man deserves to be loved if he treats someone that way! Leave him!'

'But, the children.'

'I know - you said,' he hugged her again. 'How is he with them?' Faith remembered the time when they had disturbed his hangover, 'Okay, unless they annoy him.'

'Faith!'

'No, it's fine when everything is okay – like now. He's working – no problems usually.'

Nick Wren gave her an appraising look then hugged her again. 'Listen,' he waited, she nodded against his chest. 'Listen, I am here. I believe I love you – no, don't, just listen. I would never, ever, break up a good marriage – you have to decide what yours is, but I am here. I want you to come to me *with* your children, no strings attached, if you ever need to, if you ever need to escape. Promise?'

Faith held still for a moment re-running his words.

'Promise?'

'Yes,' she whispered, then louder, 'I promise.'

'And can we meet again?' he looked at her, 'to talk more – at least to allow me to take that photograph I've been composing of your face?'

'I – I don't know,' scared of gossip, scared of her own feelings. 'Discreetly – I promise I'll never, never ask of you anything that you aren't happy with. Life has taught me that at least – but that's another part of my tales to trade.'

'I'm sure you've so much more to tell – not so me.'

'That's not an answer,' he leant down and kissed her again and her mind was made up by the previously unknown bliss that flowed through her body, she could not turn him away.

'Yes, Nick, Oh God forgive me, yes.'

chapter twenty - Faith

After the guilt of keeping Di waiting and the feeling of being caught with Nick Wren, just because Di saw them leave the lift together, Faith had hardly talked to Di on the way home. As it was she was sure that Di must be able to see that something had happened to her, that she was different somehow, especially when Di cracked the comment about not tipping Wren out of bed. Different, was how she felt. Her whole being glowed from within, a deep feeling of love and of being loved fought its way through the layers of guilt, shame and irrationality. Yet Di did not seem to notice anything, merely drove through the night absorbed in her own thoughts.

Faith cursed herself as she left Di's car and looked towards her own house. She'd meant to pick something quick up for dinner in her two hours, or get Di to stop off at the Hypermarket on the way home. She'd been so full of the turmoil that Nick had left her in that she'd completely forgotten. As she struggled with the front door she wondered what she could do quickly, there might be some pizza in the freezer, if Andy had not eaten it all already. Andy's voice rang out from the living room above the blare of the TV as soon as she'd closed the door.

'That you? I'm starving, how long for dinner?'

'Give me a chance,' Faith muttered. 'Not too long,' she called back, crossing her fingers. She was in luck; there was one last remaining pizza from the pack of six she'd bought on special offer. Not what she thought of as a proper meal but Andy was happy with pizza and it wouldn't do the children any harm as long as she didn't make it a habit.

Out of its box and cooked the pizza didn't look much, so she decided to just have the salad herself, perhaps with a piece of cheese, leaving a larger portion for Andy. Having settled in front of the TV Andy was loathed to move so Faith took him his on a tray, though she cajoled Jilly and Jon to join her at the table where they ate while watching TV with sidelong glances and quickly left to join their father in front of the set. Watching them made Faith feel sad. There seemed so little else for them as they were.

As Faith undressed for bed she found that she still had Nick's hair band around her wrist. The sight of it filled her with a sense of panic, what if Andy had seen it! Then almost as suddenly she laughed. What would he say? Nothing! He'd never suspect a hair band; he despised men who wore their hair long, considered them weirdos, wimps, hippies or gay. Besides he would probably have assumed that it was Jilly's. She pulled it from her wrist and lifted it to her nose. There was the slightest scent of a shampoo and a number of his raven dark hairs caught in the fabric. She teased them out and twisted them around her finger. Her body tightened within her as the strength of her feeling reached to her very core. Faith slipped his hair band back on her wrist as she left the bathroom and made her way to share her husband's bed hoping that he was asleep by now.

Faith woke early the next morning and instantly Nick's image was with her, the taste of his mouth, the strength of his arms. She lay gently fingering the hair band and thinking of the promise he'd made her make. If she'd been made a promise like that a week back, when Andy'd hit out at Jilly and Jon, she would have gone, but Andy had a way of being contrite when it was over. She lay there aware of the bulk of her husband beside her and made another promise to herself. She promised that she would try to be fair, she would not let her own desires rule, she'd give Andy as much chance as he gave himself. She would not leave him while things remained on an even keel, while he remembered to be gentle with them all. But if he didn't, well now she knew she had an option. Faith made herself the promise, told herself this and pretended that her heart was not aching at the decision to stay.

The next day she was desperate to get to work and perhaps see Nick. When she arrived it was to find his portfolio of work propped against her screen. Blushing she picked it up and opened it. At first she thought it was just the work that he'd brought last night, then she saw the small note clipped to the last page. She glanced round quickly. Susie had just arrived, was busy taking off her coat.. Faith just had time to read the note: *"You need to do some last minute shopping at lunch time – see you at Le Croissant."* She slipped the note quickly into her pocket and continued to peruse the contents of the folder.

'More work from the delectable Mr Wren?' Susie asked.

'Sure is – and quite a bit this time.'

'What's it about? I mean, what does he really need a secretary for?'

Faith wasn't sure how to answer as most of what she had done for Nick had been pretty trivial stuff, though now she thought she knew why there'd been so much.

'Oh, letters to magazines and things,' she replied loosely.

'Oh, yeah. I suppose.' Susie was easily satisfied, 'Would you say I look good in pale blue? I'm considering it for my going-away outfit.'

'I'd have to see the shade to be sure, but, yes, it should go well with your eyes and hair.'

'But a bit of a cliché?'

'Who cares? As long as you look stunning.'

Susie smiled happily back at Faith and set to work.

At coffee Faith was careful to mention that she had to do some last minute shopping at lunch time, so she could dash off quickly. For a moment she thought that Susie was going to accompany her when she mentioned her outfit again, but it turned out that the store where she'd seen it was on the other side of town.

'I should have got you to come with me when you had time to kill last night,' Susie sighed.

The moment lunchtime came, Faith had her coat on and was out of the door. It was all she could do to stop herself from running out of the building. Once out in the street she allowed herself to speed up to a light trot until she turned into the right street. She saw him outside 'Le Croissant' as soon as she turned the corner, her heart thumping, she watched him start to walk towards her.

'Good timing,' he said as he reached her, taking her hand and turning her to walk away from the coffee shop. Faith tugged her hand out of his, reluctantly, but he acknowledged her caution with a rueful smile.

'I want to show you my place, just in case you need to use it,' he said turning the corner and striding out so that Faith had to hurry to keep up with him.

'Your place?'

'My town flat. It's not far – next street.' Then after a few minutes, 'Here, number eleven, okay?' he flicked a look at his watch, 'Come on up.'

'Nick…'

'Just for a few minutes.'

Faith smiled, knowing her eyes gave her away. The door opened to the tapping of a keypad. The building was from the last century, heavy Victorian door and inside a staircase of marble with a mahogany balustrade.

'No lift, I'm afraid, and I'm on the top floor.' Nick led the way, the lights turning on automatically as they approached each level. Almost out of breath Faith waited while Nick unlocked his polished wood door. Inside it was light. Walls of cream were liberally decorated with photos in plain-glass mounts. Glass table tops, pale wood, a subtle lighting that made everything shine.

Nick turned to her, his eyes searching hers. Faith felt the smile on her face begin from somewhere in the centre of her being, then he smiled too. Next moment they were in each other arms, hungrily kissing, tasting each other. His hands caressed her, massaging her back, her neck, her hands sought his hair again, tugging it loose from another band, burying her face in it, breathing in the scent of his shampoo.

'My faerie Fay,' he whispered in her ear, 'I've thought of nothing else but you since yesterday. Have you thought about what I said?"

'Oh, Nick, yes but …'

'But you're not going to leave him, are you?'

'I have to give him a fair chance, for the children,' her voice nearly breaking.

'And now. This is almost too much. I asked you to come today, at such short notice, as I've got to go away for a while. I won't be back before New Year.' Faith's heart lurched; she clung to him, his arm coming round to hold her tight. 'I know it's the worst timing, but I can't help it. So look here,' he moved her away from him a small space. 'Here, my door-key, my keypad number and my mobile number. Just keep them safe with you, just in case you need somewhere to run before I get back. Since you told me – I can't bear the thought of you being hurt, Fay, I do love you.'

'How can you say that after so short a time,' Faith murmured, shaking her head, yet knowing that she loved him already, and delighting in hearing him use her favourite version of her name, unbidden.

'I was sure as soon as I held you, as soon as I kissed you.'

'Yes? And me, me too,' Faith murmured back.

'So now, be safe until I come back.'

'I don't know what to say.'

'There's no time to say anything, time has run out on us. Just remember I love you,' he checked his watch. 'Come here,' he said as he pulled her to him. They held each other tight for a moment, fixing the shape of each other in their minds. As they pulled apart Faith held out Nick's hair-band.

He smiled as he took it and snapped his hair back into it. 'I think you owe me one of these,' he said

'Finder's keepers,' she replied softly.

'Keep it well – come on, you'll be late – you'll have to run. Take this,' he said as he handed her a shopping bag.

'What is it?'

'Your shopping – that you went out for, remember?'

'Oh yes, but what?'

'You'll see,' as they ran down the stairs, 'I'll just come to the door.'

At the door he took her in his arms again, she leaned her body hard against him.

'Take care,' he kissed her again. 'Here's to the New Year.'

'Till the New Year,' suddenly a long time away.

And the next minute Faith was in the street and running. It was almost time to be back in the office and she still had four streets to go to be back at the front door.

Red faced from her exertions she stepped into the foyer to be greeted by Susie gesturing from the door of the open lift for her to be quick.

'What've you got?' Susie asked as they rode up to their floor. Faith covered herself with a coughing fit. As the doors opened she managed to say, 'Oh, you know, just some things for Christmas.'

All through the afternoon Faith kept feeling Nick's arms around her and the wonderful warmth that it spun through her whole body. She found herself sitting with a smile on her face and her fingers motionless over her keyboard and had to jolt herself back to reality and work. The thought that she would not see Nick again for nearly a fortnight focussed her mind and she allowed her hand to stray to the pocket where she had put his key to reassure herself it was all true. Touching its solidness lightly she smiled again, but by the time it came to leave work even the touching of this talisman could not drive away the sinking feeling as she prepared to go home.

chapter twenty-one - Di

It was Christmas before Di forgave Paul completely, but then she'd not had much chance to talk to him until then. He and his team had worked all hours, Paul returning shattered and filthy well after ten each evening, Di already asleep. On Christmas Day they sat together over a leisurely breakfast and opened their presents; the normal collection of over-priced and over-packaged smellies from Di's parents, silver-plated photograph frame from Paul's, the latest Delia Smith cook book from Faith and Andy, practical as ever, and then their gifts to each other. Di wondered how Faith would react to her special present when she came to it.

Di felt Paul's eyes on her as she opened the dress box and she saw him smile to himself as he caught the sparkle in her eyes. The dress was simple and beautiful, elegant and so perfect that it made her wonder how much he'd paid for it. When she lifted it from the box and saw the small jeweller's box nestling beneath she felt a short flash of anger tinge her consciousness. The deep blue box contained a pair of sparkling earrings which, like the dress, were simple and elegant.

'They are lovely!' she held them up to her ears to show him the effect, 'Oh Paul - so perfect with the dress – beautiful. Thank you.' She shook her head, 'but you shouldn't have – they must have cost a fortune.'

His tense face lightened and regained its boyish charm, 'But you are always worth it,' he beamed.

Di put on the new dress and earrings for the evening when they were visiting Paul's parents. She felt wonderful and kept checking her reflection in the mirror before they left. Paul, feeling vindicated of his extravagance, hugged her to him and nuzzled her neck promising her that as soon as they were home he'd be more interested in taking the dress off again.

Boxing Day dawned wet and cold. A fine rain from a solid grey sky cast gloom over their late breakfast. The phone rang,

Di looked at Paul and he at her and, as usual, Di went to answer it.

'Paul!' Di shouted, her tone getting his immediate attention, 'The police!'

Paul hurried over mouthing 'What?' at Di, she lifted her eyes and hissed 'The extension.' as she passed the phone to him.

'What!' Paul exploded. Di watched his face as it paled, then flushed. He put the phone down and stood just looking at it for at least a minute.

'Paul?'

He whirled. 'Vandals, they said, broke into the site,' he shook his head. 'Smashed everything up – I need to go there and see.'

'I'll come.' Di spun on her heel and raced upstairs, she dragged on her old jeans and a thick jumper. She caught up with Paul as he revved up the car.

'Right!' she said as she dropped herself into the passenger seat and felt the car surge forward.

'Perhaps it's not much,' she ventured

'Police wouldn't have made a fuss if it was minor.'

'You don't know – who reported it?'

'Nobody – some coppers saw it themselves – apparently.'

'What? Saw it happening?'

'Heard – your actual bobby on the beat – shone his torch and they scarpered.'

'So it might be okay?'

'Perhaps – but smashed was their word.'

Di's hopes were dashed as soon as they turned into the end of the street. The smashed glass glinted in the gutters even under the watery sun that now tried to break through the thinning cloud.

'Shit! Shit! Shit!' Paul muttered as he parked his car on the opposite side of the road.

'From inside.' Di said wondering at the way the windows were smashed. 'Broken out from inside!'

'Oh God!' Paul had unlocked the door and stepped into what should have been a nearly finished reception area. The beautiful elm reception bar had been splintered with a number of heavy blows, the windows, all gone, the leather seats spilled their guts onto the parquet flooring, now deeply gouged with two parallel grooves that ran a ragged circle around the room.

'Oh Paul,' Di felt the hot tears spill from her eyes, her throat too tight to say anymore. She reached out to hold him but he shrugged her away and strode towards the doors to the fitness suite.

She heard his sharp gasp before she saw the training equipment that had made the grooves outside lying dead on its side. All the machines were crippled, parts smashed off, padding ripped, tipped over. Thousands of pounds worth of equipment wrecked, the sledge-hammer that had done the work stuck up out of a weights bench in a semi-obscene gesture.

'What's that sound?' Di asked, her attention caught by a faintly musical noise. Paul looked at her then suddenly, wild-eyed, headed for the showers. Here water cascaded over the sun-bed, tinkling on the glass of the broken tubes and electrics. He went along slamming each shower off, getting himself soaked.

It was as they turned to leave that they saw the wall. Daubed in puke-green were two overlapping crosses and the word 'bastard'. Paul stood before the graffiti and his whole body appeared to go slack, the blood drained from his face.

'What does it mean?' Di murmured. Paul merely shook his head and walked slowly out of the room. Di followed , trying to make sense of Paul's reaction. The police had returned and a plain clothes detective was standing in the doorway.

'Morning sir, DC Jenkins,' he nodded to a companion, just out of sight, 'DC Hyams, may I ask your name?'

'Paul Harvey. It's my contract job – this.'

'Any means of identification?' he looked at Di as if to include her in this. Paul tugged his wallet from his back pocket.

'I'm his wife, Di Harvey,' Di filled in.

'Thank you sir, now perhaps you would run us through events from your end, then we'll look at the damage.'

'Waste of bloody time.' Paul muttered to Di, when she asked if there had been any progress with the police investigation. Four days had passed. The Leech had gone ballistic – threatening all kinds of evil on the perpetrators and failing that, threatening the full works on the contract overrun costs. 'I don't expect they'll find any links to our dear friend Billy – he'll have been far too careful for that – it's a write off.'

'And you daren't give them the hint 'cos you know it was just Billy's revenge,' Di bit back.

'Okay! Okay! Just shut it – I've heard enough.'

'You haven't heard half of it – the Leech is really on the war path – he'll do us for overrun – big time.'

'We've a week to go!'

'Get real Paul. You'll work yourself stupid and he'll still have his overrun.'

'Well standing here won't help – don't know when I'll be back – we're working late.'

The door slammed behind him yet Di heard the post drop through the letter box before she heard the car roar out of the drive. Two out of the three looked like bills. The third she opened. Her eyes raked the heading – it was one of the agencies she'd sent The Story to – scanning quickly she plucked out the words, 'fresh' 'interesting' 'but'. At that word she stopped and started again reading properly from the top.

Dear Ms Diane Faith,

Thank you for sending us your submission to consider. Our reader passed it on to me as being, in her words, 'fresh and interesting'.

I like your style and for me that is the first point I look for. The outline is interesting and you have a good voice, but it wobbles at a few specific points.

I would be pleased to read the rest of your manuscript at your earliest convenience.

A C Enderby

Di clutched the letter tightly and went off to get ready for work. Twice she picked it up again and re-read it. How much, she wondered, did a book make for an author? She had heard of vast sums being paid for some books, usually by top authors, but how much for a first novel? Money, any money, would be very welcome at this point for she knew that the Leech would much rather it was her body on the line rather than their house and though she'd hate every moment, she thought she could bear the thought of his loathsome body all over hers if it meant that they would not lose everything else. Yet – Paul had intervened and happily, foolishly, offered such good terms if they did not open on time, that the Leech had taken his offer instead. They'd not been insured against damage – they couldn't afford to be – so they were right up the creek. If the book made money, then at least they'd not be out on the streets. First things first, she'd package up the rest of the manuscript and get it sent off straight away.

chapter twenty-two - Faith

The second day of the New Year and Faith knew something was wrong as soon as she opened the door. A waft of lager fumes breathed towards her on the warm air, and it was only half past six. She closed the door quietly hoping that Andy had not heard it open over the TV. She hung up her coat, then slowly walked the short distance along the hall to the living room door. She could see the top of Andy's head slumped at one end of the sofa, the TV flickered and crashed as some bad guys blew out the end of a building. There was no sign of the children, and that rang alarm bells. Faith ran lightly upstairs. There was light coming from under their doors suggesting they were in their rooms. Opening Jilly's she looked in.

Jilly looked up from a book and smiled.

'Everything okay lovely?' Faith asked.

'Yeah, dad's watching something gross.'

'That bad, eh?' Faith made light of it. 'Had tea?'

'Sandwich.'

'Good girl, I'll get you something proper soon,' she closed the door and opened Jon's. He didn't look up from his Game Boy at first, not until she stepped into the room, then, as he realised someone was there he jumped – his eyes flashed at her, wary – then warm.

'Okay?'

'Yeah.'

'Not like Dad's film?'

'Sent me up.'

'Ah.'

'I didn't do nothing, I only asked why he was home when we got in – that's all.'

'When you came home?'

'Yeah, almost as soon as we gets to Cath's she says 'Your Dad's home – I saw him come back, you might as well go home' – so we did.'

'Right – but you're okay?'

'Starving.'

'Give me a minute. I'll call you,' Faith grinned for him and returned slowly downstairs. Andy had not moved, so she made a noise in the hall, banged open the kitchen door – as if she'd just arrived home. Right, she thought to herself, forewarned!

'That you?' Andy called.

'Of course – dinner won't be long.' Faith put the chicken pieces into roast, began peeling some potatoes. Absorbed in her work she did not hear Andy's approach.

'Bastard's laid me off,' Andy slurred.

Faith jumped. 'Pardon?' She turned to see Andy lounging against the door post.

'Billy bastard's given me my cards.'

Faith stopped peeling and shook her hands dry. Turning she could see the way anger and defeat fought within him, his body slack, his eyes blazing.

'Why? Has he laid off the whole crew?'

'Nope! Just me! And as for why – he told me to ask Paul.'

'Paul? Paul left that job ages ago!'

'Yeah well, still, he's shafted me 'cos of Paul.'

'I don't understand,' Faith said coming over to where he stood.

'P'raps 'cos you're stupid – Paul's done something to Billy – and Billy's got his own back – on me.'

'If it's not your fault can't you reason with him?'

The hand came out faster than she could have imagined possible – the slap sent her reeling.

'Reason?' he spat, as the slap echoed in their tiny kitchen. 'Hasn't Di told you what Billy's done to *them*?' Faith leant hard against the kitchen unit where the slap had sent her. She could feel her face throbbing and deep inside a hard splinter dug itself in. She didn't look at him as he asked that question or when he answered it himself, muttering, 'Nah! I guess she wouldn't tell you,' as he slouched back to the living room.

Faith stood a moment, her hand raised to her burning cheek. Was it enough? Was this past the limit she'd set herself?

'Faith,' his voice. She looked up. He was back and coming towards her. She was already back as far as she could go. 'Faith,' he opened his arms wide. 'So sorry – didn't mean to. It just, I

181

...' he shook his head as he reached her and wrapped his arms around her shivering shape. 'Didn't mean to,' he mumbled, his voice muted by his arms across her ears. Faith wriggled and he let his arms drop. When Faith looked up at him his eyes were full of tears.

'We'll manage. Billy's an idiot if he doesn't know he's lost a good site manager,' Faith found herself saying, still supplying the right words at the right time. She saw his eyes brighten and knew that he thought himself forgiven and still holding the man's place in the home – even though they were back to relying on her job again.

Faith put her decision on hold and, having splashed cold water on her face, she continued peeling the potatoes as if nothing had happened. Was it because she truly felt Andy was redeemable – that there was something worth holding on to in their twelve-year marriage, or was she just too scared. She understood herself enough to know why she felt scared of going it alone, but now she wouldn't be alone – or would she? She knew how she felt, but what of Wren? After all, a few hasty kisses and his keys did not add up to security, and that was what her psyche told her she needed. And then his insisting that he'd not pursue her, not even come near her if she just said she loved Andy and that she was happy in her marriage, what was that all about, what did that mean about the way he really felt? She put the potatoes on to boil. New Year. The first working day of the New Year and she'd been hoping all day to see him. She'd recalled his words and played them back to herself again and again and she was still not sure if he'd said after New Year or at New Year. She didn't really know him, did she, and Andy was so quick to realise his mistake, this was not the time.

Andy ate ravenously and admitted he'd done nothing more than drink since he'd come back just after nine. He said he'd just tried to blot out the day, but somehow it hadn't worked. Thankfully, as soon as his head hit the pillows, he slept.

Di seemed distracted as they drove off towards the motorway the next day but Faith wanted to pursue the clue that Andy had given her.

'Di, Andy tells me that there's been some trouble with Billy.'

Di flashed her a quick look. 'You could say that.'

'So why's it affected Andy? Did you know he's been laid off?'

'No! When?'

'Yesterday – apparently it's to do with Paul and Billy.'

'Why? Because Andy and Paul are mates?'

'That – and,' Faith hesitated then decided to follow her hunch, 'and there seems to be something else – something specific to do with Paul and whatever he's in with Billy.'

Di sighed, 'Probably. Idiot. Not you – my dear husband.'

'What's it all about?'

'Paul trying to pull a fast one over on Billy – and trying to make a quid or two more on the job he's doing for Lechwood while he's at it. Trouble is Billy got wind of the scam and has taken his revenge – big time. We are well and truly up the creek without a paddle – going to cost us thousands to the Leech in overrun 'cos the job will be well behind schedule now that Billy's sent in a mob to smash the place up and, and Andy's got the boot.'

'Just because he's Paul's friend?'

'Possibly – but I think Andy may not have realised the scam that Paul set up before he left – and that would go against him, it could look like he was in on it.'

'What do you mean?'

'That Paul was getting supplies and the bills were going to Billy.'

'Andy knew?'

'No, probably not, Paul said no mud would stick to Andy – so I think he didn't even know, it's just that he…'

'He what?'

'Well, Andy doesn't have the best overall grip – he probably just wouldn't have noticed the discrepancy in the paperwork.'

'That's – despicable. He's a friend!'

'Big words – Paul's been a bastard – and just 'cos Andy didn't notice doesn't reflect better on him.'

'No, and saying he knew nothing doesn't help him either. How could Paul do that to his oldest friend?'

'Paul? Sometimes he has no idea about real life, it's like they are still children – never grown up – everything's a big laugh.'

'But Andy's devastated – he..'

'He'll get over it. Paul will find him a new job if we ever get out of the hole – maybe even before – I'll talk to him.'

'Oh yes. Andy'll forgive him, his hero.'

'Paul tried his best.' Di sounded defensive, 'Sometimes it all goes wrong. You get nothing for nothing you know.'

There was the manila folder, propped against her computer screen. As soon as she entered the room it seemed to shine like a beacon. It was all she could do not to run over and open it but she carefully hung up her coat and her new burgundy scarf, checked her plants and turned on the computer before she allowed herself to pick up the folder. Inside were three or four sheets of handwritten letters, nothing exciting – but at the back a small piece of folded paper caught her attention. She unfolded it inside the folder – in his distinctive scrawl it simply said 'Home. Come for lunch, please. N' she slipped it out of the folder and into her pocket to dispose of later.

The morning fled as she worked quickly towards lunch. She'd laid the ground with Susie about her quick shopping trip and wondered if she needed to get something bought from a shop or leave it to luck as to whether Nick had got some. One thing she knew, if he presented her with a bag again she'd make sure she had a peek in it before she found herself in a lift with an inquisitive friend.

Three items had been in that last bag. A friendship bracelet kit, obviously meant for Jilly, a set of Pokemeon cards for Jon and a silky scarf for herself. The scarf was simple but felt so expensive. Desperately wanting to be able to wear it Faith had posted it to herself disguised as a present from Auntie Florence. Andy had not even registered it beyond saying it was the colour of dried blood and Faith replying softly that the colour was called burgundy.

Lunch time found her out of the office as soon as was possible, the silky scarf caressing her neck beneath her old sheepskin coat. She reached his door and, feeling suspicious, glanced each way for people she knew, before tapping in the number he had given her. The door swung open and to her delight he was coming down the stairs, two at a time, to meet her,

Her heart performed peculiar acrobatics in the moment it took for him to reach her, the street door closed, his arms closed around her to hold her, then he kissed her.

He took her hand and led her up the stairs to his apartment. Just inside the door they kissed again and Faith could not believe the way her body responded, as if she were both deeply contented and highly strung.

'Happy New Year,' he whispered to her.

'Happy New Year to you, too,' surprised to hear her own voice husky.

'I have missed you more than I imagined possible,' Nick said as he slipped her coat from her shoulders. A small smile lit his face as he took the two ends of her wine-red scarf and used it to draw her through to the sofa.

He tasted so good, his kisses so intense. Together they sat and kissed and caressed, barely a word spoken. Nick's hand slipped beneath her shirt to caress her bare back, Faith began, one handed, to try to undo his shirt buttons,

Suddenly she felt ridiculous and inexperienced and sat back with a laugh.

'What?' Nick looked perplexed.

Faith shook her head.

'Tell me, love, tell me.'

'I'm not very good at this. Out of practice – not much experience anyway – I don't know – it seems –teenage like.'

'It does, doesn't it?' Nick laughed lightly, 'But then again – I feel like a teenager when I'm with you.'

'Perhaps that's it then.'

'Perhaps we just need more practice,' Nick said kissing her again, mouth, forehead, eyes.

Faith winced.

'What?' Nick pushed Faith back a little to look at her, brushed back her dark fringe, 'Is this a bruise?'

'It's nothing.'

'Faith, did he?'

'Honest, it's nothing.'

Nick regarded her for a moment, his eyes focussed and grey.

'But if he did – if he started again – you do trust me – you would come?'

Faith sank back into his arms, feeling their strong warmth. Away from his gaze she sighed, 'Oh Nick, if it got that bad again, of course.'

Nick hugged her tight again, 'I wish there was more time, come on, you must eat.' He launched himself from the sofa tugging Faith after him.

The kitchen was pure designer, as if no one would ever deign to cook in there, yet there, prepared and looking marvellous were two bowls of salad. Faith felt strangely shy as she ate, finding herself watching the way Nick deftly manipulated his fork. There was a glint in his eye when he caught her watching him.

'Come on – eat,' he said, presenting her with a grape on his fork close to her lips. She opened her mouth and gently took it in, the eye contact never altered and his smile had nothing to do with food.

'How often do you think you could take a lunch break out, without looking suspicious?'

'Well, I usually never go out at lunch time,' Faith began.

'But you could start a new pattern, lunch out everyday?'

Faith thought, her heart, her body, wanted this, wanted everyday but her head told her it was silly.

'Every other day,' she suggested, and was rewarded with a smile and a widening of his eyes, 'I could need to shop – oh, but then I'll have to do some.'

'I'll arrange that – you could give me a list,' he laughed as if delighted by the prospect.

At morning break the next day Susie actually asked if she was lunching with her or going shopping. Faith coloured slightly but smiled and said, 'Lunching.'

Selecting her salad Faith sat opposite Susie. Behind Susie sat the normal occupants, the usual trio, Annie, Joan and Tommy. Once again Tommy was regaling them with some tale for both Annie, with her gorgeous mass of red curls, and the usually more dour Joan were laughing. Tommy leant back flinging one arm along the length of the seat-back to bask in their appreciation.

'Were you looking for something special yesterday?' Susie asked as she tucked into her plate of salad, eaten to aid the wedding dress diet.

'Oh no.' Faith began, ready to tell the lie she'd prepared overnight, 'It's just Di, you know Di who I get a lift in with each day? Well, Di's got a change in routine. it means I have to get the family shopping during the week. A nuisance – means I'll have to dash out every other day.'

'I'll come with you if it would help.'

'No, Oh no.' Faith cut in a little too quickly, 'It's fine really. I just sort of know what I need, what the children like,' she could feel her face begin to glow again so added quietly, 'Andy's lost his job again – got to watch the pennies.'

'Oh, Faith, I'm sorry. It's been a bit rough for you lately – I forgot – I've been so tied up in the wedding plans.'

'Yes, and thank you for the invite. How are the plans going?' Faith leapt at the chance to change the subject and there was nothing better than the wedding to distract Susie.

chapter twenty-three - Di

The phone was ringing as Di came in. She dumped the bags she was carrying and ran to answer it.

'Hello?'

'Is that Ms Diane Faith?'

Di swallowed, her mind in a whirl.

'Hello?' the voice said again.

'Yes, sorry, just catching my breath. Yes, Diane Faith speaking.'

'You're a hard one to catch – I've had my secretary ring you on and off all day – Alison Enderby, ACE Literary Agency.'

'I'm sorry – I was at work – but..'

'Never mind – I'll have fewer interruptions at home. I've read the rest of your manuscript and I think it has real potential, but it certainly can't go anywhere as it stands.'

'Already? That's great – what do we have to do then?'

'Well, taken that you agree to my conditions and rates then I will represent you and your work to the publishers. This depends, of course, on your agreeing to work on this manuscript under my guidance, for, as I said, I don't believe it'll take off as it stands.'

'Yes – we will – look I know it's crass and early days and all that but if you can sell it to a publisher, what would we be looking at, after your percentage, of course?'

'My dear Diane, that's a long way down the road, I'd have to be sure that the work could be done on the manuscript before I started hawking it around.'

'I'm sorry. I know. I understand, but I'm in a bit of a hole, financially, and I'm just clutching at straws.'

'What kind of financial mess? Sorry to sound rude but I have to consider whether you'll be able to work on this project fully. You say you work already – what time would you have to devote to a re-write?'

'A re-write?'

'Of course, it's obvious that this manuscript hasn't been re-written many times before this presentation, yet, I can see, feel, that you've got what it takes. There's the matter of the loss of voice at certain points – not least in that last chapter – but when your voice shines through it really carries the reader along. So, yes, a re-write – how committed are you?'

'Even more so without financial worries – it's my husband's firm – run into a bit of bother and a few thousand would keep the wolf from the door. No, don't worry, a re-write – I can do it!'

'Just a few thousand – well, if and when, I think you could count on ten – but don't spend it yet. Look, get yourself a pen and paper I'm going to dictate the numbers of the chapters and the areas that need working on.'

Di put down the phone, she was trembling. Quickly she ran to the office and grabbed a sheaf of copier paper and a pen. She was soon back.

'Ms Enderby?'

'Alison – if we're to work together. We are I take it? I'll send a contract by the next post. Read it – I do mean read it – sign it with a witness, witness to sign too, and send it back and we're in business. Okay?'

Di was silent, holding her breath while she tried to work out what to say. Of course it wasn't okay. Faith didn't know and she couldn't sign it as her own.

'Is there a problem Diane?'

'No, well yes. You see Diane Faith's not my real name.'

'Non-de-plume – okay no prob. Just sign the contract under your own name.'

'No, you don't get it. Diane's my name. Faith is the name of, of my…' What the hell is the word I am looking for thought Di furiously.

'Co-writer?'

'Yes. Yes, Diane Harvey and Faith Warren, you see we've been friends since forever and Faith's the one who,' Di stopped herself just in time before she admitted that it was Faith who made-up the stories, 'the one with the ideas and I, I sort of work on them to make the finished product.' Di felt pleased with herself, they sounded like an inseparable team.

'I see – so it will be two contracts, but I can't move until they are both back. In consideration of your financial worries I'll send out feelers as soon as I have the contract and the re-write of the first chapter.'

'Really? That's wonderful. There's no problem with there being two writers really.'

'None at all, as long as only one of you wants the limelight. If you're going to press as Diane Faith, a name, incidentally, I like, one of you will have to pretend to be Diane Faith at book launches and signings. An author who is not willing to get out there and sell their work is not going to be as valuable as one who will. Just look at Archer, for all his other shortcomings, he made his way into the top ten by selling himself. He never passed a bookshop without asking why his book wasn't in the window, and if it was, why it didn't have a display, and he talked, oh, he talked himself up, the book up, he used the way 'not a penny more' related to his own struggles and made the whole idea much more interesting to the buying public. So you see Diane, that would have to be a codicil to your contracts – that only one of you will be Diane Faith and all that it entails!'

Already Di was imagining what that would be like and enjoying seeing herself in that role. After all what impact would Faith make? Where as she! A photo inside the dust jacket – giving the old PR to all those people. Faith would hate it.

'I'm sure we could come to an agreement over that.' she said confidently.

'Okay, though until I see the re-write of the first chapter I'm not signing this contract, understand, so, pen ready Diane, that's right isn't it, you are Diane?'

'Yes that's right, and I'm ready.'

'So here goes. The first chapter is the most important one of the whole book. In fact the first line is the most important and luckily for you your first line hits right where it needs to.'

Di remembered the clarity of that first line in her memory. It was pure Faith – she knew that she had remembered that bit right – and here was the proof. Alison continued, 'After that the first chapter contains so many stops. Places where the language forgets what it's doing, where it causes the reader to hesitate. This is no good anywhere, but in the first chapter it can be lethal. Hey – I've changed my mind.'

'What?' gasped Di, alarmed.

'I'm not going to dictate all this mess – in the first chapter I marked all the stops. I'll have it sent. You do the business. You'll even find a few suggestions for you. Now, let's look at the rest – oh yes, the sex scenes – it needs them – that little bit of tickle – but, well, the voice is gone, it reads like a bad men's magazine.'

'I didn't think ...'

'Are you listening Diane, the idea is good – the voice is wrong.'

'Well there was a little bit of bother. Faith's sort of shy about writing that type of thing and I did that alone.'

'So the voice comes from Faith? I thought you said she was the one with the ideas.'

Di thought keenly – she'd tripped herself up. 'Well, as far as I know we both contribute to the end 'voice', as you call it.'

'But with only one of you it goes. You'll just have to get her to contribute to these bits then, even if she's shy.'

'Of course, anything else?'

'The ending – too neat, tidy and romantic – and loss of voice again.'

Di's heart sank. She'd written the last chapter herself. Taken the rough ideas that Faith had offered when pushed, and written of the glorious exposé of the city council and the leisure centre in the national press and she'd even had the happy couple riding off into the sunset together on Chris Raven's Harley. She'd only left the fate of Sherry Spencer unsettled as she was not sure what she wanted to happen there.

'The ending has to change,' Alison continued, 'and I want to make a very strong suggestion here. You two will want to write another book I'm sure. I mean – no publisher will look at you unless you do intend to do more than one, it costs money to build an author's presence in the marketplace and they're just not interested in one-offs.'

'Yes, yes, Faith's full of ideas for stories, I mean books. She always has been.'

'Good – now back to my strong suggestion – far be it for me to tell an author what to do – but Hope has to end up the heroine and Raven has to die, heroically, of course. I see Hope Jones as the heroine of a whole series of books. She can move up the echelons of journalism and meet new dangers each time – and new lovers, new partners in defence of the right. Meeting new dangers with the capable Raven in tow is too cushy. Sadly – he must die.'

'Oh, I see. I thought it was nice when they went off together.'

'Nice! Who wants nice? Leave that for the Mills and Boons, here is the chance to create a woman, feisty, sassy, sexy, who can go on to more adventures of every kind, sexy as well as investigative.'

'I see.' Di could see but wondered how Faith would take to the idea of extending the one character of Hope Jones into a series at the cost of changing the first story. 'I'm sure that'll be okay. So what needs to be done to the last chapter?'

'Scrap it – finish with them in the garage – Hope alive but wounded, give her Raven's wounds, and Raven stabbed through the heart, dying only after he tells her he loves her, has acquitted her of any wrongdoing etcetera.'

'Right, okay.' Di said scribbling frantically.

'But first start on that first chapter as soon as it arrives – and send it and your contracts back to me ASAP, I'll be hearing from you, bye now.'

'Bye – um..' but Alison had put down the phone.

Di sat and stared at her note pad. No choice now – if she wanted the chance of the money she was going to have to talk to Faith, and Faith wasn't happy with her at the moment. But, of course Faith wasn't happy because Andy had lost his job and blamed Paul, rightly or wrongly – which meant they needed the money as much as she did, Faith ought to be delighted. Di decided to talk to Faith on the way to work the next morning.

Di wondered how Faith was going to react to the news as she opened the frost encrusted door to the garage. Faith had been a little strange about the Christmas gift of her story all typed up. She'd seemed to be very shy of saying anything at first, just a 'very nice, a surprise, thank you' when they were all together. Then, on their first journey into work she'd been more inquisitive. Inquisitive, not thankful, 'how had Di remembered it all?' and Di had admitted to the tape. Faith was quiet for minutes after that and Di had to jolly her out of it by saying how much she'd enjoyed the story, and she'd kept a copy to read again because she'd enjoyed it so much. At which Faith had then thanked her again.

Now it was the matter of how to broach the subject of her having sent off the story to an agent without even asking Faith. Somehow she had the nagging feeling that Faith wasn't delighted to have had the story written down at all, let alone published for all to read. By the time she saw Faith waiting outside her place Di thought she'd come up with the recipe for her approach.

Once the heater had kicked in and the windows began to demist Di flicked a glance at Faith. She seemed to be smiling quietly to herself.

'Fay?' she said using the pet name from childhood.

'Mm?'

'Have you read your story – written up like?' Di glanced at her again to see her look flustered.

'I, er, well, not really. I've flicked a few pages, read some. It really was a kind idea Di – but I already know the story.' Faith laughed, but it sounded hollow.

'Well, as it happens Paul read it. You know he thought it was so good, brilliant really, that I thought, and he thought, it was good enough to get published. So, to prove it, I sent it off to an agent.'

'You did what?'

'It was so good Faith- you don't realise how good you are.' Di felt flustered now, then a memory came twanging back 'You see, I remembered what I'd always said, what we'd always said how one day you'd be an author, a brilliant author. Didn't we? And reading that I knew you could be, in fact, I know you can be, 'cos I saw the chance to make that dream come true. Don't be angry with me Faith, the agent liked it, she really did.'

'She did?'

'Yes, yes, she really did. There's just some bits need working on. My fault – you see I had to remember most of the first chapter and apart from the first line it seems I didn't quite get it right. I didn't have the right 'voice' she said.'

'Well, I don't suppose I'd remember it now.'

'You wouldn't have to; just retell it using your way of colouring it. And there's something else, more difficult to work on.'

'What?'

'Well – you see when I'd typed it up the story wasn't quite long enough, long enough for a book that is, so I added a few extra thousand words, to make it long enough. They may not have even looked at it if it was too short, you understand. So I wrote some, some more, you know, some sexy bits, with Hope and Raven getting it together a bit – tastefully – nothing sordid or kinky.'

Faith was silent beside her. Di flashed her a look, she was blushing. 'Faith, it's written it just needs you to make it sound right, to give it your voice.'

'No!'

'What do you mean 'No'?' Di squeaked.

'No – I couldn't, it wasn't like that in the story.'

'But Faith, it needed the extra words.'

Faith shook her head so firmly that Di saw the movement even though she was driving and began to think hard about her next words.

'Look, Faith, its not only about being an author, nor just about you – it's also about money. Look five or ten thousand pounds is going to go a long way to helping out while Andy gets another job. Look, I can help you with this bit, it's needed for the story. The agent, Alison, says it's needed for the' tickle', but the voice was wrong – please Faith?'

'We'll manage on my money - why are you so worried if I don't want to do it. Thank you for sending it off, but I don't think I can.'

'But *we* need the money!' Di blurted.

'What do you mean, we?'

'We – you and Andy, me and Paul. Oh Faith. Look you know Paul's in a bind with this job. In two weeks time we'll also be into overrun money – that's a thousand a day off our bill, and as we've been working a running total – bills direct to Lechwood, we'll end up owing him. And – and well, as I'd put the work in, extra chapters, setting it up, I sent the book off in both our names. Alison, the agent, said she really liked the name, it would look good on a cover – Diane Faith, get it? Oh, please Faith, please say you'll consider it?'

Di heard her sigh.

'I'll consider it – but I'll have to read it first.'

'There's a pal, brilliant – I always knew you had it in you. Look, you don't mind about the name do you?'

'I wouldn't want to write as Faith Warren anyway,' murmured Faith

'And you wouldn't really want all the bother of signings and publicity either would you?'

'Well – I don't know.'

'It would take time away from your writing the next novel.'

'The next?'

'Oh yes, the agent thinks Hope Jones could be the heroine of a whole series of books.'

'Really?'

'Really!'

'A series – I suppose.'

'See – it'll be great – a great team as ever. Look the first chapter is being sent back with the places I got it wrong marked – we've just got to change it, sign the agent's contracts and then she'll start to sell it to the publishers. Oh Faith, I can't wait.'

'If it took no extra time – if I could tell you the stories and you typed them up, the extra money would be worth it,' mused Faith.

'See, a great team.' sighed Di, relieved that the worst was over. She'd come to the changes to the end of the story later.

chapter twenty-four - Di

It had been a desperately busy fortnight. The chapter had come and Faith, dear Faith, had worked on it both at home and in the car. It wasn't long before they both felt it sounded just right and Di had printed it off and sent it, along with the signed contracts. Faith, blushing to her ears, had even read through the sex scenes with Di, but so often stopping to say what needed changing that in the end she said she'd take it away with her and find some time to work on them herself. Di supposed Faith would make use of the late evenings that Di was making to go and monitor the progress on the site, after all, she reasoned, two hours and the use of the office computer should go a long way towards the re-write.

The extension was still not complete; impossible for it to be when the place had been completely wrecked. Di shuddered to think what more damage could have been done if the perpetrators had not been disturbed. The suppliers that had come up trumps just before Christmas were wonderful and produced a repeat order in short time, and Paul had driven the men to work extra hours, often not returning until after midnight and without a trace of alcohol about him.

On the morning of the sixteenth Di woke knowing it was the date the building was due to be handed over. Every day after today would cost them a thousand pounds. Lechwood was already showing his malicious delight at getting the project for less than he expected and sometimes Di even wondered if he'd been behind the destruction, not Billy after all.

Just before Di hurried out, the post arrived. This time she recognised the letter from the agent even before opening it. She tore opened the letter quickly and scanned the contents. Alison was pleased, delighted, with the first chapter and was going to start 'putting out feelers' as she put it. Di felt exuberant as she drove to pick up Faith. The re-writing of the first chapter had certainly done something for Faith, she seemed to glow lately, her eyes shining in a way Di hadn't seen them for years.

'Guess what?' Di said almost as soon as Faith had buckled her seat belt, 'Got a letter from Alison the agent,' she answered her own question.

'What did she say – was it okay?'

'Was it okay – it was brilliant – here read it yourself,' Di grabbed the letter from the glove box and thrust it at Faith.

Faith opened it and read it while Di, beaming to herself, drove on.

'Well then?' she asked after a minute or two.

'Good. I only hope I can do the same with those other bits.'

'Course you will.'

'Hmmm,' Faith sounded dubious, but a quick look showed her face alight with the prospect.

'Look, I have to be home late again tomorrow, all right?.'

'Yes, okay.'

'If you take the disc in you could do some work on the story.'

'Perhaps.'

Di left it at that, not wishing to push Faith but somehow knowing that Faith would be able to perform the re-write with her usual skill. From then on, the day appeared to go downhill as far as Di was concerned; to start with, Lechwood was in the office before her. This meant she missed her early morning time to herself, and one look at his face told her he had something planned.

'Morning, my dear – no, don't remove your coat – we're off on a little visit.'

'Morning Mr Lechwood – may I ask where?'

'To see your dear husband and my gymnasium project – to see if by some miracle it is finished, which,' he smarmed as he closed the door behind them, 'I very much doubt.'

Lechwood drove his Mercedes much too fast through the city traffic, taking risks that made Di wince. From his glances in her direction she had the distinct feeling he was trying to demonstrate something to her. She gritted her teeth and forced her lips into a smile and thought him a greater fool than she'd previously imagined.

'Well, my dear, I must say that as things have turned out I'm not sure whose bargain I would have preferred to have taken. I'm not sure I'll enjoy your husband's bargain as much as I would have yours, but enjoy it I will.'

Di continued her smile and said not a word as they turned into the street where Lechwood's club was. He swung the car into the space marked 'Manager Only' and eased himself out of the car closing the door with a firm push. Di got out, closed the door and turned away from his smiling face, deciding to walk ahead of him, round the corner to the gym. She'd been there just three days before but still she found she had her fingers crossed.

The windows had already been replaced, as had the floor and the sanitary ware. They were having much more trouble getting another suitable chunk of wood for the reception desk, and the tiling wasn't quite finished. More sun beds were on order, she knew, due to be delivered in two days. Once more she cursed Paul for opting to do the whole job, finishing and fitting, if only they'd concentrated on what they knew, building work, but Paul had figured the margins were better on the fancy stuff and had put a bid in to do the lot. As it was they'd not make a penny profit having had to fork out twice for fixtures and fittings, and from now on, a whopping great loss. Di felt sick as she walked through the door and smelt the wet paint and saw the wrecked reception desk still in place.

They hadn't been there more than a minute when Paul came through wiping his hands on his trousers and offering to shake Lechwood's hand.

'Good morning.' Paul opened, his smile apparently as confident as ever, 'We've made up a lot of time since the vandalism set us back, do come and look round.' He flicked a glance at Di, who just raised her eyebrows at him.

'I intend to, Mr Harvey,' Lechwood said with a self satisfied smile.

Di was impressed, the place did look almost ready to roll, she felt her spirits lift.

'You've done well,' Lechwood muttered grudgingly, 'but you're still going to be in breach of contract which will cost you a thousand a day.'

'I realise that, sadly I did not plan for such an act of vandalism when I set my dates.'

'You agreed, no clauses, no get-outs!'

'I realise your position Mr Lechwood, but you must be able to see my predicament. It was hardly my fault that equipment was smashed, that we've run over our dates. I can assure you that we would have been ready on time if this had not happened.'

'You can *assure* me all you wish, what you should have done, boy, is to *insure* yourself against such a likelihood,' he almost chuckled at his quip.

'But,' Paul began before Di caught his eye – she shook her head, she knew that arguing with Lechwood was more than a waste of time – he could become quite obstinate if he felt he was being thwarted or crossed.

'A thousand a day, Mr Harvey,' Lechwood said, then stepping close to Paul, he growled in a low voice, 'Perhaps you should have left your wife to do the negotiating, I liked her guarantee, I'd have enjoyed myself and you could still have made a profit.' He stepped quickly back again as Paul's face clouded instantly, his neck muscles growing taut. Di could see his tightening fists and pleaded with him with her eyes, mouthing 'Leave it!' at him. She'd not been able to hear what Lechwood had said but she'd got a good idea from Paul's reaction. She saw Paul force himself to relax.

'I'll see you out,' Paul said, his voice tight and clipped.

Lechwood turned to look around him. 'Tasteful, I'll say that Harvey, tasteful,' then turned to go out the door. Di hung back long enough to get a word with Paul as they went out. Lechwood was standing in the street looking up at the fascia.

'You've done brilliantly – how long?'

'A week – with luck.'

'Five or seven days?'

'Seven.'

'Seven grand!'

Paul shrugged.

'Fine,' Lechwood boomed, 'Tasteful – can't have people thinking the wrong things just because it's attached to a nightclub. I'm sure you'll let me know when you're finished, Harvey,' he grinned, 'at a thousand a day.'

'After today,' Paul said bluntly.

'Oh yes, after today, of course. Goodbye, mustn't keep you from your work must I? Ha-ha. Come my dear, come back to our cosy little office, we'll leave Mr Harvey to get on,' and he winked at Paul. Di just shook her head at Paul once as she saw his fists tighten again, though he was probably doing it to keep himself under control.

Di was so furious with Lechwood that she barely spoke to him on the way back despite him keeping up a banter about gymnasiums he had known and how he wanted his one to be run. Di couldn't imagine that he even knew what working out in a gym was all about.

A thousand pounds a day, thank goodness for Faith's story she thought. Please God that some publisher, somewhere thinks the book is worth buying. Alison had seemed so positive, but Di had no way of knowing if this was the usual hype expected of agents or an exception. She crossed her fingers and wished, then just in case, prayed to a God who hadn't heard from her for years.

chapter twenty-five - Faith

I had been so easy to set up the lie with Susie – anyone the least bit curious would soon find out that 'Poor Faith, was having a bit of a hard time, husband out of work again, having to squeeze in her shopping at lunch time.' Susie was like that, not interested in malicious gossip but would soon put people straight if they wondered.

Faith was astonished at herself but had calmly added a shopping list to Wren's typed up work with the note that they would be collected lunchtime the following day. All the deceit was worth it once she was in Nick's arms. All her anxiety melted away as he kissed her and she responded. Oh, how she responded, as if she'd never been kissed before, she revelled in his sweet hard kisses. Her hands, his hands, traversed each others bodies, yet they remained clothed. Time stood chaperone and after a quick bite of lunch and, armed with a carrier bags of shopping, Faith had to leave and all but run to be back in the office on time. As she sat back in front of her computer screen she realised she'd not given The Story, or the amazing news about it being considered by an agent, a thought while she'd been with Nick. Besides it didn't seem real to her, more like a fairy tale, and like a proper fairy tale it was as frightening as it was magical.

When Di had first told her she had been shocked, it had seemed a bit like sharing a confidence with the whole world. Yet, hadn't that been what Faith had once wanted – to write – to be an author? Di made it all sound so easy, and when the first chapter arrived back with all those under-linings and comments Faith had decided that the only way to work on it was to read the chapter through, put it away and retell it to a tape recorder. She'd not had time to tell Wren about The Story but she'd not been inclined to tell Andy about it, but he had found out, had come across her in their room over the weekend using Di's tape-recorder, retelling that first chapter.

'What's going on?' his voice could be heard clearly on the tape, 'Have you cracked – talking to yourself?'

'No, Andy, a tape-recorder.. clunk.' The tape turned off, she'd had to explain. He'd sat his bulk on the end of the bed and listened. Faith wasn't sure if he was pleased or annoyed. She talked about the money, but his eyes slid away from her. She mentioned it helping Paul and Di and his attention was back. If Paul could benefit from Faith's work then sure as hell he could and at once he wanted to know how come Paul and Di were getting a cut when Faith was the storyteller.

Faith found herself defending Di's role in very uncertain terms, but somehow, as she explained, it became obvious to Andy. Of course, he said, it would take someone like Di to handle the stuff, sending it out to an agent, the business side of things. Suddenly Faith realised that Andy was, in fact, in love with Di, and probably always had been, though he'd never have got a look-in with his best mate Paul around. Love had been an abstract notion to Faith until she'd met Wren, now she knew what it felt like, now she knew the signs. To discover where Andy's true passion lay still came as a little bit of a shock. She wondered how much Andy had ever felt for her, she hoped for at least a fondness, though she knew now there'd not been love.

Monday had been full of wonderful news. First Di had said that the agent had loved the re-write of the first chapter, and it was true, all there in black and white, then Di had said she had to visit the site after work on Tuesday, and she hoped Faith wouldn't mind. No, she didn't mind, though Faith was not thinking of working on those other parts of the book, even if Di thought she might. She couldn't wait to see Wren at lunch time to tell him she'd have two whole hours free on Tuesday evening.

It was only as she arrived, breathless, at his apartment that she realised she'd not arranged for shopping. Annoyed with herself she tapped in the numbers and, without looking round in a suspicious manner, she entered the building.

He bounded down the steps and wrapped her quickly in his arms, then taking her hand, led her upstairs.

'A whole weekend,' he said, 'thinking of you, wanting to be with you – devastating!' and he closed his apartment door behind them and kissed her as if he was starved of her, pressing her gently against the wall. 'Oh, God, Fay, I love you. You have no idea what it's been like thinking of you and that bastard.'

'Don't, don't call him names.'

'He is, if he lays a finger on a woman or a child, he is – but all right, I won't if you don't like it.'

'I don't. Oh Nick,' she breathed as she clung to him. He caressed her back and pressed her close to him, his hardness firm against her body.

'Oh, Nick, Nick, Nick,' she whispered, her voice echoing the thrumming of her body.

'Come in here,' he tugged her away and through to the sofa, 'let me look at you.'

Faith sat beside him, half curled to look at his face, suddenly she reached forward and pulled the band from his hair. He shook it free.

'About time I had this cut to a respectable length, short, back and sides.'

'Don't you dare!' Faith retorted.

'Oh?'

'I love it, love to feel my fingers tangled in it. You know it was the first thing I noticed about you – before I knew who you were, even.'

'And me, being who I am, does that matter?'

'Not to me, but who I am does. I'm living a lie – wife and mother at home, secretary and harlot away.'

'Funny kind of harlot.'

'Not in my heart,' Faith whispered and smiled in response to the knowing sexy look he gave her. Faith hesitated a moment before telling him about Tuesday. That look said it all, her response merely confirmed it. If she came to him tomorrow after work then she knew there would be no going back. Her upbringing still strong in her veins warned, would he still want her, respect her, when he'd 'got his way'?' With one outstretched finger he stroked her face, down her neck, down to her nipple, his face full of love.

'Nick, are you at home after I finish work tomorrow?'

His eyes met hers, glowing and shining. 'Most certainly, if you are free?'

'Di's got another late meeting.'

'Wonderful.'

'I'm not sure…'

'Just come here,' he gathered her close to him, 'I love you Fay – we'll take everything slowly – as it comes. Only what you want,' Nick whispered into her hair, then his kisses travelled down her face until their lips met, tongues dipping and tasting each other. Faith felt herself melt inside, tingling, a void waiting, aching to be filled.

He found a few unopened food packets to put into a carrier for her to take back and they laughed at the games they had to play, but as Faith arrived back at the office with barely a minute to spare she knew it was the only way, that discretion was vital. In fact she realised that she'd not had any contact with Nick inside the office since she'd first visited his apartment, though he passed through her area at some time to drop off his manila folder of work for her.

She could tell Di had something on her mind as soon as she got in the car, instantly hoping it wasn't a change of plans about tomorrow. Di soon filled her in.

'Do you know what that creep did today? Only took me with him on a tour of the gym!'

'Lechwood took you along? That was a bit unnecessary wasn't it?'

'Completely – but I think he just wanted me there dancing attendance while he tried to belittle Paul in front of me. He's a snake!'

'So – you won't need to go to the site tomorrow after all?' Faith tried to keep the anxiety out of her voice.

'Won't I? Oh yes I will! Lechwood thinks he knows everything, but I saw a thing or two I want tied up pronto. Paul's got a

blind spot when it comes to the finer points of finishing off –
too used to building and handing over to decorators. This time
we're in for the lot and we can't hand over with plaster stuck
to light switches and jagged holes round where the pipe work
goes. He'll be none too pleased but it's got to be done!'

'No chance of Andy being any use?' Faith tried knowing that
Andy occupied was a happier Andy.

'Sorry Faith. Look even if we took him on at the moment I
don't know where the money would come from to pay him,
we're nearly up to the limit of our borrowings to pay the men
on site now, especially with the overtime.'

'Then take on Andy – day rate- and cut some overtime.'

'Hmm, might work – I'll talk to Paul.'

'Andy.' Faith started as she sat down to join the family eating
their evening meal, 'Di's got to go and look at the building
project after work tomorrow, so I'll be really late again.'

'What the hell! It's a bit rich keeping you away from home!'
Andy exploded, throwing down his cutlery. The children
stopped eating, mouths open and stared.

'But, you know Di's my only way of getting back,' then noticing
the children added, 'Eat your tea.'

'Bloody thoughtless. I suppose I'll have to bloody do that too,
feed them!' Andy's face was thunderous. 'No, tell her no – you
have to be home.'

'I can't Andy, be reasonable.'

'What the fuck are you going to do for two hours?'

'What do you mean?' Faith felt her face begin to colour up, 'I've
always got work to get on with,' she added as her mind cleared.

'No!'

'Andy!'

'No – I've had it with Paul. He's landed me in the shit and I've
not heard a word from him.'

'He's awfully busy, Andy.'

'Oh yes, he's awfully busy,' he mimicked her. 'He's working!'
Andy's voice became a whine.

Faith, not knowing what to say anymore, started to eat her
food, it tasting like cardboard in her mouth. As soon as she

could she slipped to the phone and called Di explaining how Andy was reacting. Something of Faith's anxiety must have transmitted itself to Di as she didn't tell Faith she was making a fuss, she just asked to talk to him. Faith suggested Paul might be better, Di seemed to have taken the hint and said she'd phone back.

Ten minutes later the phone rang, Faith, as usual, answered it, but it was Di, not Paul, asking for Andy. Andy went to the phone looking puzzled when Faith said it was Di for him. She watched him as his face softened and he nodded, she turned away, already sure that Andy would make no more trouble about her being late. She thought she must ask Di what she'd said to him.

Faith dressed with care the next morning, but in a way that would not arouse any suspicions. She wanted to look good but had to keep to her workday wardrobe, on the outside at least. It was difficult for her to concentrate on her work and nigh on impossible to respond to Susie's inane chatter over lunch. Already her heart had clattered too violently when Susie had mentioned Nick's name, and now, as the end of her working day arrived, she tidied her desk carefully and dawdled long enough to say goodbye to most of the other staff before she left the office herself. Feeling almost sick with apprehension she stepped out into the cold January night and slipped round the side of the building to make her way to his apartment.

She was at his apartment door before he appeared, he was just throwing the door open as she reached it. Wren smiled when he saw her and she knew that the worried frown that she'd worn all the way from the office had just melted away.
'Come in, my faerie Fay,' he whispered, pulling her to him, kissing her lightly, 'Come in, have a bite to eat, then we'll talk.' He led her through to where a light meal waited. Wren's eyes sparkled as he poured her a glass of white Bordeaux.
'What?' Faith giggled, 'Trying to get me drunk?'
'What else,' he smiled and lifting his glass, 'to us.'

Faith felt a shiver run through her as she lifted her glass, her 'to us' a whisper. Once she'd tasted the wine she couldn't finish her food, her throat felt too constricted with anticipation. She sipped again and again and felt the liquid warm her and his eyes, his beautiful Celtic grey-blue eyes, held her, entranced.

Nick put down his glass and stretched out his hand. Faith took it and they stood. Still holding her hand, watching her face all the time, gently he led the way through to the bedroom.

He stopped just inside the door, she knew why, her heart was beating so hard it seemed to be preventing her from taking a full breath, and the mild panic this produced must have been evident in her face. Nick stepped close to her, held her, kissed her.

'Oh Fay, I love you,' he breathed, 'I can wait if you're not sure,' and gave her no chance to answer as he kissed her mouth, caressed her neck and back, pressing her to him until her body, regardless of her panicked mind, responded, as she moulded herself to him, biting his lip, dipping her tongue.

'Yes, Oh Nick,' she broke away from him to lead him over to the bed.

He began to unbutton her blouse, until Faith took over as if she'd just decided that time was of the essence. He reached over to a switch and the lights dimmed low and golden, music played softly, something orchestral that she did not recognise. She had stripped off her blouse and bra when he stopped her by leaning forward and kissing her again, his fingers running circles around her nipples, kissing her, running his lips down her neck to her breasts, kissing, tasting, his tongue teasing her nipples and she wrested his hair from its band to cradle his head, running her fingers through and through his ebony hair.

The ache in her, the void, felt as deep as a cave, she lifted his head and kissed him fiercely, her hands pulling at his belt, then giving up, working on her own skirt, all the while kissing him, being kissed.

They lay side by side, looking into each others eyes. Nick began to stroke her naked flank, gently, then more firmly from shoulder to thigh, thigh to shoulder. Faith, feeling more daring than she could believe, reached down and felt him, subtly different under her hand to that she was used to, and the feel of him throbbing gently in her palm made her somehow desperate to feel him inside her. Her mind was on fire, never had she felt so wild, so excited or so ready.

'Oh Nick, Oh Nick.' she pushed him onto his back and slid herself astride him, he reached up his hands and, holding her at the waist, supported her as she guided herself on top of him. Precious moments he held her there, just inside, his eyes tightly closed, then they snapped open and he pushed her hips down, came thrusting up to fill that void.

She came, waves of heat flowed through her body, filled her with a sweet lassitude, yet when she opened her eyes he was smiling up at her.

'That's the most beautiful thing I've ever seen,' he murmured, 'your face, pure angelic, just then.' Which made Faith smile broadly then suddenly open her eyes wide as he gripped her hips and began to raise the tempo again and work his magic on her body until it sang and she rode him to her delight. Yet he was still there, ready for her again. Lifting her off him he laid her beside him and leant up on one elbow. Faith felt stars spin in her head and reached out to stroke his taut body, well muscled and smooth. Nick began to stroke her again, kissing her breasts, between her breasts, down to her thighs, his hair tracing lines of its own down and down her body. He kissed her back up to her lips, slipping and thrusting his tongue inside. She arched her back, held on tight to his hair with both hands, gave herself over to yet another melt-down.

He slid himself up over her, sliding deep within her.

'Are you ready Fay. I love you, I do so want you.'

'Take me,' she whispered, 'take me,' louder and louder as his speed and force increased.

'I never knew it could be so good,' Faith whispered, half to herself.

'Mmm, perfect,' he murmured affectionately in her ear, his body full on her but not his weight.

'Don't move.' Faith said, linking her ankles round his, 'I want to stay here forever.' She felt, rather than heard, his laugh. 'Bliss,' he husked, then softly slid from her and tugged the duvet to fall over them both.

chapter twenty-six - Di

Di slipped the car into a side street and was just locking up, ready to dash over to the newspaper offices when, by the glare of the street lights, she saw Faith hurrying towards her down the opposite street. Faith looked across the road and her face appeared to freeze as her eyes met Di's. Di waved and Faith checked the road again and crossed.

'Sorry.' Faith said as she waited by the passenger door for Di to unlock the car. 'I popped out for a bite to eat.'

'Are you okay?' Di asked, noticing Faith's flushed face before the car's interior light faded.

'Fine, never better, just been hurrying,' Faith replied and settled back waiting for Di to drive off.

They drove in silence for a while, Di wondering what it was that was bothering her about Faith.

'Andy okay about this evening?'

'After you spoke to him, yes,' Faith's voice was quiet and Di had to strain to hear over the engine noise. 'What did you say to him?' Faith continued.

'Pardon?'

'What did you say to him? He had such a temper on him when I asked.'

'Not much, just said it was a big favour to me. Didn't mention Paul, I got the feeling that it wouldn't have helped.'

'So you knew he'd give in for you?'

'Well,' Di hesitated, there was something strange about Faith's voice, 'he's, Andy's always been a sweetie to me – well you know that.'

'Yes, I know that,' Faith said flatly, and lapsed back into silence. Di drove on home wondering if she'd managed to upset Faith in some way and until she could decide, she didn't want to push it.

The next morning the old Faith was back. Whatever it was that Faith was in a grump about had obviously cleared, as the first thing she asked about was how Di had got on with her visit to the building site the previous evening. Di was relieved but thought it strange, as if the evening before hadn't even existed, though her visit was the reason for them being late home.

Di had her morning time in the office, sorted the mail, set the coffee percolator going, before Lechwood appeared. When he did, he paused close to her desk.

'Coffee, my dear, make it two, one for me and one for you,' he said, his voice oily and low.

Di shuddered but set about getting the coffee and took it in set on a tray. She placed it on his coffee table and started to return to her office to get her notebook.

'Where are you going?'

'To fetch my notebook, sir.'

'Don't bother, come and sit down, enjoy your coffee first,' smiled the Leech. 'I think you'll agree that there's a long way to go for completion on that job.'

'A week should see it done.' Di said boldly.

'I sincerely doubt it. I do not intend to accept it until I am satisfied that every little thing has been checked by an independent expert.'

Immediately Di could foresee problems and tried a little flattery to get her way.

'If you insist, though I would have thought, Mr Lechwood, that a man of your experience could use your own judgement, rather than spending money on someone else to do such a simple job.'

'Ah, but you forget, I do not have to worry about paying the man, after all I'm saving a thousand a day.'

'And of course he'll want to earn his fee!' Di spat, unable to stop herself.

'No doubt, so Di, my dear, this brings me back to a certain other guarantee you suggested before your husband offered terms I could not turn down.'

Di stared at her coffee cup, aware that she was beginning to colour-up, knowing that the Leech would think it was from embarrassment, yet unable to stop the fury she felt showing itself. How dare he want both their money and her body. He'd obviously not realised that the business would never have got in this position if Paul had her virtue to save, as he wouldn't have fooled around with scams then.

'Of course I would not want to seem greedy,' the Leech smarmed on, 'I am only suggesting a tête-à-tête lunch, lunch only, in exchange for say – a day's delay, a thousand pounds. A reasonable bargain, would you not say, my dear?'

Di didn't know if she could open her mouth and remain polite. Lunch, only lunch he said, for a grand, even with the news about the book a thousand pounds off would really help. Only lunch. Ridiculous to even offer to pay, a thousand pounds, why not? In the end she nodded. Yet she still felt demeaned and somehow tricked.

'Delighted, I have a place booked for lunch at the Belvedore. We will close up the office at one. Now you can go and fetch your little notebook.' Di stood, her legs carrying her mechanically as her mind raged against the man who had already booked a table for lunch before he proposed his so-called deal.

One o'clock came and Di deliberately did not go and tidy her hair and make-up. Mr Lechwood opened the door for her with elaborate charm, and the car door the same. Di felt waves of anger at his hypocrisy and flopped herself into the car seat as gracelessly as she could manage.

'Do you know the Belvedore, my dear?'

'Not at all,' Di said looking out the side window, fuming to herself that she was nobody's dear and most certainly not the Leech's.

'Ah, lovely discreet little place. Somewhat has the atmosphere of a turn of the century Gentlemen's club.' Not for you, then. Di thought – but made no actual comment. 'But they do a decent lunch, none of that public-school type of stodge you'd have got at such a club, no doubt,' Lechwood finished.

It was minutes of silence before they pulled up a side street and stopped before the porticoed entrance of the Belvedore, its blue and gold door standing open at the top of a short flight of steps. Lechwood, still the model of politeness came round to Di's door, presumably to open it for her, but she pushed it open as he arrived, climbed out and turned her back on him and closed it. He merely smiled and offered his arm, but Di ignored the gesture and strode off around the front of the car and up the steps, Lechwood actually hurrying after her.

'Relax, my dear,' he said drawing level with her at the door, 'there's no hurry, the boss isn't expecting you back in the office before he is,' and he chuckled at his own joke. Instead of turning into what was obviously the dining room Lechwood approached the desk and after a moment was rewarded with a key. Di stared, lunch with Lechwood was one thing, but a room key? What was he expecting? He came across the foyer, his slightly rolling gait reminding her of his thick meaty hands, incongruously decorated with gold rings.

'A private dining room,' he said, as he approached with the key dangling. Di didn't know what to say, a private dining room had not occurred to her – but at least it sounded safer than a bedroom. The private dining rooms were all on the first floor. Four of them, Lechwood told her as they ascended the broad staircase, often used for small meetings over lunch, anything up to a dozen, useful for business meetings of a private nature.

The room was decorated mostly in blue, with trimmings of gold fleur-de-lys. The dining table, of an extending design, must have been contracted to its minimum size and yet it still looked large set with white linen and silverware. A plush-covered chesterfield sat against one wall and a chaise-longue in the same fabric stood in the window niche.

Still with the same elaborate courtesy Lechwood ushered Di in and saw her seated at the table and indicated the menu by her place. 'Take your time choosing, my dear,' he said and sat himself down and picked up the menu, yet gave it barely a glance before laying it down again. Di looked at the list. Nothing was priced. Huh, a ladies-menu. she thought, and carefully chose what she hoped might be the most expensive dish. A waiter arrived and took their order and Lechwood began to make light conversation, trying, Di could see, to draw her out on subjects that never occurred to them in the office, which films, music and food Di enjoyed, and despite herself, with such self-centred questioning, Di ended up responding to his enquiries. All the while part of her was noticing how manipulative the man was, noting that these were techniques he was well practised in, realising that this was how he engaged his business partners and eventually got what he wanted.

They ate, with a bottle of wine on the table to share. Di eyed it suspiciously and decided to allow no more than one top up before she refused any more. What happened to the rest of the bottle she was not sure for when they ordered their desserts Lechwood ordered a second bottle, one that he waxed lyrical over, a bottle of Auslese, a special wine perfect for accompanying sweet dishes, and one that she must at least have a sip of. He over-half filled a fresh glass and handed it to her. It just wasn't in Di to simply put it down. Intrigued she took a sip, it was sweet and rich. She smiled and as she glanced up she saw her smile reflected in Lechwood's smile of triumph. The meal over, Di was aware of feeling very warm and when Lechwood suggested that she sat over by the window as it was cooler here, she acquiesced. She knew as soon as she sat down that, Don, as he insisted she call him on this occasion, would come and sit with her. What she didn't expect was, as he sat, for his hand to land on her thigh.

'Don't!' Di snapped. He didn't move his hand, merely moved his fingers, gently, massaging her leg through her skirt.

'Now then, my dear, don't play the virgin,' he murmured, 'you knew what you were doing when you made your offer.'

'One you turned down!' Di said and grabbed at his arm to tear his hand from her leg. His grip tightened even as she pulled, those massive fingers digging in deep, his weight holding his hand down on her thigh.

He laughed. 'So silly,' he said, then suddenly let go. Di flew up from her seat, whirling round on him.

'Just what did you think you were doing?

He smiled at her, 'I like a woman with spirit.'

'Spirit! This is a woman who does not take well to being treated like – like that!'

'My dear, as if I would ever treat you in any way that was not appropriate.'

'Lunch you said. Just lunch!' Di stood, hands on hips, spitting her words at him as he sat comfortably, feet firmly on the floor, legs apart, meaty hands resting on his own thighs. He pulled a face that said 'so what'

'And I thought you an – an honourable man,' Di added, seeking to wound his pride, turning on her heel and heading for the door. As she reached it she turned back to him 'And I believe it is time I was back at work,' she said, determined to leave anyway even if it meant walking back.

He laughed. The sound grated on Di, making her feel somehow silly and humiliated. He pushed himself to his feet and sauntered over to her.

'Temper, temper, my dear – I need to sign out as we go.'

In silence they descended the staircase and as Lechwood made his way to the reception desk Di went out into the cold of the January afternoon and stood shivering beside the car.

Fortunately for Di the Leech decided he had no need to be in the office for what was left of the afternoon, whether by design or discretion Di didn't care, she was just glad. She finished her work and sat for a moment wondering if she could bear working for the man any more. She felt sure that if she had not been so positive with her objections he would have pursued his own ends and the thought made her shudder. There was a difference, laying herself on the line when she knew there would be no comeback, she knew Paul would never have mucked around, never have let it happen, and having the Leech think he had the right to a free grope – urgh! Revolting!

chapter twenty-seven - Faith

Faith had realised her mistake somewhere during the night as she lay awake beside Andy's snoring bulk. She'd been so far in another world that she'd not even asked Di about the building project and Di would have found that strange, so Faith decided that on their way to work she must make sure to ask about it first thing.

Nothing seemed to really matter, at work she went through all the usual patterns, typing up correspondence, getting it signed and sent off. Chatting with Susie at break. All of it happening as if she were not really part of it. Yet as soon as lunch time came she snapped into a different mindset, everything about her body fizzed, she felt as if she were moving at such a speed that she wondered why no one gazed at her, a blur, as fingers fastened buttons, feet carried her out of the building.

She recited his door code as she marched along the streets and, heart thumping, face slightly flushed, she pressed the numbers in as if they were her own. The door swung open and she closed it tight behind her, expecting to hear his footsteps on the stairs even before she started to climb. Into the silence she stepped and briskly trotted up the stairs. She paused just before coming into sight of his door to catch her breath, sure now that he had missed seeing her arrive, knowing she was probably a few minutes earlier than he would expect. Breathing a little steadier she walked the last set of steps to his door and knocked. Silence. Then she noticed the bell-push, and feeling silly at having knocked, pressed it. Somewhere in the apartment she could hear a buzzer sounding, followed by silence.

Suddenly she did not know what to do, felt slightly silly standing there when he was not at home. At least, she thought, no one is going to walk up past me and see me standing here. The silence, made more intense by the distant roar of traffic, seemed to envelop her. She began to feel small, a sense of loss washed over her. What did she expect, a small voice hissed, after last night, after you gave him what he was after? Just another notch on the bedpost? More like a scratch, not worth a proper notch. Is that it? But he gave me a key! What do I do then, go in? But he's not there, what would be the point. Leave a note? That's it, Faith decided, her whole being aching with an ill-defined sense of rejection. She found her diary, ripped out a page and with the slim pencil wrote 'sorry to have missed you, F.' not even daring to sign it. Again she felt the wave of rejection and this time it swamped her, bringing tears to her eyes. She obviously didn't deserve love, not when she could be the cause of so much pain between her mother and father.

There was no letter box! Faith realised that the mailboxes were all downstairs, so she tried to push her note under the door. It folded up under her fingers as she tried to push it under. Frustrated she just knelt back to straighten it out when she heard him coming up the last set of steps. Her heart jolted, and tumbled over. Wren, wearing biker's leathers and carrying a helmet and a carrier bag first grinned at her, holding up the bag, then suddenly put it down and came to her.

'Fay, what is it?'

Faith just shook her head, it was just too silly to try to explain now he was here.

'Oh God!' he said as if he suddenly understood, 'Have you been here long? I'm so sorry, I'm an inconsiderate bastard – come here,' he gathered her into his arms and kissed her tears away. He lifted her to her feet, 'I went to get the shopping and got stuck in the most god-awful jam – couldn't even get the bike through,' he said, opening the door and drawing her in, dumping everything to hold her and to kiss her with all the fervour of contrition and reassurance.

Faith melted from the inside out, her core seemed to burn and she suddenly felt desperate to feel more of him. She pushed him away slightly and tugged at the zip of his jacket, opening it only to slide her hands beneath his t-shirt to run her hands over his skin, and he responded with his hands running smooth over her back.

'I love you Fay. I do. I do.'

She tipped her face and drank his hard kisses, never had she felt such a wild and desperate need to be with another person, she wanted him to take her, to make love to her, now. Her inexperience held her back but her body told her to do something before it imploded.

'Nick?'

'Mmmm?'

'Hold me.'

He tightened his grip.

'More – I need more.'

His turn to push her away a little, enough to look into her eyes. His own widening as the glint in them acknowledged her request.

'Now?'

'Now,' she sighed and taking his hand led him through to his bedroom.

'You know,' Nick said softly as then lay wrapped in each other's arms, 'every time I hold you I feel like someone just put in the last piece of the jigsaw, just so complete.'

Faith was silent for a moment, his words described the feelings she had so well, that together they became someone new. 'You feel that too?' she whispered, 'It's as if you are the other part of me.'

Nick nodded slowly, brought his hand gently beneath her chin and lifted her face for a kiss in which Faith lost touch with where she ended and he began, lost herself totally in him.

She took the bag of shopping into the kitchen when she arrived home that evening. Even holding the bag made her feel good. Andy had been home, she realised, though he appeared to be out now and there was no sign of the children either. Faith rang Cath to let her know that she was home, and Cath told her that the children weren't with her, that she'd sent them on home as Andy was at home. Faith thanked her and replaced the receiver. She began to wonder and worry where they could have gone, it was quite dark outside. She looked for a note and found none, but did find a dozen empty lager cans. There was nothing she could really do except wait until they turned up, reassuring herself that the children were with their dad – not out on their own. She began to make the evening meal, thinking that it wouldn't be long before they came back, but when all the cooking was done and they still hadn't turned up Faith began to worry in earnest, her own guilty conscience pricking her, suggesting to her that something dreadful had happened to her children and it was her fault.

At nine Faith tried Di, but Di had neither seen nor heard from Andy since that call put through to mollify him about the late night. Faith then tried Andy's parents. It was a long shot, the grandparents were fond of the children but liked prearranged visits, not approving of 'drop in anytime' visits, and apart from that they lived a good fifty miles away. Andy's mother sounded very worried when Faith asked if they were there visiting, and pursued the question wanting to know why Andy would go off with the children without letting Faith know where he was going, what was wrong? Faith explained that she'd come home to an empty house and had expected them to return any moment. It was only now that she was getting really worried. She promised that she'd phone back when she had news and decided in that moment to try casualty at the hospital. It took ages to get though, and even as she did so she thought she ought to have looked to see if they'd gone in the car. Just then the phone was answered and eventually they agreed to check if any of her family had been admitted. The message had just come back saying that no one of that name had been admitted when she heard the key turn in the latch.

Jilly ran down the hall into her arms, she was red-eyed but not crying. Jon came next followed by Andy, his trousers covered in a pink plaster dust.

'Where on earth have you been?' Faith heard herself shriek 'I've been beside myself with worry, phoned your mum, even phoned the flaming hospital!'

Andy's eyes, looking small and bloodshot, narrowed. 'Don't speak to me like that!' he snarled, and something in the way he moved made Faith push Jilly aside and behind her. 'I can go out if I like!'

'But the children …'

'They're my fucking children!' he spat and, stepping closer, pushed her with his forefinger, 'You hear, my,' push, 'fucking,' push, 'children,' push, 'and if I want them to go for a walk with me, they do!' his finger now just beneath her nose. 'Get it?'

Faith nodded just enough to show without hitting her nose on the end of his finger. He turned abruptly and stumbled off into the living room. 'And where's my tea?' he bellowed.

Faith rescued the dried-up meal and quickly took a tray in to him, telling the children to eat in the kitchen. They needed no encouragement to stay.

'What happened?' Faith whispered to Jilly.

'Dunno, Dad just said – we're going for a walk and we went. Oh Mum, we went for miles and we went out of the lights into where it was dark. Then,' Jilly whispered back.

Jon was shaking his head.

'What Jon?'

'Nuffink.'

'What then Jill?'

'Then, well, then Dad says stay there, and he left us, for a little while, then he comes back.'

'Laughing,' added Jon.

'What at?'

Jilly and Jon looked at each other, but both shrugged.

'But, you've been crying,' Faith said to Jill.

'Because she whined, and Dad fetched her a clip round the ear!' Jon hissed triumphantly. Faith's eyes felt as if they were burning.

That night, when Andy came up to bed it did Faith no good pretending that she was already asleep. He signalled his intentions as soon as she felt the bed sag on his side. His hand reached around her curled body and pulled her over onto her back. Meaty fingers slid up her legs to the top of her thighs and held her.

'Guess what,' he grunted as he heaved his body over her. Faith could not guess anything, her mind was in revolt. Andy's lovemaking had never given her any joy, just a sense of relief that he'd not squashed her, now his touch made her want to shrink away from him, made her shudder. Somewhere inside her head she was screaming No!

'I've put the shits on Billy's project,' he grunted, every word timed with a dry thrust, 'Fucking screwed him, screwed him proper, blocked his fucking drains up,' he stopped moving, held himself above her, deep and throbbing, then toppled off onto his side of the bed. Faith reached for her box of tissues, mopping herself, squeezing herself inside to expel as much of him as she could. She didn't ask exactly what he'd done to Billy. She didn't want to acknowledge he was even in the room, she felt defiled, empty and sick.

chapter twenty-eight - Di

Di slammed the door behind her. It had been a hell of a day, Monday, and the Leech had been in the office all day. Twice, *twice* he'd reminded her that their over-run on the project had saved him five thousand, and that was with their lunch-date discount. Di had fought with her sharp tongue all day, nasty snappy rejoinders echoing in her head, but she daren't do anything further to upset the Leech.

The phone started ringing as soon as she stepped into the shower but a frisson of hope made her grab a towel and rush through to their bedroom to pick it up.

'Great, caught you home at last!' Alison Enderby's voice rang out from the earpiece as Di answered the phone.

'Just got in,' Di said.

'Are you sitting down?' Alison went on, 'I've got great news. We are currently in a two house auction. It was three but Blossomhill dropped out at a hundred thousand.' Di gasped, then wondered if she understood correctly, but Alison ploughed on. 'The latest, and I suspect the last, bid is from Capricorn Publishing.'

Di waited, for how much she wondered, hardly daring to ask.

'Hello? Diane?'

'Yeah, here. Um, how much?'

'Oh, sorry – two hundred.'

'Two hundred thousand pounds?' Di said slowly.

'Yep. It's not quite that straightforward though. This would have to be for a two-book deal – fifty percent on signature on this book, fifty on approved presentation of the second book manuscript by a set date, minus, of course, my own fee.'

'Of course – and well earned.' Di was stunned. Ten grand to help them out of the hole they were in would have been great but, she quickly worked out what they would get each, ok, so forty now, forty later. She could give up working for the Leech. Faith could write – she could type. 'What happens next?' she asked.

'Next, after the finalisation of this bid the editor will want to meet both of you. Have you decided on the persona, who will be Diane Faith up front?'

'Yes, just about.'

'Great, so that's my news – I'll let you know when it's finalised.'

'Thanks, thanks. I'm just gobsmacked!'

'Well it might help with the problems you were concerned about. Just as long as you can promise that second book. By the way a brief synopsis of the next book would not come amiss, these publishers can get a little jittery at the last moment, when the heat of the auction is off, unless they've some proof that it's not going to be a one off.'

'Yes, I remember you telling me. We're loaded with ideas,' Di said, her grin subdued and her fingers crossed.

Di didn't wait to tell Faith, she rang right away. Faith sounded as disbelieving as she had felt herself, but when Di had said they could both give up work and become one writing team working from home, Faith sounded less sure. This worried Di for a moment, until she asked about whether Faith was able to think up another story for a book and Faith laughed.

'Easy as winking,' she said, and Di had explained about the synopsis. Faith had said she'd jot down a few and they could take their pick. When she rang off Di danced round the room, in her mind's eye they were meeting the publishers, she in her smartest, Faith quiet in the background, the publishers beside themselves because they couldn't decide which synopsis was best and they wanted them all, each at eighty grand a time, and they loved her persona of Diane Faith and life was wonderful, and best of all she could tell the Leech where he could shove it! At this the knot on her towel slipped and she grabbed it up and chased back into the bathroom to finish her shower.

Paul arrived home well past midnight. Di had given up waiting for him and gone to bed, the meal she had prepared left covered in the microwave. His weary footsteps on the stair woke her and she turned on the bedside light as he came in.

'Sorry,' he whispered.

'Okay, it's very late?'

'Just had to finish the bit we've been working on all day,' he slumped onto the bed bringing the scent of paint and filler into the room. 'I'll grab a shower,' he muttered and pushed himself off the bed again.

Di lay there thinking how very tired and drawn he looked, all the usual spark gone again. She felt a pang of concern, the recent memory of his fatalistic drinking flashed into her mind, but, she countered, this time it would be different. This time they'd have the stake money to set up in business again, thanks to The Story. She smiled to herself and dosed off, intending to tell Paul the good news as soon as they woke.

Someone had lit a fire right next to Di's shoulder, she could feel its heat scorching her skin, she tried to move away but there was something holding her back, something ... she woke. The heat was still there, but there were no flames. Paul was lying on his back, his face flushed, breathing laboured, his body radiating heat. Di hardly had to put her hand to his forehead to check his temperature, but she did so out of some kind of ritual. It was burning.

'Paul,' she whispered, 'Paul? Paul? Wake up!'

He barely moved, his eyelids flickered, his lips moved together and apart again. Suddenly worried Di shook him and told him to wake up again. This time, with a shake of the head Paul opened his eyes.

'God, I feel rough,' he muttered.

'That's nothing to how you look,' Di said with a smile. 'I think we'll get a couple of paracetamol down you and I'll bring you a nice hot cup of tea.'

'No good – I've got to get going.' He hauled himself up the bed, the effort causing a sweat to break out all over his frame.

'I know – but have the tea and paracetamol first,' Di said firmly and went downstairs. As the kettle boiled she wondered how much work there was left to do, whether the boys could get on with it in his absence and whether they'd put in the graft without the boss around. She hoped they would, as she'd only seen Paul looking as bad as this once before, when off the booze, and that time he had flu and was truly laid up for a week and barely operational for a second week.

She had to wake him again to get him to take the tablets and drink the tea. Looking him straight in the eye she told him she didn't think he was fit to go into work today.

'I've got to love. Were so close, and you know that every day counts.'

'I know, of course I know. Though things aren't as bad as they seem.'

'Oh yes they bloody are!' he spat, bloodshot eyes bulging with anger. 'It'll be all this effing work and deeper in debt than when we effing started.'

'No!'

'Yes!'

'No – this time we've got a miracle to bail us out.'

'It'll take a miracle.'

'Remember that story – Faith's and ours? You know you said to send it off to someone? You know I did?'

He nodded.

'That's the miracle – it's been in an auction between interested publishers and they've bid two hundred thousand pounds for the book. Two hundred thou! That'll be eighty odd for us, eighty odd for Faith.'

'You're joking?'

'Not a bit – okay so it's for a two book deal – that is Faith's got to write another one, and it's in instalments, half now half later, but we can live with that – it'll pay off the Leech and give us a little stake money.'

Paul sighed, his breath ragged, and leaned back on the pillows. 'You are a wonderful woman, know that?'

Di smiled, 'And you are not going anywhere today – I'll go into the site before work, chivvy them up a bit, anything I must get them doing they won't think about for themselves?'

'I'm sorry it was such short notice for going in early Faith,' Di said as Faith climbed in the car, 'but Paul's really sick, probably flu, remember about four years ago when they both got it?'

'Umm?'

'Well there was no use in letting him go in the state he was in – burning up – so I've just got to let the fellas know what he desperately wants done today – and from the list he's given me that's just about everything.'

'Will they work while he's off?'

'Damn well hope so! Oh, Paul couldn't believe the news about the book either. Dumbstruck! What did Andy think?'

'I er, I it wasn't convenient to tell him last night. Besides, I don't think I believe it myself – quite.'

'But you've started thinking about some ideas for this second book, haven't you?'

'Oh, yes, that, of course, do you want to hear some, roughly?'

'Are they sequels? You know – taking Hope Jones into some new adventure?'

'Well, I'll do one like that, but the ones I've jotted down don't involve her, that story seemed to come to a neat end.'

'What? You left them in the garage – I had to finish it off – riding into the sunset and stuff.'

'Oh!'

Di could tell by the sharp gasp that she'd blundered. She'd forgotten that she'd not mentioned the ending to Faith yet, nor the need for it to be rewritten in the 'voice' and with the demise of the delicious Raven. She laughed. 'Well it was a bit like the sex scenes, I added more to make up the number of words, but you were completely right, the agent said it was all too tidy and Mills and Boony, in fact she wanted us to go over the ending again to make it more – raw and – edgy and to leave it with maximum potential for sequels. So you're right again, it was tied up too much for a sequel but with the ending that Alison has asked for it wouldn't be? Do you see?'

'Yes, I think so? When do I hear the new ending?'

'Whenever you like, only not this morning, let's have a look at the stuff I sent off and how much better this would be, over a glass of wine one evening, soon?'

'Okay.' Faith said quietly, so quietly that Di took her eyes off the road to steal a good look at her friend to make sure she wasn't crying. Damn Paul being ill, if she'd not been so distracted she'd never have blurted out the truth.

'Hi Andy? It's Di. Look I need Faith's advice on something, be a love, see if she could come over this evening for an hour or two?' ....

'Thank you, you're so kind to me. Look Paul's come down with flu, I know he was going to get in touch to see if you wanted a bit of work, while we've still got it, perhaps you wouldn't mind being boss in his place for a few days, basic rates I'm afraid, you know we're into overrun time, a thousand a day?' .....

'Great, I'll put Paul on the line, he'll tell you what wants doing, tell Faith I'll see her about half seven then, bye, thanks Andy, here's Paul.'

'I can't write that.' Faith's colour was high from reading the sex scenes that Di had added. The truth was that they reminded her too much of her relationship with Nick Wren.

'Of course you can Di said smiling 'You can do anything with words. Look, I knew you wouldn't like it that's why I tried, but every bit I tried on my own wasn't quite right for Alison, she says that these bits don't have 'the voice' – yet she wants this bit in.'

'I don't see that it's necessary to the story.'

'It probably isn't, but it is necessary to the sales figures – you see the story has everything else – intrigue, violence, murder but, apart from a friendly interest, it hasn't got the sex – and it needs it – those two, they're made for each other.'

'Well,'

'You only have to rewrite what I've done – give it your voice.'

'All right, I give in – but what about the new ending – you haven't told me about that yet.'

'All in good time Fay, let's get this sorted first, eh, I'll fetch us a glass of wine.'

'Whew!' thought Di as she got yet another refill of wine, 'Who'd have thought it – perhaps Andy was better in bed than he looked.' Faith's re-rendition of the sex scenes had added something indefinable but enough to make a tingle of sexual excitement run through Di as she re-read it. Now for the really tricky part she thought to herself as she returned to the study where she'd left Faith reading the amended ending asked for by Alison. As she entered she knew they had a problem – Faith was sitting stock still staring at the manuscript.

'Okay?' Di asked with as carefree a voice as she could muster. 'Does he have to die?'

'Well, apparently, yes.' Di began, then rushed on before Faith could add anything else. 'It's all to do with having a sequel at some point – or even a whole series – you see Alison sees this character as the mainstay of a series of adventures – like Poirot, or - or that forensic scientist woman, you know, imagine it, your creation – a whole series – perhaps TV might get interested.' she added as the inspiration hit her. Di stopped, there were tears in Faith's eyes. 'What's wrong? You're supposed to be happy?'

'It's silly,' Faith sniffed, 'ignore me.'

'Of course not. What is it?'

'Well these characters – they've become so real, you know, it hurts to lose one, to be killed like that.'

'But you've got horrible things happening to others!' Di said surprised out of her comforting frame of mind.

'Yes, but that's different, that's what they were made for – Raven wasn't – he just wasn't. It's so silly – ignore it. It's too important. You need the money and if this will do it – Wren must die.' She faced Di – her eyes shining. Di had heard Faith say Wren and for a moment had not recognised Faith's mistake, intent on hearing only that Faith would re-write, but the slip of the tongue made Di wonder if every character had been based on someone that Faith knew, not just herself and Faith. None of that mattered though, as the important thing was that Faith had said 'Yes' and she was ready to re-write the ending.

Di shuddered a little as she read the new ending. She knew what was coming – should have known as Alison had plotted it out, but what Faith had done with it was wonderful. Suddenly she could see it all happening, feel the knife slide in past the leather of his coat, the first surprise of pain, the second deep malicious thrust as the knife found his heart, the wrenching free as he toppled back – and the blood. The blood and Hope's anguish. Di shook her head, the pictures and the feelings were too vivid she wanted to shake them from her head.

'Absolutely brilliant,' she murmured. And that was not all, Faith had left Hope there with the dead and injured women, Chris Raven, dead, his head cradled on her knee – it cried out for a sequel, even Di wanted to know what happened to Hope next, where the next book was. It was pure magic. 'I'll send it off to Alison first thing.' She grinned. Faith beamed back, her face flushed.

'Di!' Alison's voice rang out loud and clear through the phone a couple of days later. 'Wonderful ending – couldn't have done better myself – ha ha – now look, it is imperative that we get you both up here, pronto, papers to be signed, people to meet. When can I arrange it for, is next Wednesday suitable?'

'Well, I would have thought so. I'll check with Faith but I think she should be able to get time off work for then.'

'Good, do it – if I don't hear from you by tomorrow afternoon I'll go ahead, okay?'

'Okay. Um, how long will we need to be in London?'

'I'll book you in somewhere, get the morning train down and reserve a ticket back for the next day – I'll get you booked in for a tart-up and bring your best to wear – we'll see.'

'Pardon?'

'They may need publicity shots while you're here, might run a pre-publishing promo on you. Always worth being ready.'

'Of course.' Di replied, her head spinning with the promise of the whole adventure.

Di couldn't leave the subject any longer. They were already more than half-way to London and she'd not got Faith's go ahead to be the public persona of Diane Faith.

'Fay? You know they want one person to represent the persona of Diane Faith to the public?'

'You said something before.'

'Yes, well, it's very important that the public have someone they can relate to when they think of the author. I thought that you might like me to do it for you, it would take up a lot of writing time, and it means a lot of talking in public, which you don't like much.'

'I don't know about that.'

'Oh, come on – you go all red at the first hint of having to say something to someone you don't know,' Di retorted, and instantly wished she hadn't as she saw the look of determination settle on Faith's face. She recognised it from old – Faith in fighting mode. 'Well, of course you *can*, you can do anything you set your heart on, I know that better than anyone, but would you really want all that hassle?'

'But they're my stories. How could you possibly talk about them?'

'That's not what its about – publicity – it's more about shaking hands with people, signing books, smiling a lot – you know.'

'I'm still not sure – I'd like to be myself. Can't they have both of us?'

'Apparently not. Alison says that co-authors are not liked – that is - for publicity purposes.'

Faith was quiet for a while. She closed her eyes. Di sat watching her, waiting for her answer, knowing that she'd said as much as Faith would allow her for the moment, praying that Faith would see reason and give in – after all it did make sense and, as far as Di was concerned it meant that Faith's good fortune would forever be linked to her – after all any publisher would surely baulk at a change of the persona at a later date.

The train rumbled on and after a while, when Faith had given no answer, Di ran through as many different arguments as she could think of, to persuade Faith that she was right. Faith listened but did not argue the case either way, so Di decided to change her talk to inconsequential things in case she was only making things worse for herself.

'Okay,' Faith said as the announcement came for their station. 'though on one condition.'

'Pardon?' Di had in the intervening desultory chatter about the journey lost the question that Faith was suddenly answering, though in truth it was all that had been on her mind.

'You can be the persona of Diane Faith but I want my own and full name to be acknowledged in the credits.'

'I don't know – I suppose – we'll ask Alison,' Di finished lamely, hoping it could be sorted out somehow.

chapter twenty-nine - Faith

The first day back at work after the London trip seemed like a
fantasy in itself. London had been weird, a whirlwind of
meeting people, of listening to advice, of making decisions and
of fighting. Faith read the contract offered her after Alison had
explained it, had asked questions until she felt she really
understood. She could tell that no one seemed to like her taking
up so much time but it was important to her, so she ploughed
on. Eventually she explained that she needed to have her own
identity in evidence on the book somewhere, Faith Evans –
writing as Diane Faith, or some such declaration. Alison had
taken her aside, leaving Di behind this time, and talked deeply
and frankly to her about the book trade and the personality cult
of the author. Faith had simply replied that in truth Di had been
no more than a scribe, and, though she loved her dearly and
would not exclude her from either this or the second book in
the deal, she wasn't sure that it would go on forever.

The look on Alison's face had at first been thunderous, but
as she stood and regarded Faith she began to smile, albeit a little
grimly.
'Lifelong friends, eh, but she's not above taking advantage, is
that it?' she asked slyly.
'Lifelong friends,' agreed Faith. 'But my life may not always
follow the same lines as hers, I'm being realistic. Look, I'm
grateful to her for this, for finding you, I probably would never
have got the courage to do it, which is why she's in for a half
cut on this deal, but would you tie yourself to someone if you
didn't have to?'
At that Alison nodded. 'Okay, you're on – though you'll have
to be willing to promote your books yourself – no way will they
wear you changing from a tall blonde to a petit brunette
between books.'
'Fine, I'll learn to do that.' Faith answered
'And I think the non-de-plume Diane Faith may have to stick,
it has a certain ring about it that I think you'd be wise to keep.'

Faith thought a moment – at least the name held neither Di's surname nor her own married surname, she'd decided against that earlier and had planned to use her maiden name – Diane Faith? Hadn't she often wished she was Di. She'd smiled to herself and nodded. 'Fine,' she said then gritted her teeth ready to face Di.

Di was not happy with the decision. Faith could tell that her friend had been looking forward to the role, but in her deepest bones Faith knew she had done the right thing for a change, and this was such a change, to do something for herself *and* to risk upsetting Di, an unprecedented combination.

After all that had happened the office seemed so dull and common-place, she longed to tell everyone and say goodbye to the sneering Ms Robertson and the pedantic Mr Watson, but Alison had asked for her to wait just a short while, only a month, it didn't seem long when said but already Faith could tell that it would be a month made up of very long days.

Susie arrived a little late and squealed with delight to see Faith. 'Oh! You're back, good!' As if she'd been away a week instead of just two days. 'I thought you might not be in until Monday and I just can't wait to show you – look!' She held out her left hand, the delicate elegant fingers waved and the third one was now decked with a stunning engagement ring.
'Wow, at last,' breathed Faith, for the search for the perfect ring had taken ages, until Susie's fiancé had taken her off to a craftsman jewellers and they had a special one designed and made, and here it was, a little over elaborate for modern tastes perhaps, but a truly formidable engagement ring.
'Isn't it just beautiful?' Susie said holding out her hand at arms length and admiring the ring, 'John was so particular, it had to be something unique.'
'Well he sounds an all round unique person himself Susie, I'm so pleased for you.'

'You are? You really are? I had wondered sometimes whether you were, you've been sort of distant since I told you we were getting engaged.'

'Oh Susie,' Faith hugged her friend, feeling guilty as she was well aware what and who had been preoccupying her thoughts, 'Of course! I've just had other things on my mind recently – that's all. I am really and truly pleased for you. Have you named the happy day?'

Lunch time came and Faith quickly grabbed her coat and bag and left with a wave to Susie and a mouthed 'shopping'. As usual she walked briskly to Wren's place and punched in the entry numbers. Once inside she breathed easier and trotted up the stairs. Alison had said not to tell anyone about the deal yet, but Faith was going to make an exception. In fact she was wishing that she'd talked to Nick about the book deal before she went, she'd signed the deal along with Di, the two book deal with Di taking half, she knew she was morally right to do so but was concerned that she may have made a mistake, that Di could have some hold over her future deals, Nick would have known what to do. She knew that to anyone else she would seem crazy to split the money evenly, but to Faith it seemed so much money and she knew she wouldn't have had any of it, if it hadn't been for Di's initiative and instinct. She'd only seen Nick once between Di asking her to get the day off and the trip, and somehow she'd not mentioned it. She wasn't sure whether it was because she couldn't believe it herself or just the sheer fact that their limited time together meant that conversations were kept to a minimum. Whatever, today she would tell him.

She rang the bell and turned her key for his door simultaneously. She knew that the look on her face must have been as shocked as that on the face of the beautiful young woman who was walking towards the door to open it. Tall and dark she stopped and took a step back, one hand instinctively going to her chest the other touching the wall as if for balance.

'Oh, sorry,' Faith said without thinking, her mind too busy whirling with different meanings. She must be in the right apartment. So where was Nick and who was this? A new conquest? Certainly not the cleaner.

'You must be Faith,' The young woman said, her voice slightly accented with American tones.

Faith nodded, she did not trust her voice further, though she doubted that a new conquest would have used her name so lightly.

'Nick said you'd probably be over, he should be back any moment, something about getting some shopping – he flew out of here like a banshee. Come in, make yourself comfortable.'

'Yes, he does some shopping for me,' Faith said stupidly as she sat down on the edge of the sofa.

'Strange, but then he's been most mysterious about you,'

'He has?'

'Oh yes. Look Angel, he says, I've met someone special, but it's very complicated, when you meet her you must be very discreet. Now that's something that makes me very curious.'

'So is your curiosity satisfied?' Faith asked, quietly adding, 'Mine isn't.'

'Yours? Oh, let me guess – you have no idea who I am. Oh, gosh, I'm sorry.' Angel laughed, 'Faith, I'm Nick's daughter, Angie.'

'Oh!' not something that Faith had considered, Nick not having mentioned any family, instantly she wondered about his wife and whether that was the reason he'd not said anything.

'And you didn't know about me, did you?' Angie added perceptively.

'Huh! No, obviously I don't know much about your father at all.'

'Sounds like Dad, though he wasn't always like this,' Angie's voice dropped to a whisper.

'Like what?'

'Like quiet and secretive.'

'I see,' Faith began but her next words were taken from her as the door burst open as Nick returned.

'Has she – oh yes, sorry I wasn't here Faith,' he dumped a bag of shopping by the chair and leant over Faith giving her a gentle kiss on her temple. 'You've met Angie – I see. I really had hoped to be back before you arrived, like an idiot I lost track of time.'

'You could have left the shopping,' Faith said softly, wishing he had been there from the start and suspecting he'd arranged to be absent.

'No, it might give you problems.' Faith nodded and smiled, he was right of course. Angie was watching them her dark eyes bright, a smile on her face. Glancing at her Faith recognised the family likeness.

'You didn't tell me about Angie,' she said softly.

'I thought the idea of a nineteen year old daughter might frighten you off,' Nick said with a laugh, but one look at his eyes and Faith knew that there was more than a grain of truth in what he was saying.

'Yet you knew all about Jilly and Jon.'

'You've got children?' cut in Angie, her eyes flicking from Nick to Faith and back to Nick.

'Yes,' Nick answered, 'and, no I didn't tell *you* about them either. One thing at a time, eh?'

'Oh you're really too much sometimes. I don't suppose you'd had even told me about Faith here, if she hadn't been going to come round today and I just inconveniently happen to be here.' Angie's eyes flashed with a childish petulance.

'You're possibly right. As I told you love, this is complicated, and we need to be discreet and ..'

'Ahh! And a husband! I get it.' Angie's eyes were sharp and Faith felt them scour across her, re-evaluating her.

'Angie, please.'

'And I thought her so nice.'

'She is.'

'But you're a hypocrite!' she spat and turned to face Faith, 'Said he'd never, *never*, break up anyone's marriage. Isn't that right?'

'He isn't,' Faith said softly, suddenly knowing that this was the truth. Angie's eyes narrowed.

'Divorced?'

'No. Just..'

236

'Just you met Dad and suddenly you want out.'

Faith shook her head. 'It's far too long a story to tell you, but it wasn't good, long before I met Nick,' she said, a catch in her voice.

Wren slid down beside her, his arm round her, holding her gently; he looked across at his daughter. She stared back at first, then lowered her eyes.

'Okay, if you say so. You're too damn secretive, you know that. It only makes people suspicious,' she said. Nick continued to look her in the eye. 'And I'm sorry for,' Angie began.

'For the unpleasant way I've treated you both?' Nick suggested.

'I'm not a little girl! I'm sorry I didn't think before I spoke. Perhaps I should have known better, but, Faith, get Nick to tell you everything. Get him to tell you about Mom, about Ethiopia and the farm before you commit yourself to anything,' she added quickly, her eyes flicking from Nick to Faith and back as if expecting an interruption.

'She's right, I ought to tell you everything – and would if ever we have the time.'

'Time!' Faith yelped as she suddenly looked at her watch. She had less than a quarter of an hour to be back in the office.

'I'm sorry, love, this hasn't been the most – relaxing of lunch-breaks – and you've not even had anything to eat.'

'Never mind,' Faith smiled, 'I can do without, I have to go. It's been good to meet you, Angie. I hope we'll see each other again, and thank you.'

Angie smiled back at her. 'I think we may, bye, but don't let him bully you.'

'No chance,' Faith said softly, then turning to Nick, 'walk me down?'

'Of course,'

As they left his flat Wren turned Faith around and kissed her, whispering, 'Sorry, for all that. I should have told you before – there just didn't seem to be a right time.'

'Know what you mean, where does our time go?' Faith whispered, 'and I've something important to tell you.' They'd reached the last landing and Nick turned a concerned face towards her. 'Don't look like that, it's not bad.'

'Phew!'

'I've just got to tell someone. You won't believe it though.' About to tell him that she'd just signed half of a £200,000 book deal it suddenly struck her again as quite unbelievable.

'Of course I will.'

'I've written a book, and, and yesterday I signed a two book deal that's worth,' she opted to mention only her own income, 'ninety thousand pound to me.' The look on Nick's face made her laugh. 'I said you wouldn't believe me.'

'You say so, I believe you and it's wonderful, but – you never said anything about writing.'

'Ah, and you never said anything about a daughter, or any of the rest of it – I've got to go. Love you, see you Monday?' She kissed him quickly before running down the stairs. He caught her up at the door, pressing his hand against it.

'You can't just go, what's the book about?'

'It's just a story, a novel. I must go, I'll be late.'

'What does it matter, they won't sack you, and if they did, it wouldn't matter now, would it, tell me?'

'It matters Nick, love you, bye.'

'As ever – take care.' Nick kissed her quickly as she slipped out of the door, clutching her shopping tightly, ready to run.

The weekend swept by, Andy was in a good mood, working as boss in Paul's place had made him feel big and needed, and then Paul had kept him on when he returned. He had worked the men hard for Paul then had gone straight to Paul's home each evening to report on progress and get any new orders. Paul, no longer anxious about the money, had been pleased to have Andy oversee the work, feeling as grotty as he did. He was just about recovered, though his exhausted state before he went down with the Flu had exacerbated the symptoms, but with Andy's help he had offered Lechwood the Wednesday as hand-over day. He figured that it would have cost him twelve thousand in 'fines' plus overtime for the lads, but with the money coming in from the book deal Paul wasn't over worried, Andy said. Andy was sure that Paul was on the up again, and that the money from the book deal was going to mean a new era of Paul and Andy as partners.

Andy even talked of investing half of their share of the book deal so that he and Paul could be real partners in the next venture. This happy Andy was the one Faith had known in the early days, but the difference was she now knew that she had no love for him, that he had probably not loved her and the old sense of relief at being chosen and not harmed was not enough, and not even true. The knowledge that she could make her own living, not just surviving on her secretary's pay, but a living where she could be at hand for Jilly and Jon as well as earning enough to support them well, made her look at life from a new perspective. It was as if she had only just grown up, that she had been a long time growing.

Monday dawned as one of those crisp blue-skied days that herald a beautiful but cold day. The light broke as they made their way up the motorway and made Faith think of the coming spring and deep inside she felt both happy and excited. She left the muggy warmth of Di's car just outside the newspaper offices as usual, and with a wave and a shiver she trotted to the doors. Inside the heating was on full blast sending wafts of hot air down the inner face of the door. She was soon hanging up her coat and scarf, turning on her computer and checking on her plants. She watered each of them then settled down to see what work had been left for her to do. Mondays were often busy as both editors had time to build up a backlog of work for her.

She was halfway through her first letter when she began to wonder where Susie was. Though Susie was sometimes a little late it was way past that sort of time. When she hadn't appeared by break time Faith assumed that Susie must be ill or something. As she collected her coffee, Annie Morcambe was just behind her.

'Isn't it awful about Susie,' Annie whispered to Faith, her long red hair rippling as she shook her head as if in disbelief.

'What?' Faith asked quickly, 'What's happened?'

'Oh, sorry. I thought you'd know already. Susie phoned us in personnel to say she wouldn't be in for a while, she can't type you see. Her hand was crushed.'

'Oh, God! Poor Susie, how did it happen?'

'I don't know, I don't think they asked. Apparently she's distraught, her new ring was wrecked.'

'Grief!' Faith gasped. 'Poor Susie!' She left her coffee and headed back to her desk. Once there it didn't take long to find Susie's number and dial it.

'Susie, it's Faith. I just heard, you poor thing.'

'Oh, Faith, it's nice of you to call. I can't really believe it happened.'

'What did happen?'

'I'd just gone over to see John, but the roads round his way were ever so busy, parking I mean, and I had to park a few streets over. I never like doing that, it means a long walk to his place. He's always told me to call him on the mobile he's given me if I want him to walk me round, but I never do, it seems too silly. But I'll never think it's silly again.'

'Why.'

'Well I was just getting my bag out of the car when these thugs came by. I didn't see them, you understand, but one nudged the door and it pushed me over. I was annoyed and said they were stupid. I know, I know, it was stupid of me, but I didn't think. Next thing I know they're kicking at the door, and my left hand was still holding it.'

'Christ!'

'I screamed, the ring bit right into my finger, buckled. They ran off. I think it was the screaming did that.'

'So it was mostly the ring?' Faith said softly.

'No, I called John. He was so angry with me for not calling him before, but we went to casualty and they've put my whole hand in plaster.'

'Oh, Susie! What about the thugs?'

'Oh well we told the police all about it, but John doesn't hold out much hope. When we're married we're getting somewhere away from that type.'

'I'll keep in touch, Susie, got to go now.'

'Thanks for calling.'

Poor Susie, Faith thought with a shiver, it reminded her of what happened to the Susie in The Story.

chapter thirty - Faith

Faith's lunch-date with Nick went all too quickly, wrapped in each other arms she told him briefly about the way the story was told and was captured by Di. How Di had sent it off and the deal she'd signed, giving Di a half share. Nick seemed surprised and not surprised at Faith's generosity to her friend, saying it was just like her, as if he'd known her forever. She didn't mention Susie, there wasn't time, nor to quiz him about 'Mom, Ethiopia and the farm' as she'd been told to. It was enough to feel his breath against her cheek, his lips on hers.

'Faith,' he whispered in her ear, 'can you arrange another late evening – I really do have to tell you about all that stuff Angie said, it's only fair, but it's a hell of a long story,' as if he'd read her mind.

'Oh, Nick. I don't know, it was pure luck that we were ever late, only when Di had to look over the job that Paul was doing, and on Wednesday they'll have the handover. The end of the job.'

'I see, and there's no other way you'd be late?'

'Not really, I'm dependent on Di for transport. Unless …'

'Unless what?'

'Unless the handover means a late evening, Di's not said anything though.'

'I'll keep my fingers crossed, let me know at lunch, I'll see you then anyway, won't I?'

'Of course, of course.'

Di was agitated on Wednesday; she arrived early, even before Faith had stepped outside the door, and tooted her horn. Faith ran from the house and, flustered, scrambled into the car.

'Sorry, sorry, I didn't think I was late.'

'You're probably not,' Di said briskly, 'but once I was ready I just couldn't hang around any more.'

Faith looked over at Di. Usually well dressed she was ultra smart today, wearing a suit that Faith remembered as costing a fortune in their affluent days. She realised that as today was the day that they hoped to hand over the job to Lechwood, Di was dressed for battle. Faith had thought little about the handover since Di had asked her to arrange to be late again. 'For the last bloody time, I hope,' she'd said, and Faith had instantly thought of the chance of seeing Nick and of little else.

'Do you think it'll all go okay today?' Faith asked after they had driven in a fierce silence for a while.

'Quite honestly, no. I think the Leech would pay his own man a thousand bonus just to find something to stop the handover. I never realised what a spiteful prick he was until this. I really wish I'd never had the idea that we could work for him. I wish I'd never worked for the creep, ever.' The tirade was said with such venom that Faith just looked at her friends profile in astonishment.

'Is it that bad?'

'It's the constant crowing and innuendo that's really got to me, thank goodness for your story, at least I can tell him where to shove it at the end of the week.'

'Yes, there's that.'

'When are you giving in your notice?'

'What? Oh, I don't know, I thought I would work on for a bit.'

'But you've got to get that next book written.'

'I know. I had thought I could tape it, maybe that would be the best way.'

'Yeah, I suppose, but won't that take time too?'

'Yes, but I need to know the money's there, that we've got some coming in regularly. Then I'll give up.'

'What does Andy think?'

Quite, thought, Faith. What Andy thought was that the first half of the money should go into making a partnership with Paul, that they'd soon be making enough to buy a house as good as Paul's, run a couple of cars, whatever. Andy was dreaming already and Paul had not even agreed to the idea, let alone Faith. No, Faith wanted to hang on to her job, though she had to admit to herself that it wasn't just for the security.

'Well, he has hopes of going into partnership with Paul,' she began hesitantly.

'Oh, yes, I know. He has it all worked out,' Di replied briskly.

'You know?'

'Yes, Andy called me and explained all about it, oh, last Friday.'
'Friday!' Faith gasped, Friday; before he'd even spoke to her about the idea.
'Yeah, think so, must have been 'cos I was trying to get the dinner cooked, and I remember it was the fish.' And I was running Jilly and Jon to their sports club, Faith thought to herself, and would I even be bothered if it wasn't for my own guilty conscience?
'What does Paul think?'
'Don't know yet, he's concentrating on getting this job finished, one thing's for certain, he'll never offer to do the whole job again, he's not cut out for the finishing work, and it's driving him crazy.'
'What time do you think it'll be over, I may go out for a bit of window shopping.'
'Oh, right, hadn't thought about that, thought you'd be sitting in your office like, and I could get reception to buzz you?'
'It depends, it depends how much work I've got hanging about and how long this is likely to take.'
'Right, look let's say it'll be at least an hour, so if you feel like getting out of the office you know you've that long at least, how's that.'
'Okay, fine.' Faith said, her heart sinking a little, she'd been so looking forward to being with Nick for a long time.

Lunch time came and with no Susie to fool Faith just left the office and made it round to Wren's in record time. He must have been watching for her again as the door opened as she reached it. He swept her in and hungrily kissed her.
'Any news of this evening?' his bright eyes scanned hers. She couldn't help but smile, even though the news wasn't as good as she'd hoped.
'An hour this evening, not that long, but better than a kick in the teeth.'
'An hour, then I'd better begin the story now, while we eat,' he said, his face serious.
'If you want?' she said, feeling just a little wary.

They moved to the kitchen diner and sat opposite each other where Nick had a goat cheese salad already prepared, warm focaccia bread scented with rosemary and a glass of white wine for each of them.

He took a sip of wine and broke off some of the warm bread. 'It goes like this. And this time you can ask questions. No game of hide and seek this time. I met Angie's mum in the US, that's where she gets the accent. Valerie was a make-up artist with one of the movie makers, Belmont, she was doing the works on a couple of the artistes that I was shooting. Basically, I was a cocky British upstart, oh, they wanted my name, they'd called me over to do the shoots. That makes your head swell when you're just nineteen. Imagine that, me at nineteen, I thought I could do anything then, I'd snapped any pop star that was worth taking a picture of in England and they'd called me over to shoot some of their film stars.'

'Must have been incredible.'

'Yeah, but I don't think they'd ever looked at a picture that I'd taken. The shots I was known for were quite raw. I used the people as they were, no touching up, just used lighting in particular ways. More than that, my shots took time. I'd talk to the person, try to get under the image, find out something about them that I wanted to show. Most, those that had been in the business long enough, appreciated that, opened up for me. They get to a point where they get surrounded by two types, sycophants and spongers. I was neither, sure I wanted something from them, their picture, but that was what they wanted too, I could talk to them in ways they'd almost forgotten and then they'd let me see the person I wanted to photograph. Do you get it?'

'I think so.'

'Well, there's this Hollywood star all pasted up to the nines and with a fifteen minute slot to fit me in for a shoot! She looked terrible, face a pastiche. I said something along the lines of 'she needed to scrape some of the muck off her face before I'd take her photo'. She said 'What's wrong? Valerie always does my make-up and it's always perfect for the shoot.' To which I believe I said, 'If that's perfect then Valerie must be as blind as a bat'.' Nick grinned and gave a half laugh, 'Next thing I knew I got a whack across the head, made my ears ring. Valerie, this lovely girl, had been standing right behind me and had whacked me with a wet towel she was carrying. I have to say it was magic. We fought like cat and dog but there was no denying the attraction. We got married before I finished the job for Belmont. A whirlwind romance they call it.'

'What was she like?'

'Truthfully? Beautiful. Not in a English way, in that wide-mouthed, brash American way. She never did take to England much, but then we were on the move a lot to begin with, and then pretty soon Angie came along. She changed everything, Valerie wanted to settle down so we bought a little place in California, so she could be near to her folks, and life meant circulating from California to England and back. My fame,' again the half laugh, 'was still carrying me from star to star.' Nick stopped talking and stared at the crumbled bread in his hand.

'And?'

'And Valerie took up with her childhood sweetheart. Sounds corny as hell doesn't it. Okay, so I wasn't around most of the time, it was the nature of the work, but I wasn't messing around. *I wasn't*, though every other scandal sheet had a snap of me with my latest 'lover' and it's amazing how many of those papers happened to find their way to a small town in California.' He glanced at his watch, the time had passed quickly. 'Angie was twelve before I realised, no let's be honest, I knew something wasn't right but I blamed myself, the dashing around the world, the photos of me with the stars I'd gone to photograph, I didn't think at first that it could be someone else. Big headed of me, I knew there wasn't anyone around that was as exciting as me. Funny? Eh?'

Faith could see that he was upset but she sensed that she'd not heard the most important part of this story yet, she found herself biting her bottom lip.

'So, the idea of the divorce hit me hard, what do they say 'pride goes before a fall'. Well I fell.'

'And when Angie accused you of being a hypocrite, what did she mean?'

'That was because of the number of times I've told her that breaking up someone's marriage is despicable, that I'd never do that, no matter how much I ran around, 'cos that's what I did after the divorce, I made sure that I did everything they'd accused me of. Starlets, Stars, pop or film, anyone, tried anything to make me forget. That was what I like to think of as Phase One. Hearing that Valerie had cancer put a whole new set of emotions in train.'

'Oh, my God!'

'I didn't know what to do. You see I still saw Valerie, well I saw Angie, as often as I was in the States. It wasn't as if I had no contact.' He dropped the bread onto his plate and took a sip of wine. 'And our lunch time has almost gone, and you've not eaten much.'

'I couldn't,' Faith said and swallowed, unaccountably she had a lump in her throat.

'You can see why I didn't tell you all this before, can't you?' Faith nodded, it would have been a hard base to start out from. 'And like Angie said, I haven't finished yet, eat something, please. Perhaps I can finish off this sorry tale quickly this evening,' he added with a smile that reached right into Faith and made her shiver with anticipation.

By the time Faith reached Wren's door that evening she was aching to hold him, all afternoon she'd relived parts of his story and felt his anguish in the telling. He hadn't hidden his sensitivity or his own brashness from her and somehow it made him seem more vulnerable.

She knocked and let herself into the flat, he was just coming out of the bathroom, his shirt off. Faith stripped off her coat and let it fall as she went into his embrace, she drank in his scent. She smiled to herself as she half dragged him through to his bedroom.

Sated and snuggled up against him in the untidied bed she whispered, 'And now you can tell me the rest.'

'It's difficult. Doesn't feel right like this, I can't watch your face.'

'You don't need to,' she kissed him just beneath his ear.

'Okay, as you wish. Yep, I got told that Valerie had cancer; it was inoperable and fast moving. We made sure she had the best care but there wasn't anything that could help what she had to go through. Larry just gave up on her.' Faith felt him tense. 'I tell myself now he couldn't bear to see her suffer, but at the time I just thought he was a rat, patted myself on the head for being there.' Faith felt a huge sigh escape him and touched him on his chest. He responded by pulling her tighter to him. 'It took two months from when she went in to hospital. I believe in euthanasia now, it wasn't fair on her, or anyone. When it was over, funeral and all that, I got a sense of my life being a waste, photographing ephemeral trash! I took off for some of the areas of the world that need to be shown. Went with Princess Di to take photos for the International Red Cross anti-landmines campaign, then set off for Ethiopia.'

Faith felt him sigh. 'It happened gradually, I was taking shots for various aid agencies. I didn't need to get to know these people before I took their pictures, all their hopes were painted in stark lines on their faces, in their over-large eyes. It got that I couldn't take the pictures. It seemed too painful. To them? To me? I still don't really know. I just froze. I couldn't press the shutter, I couldn't focus on the pain. It probably wasn't the right place to be after Valerie's death, who knows, it was probably some kind of breakdown, though I've never admitted that to anyone else.' Faith squeezed him, her face pressed against his naked chest, kissed him. 'I came home, sold my apartment in California, the town house in London, bought a small farm in Devon and disappeared for a bit.

'And Angie?' Faith whispered.

'Angie stayed with her Gramps and Grandmama in California. That was best all round, then she got herself a place at college, sold the house and bought one near campus. She's got a good head on her, knows that she'll be able to sell as easy as winking when she's ready. Since Ethiopia I haven't been moving round the world much, so she's taken to coming over to see the poor old man.'

'Worried about you?'

'Probably. So, that's the story. I'm sorry, I couldn't have told you before.'

'No, I understand that, but you would have, even without Angie pushing you?'

'Yes, of course, when it was right,' he hugged her tight, one hand smoothing her flank. Faith found herself moving against him, her body singing its own tune.

'Oh God, I love you,' Nick said, his voice husky with desire, lifting her to lie over him. She slid her body up his then poised herself to take him in. 'Love you! Love you, love you,' he repeated as he responded to her urgent demand to take her.

Lying moulded to his body Faith's head turned to one side, she noticed the time on the clock and her whole body jerked. She'd been at Wren's for an hour and a quarter, long past the time she'd said she'd be back at the office.

'What's wrong?' Nick said as she rapidly slid from him and scrambled from the bed.

'The time!' Faith said, hurriedly finding the clothes she'd discarded in her initial passion to have him to herself. Nick watched her for a moment then swung himself out of bed and pulled on his jeans.

'Are you going to be okay?'

'Yeah. Just, just I don't want any questions. I go red when I have to make up an excuse. See you on Friday?' she said as she tugged on her coat, glancing in a mirror as she did so.

'There's a problem with Friday, I'm following up some work and may not be back. Most probably won't be back, so it'll have to be Monday, can you make that?'

'Of course,' Faith, hair tidied, went to him and reached up to kiss him, 'can't wait,' she whispered.

Faith left the front door at a run for the second time that week. She slowed only when she got near the newspaper offices, then continued in a brisk walk. Just as she turned the corner to go in, thanking her lucky stars that Di must have been kept longer at the handover, she almost bumped straight into Andy. His face was thunderous.

'Where the fuck have you been?' he snarled.

'Just, just window shopping,' Faith blurted, her face glowing. 'I didn't notice the time, been running to get back quickly.' She added hoping that the truth would hide the heat she felt rising up her neck. 'Where's Di?'

'Round the corner in the car, just as well I said I'd come with her, I wouldn't like to think of her hanging around waiting for you all this time on her own,' Andy said as he stomped of in the direction he'd indicated. Faith followed meekly behind, feeling wretched. As she watched Andy move in front of her she felt a shudder run through her. She desperately wanted to turn round and return to Nick, to live in that other world where she was loved and cherished.

'Faith!' Di said as Faith clambered in the back seat, 'You had us worried!'

'I just lost track of the time,' Faith muttered, 'When I realised I ran all the way back.'

'It was the third time I'd sent Andy out to look for you.'

'Okay, thanks, I'm sorry.'

Di put the car into gear and pulled away. There was nothing but the sound of the engine for a few moments. Faith collected her thoughts, felt a shiver of delight flow through her as she heard Nick's 'I love you' again.

'Well?' Di broke into Faith reverie. 'Aren't you going to ask how it went?'

'Oh, yes, of course, how did it go? Did the Leech double cross you as you thought he might?'

'Amazingly, no. He accepted the report from his man that all was well and accepted, though the bastard couldn't stop himself gloating over the fines we're paying.'

'Bastard,' echoed Andy.

'Thank God for our book deal, I really think Paul might have punched him in his slimy face if he'd been facing disaster and the Leech had said that, as it was I could see him gritting his teeth.'

'What was the final loss then?' Faith asked, wondering how much Di and Paul would have left to put into the new partnership that Andy was angling for.

'Fourteen and a half thou on fines and overtime, plus the replacement of the fixtures that were wrecked.'

'You didn't have insurance?'

'Couldn't afford that on top of the basic site insurance, mistake!'

'So?'

'So, all that work and we made a loss of five grand. Like I said, thank God for the book deal. You know the money's arrived in our bank accounts?'

'Yes.' 'No, I didn't.' Andy and Faith said simultaneously.

'Alison says to remember that the tax man will want some and not to spend it all.'

'Right,' Faith said softly.

Faith rang Susie on Thursday evening to see how she was getting on. Susie was pleased to hear from her and reported that the ring was repaired, nothing had been heard about the thugs, and that she wasn't over surprised.

Friday came without the usual frisson of excitement and Faith decided to have lunch in the cafeteria rather than go out and collect some non-urgent shopping. Only Susie would have noticed if she'd changed her new routine. Faith collected a salad and took it over the seats that she usually shared with Susie. It wasn't long before Tommy and Joan came to sit facing her on the adjoining table, followed by Annie.

Faith glanced up just as Annie was sitting down, she smiled briefly at Faith and then turned and sat, her back towards her. Faith stared. Annie's glorious red locks were gone. In their place was a tight neat crop, tapered close to the neckline. It was such a dramatic change of style, Annie didn't even look like herself anymore. Joan, facing Annie, facing Faith, caught Faith's eye and Faith realised she must have been gaping at the back of Annie's head since she sat down. She blushed and quickly busied herself with her food.

'Suits you though,' she heard Tommy say in his over-loud way.

'Well, I've either got to get used to it or start growing it all again.'

'I'd have thought they could have made it a bob, given you more of a start,' Joan piped in, 'I mean, it looks terrific but if you want to grow it back again.'

'Oh, they couldn't, some was singed almost to the scalp. I think he did the best he could, after all when someone walks in with half their hair burnt away you don't have much left to work with.'

'Must have been terrifying,' Tommy said, leaning back as if enjoying himself.

'Oh, don't. If Matt hadn't reacted so quickly…' Annie shuddered.

Faith was listening. Her forkful of salad poised half way to her lips. *Singed. Hair burnt-away.* Joan was looking at her again. She flicked an acknowledging smile, put the food in her mouth.

'Have you heard from Susie?' Joan said across the void. Faith swallowed, nodding.

'How is she?'

'Fine, apart from her hand, the ring's been repaired.'

'Did you hear what happened to our poor Annie here?' Tommy added. They were all looking at her now.

'No, just, I caught a bit of what you were saying. The new style does suit you, Annie, it was just a shock – you know - the difference. What happened?' Faith found herself asking, though something in her was saying she didn't want to know details.

'I was late, Matt was already sitting at the table in the restaurant, so I leant over to kiss Matt a sorry for being late and suddenly, whoosh, my hair goes up in flames. I'd not noticed the candle. He was so quick, doused the flames, but the damage was done. We didn't eat, went straight round to his friend's, a hairdresser. I've never been so terrified or so embarrassed in my life!'

'Thank God he was quick!' Faith said with a shiver, her thoughts reeling at the consequences if he hadn't been.

'We're getting a bit accident prone round here,' laughed Tommy, 'think I'll start looking for a job somewhere else.'

The image of breaking glass flashed through Faith's mind and as quickly she drove it away.

chapter thirty-one - Faith

Faith had bad dreams that night, everyone she knew was gathered together in a huge bonfire and she was trying to drag them out, but no sooner had she let go of one she'd rescued than they were drawn back into the flames.

'What was wrong with you last night?' Andy said over breakfast, 'Didn't let me get to sleep.'

'Oh,' Faith said. 'Why not?'

'You just didn't keep still, and talking, muttering away.'

'Sorry. I had a bad dream, I know that.'

'Huh, I'll wake you up next time then.'

Talking about it brought the nightmare back into Faith's mind, and for a brief moment she saw the flames and the sheets of blackened paper that whirled up in the smoke. She shook herself, it was nothing but her overactive imagination, time she wrote that next story.

Saturday was filled with the usual domestic routine; the washing had to be done, beds changed, vacuuming and dusting. Faith's day disappeared as usual until the evening when, tired, she just had the ironing to do. Andy had gone over to Paul's just after lunch and Jilly and Jon had played with friends down the street. Faith had been alone most of the day but had deliberately kept herself from thinking about The Story or the people she knew at work. Briefly she'd wondered about starting the next book, but as soon as she'd let her imagination go it twisted itself back round to The Story. The publishers had chosen a sequel to The Story but had made sure that Faith understood that it had to be able to be read as a stand-alone, that anyone could pick it up and enjoy it even if they hadn't read the first one. Not so much a sequel but one in a series, they predicted, of 'Hope Jones – investigative reporter' books. No wonder she couldn't drag her mind away from The Story, as soon as she thought of Hope Jones she saw her with Chris Raven, saw his long dark hair caught back in a band, saw his coruscating eyes, felt his touch, knew the scent of him, and told herself that he couldn't be in the next book because he was dead.

After the children had gone up to bed Andy took up a place on the sofa, and Faith, when she'd completed the ironing, knowing what it meant felt nauseous as she curled up at the other end from him but this time he didn't pat the space beside him so then Faith didn't know where she was.

'Been discussing the partnership deal with Paul,' Andy said after a while, not even looking at Faith, his eyes still watching the TV.

'What does he say?'

'It's all fixed. We're going to be partners, its Harvey and Warren, builders, from now on.'

'All fixed?' Faith said startled. 'Why didn't you talk to me first? How much are you putting in?'

'What for? Are you some kind of expert on building work or something?' he glared at her now.

'No, but …'

'And we've put the same amount in as Paul, so we're equal partners.'

'How much is that?'

'Thirty-five grand,' Andy said defiantly.

Faith looked at him for a moment. 'Surely they didn't have that much spare with the deficit from the gym job.'

'Well, yes and no.'

'What?'

'There's some balance to be carried over, Paul said, that it would be settled up as the money started to come in.'

'So,' Faith said her voice taking on a sharp note despite herself, 'Paul has brought a debt as part of his contribution to this new partnership.'

'What do you know?' Andy snarled back, his neck reddening, 'Since when did you become interested in business?'

'Since it was my money!' Faith spat back and in the instant knew she shouldn't have as his arm swung round and the flat of his huge hand caught her square on the side of the head.

'Shut it!' he shouted, 'The business will make more money that your scribbling ever will, I don't think you could have done it without Di, she probably wrote most of it anyway,' as Faith leapt from the sofa and backed away to the door.

'You're *so* wrong, and Paul has taken you for a sucker like he always does,' she said recklessly.

'Bitch! Paul's the best mate anyone could have, what d'you know 'bout that? You'd never have had any if Di hadn't taken pity on you, huh?' Andy knew how to hurt with words as well as fists, Faith thought, but now she had cooled down and was out of arm's reach she decided to try reasoning with him.

'You can't give Paul all our money,'

'It's not all, and it's not given. You see you don't know anything. It goes into the business, a separate account, not Paul's. As soon as we start making money we draw a wage, that's how it works. I gave Paul the cheque already.'

'Paul! Who's it made out to?'

'To Harvey and Warren, idiot.'

'And he's going to open the account on his own? Who gets to sign the cheques?'

'No, he's not. Di is, and Di signs everything for the firm. She knows how a business works.'

'Paul's wife.'

'What the hells wrong with you? Don't you trust your *only* friend?' Andy sneered. 'So, that's the way it is. You should be pleased, I'm on the up now.'

Monday came like a dream. Everything seemed different and mainly because Faith had to drive herself into work. Di had quit her job in a spectacular manner on Friday, apparently saying all the things she'd been bottling up since she'd started working for Lechwood, and topping it off with a threat of reporting him for sexual harassment if she had any problems through his influence in the future. Di had chatted wildly about it all the way home on Friday and Faith had been grateful as she didn't want to think because whenever she did her thoughts kept returning to Annie's glorious hair going up in flames and Susie's lovely long fingers crushed in a car door. Andy wasn't happy that she had to take the car, and muttered about getting her a small car for the journey. He hadn't suggested that she stop work, Faith noticed, and she was glad not to have to fight that battle. It felt strange and good to be setting off on her own, as if she was in control of her own life in a sense. She turned on the radio and listened to Radio Four, news and commentary on the news, all words, all enough to keep her mind from slipping into thinking about The Story and its characters. The nightmare had come again last night, and she had the strange feeling that she'd even recognised its coming and had tried to wake herself up, wishing that Andy had been as good as his word and had woken her.

Morning coffee time came and she took her drink and, out of habit, wandered towards the place she usually shared with Susie. Annie and Joan were already 'next door' talking animatedly.

'Sit here, if you like.' Joan said as Faith was about to sit down. Faith looked at them both then quickly smiled and saying 'Thanks' sat with them.

'Plenty of room today,' Joan added, 'Tommy's off.'

'He's hurt himself,' Annie added.

A wave of heat swept through Faith, it was as if she could not breathe properly.

'You okay?' Joan was looking at her closely.

Faith could only shake her head for a moment, then recovered enough to whisper 'How?' glass flashed across her inner eye, glass tinged with pink, red drops pooling themselves on a white shirt.

'Seems he was at a really wild party on Saturday night.'

'Probably plastered, or high,' added Annie.

'And he went through the glass on the kitchen door.'

'No!' Faith gasped.

'Can't have been safety glass.'

'His face and arm were badly cut up.'

'He was lucky, a cut only had to go in the wrong place and he could have died!'

The room swam, Faith felt sick and faint.

'You okay?' Joan said again. Faith nodded, though she could feel her heart beating fast and there were black edges to her vision. She closed her eyes to steady herself.

'Drink some of your coffee,' Joan ordered. It was something to focus on, Faith drank and felt a little more stable

'Okay?' Annie asked.

'Yes, okay now. It was just a bit of a shock!' Faith turned with a small smile to Annie to prove it, and just caught the 'raised eyebrows' look that Joan sent to Annie.

'Poor Tommy,' Faith said, thinking of the scars. Though Tommy might even turn them to his advantage, with his sweet-talking way with words.

'And fancy, he was only saying on Friday about us being accident prone, said he was going to look for a job somewhere safer!' Annie laughed, 'You two had better watch out!'

'No, we should be all right, these things always go in threes,' Joan said with a smile, 'Susie, You and Tommy, we'll be alright, won't we Faith?'

'Yes,' Faith said, not smiling, 'Yes, we should be alright.' She glanced at her watch, 'Thanks, got to get back now, see you, oh and if anyone's going to see Tommy, send him my best,' her voice cut itself off as the need to cry tightened her throat and forced her to leave quickly.

'Perhaps she fancies him?' Faith heard Joan say in an undertone as she went.

'Perhaps he's already..' the rest of Annie's reply was lost.

Oh, my God, more bloody rumours, Faith thought as she brushed away the tears and fought to remove the lump in her throat. It has to be coincidence. Things don't happen because they're in a story. Poor Tommy, he's the worst hit, probably scarred for life. Annie can grow her hair back, Susie's finger's will mend but – oh no! Alun Watson. No she wouldn't even think about it. That was what she did last time, thought about the glass and Tommy's face. No, no thinking, 'Frère Jacques. Frère Jacques, Dormez vous, Dormez vous,' she sang the first thing that came in to her head, lining up some other song to fill her head as soon as she'd reached the end.

257

Back at her desk she plugged in the headphones and began to type up Mr Watson's letters for the day, concentrating on their content, not on the author.

Just before lunch she took the sheaf of letters to Mr Watson to sign. As he read and signed each letter she let herself look at his room again. Too much paper, too much stuff that could burn she thought and even as she did so wished she'd not even let the thought creep in.

By the time Faith saw Nick again she was feeling the strain. The nightmares had wracked her every night, to the point where she was beginning to dread falling asleep. The news about Tommy had been as good as could be expected, he was, apparently, dealing with the tragedy in as humorous a way as was possible. Yet still Faith felt guilty.

Wednesday came and Faith worked impatiently, the minutes dragging by until lunchtime. With no Susie to give explanations to again, Faith was swiftly out of the building and once out of sight she broke into a trot and arrived at Nick's door slightly out of breath.

He was there, waiting for her at the top of the stairs. She threw herself into his open arms and squeezed him so tight, burying her face in his shoulder.

'What it is it, love?'

Faith shook her head against the thick wool of his jumper.

'Come in, tell me all about it,' his voice gentle and inquiring.

Faith broke away enough to receive a kiss and to go inside. The brightness of the room lifted her slightly, as if all these clear-cut lines could sort everything out.

'You'll think me mad - probably am,' she said quickly, 'but something extraordinary seems to be happening.'

'Go on,' he said leading her to sit down.

'You remember my story? The book deal?'

Nick nodded 'How could I forget?'

'I never did get to tell you the whole story. I've brought you a copy. Listen, when I told that story I used people I know to hang the characters on. Yeah? Just, just to make it easier to keep it all in my head. Remember, I didn't know it was ever going to be written down.'

'Is someone trying to sue you for libel?'

'What? Oh, God, no I hadn't thought of that. No, it's…' Faith searched for some way to explain so that it didn't sound quite so wild. There wasn't any so she ploughed on, 'These characters, in the book, some of them had rather nasty things happen to them – you know they had to for the story – and, and now some of these things are happening in real life.' Faith stopped and looked hard at Nick and saw in his eyes some confusion. 'Like, Susie, she was persuaded to tell the gang what they wanted by them crushing her hand in a car door, and that's just happened to her – and Annie, Annie with her long, beautiful red hair, I made them burn her hair, set it alight to scare her and that happened to her,' she could hear her voice getting higher. 'I told you it sounded mad.'

Nick pulled her to him, held her close. 'Coincidence?' he murmured into her hair.

Faith shook her head, pulled back a little, 'Oh, and now, now I had them cut up Tommy's face with window glass and Tommy's cut his face to pieces on a glass door. Three? Coincidences?' she swallowed, 'It doesn't feel like it.'

'Even so love?'

'Look, our time's running out. It's not all, I've brought you a copy. Please read it, you'll see what I mean. Then, oh God Nick – I hope you can persuade me I'm imagining things,' she shuddered involuntarily and Nick drew her even closer again, kissing the top of her head.

'Okay, but for now I think you need some lunch, and I need a proper kiss,' he said tipping her face up towards him.

chapter thirty-two - Faith

The next morning at ten-thirty Faith was shocked to find Nick at her elbow. He had with him the manila folder that contained her book. Feeling as if every eye in the place was on her she looked up at him and suddenly it really didn't matter.

'I've brought you some work,' he said, clearly enough for anyone who wanted to overhear to hear.

'Does it have a deadline, Mr Wren?' she heard her own voice sound prim and distant.

'Yes, I've included a note to that effect. Can you do it in time?' Faith opened the envelope and looked at the note – it said 'Lunch today?' 'Yes, sir, I think I can do that in time.'

'Fine, Thank you,' he said and slipped away. Why had he brought her the manuscript? Was that some message in itself – that it really wasn't worth considering – that he thought her too silly? She opened the flap again and looked at the pages, they seemed neat enough – though perhaps not as tidy as when she'd put them in for him to read. Lunch, though soon, seemed an age away.

Still without Susie to make excuses to she slipped out of the office and away as soon as lunchtime arrived. He was there, waiting for her as she climbed the stairs.

'Come here!' he said, pulling her to him, kissing her lightly, drawing her inside.

'Well?' she began, then wondered again if he'd read the whole thing in the time.

'Well, my love, you are a fantastic storyteller. You know I didn't put it down until I'd finished. Quite forgot that I was supposed to be looking out for certain characters. In fact – I had to go back and check out one of them.'

'But what do you think – the coincidences?'

'Probably just that. Things don't usually happen because someone had written them in a book. Though I have my doubts about that Raven character and the lovely Hope,' he grinned.

'Oh, well, that just happened. I didn't mean to peg a character on you – it just happened.'

'And on you?'

'That was deliberate – I told you, stories featuring Di and me, that's all they were, before this one.'

'Well they'd better be coincidences,' Nick laughed, 'after what happens to me at the end.'

'No! No don't say that – that wasn't my original ending – that was the agent, she insisted that Hope had to be free of ties ready for the next book, that Raven had to die,' Faith felt herself go cold inside. 'No, that couldn't happen.'

'So, it's not what is in the book, just the parts you made up?' Nick looked at her closely, 'Faith, love, I think you are feeling guilty about us and these coincidences are playing on your mind.'

'So I'm mad to think it?'

He drew her close and hugged her gently, 'Mad in the best possible way, madly in love, I hope.'

'Just coincidence,' she murmured into his chest and sighed, 'Please let there be no more then, I don't think I could bear any more.' Though there were flames licking at the edge of her imagination.

'I'm glad you could come today,' Nick whispered, 'I've got to go abroad for a few days – there's a problem I need to sort out.'

'Oh!' a sinking feeling filling her, 'Okay, when will you be back?'

'Probably on Monday. Will you be all right?'

'How do you mean?'

'Well I can tell you are still worried about these coincidences.'

'Mmm. But I'll be okay.'

'And you've got my number.'

'In a secret code,' Faith smiled up at him, in his arms she felt totally safe, in a separate world where nothing else mattered.

It was just that feeling that Faith tried to conjure when she was alone for a few hours on Saturday. Andy, feeling pleased with himself, had decided to take Jon to the football and Jilly was round at a friend's, giving Faith an unaccustomed spell of time in which she continued to catch up on her weekend chores but let her mind drift in between . She switched on the radio, began bopping to the music as she worked and was happy just thinking of Nick and how being with him made her feel.

'Four o'clock and time for all the news and especially all the local news – from Second City Radio! Headlines today: Reports of a military coup in Niger, Ministry of Transport denies rumours of a change of policy on car tax and locally, an update on the fire at the Central News building earlier today.'

Suddenly Faith felt dizzy. No, she couldn't have really heard what she thought she had heard, could she? Her hands shook as she turned the radio up, tapping her foot with impatience as the news trawled slowly through the international and national items. Faith was conscious of her heart beating faster as the time came nearer, still telling herself she must have misheard.

'And the fire that seriously damaged a suite of offices at Central News and left a senior editor with severe burns is officially extinguished. The disaster did not prevent Evening Central going to press on time with the burning of its own building as headlines. Earlier our news team interviewed Ms Robertson, senior editor of Evening Central. 'Ms Robertson, though the fire is stated to be extensive it has not stopped you from bringing out this afternoon's copy.' 'Well, no, of course not – after all the only really bad news is no news… of course we are all tremendously upset by the injuries suffered by Mr Alun Watson in the fire but in our -'

The rest was lost in the pounding and rushing in her head, she sat down, tried to focus and listen, but now they were playing music again and it was lost.

'No. No. It can't be. Impossible, how could it happen? I know – I'll call the office and find out how it happened, how Mr Watson is.' Faith stood to go to the phone, only to find everything waver, she sat again for a moment, then steadying herself she went and phoned, her fingers stumbling over the numbers.

'Central News.'

'Hi, it's Faith Warren here,'

'I'm sorry, who did you say you wanted?'

'I. I didn't, um, who is that please?'

'Reception at Central News.'

'No, look I work at Central News, for Mr Watson, I want to know how he is, what happened?'

'The fire is officially extinguished and the paper will be put out as usual in the morning, Mr Watson is said to be comfortable in hospital, thank you for calling, goodbye.'

'But..' the phone line hummed in her ear. Faith started to redial, then stopped, perhaps they had been inundated with people calling, there had to be a better way. She dialled straight through to Ms Robertson's editorial assistant.

'Yup?'

'Julie? It's Faith Warren. I've only just heard the news.'

'Oh, Faith, I'm surprised no one called you. But then it's been all hell broken loose here, as you can imagine?'

'How's Mr Watson?' Faith heard her own voice sound faint and tremulous.

Julie's voice when it came back was soft and low, 'Oh Faith, it seems he's going to be okay, but he'll be off for quite a while.'

'How?' the word barely a whisper.

'How did it happen? Well, they won't know until the fire brigade forensics have done their bit – but they say it started in Mr Watson's office, that he went back in to try to put it out, or get his cuttings, they say he had is arms full of them, who knows, then the flames got him trapped, so he was in a bad way. I wasn't here, all those who were have been sent home, the firemen got him out, but, well, that's how comes he's in hospital. The Royal, by the way.'

'Thanks. Thanks, I still can't quite believe it,' Faith said, believing it only too well, feeling her whole body begin to tremble.

This was just too much. Too much of a coincidence. She heard Nick's reassuring voice saying that it could only be coincidence – highlighted by her guilt feelings. But this was one coincidence too many, she had to talk to someone, she had to do something. Nick! Shaking, she dialled in the number he'd given her to contact him on his mobile whenever and wherever he was. A ring. A recorded message – please leave a message after the tone. What to say when there was no way he could call her back. 'Oh, Nick. It's happened again – another coincidence – I – I - something must be done to stop it,' she stopped – there was no point in leaving a message like this, she rang off. Faith sat hands pressed together, eyes closed, trying to think her way through, yet the images of the burning of her character Alun Holmes kept flashing into her mind and a small insidious voice said that four coincidences could not be just that – coincidence – there had to be some kind of link. Still she sat there, her fingers growing numb with the pressure, her body beginning to feel cold. The story played on, the near fatal injuries of Professor Holmes, the gang capturing Hope, preparing their suicide scenario, the rescue by Raven and, and, and, great walls of blackness, no ending, nothing.

Di! At least Di knew the whole story, knew what she would be talking about when she tried to explain about the coincidences. Finding it hard to move again Faith reached out and dialled Di's number. The phone rang and rang until Faith believed she could still hear it even after she had put it down.

Before Faith could think about what to do, or do anything else the back door crashed open and Andy and Jon returned.

'Got something to eat? I'm starved,' Andy called as they came into the living room and collapsed on the sofa, Jon the perfect mimic of his dad.

Faith just looked at them, could see the way that Jon was growing up and shuddered.

'What's the matter with you? Cat got your tongue? I asked you a question.'

'There's been a fire,' Faith said quietly, feeling the tears that had been held at bay by sheer panic come rising through her frame.

'Cor, where? Was it big?' Jon began.

'Well then?'

'At the newspaper, Mr Watson's been burned – badly.'

'Oh yeah, saw that on the newspaper stand headline,' Andy said off-hand as he picked up the remote for the television, 'Did you know this guy?'

'Andy! He's one of the two people I work for!'

'Well, it wasn't your fault – don't know why you're getting so het up.'

Faith stood shakily, 'I'm going to try to call Di again.'

'Won 't be in.'

Faith looked at him, 'How do you know?'

'Di and Paul were at the game, were going on to eat out somewhere they said.'

'Aunty Di's got a new mobile phone, she showed it to me!'

'Has she?' Faith's tone was flat, she moved automatically towards the door. Perhaps Di wasn't the one to talk to after all. 'While you're out there, get us some grub. Footy's hard work, innit Jon?'

'But Dad we was watching not playing.' Faith heard her son say as she turned into the kitchen and started to make some sandwiches.

'Bastard, bastard, Cold hearted bastard,' she muttered to herself as she slapped margarine onto slices of bread and found some sliced ham to put in them. She cut them across and put them on a plate. Already Jon and Andy were engrossed in the television, so she placed the plate on the table in front of them and returned to the kitchen.

Feeling hot all over Faith picked up the phone, she just had to try Nick's number again. Her heart was thumping as she pressed in each digit, and still there was no Nick, still out of contact. She picked up the handset again and held it so long that the 'off hook' whistle started. She looked at the phone for a moment before she realised what it was, then hurriedly put it down.

Faith shook herself and made a decision, she would talk it through with Di – she'd leave a message on Di's answer phone if it was on, to call her back when she got in.

chapter thirty-three - Di

'It was so nice to eat out for a change!' Di said as they arrived home.

'The first of many more – I've a feeling we are on the up again,' Paul said as he slipped his arm around Di's waist. 'Answer phone's blinking.'

'Yeah, let's see,' Di reached out her arm and switched playback on, only to hear Faith asking in a bit of a weird voice to ring her back as soon as she got in, about the book, she said, urgently.

'Forget it, you can chat to her tomorrow,' Paul nuzzled Di's neck.

'But she said it was about the book.'

'So?'

'And she sounds pretty odd to me, don't you think?'

'Always sounds odd to me.'

'Paul! Look I'm sure it won't take long, you go and pour us a couple of drinks,' Di said, picking up the phone and turning to him with a smile.

She dialled Faith's number, only to find it answered almost at once.

'Faith, that was quick!'

'Oh, I was just here.'

'Well, what is it you need me for about the book?'

'Can I come over and talk about it, I don't want, I don't want to talk on the phone.'

'Must you, I mean, of course we can talk but must it be this evening?'

'Yes I really think it must – did you hear about the fire at the newspaper offices today?'

'Well, I did see something – but I didn't really know what – is that what this is about?'

'Sort of, I'm coming round.'

'Faith, wait …' Di looked at the receiver, the hum of the disconnected line letting her know Faith wasn't going to be put off, and now she had to break the news to Paul.

Paul had just about accepted that their evening together was ruined and had sloped off into the sitting room with his drink when Faith arrived.

'Come through here,' Di said leading Faith into the dining area, 'Would you like a glass of wine?'

'No, oh well yes, if you're having one.'

'Faith, what is it, you look white as a sheet, sit down,' Di said as she looked at Faith properly in the light. 'What is it?' she said as she sat beside her, their wine glasses placed side by side on the table.

'Di, remember when I was telling you the story?'

'Of course.'

Faith shot her a fierce glance, 'Remember I said I was using some people I knew to be some of the characters in the book?'

'Did you?'

'Yes! Remember, I said that Susie Moore in the story was based on Susie, the Susie I work with, I just changed the name a bit – Dudley to Moore, and Tommy Trout in the story is Tommy Salmon, though he's in sales, and..'

'Woah! You never did tell me, 'cos if you did it would have been on the tape – does it matter if you told me?'

'I didn't tell you about – any of them?'

'Well I guessed you and me – of course.'

'So – oh, well I'm telling you now. There were those two, and also Annie Wise was based on Annie Morecombe from personnel and Professor Alun Holmes was from one of the senior editors I work for Mr Watson. Now this is important, can you remember what happened to these characters in the Story? I mean what the gang did to them to get them to talk?'

'Well, yes,' Di was looking hard at Faith, her face seemed flushed and her eyes strangely bright and there was an unaccustomed crispness to her voice.

'So, tell me what happened to Susie?'

'They crushed her hand in the car door.'

'Correct, and not two weeks ago a gang of thugs did exactly that to the real life Susie!'

'Faith, it's horrible but…'

'What happened to Annie Wise?'

'Faith?'

'Annie Wise?'

'She, they burnt her hair.'

'Burnt her lovely long red hair! And that's what has happened to Annie Morecombe – accident – but still, and Tommy?'

'Tommy, let me see, Faith this is nonsense you know, just coincidences.'

'Tommy they sliced his face with glass from the door, and real life, living and breathing Tommy has fallen through a glass door and sliced up his face. And now, now,' her voice rising all the time.

'Faith, shhh!'

'Di, the fire, the fire at the news room.'

'It was your Mr Watson wasn't it?'

'You see - you can see it too, it can't be coincidence any more, we have to stop it going any further.'

'But Faith, even if it was like that, like some coincidences linked to your story, look, who is there left, that's all the people the gang made to talk.'

'Not to talk.'

'You? Come on Faith , you're not about to put yourself in a car with a hosepipe attached, are you?'

'No.'

'So what else could happen?'

'There's, there's Raven.'

'But you didn't say he was based on anyone just now. Was he?'

Faith went very still, her eyes shut.

'Faith?'

'Not in the same way, not deliberately, but he was based on someone.'

'Well, anyway – if it got that far you'd not be able to put a stop to it,' one look at Faith's face and Di added quickly, 'Ha ha, joke!' Faith still remained immobile. 'Look Faith, perhaps you're overwrought, with hearing about the fire and things, I'm sure there's nothing in it – they are just very unhappy coincidences.'

'That's what Nick said,' Faith murmured.

'Who said?'

'Never mind, someone.'

'Well a very sensible someone.'

'But when he said it, there were only three.'

'Three, four, it can only be coincidence - look at it logically, things just do not happen because someone else tells them that way in a story – look at me Faith – do they?'

'No, not usually.'

'There you are then!'

'There I am. Thanks. Sorry to have disturbed your evening,' Faith stood, her glass of wine untouched, she turned woodenly and left the house.

Di watched her go and as she did so hoped that she was fit to drive, Faith appeared to be almost in shock. Di resolved to call her in the morning and check that all was well.

Sunday morning didn't get off to the early start that Di had planned for herself, to begin with Paul had been very persuasive about staying in bed late, and even coming back to bed once she'd made coffee and collected the Sunday papers. All in all it wasn't until eleven that she called, only to be told by a grumpy sounding Andy that Faith had gone off to the hospital to visit that boss of hers. Di said she'd call back later; however it was nearly three in the afternoon when she remembered she was going to call Faith. As she reached for the phone it rang. She fully expected it to be Faith so it took a moment or two to register the voice as Alison Enderby's

'Diane?'

'Yes?'

'Thank goodness. I've just had Faith on the phone, talking nonsense about wanting to pull out of the publishing deal. Something to do with coincidences that aren't. I have told her it is not possible without dire consequences at this stage, least of all the fact that no-one would ever publish her again, but she claims she's thought it all through and she wants out. So what's it all about?' Alison paused for breath.

'Oh, God! Well she did tell me about the coincidences, pretty creepy really, but it just can't be anything else. I thought yesterday I'd talked her round.'

'Then you'd better do some more talking and fast, my reputation is on the line here too you realise, to say nothing of your own predicament, the publishers would want all the money back with interest.'

'I'm well aware.'

'Thank goodness I happened to be in the office catching up, listened to the start of her message then cut in – if she'd gone to the publishers, it doesn't bear thinking about.'

'Look, I'll sort it,' Di said crossing her fingers, 'She's just pretty overwrought because one of the people she works for was badly burned in the fire at the newspaper offices.'

'That's what she meant about one of her people being burned?'

'Well, yes and no, she'd based one of her characters on him a bit, the Professor who was burnt by the gang in the fire.'

'Sorry, can't place him, can't remember all of them, well, get back to me as soon as it's sorted, whatever, don't let her ring the publisher!'

'I'll do everything in my power,' Di said already thinking hard.

'Who was that, love?' Paul asked as he sauntered in.

'Alison Enderby, our agent. We've got a problem.'

'With the book?'

'With Faith.'

'To do with all that stuff you told me she'd come up with yesterday?'

'Yep, only now she's rung the agent and said she wants out of the contract. And out of the contract means no money now, and never any money from Faith's writing ever again, and everything paid back with interest'

'Shit! So what now?'

'Luckily the agent doesn't want this to hit the fan anymore than you do, my sweet. She's asked me to make sure Faith doesn't pull out and doesn't contact the publishers direct.'

'But you talked to her yesterday, and obviously that didn't do any good,'

'Thank you for that vote of confidence. And Alison told her the money side of things.'

They looked at each other for a while.

'Andy would sort her out, she's always done whatever he's said, meek as a kitten.'

'Mmm, I hope so, there's been something different about Faith lately, but it's worth a try.'

'Andy won't like the idea of the partnership going down the pan.'

'No, he certainly won't. Look, you ring him Paul, Faith will be much less suspicious if you ask to talk to Andy than if I do.'

'Fine, give us the phone.'

chapter thirty-four - Faith

'Andy, phone for you, it's Paul,' Faith, handed the phone to Andy as he lumbered in,

'What can I do for you mate?' Andy said and stared at Faith until she walked away, although Andy's half of the conversation was still clear in the other room.

'Problem?' followed by a very long silence. 'She what?' ….
'Don't you worry, I'll sort it.'

Faith was folding ironed clothes from the airer when Andy crashed back into the room, the door bouncing on its hinges. Faith looked up startled.

'What the fuck's all this nonsense about not publishing your crappy book?'

'How do..?'

'Never you mind how, just get this into you pitiful little brain, that book goes ahead, and our partnership goes ahead.'

'That's all you care about isn't it. Big Andy and his mate Paul as partners. You know nothing! You don't know why the book mustn't go out. You don't care that people are getting hurt!'

'Hurt? Hurt, there's only one person round here that's going to get hurt if you don't see sense!'

'Andy! I mean half burnt to death – you didn't see Mr Watson this morning. It was awful, more bandages than face, and his hands and arms.'

'What is it, what is he to you? Chats you up does he, sticks his hand up your skirt, you his bit of stuff?'

'Andy!'

'Got to be something, the way you've been lately, so now he's fried, you feeling all guilty and want to quit your book.'

'Lies, lies, shut up,' Faith hissed. 'He's just someone I based a character on – it's no use telling you who, you haven't even bothered to read the story - but someone who gets burnt, badly, and now he has, and that, that's just too many times for this to happen. It's got to stop!'

In a step Andy big hands clamped round Faith's shoulders, he hauled her up to him, face close to his, she tried to look away but he shook her. 'Look at me! Look at me! Look, you're just being stupid and hysterical,' he shook her again and set her down, her feet fully on the floor. 'Now, you're *not* going to pull out from this book deal, 'cos you're *not* going to wreck my chances, and that's final, so if you think you can get your own back on me that way you better think again.'

Behind Andy, Faith saw Jilly and Jon, their faces pale and worried, her face must have registered something because Andy turned and saw them too.

'You two get the fuck upstairs and I don't want to hear a word, we've just got something to sort out, got it?' The children didn't move. 'GO! And don't come out of your room till I tell you!' Andy shouted at them. They ran, Andy kicked the door closed behind them.

'All settled then, now you ring that agent woman and tell her you were mistaken, that there's no problem.'

Faith just shook her head. In her minds eye she could see Mr Watson, and the story kept running on to its blood soaked conclusion, she wasn't looking up so she didn't even have a chance to move. Andy's hand hit her off her feet in one fell swoop, his voice roaring at her, almost unintelligible. 'You'll do what the fuck I say.' Then his hands picking her up, shaking and throwing her down across the armchair so it toppled back taking her with it, 'And you'll do it today!' She struggled to get to her feet, but Andy reached over and grabbed one ankle, yanking her back, her body folded back over the fallen chair. She could hear herself screaming so loud, 'Don't, it hurts! Oh God!' but somehow it seemed as if someone else had to be screaming these words, she didn't know how to be so loud. He pulled her to her feet again, brought his head down near hers; spittle was gathering at his lips, his face was red. 'Now fucking say it, there's no problem, it can go ahead as before.'

Faith, breathing hard, stared right back at him, her lips a tight line.

'Bitch! Say it!' he shook her with every word. His eyes narrowed, his hand came up and slapped her round the face, once, twice. 'Say. It!'

Faith felt her neck muscles twang, her face burn and sting. 'No,' she whispered.

He looked at her again. 'I know,' he said and let her drop. Instantly she raised her hand to her face to rub at the burning places, Andy moved toward the door and opened it again. 'Jilly, Jon,' he called, his voice loud enough to carry, soft enough to sound controlled. Faith heard the scuffle as they left their rooms, and saw the look in Andy's eye as he turned his head to face her.

'You wouldn't?'

'Wouldn't what?'

'Jilly, Jon, run! Run out the back!' Faith screamed as she heard them clattering down the stairs.

'No you don't.' Andy turned and tried to catch them, Faith flung herself at him, being thumped in the face as he tried to free himself from her. They slipped under his grip and Faith, hearing the back door bang, sank to the floor.

He turned back to Faith, 'Now or later, they can't stay outside forever.'

Faith came to a decision.

'Okay, okay, I give in – I'll phone the agent back.'

'Now!'

'Now, just leave them alone, I'll phone now.'

'Let's see you then.'

So Faith phoned Alison Enderby, surprised to find her still in the office so late on a Sunday, and told her she'd made a mistake, that it was okay for the book to go ahead. She hardly listened while Alison prattled on about authors who get so involved with their characters that they seem to come to life, hearing instead only the thump of her own heart.'

'That's better, stupid, I knew you'd see sense,' Andy said, a self satisfied smirk on his face.

Yes, Faith thought, at last I see sense.

'Right, that's it, mission accomplished, ha, think I'll go and report back in person.'

Faith said nothing, she didn't trust herself and the thing she wanted most was for Andy to go away, anywhere, fast. She was still standing there when she heard him shout, 'What the fuck you looking at?' from out the front, and stepped closer to the window to see what it was about. Two neighbours were standing outside, more in front of the next house than theirs, but still looking at their house, one had flushed bright red, the other stood hands on hips in fighting mode, they didn't move off, even when Andy roared out of the drive.

Faith first went to the back door and called Jilly and Jon, they were standing together just round the corner, hunched against the wall, their eyes wide with fear.

'Dad's gone – to Aunty Di's – and we're going on a trip too. Surprise trip, come on.'

The children stood frozen to the spot.

'Come on, Dad's not here, and we must hurry.'

'Will Dad come back?'

'Yes, and perhaps very soon, but I want us to be away when he gets back, because he's not very happy at the moment.'

'No, he's being a beast!' Jon said boldly.

'Where are we going?' Jilly asked, shaking herself and moving towards the door.

'Well, first to a friend's flat in town, then, well.' Where might sound enticing, suddenly Faith recalled the Devon farm, 'I'm not sure, perhaps to a farm, in the country.'

'With animals?'

'And tractors?' added Jon.

'Probably, come on.' Faith felt her spirits lift as the children became interested. Just then the door bell rang. Faith tugged her fingers through her hair to tidy it and went to the door. After a fight it opened, there stood her neighbours.

'You okay love?'

'Yes, now, thanks.'

'Your husband sounded, well, angry.'

'Yes.'

'You're not all right are you?' the other said, 'You've got a huge welt coming up under your eye'.

'It's all over now, thank you,' Faith said, cursing them for holding her up, 'I really must go, packing to do.'

The neighbours looked at each other, and raised eyebrows, 'If you're sure, then.'
'Yes thanks.'

Faith closed the door. Time was against her she knew. She scooped Jilly and Jon ahead of her upstairs, threw them a large holdall each and told them to stuff as many clothes as they could in them. She ran into her room and started to do the same with her own. She ran back downstairs and called a taxi to collect them as soon as possible, which turned out to be in ten minutes.   Hoping that Andy would stay and have a drink or something with Di and Paul, she grabbed a handful of carriers and took them to the children's room.
'Here, pack what you can in toys and stuff in these, I know it won't all fit, take the most important things,' she called as she returned to do the same for herself. She looked around, what was precious to her? Barely anything, then she remembered the baby books and the photo collection, these she stuffed in her carrier and dragged the lot downstairs.
'Jilly, Jon, come on, bring your stuff down.'
'I can't,' came a sob from Jilly.
Faith flew back upstairs, Jilly was crying great tears and trying to put all sorts of stuff in her bag, most of which was fluffy toys she'd had since she was small. 'Mum, they're all important,' she wailed.
'Don't worry, I'll get you more bags!' Faith said dashing down the stairs again. A toot of a horn signalled the taxi arriving. 'Jilly, grab these bags,' she called, throwing them on the foot of the stairs. She went out to the cab with her bags in tow. 'Thanks, just the children and their bags to come,' she said, casting a worried glance down the street, expecting to see Andy returning too soon. The neighbours were still there, further off now, but still watching.

Back in the house Faith ran up the stairs again, hustling Jon with his two carrier bags, Jilly with her three and grabbing their holdalls herself, she shepherded them down and out of the door.

'Quick, over to that car,' The cab driver had got out and was ready to finish loading his boot.

In minutes they were on their way, Faith could barely believe that they'd made it, and thanked God that Andy had taken his time. Her heartbeat had just about returned to normal, and Jon was just beginning to whine asking how long until they got there, when the driver spoke.

'Where shall I drop you then Mrs? Right outside the newspaper office building? Did you hear about the fire they had there then?'

'Yes, I work there.'

'Right, I see, there then.'

Faith thought again, true most of those who worked at weekends there weren't the same people that worked there during the week, but some were, and what would she say if they recognised her. Yet she didn't want to go straight to Nick's place, she had ideas that they might track her by the cab she used, like they do in stories.

'No, the street behind please, it's quieter there, less traffic,' she gave as a reason.

It was quiet there, late on a Sunday afternoon, just the odd pedestrian wandering along. She got the children out; their luggage piled haphazard around them, then paid the driver. She watched him go before loading herself and the children like packhorses and leading them away.

'Who's this friend Mum? Susie?'

'No, not Susie, it's a man, his name is Nick and he's very kind, and gentle.'

'And he doesn't shout?'

'I don't think so, my lovely.'

They reached his door and Faith unloaded her weary arms and punched in the number. Gazing around as they entered, the children followed their mother and began climbing the broad marble stairs.

Faith rang the bell but then let herself into the flat. 'Mind you don't make it all too messy,' she said, with a look at Jon.

'Wow, it's lovely Mum,' Jilly sighed, 'like in a magazine.'

'Where do I sleep?' Jon asked sticking his head through Nick's bedroom door.

'I'm not sure – hang on,' Faith went on past the kitchen and sure enough there was a twin bedded bedroom. 'In here probably, best put your stuff in here anyway.'

'Where will you sleep then Mum?'

Faith felt herself colour up, 'Don't you worry about me, I'll be okay. Now let's see if we can find anything for tea.'

A tea of breakfast cereals and an evening watching the TV was followed by the children going to bed, even though Faith could hear them talking long after. She went to the phone and tried Nick's mobile again. This time it was answered.

'Nick Wren'

'It's Faith.'

'Faith, Faith, are you all right? I got some kind of message, didn't make a lot of sense, what's happened? And you're at my place!'

'How do you know?'

'My mobile said my home number was calling!'

'Oh! well, yes, we all are.'

'All?'

'Oh, Nick, I've taken the children and run! It was too horrible; I'll tell you when you get back.'

'Tomorrow, about three in the afternoon, are you okay?'

'Bruised – but he, he …' At the thought of Andy threatening the children the words caught in her throat, leaving only hiccupping cries.

'Faith, you're okay there, he can't find you, only you and I know where you are and as soon as I get back we'll go down to Devon.. Is that right, that what you'd like?'

'Oh please,' she took a deep breath, 'I'll be waiting for you.'

'As soon as I can.'

In the morning Faith called in sick to the office, saying she had no idea how long she'd be away as she felt so bad. Then she left the children for a short time while she went on a food, toothbrush and toothpaste shopping foray, with strict instructions not to open the door, answer the phone or even touch the phone while she was out. She wore clothes she didn't wear to the office and kept her eyes on the floor whenever she could and was as quick as possible to make sure that she saw no-one she knew. There was a tangible sense of relief when she returned loaded with stuff and safe again.

Nick walked in just before three, and it was all Faith could do to stop herself bursting into tears and running into his arms. 'My God! Let me look at you! Your poor face.' The slaps has blossomed into large pale bruises, the thumps into deeper purple patches.

Despite herself the tears began to well in Faith's eyes. 'Let me introduce my children,' she said softly, she knew they were standing behind her, just a little way back.

Nick smiled, the light making his eyes sparkle, 'You must be Jilly, and you must be Jon,' he said holding out his hand to shake theirs, 'and I'm called Nick, and I'm a special friend of your Mum's.'

Neither child came to shake his hand so he crouched down and asked them if they thought they'd like to visit his farm. That started them off and in moments they were right up close and had beaming smiles on their faces. Faith just felt her heart squeeze with the love she felt for the trio in front of her.

Later that night Faith explained what had happened while Nick had been away, and how seeing Mr Watson had made it all so vividly terrible that she'd tried to get the book stopped. Nick listened and hugged her, and at last asked if she wanted his opinion.

'Of course. That's why I called so often.'

'Sorry about that, apparently we were in a signal blind spot, nothing in or out of there for ten miles or so around.'

'Well?'

'Let the book go ahead. After all it's your baby.'

'But, what if the things keep happening?'

'I'm willing to risk it that they won't, and it looks like I've got most to lose,' he hugged her tight and kissed her hair as he said it, 'And, besides, you are so good at writing I'd hate for you to have to give it up before you started, because they'd never take you on again.'

'That's what the agent said.'

'Faith, you deserve the break! You're a brilliant writer and as the one victim left I vote the book goes ahead.'

'Really?'

'Really! I'm sure you can keep me safe from fiends with knives,' he chuckled.

'Okay, I'll leave it as it stands. Though the rest of my money comes to me, not Andy! I suppose I'd better get myself a bank account.'

'And tomorrow we'll go down to Devon, and no-one need know where you are, except your agent, but then she can have my mobile number as a contact, that will fool them!'

'I do love you, Nick.'

'I know, and I'm so glad you came to me.'

chapter thirty-five   -   Di

'Oh my God! Paul, here comes Andy again.' Di sighed as she looked out of the window. 'I'm getting really cheesed off with him living in our pockets!'

'He's had a hard time.'

'Hard time, the idiot! What did he expect if he beats his wife up?'

'It got what we wanted, didn't it? The book deal's still on,' Paul hissed. 'Hi Andy, come on through. Any news?'

'Nah, she's not tried to use her bank card or anything. You'd think the coppers would be worried about that, a whole week, and her with the kids to look after and all.'

'But you know what they said, having talked to your neighbours, they reckoned she'd gone to a refuge or to a friend or relatives. Now you've tried the few relatives and any friends you know of, and refuges just aren't going to talk to a husband,' Di cut in, her eyes narrow, she'd looked at Andy in a different light since Faith had run away and the truth about that afternoon had come out.

'I had a thought though. She's not told them to stop the book again has she?'

'No, I'm sure Alison would be on to me like a shot if she did.'

'Would that woman know where she was?'

'Who, Alison?' Di thought for a moment or two, the publishing date was drawing near, Alison probably had lots of things she'd need to talk to Faith about. 'You could be right, it's worth a try.' Di said getting up and going over to the phone. Before she picked it up she had second thoughts about calling in front of the pair of them and said, 'Oh, the number's upstairs, I'll call from there,' and trotted quickly upstairs. She dialled the number and waited.

'Alison Enderby, ACE Literary Agency.'

'It's Di Harvey, Alison.'

'Yes, what do you want?'

From Alison's tone Di suspected that Alison had been filled in on the happenings. 'Um, are you in contact with Faith?'

'Of course.'

'You see I'm terribly worried about her, and the children, nothing to do with their Dad, I just want to know if she's okay, and how I can contact her, you know, I am her oldest friend.'

'I know, she told me as much. She's fine. I would have thought she'd contact you if she wanted to.'

'But she'd be worried that she might get my husband, he *is* close to her husband, a phone number would do.'

'Well, I do have a number for contact, it's not hers though.'

'Someone close, she said there was someone close she could turn to,' Di lied, fingers crossed.

'It's a mobile number, I suppose it can't hurt to give you that, but for heaven's sake don't let that brute get hold of it.'

'Of course not. Faith's my friend,' she said as she scribbled the number down. She had no intention of letting Andy get hold of this number, she wanted to do some sleuthing on her own and then decide if she'd share, and there was no time like the present, she pressed in the numbers she'd just written down and waited, heart thumping.

'Nick Wren' a warm rich masculine voice answered the phone.

'Oh! um, is Chris there?' Di pretended to be a confused caller, using the first name that came into her head.

'No, sorry, you must have the wrong number.' And the line went dead.

Di cradled the handset for a moment looking at it in amazement then put it down. Nick Wren. Nick Wren. What the hell, this was almost as unbelievable as one of Faith's stories. The Story! Oh, yes, Chris Raven, hmmm, Nick Wren would probably fit the bill, no wonder Faith was in so much of a tizzy, talk about a dark horse! But what to do now, taken that all she was guessing was right, did it make any difference? Di decided to sleep on it and see what she thought in the morning.

When she woke Di knew exactly what she was going to do, though she wasn't sure of her own motives. The evening before she'd lied to Andy and Paul and said that Alison only had a box number to send to, and that had settled that idea, so it wasn't as if Andy was pursuing that line of enquiry. She waited until nine-thirty then rang the newspaper offices and asked to be put through to Mr Wren. She was passed on to someone who informed her that Mr Wren was away for a week or so, but that anything urgent could be forwarded. Di tried to extract an address, saying she'd save them the bother but that was a definite no-go area, so she said in that case she'd send a letter to be forwarded and thanked them for their help.

She jotted down, 'Nick Wren – away for week or so.' on some paper near the phone, then dialled the newspaper offices again and this time asked for Faith's friend Susie, wondering if she would be back in work yet. As she waited to be put through she tried to imagine this girl that Faith had sometimes told her about, the one who had so recently had her hand crushed just like the Susie in The Story.

'Susie Dudley.'

'Hi, you don't know me, but I'm a friend of Faith's, Sherry, and I haven't been able to get hold of her at home, I was wondering if you knew how to contact her.'

'Oh, no, I'm sorry, I really don't. It's been terrible, I only came back yesterday to try to cover some of her work, she rang in sick at first, then,' it was as if Susie had suddenly remembered caution, 'do you know about what happened?'

'Oh, yes, her brute of a husband beat her up and she's run off with the children,' Di said putting herself firmly on Faith's side.

'Well, yes, and we even had the police round wondering where she'd gone and the like.'

'Well, where would she go? She could have come to me, as a friend, or you.'

'But she didn't.'

'She must have gone to another friend, anyone you can think of?'

'Not from work, Faith was a lovely person but, as you'll know, not one of the gaggle.'

'She did hint she had a particular male friend at work, Nick or something?' Di tried.

'Nick? Nick? No,' then Susie laughed. 'Nick Wren! Oh that was *so* funny, he did offer to buy her lunch and she turned him down – said she always had her lunch with a friend – meaning me! I bet he's never been turned down in his life before! But it can't be him, she just does his typing.'

Oh can't it? Di thought, remembering seeing Faith and Wren exiting the lift together that evening. 'Not *the* Nick Wren, photographer to the stars?' she asked innocently.

'The very same!'

'And our Faith turned him down! What a girl,' Di said with feeling, 'Well, thanks anyway. If you do hear from her, send her my love.'

'Oh, I will, bye'

Di jotted down, Nick Wren – lunch? and Wren = Chris Raven – identical!

She looked at her notes. Nothing concrete but she was certain that Faith was with Nick Wren and small indicators, that she'd totally missed at the time, came sneaking back into Di's memory, like the monumental blushes or Faith's eyes alight as she retold certain sections of The Story. She'd misread them totally, rather like those others signals she'd only noticed in retrospect, after hearing about Andy's treatment of Faith, of Faith looking hurt and hunched-up some mornings, incommunicative, pale. No, Faith was happy now, she felt sure, and though she'd cut Di out of a lifetime of being Diane Faith, she'd still split the money on the first two books. Di decided she wouldn't tell what she thought she'd found out, she screwed her notes up and threw them in the bin.

'Di, have you seen a sheet of figures around?' Paul called from the bedroom.

'What type of figures?' Di called back from the kitchen.

'Just a list, in pencil, I thought I'd left it up here. Oh, never mind, I've found it, flipping screwed up.'

'What?'

'Never mind.'

Di continued to unload the shopping and put it all away.

'Di?'

'What now?'

'What's all this?'

'What?'

Paul appeared at the kitchen door. 'This.' In his hand he held a screwed up sheet of paper. Di could clearly see her notes from the day before scrawled across the top, she felt herself begin to blush and turned to carry on putting the shopping away.

'Well?'

'I don't know, nothing.'

'Di, it's your writing, who is he?'

'Who?'

'Don't play me for a fool!' Paul suddenly shouted, 'This, this guy, Nick Wren or is it Chris Raven?'

'Paul, listen.'

'Raven, that's the guy from the book, isn't it. And this Wren is the same person. Like those others Faith paired up.'

'Well, I think he is.'

Paul stared at her for a long moment. 'And what, you think that's where Faith is?'

Di couldn't stop her face betraying her, Paul knew her far too well.

'All of it?'

'What?'

'All that stuff, in the book, Faith and this bloke? Faith, having an affair?'

Di shrugged her shoulders.

'God! What'll Andy make of this?'

'He can't know – don't tell him!'

'I think he has a right to know – don't you? No, obviously you don't as you threw this away.'

'Paul, he'll, he'll go ballistic.'

'At least he'll know! Everyone should know that she wasn't all sweetness and light like they're making her out to be.'

'Paul, I really don't think it's a good idea to tell Andy.'

'Well, it isn't you that's going to, is it?'

'Tell me what?' Andy said as he opened the back door, 'I could hear you two half way down the street. You'll have the neighbours out if you're not careful,' he added with a snort of a laugh.

Di mouthed, 'No,' and shook her head at Paul.

'Well Andy, seeing as you asked,' he shot a look at Di, 'Di's been doing some sleuthing and it seems that your Faith wasn't as sweet and good as all those busybodies are making her out to be.'

'What the hell you talking about?'

'Seems as if Faith's been having it off with this guy called Wren, and that's probably where she's gone.'

Andy's face drained of colour, he stared at Paul, then switched his gaze to Di, suddenly the colour rushed back into his face, his eyes seemed to bulge. Di took a step back and found herself leaning hard into the kitchen unit.

'Bastard! I'll get the fucker and kill him! No, I'll skin him alive, the bastard! Who is he? Where's he live. I'm getting her and the kids back and he'll regret it.'

'Andy, Andy, calm down,' Di pleaded

'Calm down? Oh, I'm calm enough. I'll kill him, so help me God, I'll kill him.'

'Just forget them, all of them, you're better off without them, aren't you?' Paul tried

'What the hell would you know? You've always had what you want, you've got Di. Faith was *mine*! The bloody kids are *mine*! No other fucker's going to have them.'

'But if she'd treated me like that I wouldn't want to know her anymore.'

'He'd have led her on – she'd never have even thought of it. No, he's the one.'

'Andy, wake up, she's not the angel they're all painting.'

'Fuck off, Paul,' Andy spat and left slamming the door behind him.

'That was great, wasn't it? What do you think he'll do?' Di said after the reverberation had faded.

'Who knows? Did you have any luck trying to find out where this bloke Wren lives?'

'No.'

'Then I don't suppose Andy will. He'll get over it, calm down, then he'll see that what I said makes sense.'

chapter thirty-six - Faith and Di

'I am just so nervous!' Faith fidgeted as they drove to the launch party for her first book.

'But no more worries about the coincidences?' Nick asked with a glance towards her.

Faith smiled, 'Well after six weeks of peace and tranquillity and nothing fiercer than your neighbour's cows, I think you were right after all!' though she still could not prevent herself from crossing her fingers as she said it.

Alison had said that publishers rarely push the boat out for any author unless they're guaranteed to be bestsellers but they'd stumped up on this one, enough to hire a good catering firm and enough booze to go round. The idea and provision of the venue, the headquarters of a major National Daily, incidentally owned by Lord Boulder, had been Nick's contribution.

They drove straight round to the management parking area and climbed out. Jilly was looking very grown up and Jon, though resisting looking pleased, was about as smart as Faith had ever been able to get him.

Alison came hurrying over to them. 'Oh good, in the nick of time, are these your children?'

'Yes, Jilly and Jon, this is Ms Enderby, my agent.'

'Hello,' Jilly said shyly, Jon just looked at the floor.

'And, Mr Wren!' Alison said, 'I did so like your photo for the inside jacket, you really captured Faith's fragile beauty but still showed her inner core of strength, she can be a very determined woman when she chooses to be, I should know.'

'Thank you, shall we go in?'

'Of course,' Alison looked at them again as Nick squeezed Faith's hand in encouragement.

'And, if I'm not being too presumptuous, would you say you two were an item? I ask in a professional way, you know how useful this would be to book publicity and promotion in the future?'

'You are being presumptuous and Faith's writing will speak for itself,' Nick said, and squeezed Faith's hand again and when she looked up at him, planted a kiss on her lips.

'Now, the programme will run something like this, everyone has got a glass of something as they arrived, they've been mingling and chatting, as usual, now you're here your editor will call everyone to order and introduce you and tell them about your book. She's going to lay it on thick about how you always wanted to be a writer since you were a child but had opportunity denied you, about your friend and how she taped your story and typed it up for you and the rest is history, okay with all that?' Alison said as they stepped into the crowded room.

'Is Di here?'

'Well, I hope so, I invited her to come, she's part of the editor's presentation. Come on, look Julie Munro's signalling to you, she's ready.'

'Look after the children, wish me luck,' Faith said looking at Nick for reassurance.

'You're a star, my love, go show 'em.'

'Ladies, Ladies and Gentlemen, thank you. Welcome to the launch of The Story, based in a newspaper office, launched from a newspaper office!' Julie Munro stopped for the ripple of polite laughter. 'A Story that may never have come to light if it hadn't been for an unusual idea and a good friend. But first our author, please welcome Diane Faith.'

Faith stayed still for a second, then realised it was her, not Di they were waiting for. She stepped up to a gentle round of applause, feeling her cheeks burn as she did so, once beside Munro, the speech continued. 'Diane Faith is one of those natural born storytellers who were telling stories from the time they were very small. Good, imaginative, inventive stories told to amuse and entertain her friends. She had dreams of going to university and one day being a writer, but fate took an unfortunate turn and this was not to be. However, one day, while sharing a lift to work with her friend she began to tell The

Story, a story that so gripped this friend that, where is she? Come on up!'

Di, who had moved forward when the speech began, found herself standing a little way behind Wren and the children. She looked at the trio, noting that, despite the unusual setting that both children were looking remarkably calm. Jilly was almost leaning on Wren, and Jon, looking very smart, had a smile on his face the time he turned to Wren and said something, Wren ducking his head to be nearer the boy's height in answering him, turned, showing Di his profile. And of course it was Wren, as she'd deduced, and looking altogether too hunky for words. Suddenly she heard her name, or thought she did, she started, then realised it was the name Diane Faith that had been called. She watched as Faith went forward from a hidden position even nearer the front, and stared. What had happened to Faith in the missing weeks, the woman who stepped forward was - beautiful. It wasn't just the hair, worn up in an artless way as if she'd just stepped out of a love bed and pinned it up, yet obviously perfectly contrived to look just that seductive, nor the superbly fitting clothes, there was more. Di noted that Faith still had her blush, but now it was more of a glow that heightened her bone structure, and Faith, petite as ever, was standing tall, every inch elegant and in control.

Then Di realised she *was* being called, 'Come on up!' the editor said and Di went forward and joined them, and as she reached Faith she touched her shoulders and gave her the double air-kiss of celebrities everywhere, noticing the sparkle in her eyes.
'This friend,' continued the editor, 'was so gripped by what she heard that she secretly taped the whole story, then typed it all up to give back to Diane as a present. Only when she'd got it all typed up she realised that this was something special and sent it away to an agent. Who, wisely, took it up straight away! The fairytale came true, Ladies and Gentlemen! As I'm sure you will soon find out, this book, The Story is both gripping and sexy, with a new type of hero, a sassy, sexy, female investigative journalist, determined to make her way in the

tough world of newspapers and, after you've read this book, I'm sure you, like me, will not be able to wait for her next adventure. Thank you.'

The guests were beginning to turn away, looking to refill their glasses, the doors at the back opened and waiters, carrying trays of canapés, started to come in.

Di looked at Faith, she knew Faith was truly happy, just by her face.

'Faith, I've missed you,' she heard herself say. 'You look wonderful, I can't quite...' Her words were cut short by a crash as a tray clattered to the floor, heads turned, a waiter was struggling to get up, and in the centre of the commotion stood a large angry man with a knife glinting in his fist. A woman started screaming. Andy, sweeping the knife from side to side, glared round the room then fixed his eyes on Faith.

The hysterical woman continued screaming as Andy, still sweeping the knife from side to side to keep everyone at bay, lunged through the room towards the makeshift stage and mounted the steps. Di and Faith had unconsciously backed away and came up against the back wall as Andy paused on the edge of the stage, his chest heaving, his skin shining with sweat and shaking his head like a tormented bull.

Then a number of things happened at once, Jon shouted 'Dad!' and Jilly screamed, 'No! Dad, no!' Andy turned his head towards their voices and at that moment Nick Wren said something to the children, swept them behind him and started headlong for the stage.

It was as if Andy had been waiting for the signal, his body snapped into an attacking stance, the knife weaving menacingly.

'Wren?' he snarled. Nick glanced towards the sound of his own name as he darted across the stage, putting himself between the women and Andy. Taking her eyes off Andy for a few precious seconds Faith could see the guests being ushered out of the room by someone in uniform and felt a new note of panic hit her but then saw Alison had taken the children by the hand and was leading them away, their eyes drawn back to the scene on the stage, Faith lifted her chin and gave a brief nod of encouragement to them.

'You cunning bastard!' Andy sneered, his eyes flickering between Wren and Faith. 'She's mine, y'know! And the bloody kids are mine! And anything she's got is mine! Got that?' He stepped forward, the knife weaving a tight figure of eight.

'Don't Andy,' Di tried. 'Don't do anything stupid!'

'Stupid? Stupid?' his reddened eyes found Di's. 'That's what you think of me, isn't it? And I used to think you were really something special, but you don't care shit.' And all the time the knife was moving, flashing messages of fear, mesmerising.

'Look,' Nick said, his voice reasonable and low, 'why don't you put the knife down before you do something you regret?'

Andy's eyes hardened as he took another step forward, Faith and Di shrank back into the corner, Nick shielding them.

'No mate, it won't be like that, you've fucking got it coming, you thieving fucking bastard!' And he suddenly lunged, slashing with the knife. Faith screamed 'No!' as Nick leapt forward. The knife struck deep into his flesh as he shoulder-charged Andy off his feet. Andy crashed back onto the floor, the bloodied blade still tight in his grip.

As if from nowhere two uniformed security guards appeared, one stood on Andy's wrist yelling 'Drop it' until he released the knife, the other flattened himself over Andy until they could both deal with him.

Nick staggered back against the wall clutching his arm across his chest, Faith ran to him, tears running down her face. She tore his jacket open sobbing, 'Where? Where?' Blood blackened his sleeve and began trickling down his wrist, dripping bright on his hand. As she saw it Faith hugged him tight sighing, 'The first ending, thank God, the first ending.'

Acknowledgements:

To the many friends with different life skills, occupations and experiences of whom I asked so many strange questions in order to help get things right, thank you! Any remaining errors are my own.

To **The Western Morning News** for allowing me to see behind the scenes at their newspaper offices and for answering my odd questions while researching this novel. Grateful thanks also to Christine Haywood , Dorothy Silverstone & Ian MacDonald for invaluable help along the way.

Thank you for reading **Some Kind of Synchrony**
by Ann Foweraker
You may review this book and the others written by the author on Amazon, Goodreads or Annmade.co.uk - where they are also available to purchase in all e-formats

Other novels by ANN FOWERAKER

Nothing Ever Happens Here

Living in London suddenly becomes too uncomfortable for the attractive Jo Smart and her sixteen year-old son, Alex, after he is beaten up. so when they are offered the chance to take an immediate holiday in a peaceful Cornish town they jump at it. But not all is as peaceful as it seems as they become involved in a murder enquiry, drug raid and abduction.

DI Rick Whittington has also escaped from London and the reminders of the death of his wife and child, and through his investigations finds himself meeting Jo and being drawn into the events surrounding her.

This is a light thriller, set in the early 1990s, which combines the historic Cornish love of the sea and smuggling with romance and hard faced twentieth century crime and detection.

Divining the Line

The first time it happened it felt like stumbling across another avenue to an ancient monument, but this one pulled at more than just his head, there was a tightness in his chest, the lights twinkled and flashed inside his mind, the intensity giving Perran a firework of a headache. Following the line - years later in the early nineties - leads him into Liz Hawkey's ordered life, and together they discover the source of the line. A story of family, love and loss set in the early 1990s, Divining the Line brings the ordinary and the extraordinary together into everyday life.

The Angel Bug

'These memoirs may be the only evidence left of what really happened, where it came from and how it spread.'

When Gabbi Johnston, a quiet, fifty-something botanist at Eden, was shown the unusual red leaves on the Moringa tree, she had no idea what was wrong. What she did know was that the legendary Dr Luke Adamson was arriving soon - and that he would insist on investigating it.

This is the unassuming start to a maelstrom of discovery and change - with Gabbi swept up in it. What starts out as an accident turns into something illicit, clandestine and unethical – but is it really, as Adamson claims, for the good of all mankind?

***

'The Angel Bug', Ann Foweraker's fourth novel, is set mainly at the Eden Project in Cornwall, UK. This is a contemporary novel combining science fact and fiction, told by the people at the heart of the discovery.

About the Author

Though a writer of poetry and short stories since my teens I also love passing on knowledge so I became a teacher, gaining my BEd degree in the seventies. Teaching is still in my blood - give me half a chance and I'll teach you everything I know. Marriage took me from Berkshire, where I was born, to live in Cornwall and the novel writing began while taking an extended break from teaching to bring up our four boys.

My books are all available to order from all bookshops and from PendownPublishing.co.uk as well as in in various e-formats and are also available at Amazon for Kindle.

Please follow my blog on annfoweraker.com where you'll get an insight into the things I'm in to, from belly dancing to sandsculpture and, of course, writing.
Follow me on twitter at @AnnFoweraker for tweets on life, Cornwall and writing, and Like my page on Facebook 'Ann Foweraker' for more info and thoughts.

Lightning Source UK Ltd.
Milton Keynes UK
UKOW02f0749170914

238689UK00001B/1/P